Oscar Wilde 著

巴金 譯

THE HAPPY PRINCE AND OTHER TALES

快樂王子

書　　名：*The Happy Prince and Other Tales* 快樂王子

作　　者：Oscar Wilde

譯　　者：巴　金

責任編輯：黃家麗　　王朴真

封面設計：張　　毅

出　　版：商務印書館 (香港) 有限公司

　　　　　香港筲箕灣耀興道 3 號東滙廣場 8 樓

　　　　　http://www.commercialpress.com.hk

發　　行：香港聯合書刊物流有限公司

　　　　　香港新界大埔汀麗路 36 號中華商務印刷大廈 3 字樓

印　　刷：中華商務彩色印刷有限公司

　　　　　香港新界大埔汀麗路 36 號中華商務印刷大廈

版　　次：2019 年 10 月第 1 版第 2 次印刷

　　　　　© 2013 商務印書館 (香港) 有限公司

　　　　　ISBN 978 962 07 0352 2

　　　　　Printed in Hong Kong

Publisher's Note 出版說明

　　快樂只在於無憂無慮，還是像快樂王子一樣關心他人？夢境與現實縱橫交錯，愛麗絲夢醒之後，仍是天真無邪，卻已有對現實的感悟。童話字字璣珠，更啟發對人生的思考。

　　使用本書時，先閱讀英文原文，如遇到理解障礙，則參照中譯作為輔助。如有餘力，可在閱讀原文部分段落後，查閱相應中譯，觀察同樣詞句在雙語中不同的表達，從而體會如何用優美達意的中文表達英語文學中的深意。

　　文字優美，寓意深刻，啟迪智慧，是為特點，能為初、中級英語程度的讀者提供經典的文學，更帶來對生活的啟發。

商務印書館（香港）有限公司

編輯出版部

Contents 目錄

Preface to the Chinese Translation　　中文譯本序　*1*

The Happy Prince and Other Tales / 快樂王子

The Happy Prince / 快樂王子　*11/184*

The Nightingale and the Rose / 夜鶯與薔薇　*25/195*

The Selfish Giant / 自私的巨人　*35/202*

The Devoted Friend / 忠實的朋友　*43/207*

The Remarkable Rocket / 了不起的火箭　*59/220*

A House of Pomegranates / 石榴之家

The Young King / 少年國王　*77/236*

The Birthday of the Infanta / 西班牙公主的生日　*95/251*

The Fisherman and his Soul / 打魚人和他的靈魂　*119/271*

The Star-Child / 星孩　*163/310*

Notes / 註　*182/327*

Preface to the Chinese Translation
中文譯本序

一

王爾德於一八五四年生於愛爾蘭的首府都柏林。王爾德這名字挺中國化的，其實他有一個連西方人都少有的大長名字：奧斯卡·芬格爾·奧弗拉赫蒂·威利斯·王爾德！

王爾德的父親名叫威廉·王爾德，是一位十分著名的外科醫生；他母親是作家，又是有名的文學女主持人，經常主持倫敦詩歌戲劇沙龍，曾使用"斯珀蘭扎"的筆名發表過許多文學作品。王爾德早年在都柏林三一學院研習古典名著，而後到牛津馬格達蘭學院就讀，因成績優秀顯露頭角，成為有名的學生，並因他的詩《拉凡納》獲得紐迪蓋特獎。在牛津求學期間，他穿着花裏胡哨，極力張揚唯美主義，即"為藝術而藝術"，而成為公眾矚目的人物，但不少守舊人士對他的做派和主張懷有成見。敏感的王爾德針對此世俗之見曾戲言說："我王爾德要麼臭名昭著，要麼名揚天下。"

王爾德天分極高，談吐機智幽默，話鋒不遜，寫作標新立異，很快走運倫敦及英國文壇，成為文學名流。一八八一年，他出版他的第一部集子《詩集》，廣受歡迎，並由此導致他首次赴美巡迴講學一年。初登美洲大陸，帶着英國人的傲慢和他特有的表現方式，他在紐約海關登記處留下了那句極具個性的名言："我需要申報的只有我的天才"（I have nothing to declare but my genius.）。一八八四年他和康斯坦絲‧洛伊德喜結良緣。婚後生有二子。正是由於對兒子的愛，王爾德曾致力於兒童文學創作，其中主要是童話故事。

進入十九世紀九十年代，王爾德迎來了他的創作高峰。先是他的唯一一部長篇小說《道連‧格雷的畫像》於一八九一年發表，接着他走紅倫敦舞台：《溫德米爾夫人的扇子》（1892）、《一個無關緊要的女人》（1893）、《理想丈夫》（1895）、《認真的重要》（1895），以及他的最後一部用法語寫的象徵主義悲劇《莎樂美》（1895）。《認真的重要》被認為是其戲劇創作上的代表作。

至此，王爾德一直是生活的寵兒，一路順風，幾乎每涉及一個文學領域、每創作一部作品，都會取得極大成功，贏得一片喝彩，真可謂"名揚天下"了。

如同在不同文學體裁的作品裏所反映的，王爾德讚美友誼，珍視友誼，與他喜愛和敬重的人建立友誼。在他的種種友誼中，有一例稱得上是"友誼中的友誼"，那便是他和他的親密朋友艾爾弗雷德‧道格拉斯勳爵的友誼。應該指出的是，他們的這種友誼包含着王爾德對男性美的一種追求。他們兩個都算得上年輕貌美，彼此吸引，雙雙出入倫敦上流社會以及劇院、酒店、餐館和咖啡廳這些公共場合，構成了倫敦社會的一道風景。然而，這道風景在倫敦上流社會並不受歡迎，認為它傷風敗俗之舉的大有人在，其中道格拉斯的父親昆斯伯里侯爵就是深惡痛絕者之一。這位侯爵的深惡痛絕本源自他和兒子的矛盾，當然也包括反對兒子和王爾德的交往。這導致了一場官司，而且，在法庭取證時小道格拉斯倒向親情一邊，王爾德終因同性戀之罪被判刑兩年。這場官司致使他家破財散，兩年的監獄苦役和精神折磨摧毀了他的身體，此時的王爾德從天堂掉入地獄，又可謂"臭名昭著"了。

出獄後，在朋友們的慷慨贊助下，他移居法國，用"塞巴斯蒂安‧梅爾莫斯"這一名字繼續寫作，其中最著名的是他的長詩《雷丁監獄之歌》。他在牢中以懺悔之心、友愛之情寫給艾爾弗雷德‧道格拉斯的信，後結集出版，名為《從深處》(1905)。此階段的作品，是王爾德最具現實主義的創作，但王爾德"為藝術而藝術"的主張不僅未改，反而具有了新的內容。

二

王爾德的第一部童話集名《快樂王子童話集》，內收有"快樂王子"、"夜鶯與薔薇"、"自私的巨人"、"忠實的朋友"和"了不起的火箭"，於一八八八年出版。第二部童話集名為《石榴之家》，是題送他妻子的。石榴在中國有"多子"象徵之意義，不知王爾德將這部童話取名《石榴之家》並呈獻給妻子，是否有這層意思。不過王爾德對石榴樹及石榴果情有獨鍾，在不同作品中多次以美的形象提及。這個集子裏包括"少年國王"、"西班牙公主的生日"、"The Fisherman and his Soul"以及"星孩"，出版於一八九一年。

就王爾德的童話總體創作來看，他仍遵循了一般童話中應有的懲惡揚善、鋤強扶弱、劫富濟貧以及褒美貶醜等主題，無論是悲劇類的還是喜劇類的，都會有一個充滿希望的結尾。這點在他的第一部童話集《快樂王子童話集》的所有五個故事中都很明顯。需要特別多說幾句的是"快樂王子"和"夜鶯與薔薇"兩篇。毫無疑問，"快樂王子"是王爾德童話中流傳最廣、最受孩子們喜愛的童話。王子活着時生活在"無愁宮"裏，無憂無慮，衣來伸手飯來張口，因而認為世界上所有的人都像他一樣過着幸福的生活。然而，他死後他的塑像被安放在一根高高聳立於城市上空的立柱上，他才俯瞰到了人間的種種苦難與不幸，因而傷心難過，決心盡可能幫助那些最不幸的人。一隻快樂的小燕子幫了他的忙。小燕子無私地一次次捨棄到南國避寒的機會，把王子的寶石、眼珠和身上的一片片金葉子，送到了那些最需要幫助的不幸的人手中，結果凍死在快樂王子的腳下，快樂王子因此痛碎了一顆鉛製的心！一則童話到此已十分完整，但王爾德沒有忘掉他對美的探討：一尊沒有眼珠、沒有金葉裹身的塑像和一隻死鳥，還美嗎？世俗之人認為不美，但上帝認為仍然很美，於是"鉛心"和"死鳥"都進了天堂。最後王爾德還留給大小讀者一個歷來不受重視的問題：快樂王子"幸福"嗎？他曾經幸福過；自從了解到民間疾苦後他不幸福了；為不幸的人們解除痛苦後，他終於又幸福了。這樣，作者把甚麼是幸福這一命題很富於哲理地予以闡述，並把這一命題與他的唯美主義以及"心之美"聯繫起來，一起進行探討。這又是王爾德童話高明與不朽的一面。

"夜鶯與薔薇"以愛情為主旋律：一隻夜鶯為成全一對青年男女的愛情，不惜用牠心裏流淌的血，通過刺入牠心臟一根尖利的薔薇刺，給薔薇樹提供血汁，讓它開出一朵鮮豔無比的紅薔薇。這是"心之美"的形象化體現。但那年輕女子看不上這朵無比珍貴的薔薇花，看重的是名望地位和物質享受；一隻鳥裏的“心之美”和人類的“利慾薰心”，形成了強烈的對照。王爾德在這裏探討的是他的唯美主義的內容之一，表達方式近乎殘酷（一根利刺直插一顆完美的心），象徵一種不折不扣的美，這顯然是一般童話所沒有的。

僅此亦不難看出，王爾德在他的童話世界裏，除了表現一般童話裏的主題，總還會以他的唯美主義觀點，探討“幸福”、“心之美”等重大命題。這種探討在《石榴之家》這個童話集中深入開展，並從童話寫作形式和內容表達兩方面都取得突破，取得實績。

僅就形式而言，“西班牙公主的生日”是最值得注意的：西班牙小公主美麗至極，在她隆重的生日慶典上，她享受到了許多美的東西，其中包括一個小矮人獻舞。小矮人長得畸形醜陋，但他自己並不知道。最後他在一面大鏡子裏看見了自己，自慚形穢，心碎而死。故事裏美醜分明，但醜也可以給人帶來歡樂，而美如果以別人的痛苦為樂，美也顯得醜陋。從寫法到表現內容，這則童話都更像一個現代派短篇小說；其中有象徵，有寓意，有哲理，讀來令人對作者的豐富想像和天才的創造力感到由衷的佩服和驚歎！

“The Fisherman and his Soul”是王爾德童話中最長的，這恐怕是王爾德試圖通過童話形式探討靈、肉、心三者之間關係的結果。靈與肉的問題，是幾乎所有文學大家都試圖說清的命題。一般論點或說絕大多數論點都認為，肉即肉體，是物慾之物，世俗之物；靈即靈魂，不得不時時刻刻陪着它，管它吃管它喝，管着它別讓物慾引誘太深，掉進罪惡的深淵。但王爾德在這個童話裏持有正好相反的觀點：肉物只享受自然之物，比如愛情；而靈魂卻在支配肉體去尋歡作樂，作惡犯罪。心在肉與靈之間扮演着愛的角色，象徵着愛。靈魂脫離肉體時是從心那裏走了，但回來時卻因為漁夫對美人魚的"愛"太偉大，再也回不到心裏去了！多麼奇特的想像和探討！正是通過這篇童話，王爾德初步闡明了他的一個關於美的著名論點：藝術優於生活，即他的唯美主義。藝術沒有甚麼實用的價值，但人類應該為藝術而藝術地生活，不應該為生活而生活。這正是王爾德童話世界裏的主要特色，魅力所在，永恆所在！

三

王爾德除了利用童話闡述他的唯美主義，更多也是成功地在創造美。他的童話講究結構，語言詩化；童話世界裏的人物、鳥獸、草木、宮殿以至一物一事，他都盡力從美的角度去挖掘，尤其從內在美的角度。"自私的巨人"因最後變得無私而進入天堂："那天下午小孩們跑進園子[1]來的時候，他們看見巨人躺在一棵樹下，他已經死了，滿身蓋着白花。"多美的結局呀！"忠實的朋友"中的小漢斯至死都不肯承認他的朋友那個磨坊主的自私、卑鄙和貪婪，但他留給世界的是溫暖的忠誠，雖死猶生，營造了一種悲劇美。"了不起的火箭"一生以非凡自居，卻始終沒有表現出他的非凡之處。但是他堅定地相信"像我這樣的天才總有一天會給人賞識的"（Genius like mine is sure to be appreciated someday.），後來被拆得七零八落，扔在篝火裏引爆了火藥，他仍興奮地嚷叫説："我早知道我會大出風頭的。"這種不折不扣的虛榮也不失為一種病態美吧。"少年國王"表現的是一種屢經磨難後的成熟美，內在美。"星孩"所表達的內容與"少年國王"有相同之處，但在表現方法上迥然不同，顯示出王爾德駕馭童話的高超手法。

王爾德對大千世界裏美的東西，好似具有第六感官，只要稍有機會，他就會如數家珍般地寫進故事裏，尤其對植物的鍾愛：石竹、玫瑰、羅勒、紫羅蘭、桂竹香、鳶尾花、麝香石竹、美國石竹、深斑玫瑰、草地虎耳草、美洲耬斗菜、黃花九輪草以及布穀鳥剪秋羅，等等。他這種時候全然忘了他給孩子們和讀者帶來了許多冷僻的生字，犯了童話創作的大忌。在他眼裏，每一種美的東西就是一首詩，一幅畫，完全可以囫圇吞棗全盤接受，等閒下來再慢慢消化，細細品嚐它們的美汁美味。

很可惜，王爾德出獄後身心交瘁，一直沒有能徹底康復，出獄後三年多便在巴黎客死他鄉，只在人間活了四十六年。他留給世界文壇不足兩百萬字，他的童話創作充其量只佔他全部創作量的二十分之一。然而，我們僅從這些作品中便不難看出他給讀者帶來多少美的享受。二〇〇〇年是王爾德去世一百週年，英倫三島曾經掀起"王爾德熱"，僅一本《王爾德妙語集》便行銷一百多萬冊！進入二十一世紀，王爾德依然是英美文壇研究的熱點。我們有理由相信，他的童話將會一如既往地給中國大小讀者帶來福音。

蘇福忠

The Happy Prince
and Other Tales

The Happy Prince

High above the city, on a tall column, stood the statue of the Happy Prince. He was gilded all over with thin leaves of fine gold, for eyes he had two bright sapphires, and a large red ruby glowed on his sword-hilt.

He was very much admired indeed. 'He is as beautiful as a weathercock,' remarked one of the Town Councillors who wished to gain a reputation for having artistic tastes; 'only not quite so useful,' he added, fearing lest people should think him unpractical, which he really was not.

'Why can't you be like the Happy Prince?' asked a sensible mother of her little boy who was crying for the moon. 'The Happy Prince never dreams of crying for anything.'

'I am glad there is some one in the world who is quite happy,' muttered a disappointed man as he gazed at the wonderful statue.

'He looks just like an angel,' said the Charity Children as they came out of the cathedral in their bright scarlet cloaks and their clean white pinafores.

'How do you know?' said the Mathematical Master, 'you have

never seen one.'

'Ah! but we have, in our dreams,' answered the children; and the Mathematical Master frowned and looked very severe, for he did not approve of children dreaming.

One night there flew over the city a little Swallow. His friends had gone away to Egypt six weeks before, but he had stayed behind, for he was in love with the most beautiful Reed. He had met her early in the spring as he was flying down the river after a big yellow moth, and had been so attracted by her slender waist that he had stopped to talk to her.

'Shall I love you?' said the Swallow, who liked to come to the point at once, and the Reed made him a low bow. So he flew round and round her, touching the water with his wings, and making silver ripples. This was his courtship, and it lasted all through the summer.

'It is a ridiculous attachment,' twittered the other Swallows; 'she has no money, and far too many relations;' and indeed the river was quite full of Reeds. Then, when the autumn came they all flew away.

After they had gone he felt lonely, and began to tire of his lady-love. 'She has no conversation,' he said, 'and I am afraid that she is a coquette, for she is always flirting with the wind.' And certainly, whenever the wind blew, the Reed made the most graceful curtseys. 'I admit that she is domestic,' he continued, 'but I love travelling, and my wife, consequently, should love travelling also.'

'Will you come away with me?' he said finally to her, but the Reed shook her head, she was so attached to her home.

'You have been trifling with me,' he cried. 'I am off to the Pyramids. Good-bye!' and he flew away.

All day long he flew, and at night-time he arrived at the city. 'Where shall I put up?' he said; I hope the town has made preparations.'

Then he saw the statue on the tall column.

'I will put up there,' he cried; 'it is a fine position, with plenty of fresh air.' So he alighted just between the feet of the Happy Prince.

'I have a golden bedroom,' he said softly to himself as he looked round, and he prepared to go to sleep; but just as he was putting his head under his wing a large drop of water fell on him. 'What a curious thing!' he cried; 'there is not a single cloud in the sky, the stars are quite clear and bright, and yet it is raining. The climate in the north of Europe is really dreadful. The Reed used to like the rain, but that was merely her selfishness.'

Then another drop fell.

'What is the use of a statue if it cannot keep the rain off?' he said; 'I must look for a good chimney-pot,' and he determined to fly away.

But before he had opened his wings, a third drop fell, and he looked up, and saw—Ah! what did he see?

The eyes of the Happy Prince were filled with tears, and tears were running down his golden cheeks. His face was so beautiful in the moonlight that the little Swallow was filled with pity.

'Who are you?' he said.

'I am the Happy Prince.'

'Why are you weeping then?' asked the Swallow; 'you have quite drenched me.'

'When I was alive and had a human heart,' answered the statue, 'I did not know what tears were, for I lived in the Palace of

Sans-Souci, where sorrow is not allowed to enter. In the daytime I played with my companions in the garden, and in the evening I led the dance in the Great Hall. Round the garden ran a very lofty wall, but I never cared to ask what lay beyond it, everything about me was so beautiful. My courtiers called me the Happy Prince, and happy indeed I was, if pleasure be happiness. So I lived, and so I died. And now that I am dead they have set me up here so high that I can see all the ugliness and all the misery of my city, and though my heart is made of lead yet I cannot choose but weep.'

'What! is he not solid gold?' said the Swallow to himself. He was too polite to make any personal remarks out loud.

'Far away,' continued the statue in a low musical voice, 'far away in a little street there is a poorhouse. One of the windows is open, and through it I can see a woman seated at a table. Her face is thin and worn, and she has coarse, red hands, all pricked by the needle, for she is a seamstress. She is embroidering passion-flowers on a satin gown for the loveliest of the Queen's maids-of-honour to wear at the next Court-ball. In a bed in the corner of the room her little boy is lying ill. He has a fever, and is asking for oranges. His mother has nothing to give him but river water, so he is crying. Swallow, Swallow, little Swallow, will you not bring her the ruby out of my sword-hilt? My feet are fastened to this pedestal and I cannot move.'

'I am waited for in Egypt,' said the Swallow. 'My friends are flying up and down the Nile, and talking to the large lotus-flowers. Soon they will go to sleep in the tomb of the great King. The King is there himself in his painted coffin. He is wrapped in yellow linen, and embalmed with spices. Round his neck is a chain of pale green jade, and his hands are like withered leaves.'

'Swallow, Swallow, little Swallow,' said the Prince, 'will you not stay with me for one night, and be my messenger? The boy is so thirsty, and the mother so sad.'

'I don't think I like boys,' answered the Swallow. 'Last summer, when I was staying on the river, there were two rude boys, the miller's sons, who were always throwing stones at me. They never hit me, of course; we swallows fly far too well for that, and besides, I come of a family famous for its agility; but still, it was a mark of disrespect.'

But the Happy Prince looked so sad that the little Swallow was sorry. 'It is very cold here,' he said; 'but I will stay with you for one night, and be your messenger.'

'Thank you, little Swallow,' said the Prince.

So the Swallow picked out the great ruby from the Prince's sword, and flew away with it in his beak over the roofs of the town.

He passed by the cathedral tower, where the white marble angels were sculptured. He passed by the palace and heard the sound of dancing. A beautiful girl came out on the balcony with her lover. 'How wonderful the stars are,' he said to her, 'and how wonderful is the power of love!'

'I hope my dress will be ready in time for the State-ball,' she answered; 'I have ordered passion-flowers to be embroidered on it; but the seamstresses are so lazy.'

He passed over the river, and saw the lanterns hanging to the masts of the ships. He passed over the Ghetto, and saw the old Jews bargaining with each other, and weighing out money in copper scales. At last he came to the poor house and looked in. The boy was tossing feverishly on his bed, and the mother had fallen asleep, she was so tired. In he hopped, and laid the great ruby on the table beside the woman's thimble. Then he flew gently round the bed, fanning the boy's forehead with his wings. 'How cool I feel!' said the boy, 'I must be getting better:' and he sank into a delicious slumber.

Then the Swallow flew back to the Happy Prince, and told him what he had done. 'It is curious,' he remarked, 'but I feel quite warm now, although it is so cold.'

'That is because you have done a good action,' said the Prince. And the little Swallow began to think, and then he fell asleep. Thinking always made him sleepy.

When day broke he flew down to the river and had a bath. 'What a remarkable phenomenon!' said the Professor of Ornithology as he was passing over the bridge. 'A swallow in winter!' And he wrote a long letter about it to the local newspaper. Every one quoted it, it was full of so many words that they could not understand.

'Tonight I go to Egypt,' said the Swallow, and he was in high spirits at the prospect. He visited all the public monuments, and sat a long time on top of the church steeple. Wherever he went the Sparrows chirruped, and said to each other, 'What a distinguished stranger!' so he enjoyed himself very much.

When the moon rose he flew back to the Happy Prince. 'Have you any commissions for Egypt?' he cried; 'I am just starting.'

'Swallow, Swallow, little Swallow,' said the Prince, 'will you not stay with me one night longer?'

'I am waited for in Egypt,' answered the Swallow. 'Tomorrow my friends will fly up to the Second Cataract. The river-horse couches there among the bulrushes, and on a great granite house sits the God Memnon. All night long he watches the stars, and when the morning star shines he utters one cry of joy, and then he is silent. At noon the yellow lions come down to the water's edge to drink. They have eyes like green beryls, and their roar is louder than the roar of the cataract.'

'Swallow, Swallow, little Swallow,' said the Prince, 'far away across the city I see a young man in a garret. He is leaning over a desk covered with papers, and in a tumbler by his side there is a bunch of withered violets. His hair is brown and crisp, and his lips are red as a pomegranate, and he has large and dreamy eyes. He is trying to finish a play for the Director of the Theatre, but he is too cold to write any more. There is no fire in the grate, and hunger has made him faint.'

'I will wait with you one night longer,' said the Swallow, who really had a good heart. 'Shall I take him another ruby?'

'Alas! I have no ruby now,' said the Prince; 'my eyes are all that I have left. They are made of rare sapphires, which were brought out of India a thousand years ago. Pluck out one of them and take it to him. He will sell it to the jeweller, and buy firewood, and finish his play.'

'Dear Prince,' said the Swallow, 'I cannot do that'; and he began to weep.

'Swallow, Swallow, little Swallow,' said the Prince, 'do as I command you.'

So the Swallow plucked out the Prince's eye, and flew away to the student's garret. It was easy enough to get in, as there was a hole in the roof. Through this he darted, and came into the room. The young man had his head buried in his hands, so he did not hear the flutter of the bird's wings, and when he looked up he found the beautiful sapphire lying on the withered violets.

'I am beginning to be appreciated,' he cried; 'this is from some great admirer. Now I can finish my play,' and he looked quite happy.

The next day the Swallow flew down to the harbour. He sat on the mast of a large vessel and watched the sailors hauling big chests out of the hold with ropes. 'Heave a-hoy!' they shouted as each chest came up. 'I am going to Egypt!' cried the Swallow, but nobody minded, and when the moon rose he flew back to the Happy Prince.

'I am come to bid you good-bye,' he cried.

'Swallow, Swallow, little Swallow,' said the Prince, 'will you not stay with me one night longer?'

'It is winter,' answered the Swallow, 'and the chill snow will soon be here. In Egypt the sun is warm on the green palm-trees, and the crocodiles lie in the mud and look lazily about them. My companions are building a nest in the Temple of Baalbec, and the pink and white doves are watching them, and cooing to each other. Dear Prince, I must leave you, but I will never forget you, and next spring I will bring you back two beautiful jewels in place of those you have given away. The ruby shall be redder than a red rose, and the sapphire shall be as blue as the great sea.'

'In the square below,' said the Happy Prince, 'there stands a little match girl. She has let her matches fall in the gutter, and they are all spoiled. Her father will beat her if she does not bring home some money, and she is crying. She has no shoes or stockings, and her little head is bare. Pluck out my other eye, and give it to her, and her father will not beat her.'

'I will stay with you one night longer,' said the Swallow, 'but I cannot pluck out your eye. You would be quite blind then.'

'Swallow, Swallow, little Swallow,' said the Prince, 'do as I command you.'

So he plucked out the Prince's other eye, and darted down with it. He swooped past the match girl, and slipped the jewel into the palm of her hand. 'What a lovely bit of glass!' cried the little girl; and she ran home, laughing.

Then the Swallow came back to the Prince. 'You are blind now,' he said, 'so I will stay with you always.'

'No, little Swallow,' said the poor prince, 'you must go away to Egypt.'

'I will stay with you always,' said the Swallow, and he slept at the Prince's feet.

All the next day he sat on the Prince's shoulder, and told him stories of what he had seen in strange lands. He told him of the red ibises, who stand in long rows on the banks of the Nile, and catch goldfish in their beaks; of the Sphinx, who is as old as the world itself, and lives in the desert, and knows everything; of the merchants, who walk slowly by the side of their camels and carry amber beads in their hands; of the King of the Mountains of the Moon, who is as black as ebony, and worships a large crystal; of the great green snake that sleeps in a palm-tree, and has twenty priests to feed it with honey-cakes; and of the pygmies who sail over a big lake on large flat leaves, and are always at war with the butterflies.

'Dear little Swallow,' said the Prince, 'you tell me of marvellous things, but more marvellous than anything is the suffering of men and of women. There is no Mystery so great as Misery. Fly over my city, little Swallow, and tell me what you see there.'

So the Swallow flew over the great city, and saw the rich making merry in their beautiful houses, while the beggars were sitting at the gates. He flew into dark lanes, and saw the white faces of starving children looking out listlessly at the black streets. Under the archway of a bridge two little boys were lying in one another's arms to try and keep themselves warm. 'How hungry we are!' they said. 'You must not lie here,' shouted the watchman, and they wandered out into the rain.

Then he flew back and told the Prince what he had seen.

'I am covered with fine gold,' said the Prince, 'you must take it off, leaf by leaf, and give it to my poor; the living always think that gold can make them happy.'

Leaf after leaf of the fine gold the Swallow picked off, till the Happy Prince looked quite dull and grey. Leaf after leaf of the fine gold he brought to the poor, and the children's faces grew rosier, and they laughed and played games in the street. 'We have bread now!' they cried.

Then the snow came, and after the snow came the frost. The streets looked as if they were made of silver, they were so bright and glistening; long icicles like crystal daggers hung down from the eaves of the houses, everybody went about in furs, and the little boys wore scarlet caps and skated on the ice.

The poor little Swallow grew colder and colder, but he would not leave the Prince, he loved him too well. He picked up crumbs outside the baker's door when the baker was not looking, and tried to keep himself warm by flapping his wings.

But at last he knew that he was going to die. He had just enough strength to fly up to the Prince's shoulder once more. 'Good-bye, dear Prince!' he murmured, 'will you let me kiss your hand?'

'I am glad that you are going to Egypt at last, little Swallow,' said the prince, 'you have stayed too long here; but you must kiss me on the lips, for I love you.'

'It is not to Egypt that I am going,' said the Swallow. 'I am going to the House of Death. Death is the brother of Sleep, is he not?'

And he kissed the Happy Prince on the lips, and fell down dead at his feet.

At that moment a curious crack sounded inside the statue, as if something had broken. The fact is that the leaden heart had snapped right in two. It certainly was a dreadfully hard frost.

Early the next morning the Mayor was walking in the square below in company with the Town Councillors. As they passed the column he looked up at the statue: 'Dear me! how shabby the Happy Prince looks!' he said.

'How shabby, indeed!' cried the Town Councillors, who always agreed with the Mayor; and they went up to look at it.

'The ruby has fallen out of his sword, his eyes are gone, and he is golden no longer,' said the Mayor; 'in fact, he is little better than a beggar!'

'Little better than a beggar,' said the Town Councillors.

'And here is actually a dead bird at his feet!' continued the Mayor. 'We must really issue a proclamation that birds are not to be allowed to die here.' And the Town Clerk made a note of the suggestion.

So they pulled down the statue of the Happy Prince. 'As he is no longer beautiful he is no longer useful,' said the Art Professor at the University.

Then they melted the statue in a furnace, and the Mayor held a meeting of the Corporation to decide what was to be done with the metal. 'We must have another statue, of course,' he said, 'and it shall be a statue of myself.'

'Of myself,' said each of the Town Councillors, and they quarrelled. When I last heard of them they were quarrelling still.

'What a strange thing!' said the overseer of the workmen at the foundry. 'This broken lead heart will not melt in the furnace. We must throw it away.' So they threw it on a dust-heap where the dead Swallow was also lying.

'Bring me the two most precious things in the city,' said God to one of His Angels; and the Angel brought Him the leaden heart and the dead bird.

'You have rightly chosen,' said God, 'for in my garden of Paradise this little bird shall sing for evermore, and in my city of gold the Happy Prince shall praise me.'

The Nightingale and the Rose

'She said that she would dance with me if I brought her red roses,' cried the young Student, 'but in all my garden there is no red rose.'

From her nest in the holm-oak tree the Nightingale heard him, and she looked out through the leaves and wondered.

'No red rose in all my garden!' he cried, and his beautiful eyes filled with tears. 'Ah, on what little things does happiness depend! I have read all that the wise men have written, and all the secrets of philosophy are mine, yet for want of a red rose is my life made wretched.'

'Here at last is a true lover,' said the Nightingale. 'Night after night have I sung of him, though I knew him not: night after night have I told his story to the stars and now I see him. His hair is dark as the hyacinth-blossom, and his lips are red as the rose of his desire; but passion has made his face like pale ivory, and sorrow has set her seal upon his brow.'

'The Prince gives a ball tomorrow night,' murmured the young student, 'and my love will be of the company. If I bring her a red rose she will dance with me till dawn. If I bring her a red rose, I shall hold her in my arms, and she will lean her head upon my shoulder, and her hand will be clasped in mine. But there is no red rose in my garden, so I shall sit lonely, and she will pass me by. She will have no heed of me, and my heart will break.'

'Here, indeed, is the true lover,' said the Nightingale. 'What I sing of, he suffers: what is joy to me, to him is pain. Surely love is a wonderful thing. It is more precious than emeralds, and dearer than fine opals. Pearls and pomegranates cannot buy it, nor is it set forth in the marketplace. It may not be purchased of the merchants, nor can it be weighed out in the balance for gold.'

'The musicians will sit in their gallery,' said the young Student, 'and play upon their stringed instruments, and my love will dance to the sound of the harp and the violin. She will dance so lightly that her feet will not touch the floor, and the courtiers in their gay dresses will throng round her. But with me she will not dance, for I have no red rose to give her;' and he flung himself down on the grass, and buried his face in his hands, and wept.

'Why is he weeping?' asked a little Green Lizard, as he ran past him with his tail in the air.

'Why, indeed?' said a Butterfly, who was fluttering about after a sunbeam.

'Why, indeed?' whispered a Daisy to his neighbour, in a soft, low voice.

'He is weeping for a red rose,' said the Nightingale.

'For a red rose?' they cried; 'how very ridiculous!' and the little Lizard, who was something of a cynic, laughed outright.

But the Nightingale understood the secret of the Student's sorrow, and she sat silent in the oak tree, and thought about the mystery of Love.

Suddenly she spread her brown wings for flight, and soared into the air. She passed through the grove like a shadow and like a shadow she sailed across the garden.

In the centre of the grass-plot was standing a beautiful Rose tree, and when she saw it she flew over to it, and lit upon a spray.

'Give me a red rose,' she cried, 'and I will sing you my sweetest song.'

But the Tree shook its head.

'My roses are white,' it answered; 'as white as the foam of the sea, and whiter than the snow upon the mountain. But go to my brother who grows round the old sundial, and perhaps he will give you what you want.'

So the Nightingale flew over to the Rose tree that was growing round the old sundial.

'Give me a red rose,' she cried, 'and I will sing you my sweetest song.'

But the Tree shook its head.

'My roses are yellow,' it answered; 'as yellow as the hair of the mermaiden who sits upon an amber throne, and yellower than the daffodil that blooms in the meadow before the mower comes with his scythe. But go to my brother who grows beneath the Student's window, and perhaps he will give you what you want.'

So the Nightingale flew over to the Rose tree that was growing beneath the Student's window.

'Give me a red rose,' she cried, 'and I will sing you my sweetest song.'

But the Tree shook its head.

'My roses are red,' it answered, 'as red as the feet of the dove, and redder than the great fans of coral that wave and wave in the ocean cavern. But the winter has chilled my veins, and the frost has nipped my buds, and the storm has broken my branches, and I shall have no roses at all this year.'

'One red rose is all I want,' cried the Nightingale, 'only one red rose! Is there no way by which I can get it?'

'There is a way,' answered the Tree; 'but it is so terrible that I dare not tell it to you.'

'Tell it to me,' said the Nightingale, 'I am not afraid.'

'If you want a red rose,' said the Tree, 'you must build it out of music by moonlight, and stain it with your own heart's blood. You must sing to me with your breast against a thorn. All night long you must sing to me, and the thorn must pierce your heart, and your life-blood must flow into my veins, and become mine.'

'Death is a great price to pay for a red rose,' cried the Nightingale, 'and Life is very dear to all. It is pleasant to sit in the green wood, and to watch the Sun in his chariot of gold, and the Moon in her chariot of pearl. Sweet is the scent of the hawthorn, and sweet are the bluebells that hide in the valley, and the heather that blows on the hill. Yet Love is better than Life, and what is the heart of a bird compared to the heart of a man?'

So she spread her brown wings for flight, and soared into the air. She swept over the garden like a shadow, and like a shadow she sailed through the grove.

The young Student was still lying on the grass, where she had left him, and the tears were not yet dry in his beautiful eyes.

'Be happy,' cried the Nightingale, 'be happy; you shall have your red rose. I will build it out of music by moonlight, and stain it with my own heart's-blood. All that I ask of you in return is that you will be a true lover, for Love is wiser than Philosophy, though he is wise, and mightier than Power, though he is mighty. Flame-coloured are his wings, and coloured like flame is his body. His lips are sweet as honey, and his breath is like frankincense.'

The Student looked up from the grass, and listened, but he could not understand what the Nightingale was saying to him, for he only knew the things that are written down in books.

But the Oak tree understood, and felt sad, for he was very fond of the little Nightingale, who had built her nest in his branches.

'Sing me one last song,' he whispered; 'I shall feel lonely when you are gone.'

So the Nightingale sang to the Oak tree, and her voice was like water bubbling from a silver jar.

When she had finished her song, the Student got up, and pulled a note-book and a lead-pencil out of his pocket.

'She has form,' he said to himself, as he walked away through the grove— 'that cannot be denied to her; but has she got feeling? I am afraid not. In fact, she is like most artists; she is all style without any sincerity. She would not sacrifice herself for others. She thinks merely of music, and everybody knows that the arts are selfish. Still, it must be admitted that she has some beautiful notes in her voice. What a pity it is that they do not mean anything, or do any practical good!' And he went into his room, and lay down on his little pallet bed, and began to think of his love; and, after a time, he fell asleep.

And when the moon shone in the heavens the Nightingale flew to the Rose tree, and set her breast against the thorn. All night long she sang, with her breast against the thorn, and the cold crystal Moon leaned down and listened. All night long she sang, and the thorn went deeper and deeper into her breast, and her life blood ebbed away from her.

She sang first of the birth of love in the heart of a boy and a girl. And on the topmost spray of the Rose tree there blossomed a marvellous rose, petal following petal, as song followed song. Pale was it, at first, as the mist that hangs over the river—pale as the feet of the morning, and silver as the wings of the dawn. As the shadow of a rose in a mirror of silver, as the shadow of a rose in a water pool, so was the rose that blossomed on the topmost spray of the Tree.

But the Tree cried to the Nightingale to press closer against the thorn. 'Press closer, little Nightingale,' cried the Tree, 'or the Day will come before the rose is finished.'

So the Nightingale pressed closer against the thorn, and louder and louder grew her song, for she sang of the birth of passion in the soul of a man and a maid.

And a delicate flush of pink came into the leaves of the rose, like the flush in the face of the bridegroom when he kisses the lips of the bride. But the thorn had not yet reached her heart, so the rose's heart remained white, for only a Nightingale's heart's-blood can crimson the heart of a rose.

And the Tree cried to the Nightingale to press closer against the thorn. 'Press closer, little Nightingale,' cried the Tree, 'or the Day will come before the rose is finished.'

So the Nightingale pressed closer against the thorn, and the thorn touched her heart, and a fierce pang of pain shot through her. Bitter, bitter was the pain, and wilder and wilder grew her song, for she sang of the Love that is perfected by Death, of the Love that dies not in the tomb.

And the marvellous rose became crimson, like the rose of the eastern sky. Crimson was the girdle of petals, and crimson as a ruby was the heart.

But the Nightingale's voice grew fainter, and her little wings began to heat, and a film came over her eyes. Fainter and fainter grew her song, and she felt something choking her in her throat.

Then she gave one last burst of music. The white Moon heard it, and she forgot the dawn, and lingered on in the sky. The red rose heard it, and it trembled all over with ecstasy, and opened its petals to the cold morning air. Echo bore it to her purple cavern in the hills, and woke the sleeping shepherds from their dreams. It floated through the reeds of the river, and they carried its message to the sea.

'Look, look!' cried the Tree, 'the rose is finished now;' but the Nightingale made no answer, for she was lying dead in the long grass, with the thorn in her heart.

And at noon the Student opened his window and looked out.

'Why, what a wonderful piece of luck!' he cried; 'here is a red rose! I have never seen any rose like it in all my life. It is so beautiful that I am sure it has a long Latin name;' and he leaned down and plucked it.

Then he put on his hat, and ran up to the Professor's house with the rose in his hand.

The daughter of the Professor was sitting in the doorway winding blue silk on a reel, and her little dog was lying at her feet.

'You said that you would dance with me if I brought you a red rose,' cried the Student. 'Here is the reddest rose in all the world. You will wear it tonight next your heart, and as we dance together it will tell you how I love you.'

But the girl frowned.

'I am afraid it will not go with my dress,' she answered; 'and, besides, the Chamberlain's nephew has sent me some real jewels, and everybody knows that jewels cost far more than flowers.'

'Well, upon my word, you are very ungrateful,' said the Student angrily; and he threw the rose into the street, where it fell into the gutter, and a cartwheel went over it.

'Ungrateful!' said the girl. 'I tell you what, you are very rude; and, after all, who are you? Only a Student. Why, I don't believe you have even got silver buckles to your shoes as the Chamberlain's nephew has;' and she got up from her chair and went into the house.

'What a silly thing Love is!' said the Student as he walked away. 'It is not half as useful as Logic, for it does not prove anything, and it is always telling one of things that are not going to happen, and making one believe things that are not true. In fact, it is quite unpractical, and, as in this age to be practical is everything, I shall go back to Philosophy and study Metaphysics.'

So he returned to his room and pulled out a great dusty book, and began to read.

The Selfish Giant

Every afternoon, as they were coming from school, the children used to go and play in the Giant's garden.

It was a large lovely garden, with soft green grass. Here and there over the grass stood beautiful flowers like stars, and there were twelve peach trees that in the spring time broke out into delicate blossoms of pink and pearl, and in the autumn bore rich fruit. The birds sat on the trees and sang so sweetly that the children used to stop their games in order to listen to them. 'How happy we are here!' they cried to each other.

One day the Giant came back. He had been to visit his friend the Cornish ogre, and had stayed with him for seven years. After the seven years were over he had said all that he had to say, for his conversation was limited, and he determined to return to his own castle. When he arrived he saw the children playing in the garden.

'What are you doing here?' he cried in a very gruff voice, and the children ran away.

'My own garden is my own garden,' said the Giant; 'any one can understand that, and I will allow nobody to play in it but myself.' So he built a high wall all round it, and put up a notice-board.

```
TRESPASSERS
WILL BE
PROSECUTED
```

He was a very selfish Giant.

The poor children had now nowhere to play. They tried to play on the read, but the road was very dusty and full of hard stones, and they did not like it. They used to wander round the high walls when their lessons were over, and talk about the beautiful garden inside. 'How happy we were there!' they said to each other.

Then the Spring came, and all over the country there were little blossoms and little birds. Only in the garden of the Selfish Giant it was still winter. The birds did not care to sing in it as there were no children, and the trees forgot to blossom. Once a beautiful flower put its head out from the grass, but when it saw the notice-board it was so sorry for the children that it slipped back into the ground again, and went off to sleep. The only people who were pleased were the Snow and the Frost. 'Spring has forgotten this garden,' they cried, 'so we will live here all the year round.' The Snow covered up the grass with her great white cloak, and the Frost painted all the trees silver. Then they invited the North Wind to stay with them, and he came. He was wrapped in furs, and he roared all day about the garden, and blew the chimney-pots down. 'This is a delightful spot,' he said, 'we must ask the Hail on a visit.'

So the Hail came. Every day for three hours he rattled on the roof of the castle till he broke most of the slates, and then he ran round and round the garden as fast as he could go. He was dressed in grey, and his breath was like ice.

'I cannot understand why the Spring is so late in coming,' said the Selfish Giant, as he sat at the window and looked out at his cold, white garden; 'I hope there will be a change in the weather.'

But the Spring never came, nor the Summer. The Autumn gave golden fruit to every garden, but to the Giant's garden she gave none. 'He is too selfish,' she said. So it was always Winter there, and the North Wind and the Hail, and the Frost, and the Snow danced about through the trees.

One morning the Giant was lying awake in bed when he heard some lovely music. It sounded so sweet to his ears that he thought it must be the King's musicians passing by. It was really only a little linnet singing outside his window, but it was so long since he had heard a bird sing in his garden that it seemed to him to be the most beautiful music in the world. Then the Hail stopped dancing over his head, and the North Wind ceased roaring, and a delicious perfume came to him through the open casement. 'I believe the Spring has come at last,' said the Giant; and he jumped out of bed and looked out.

What did he see?

He saw a most wonderful sight. Through a little hole in the wall the children had crept in, and they were sitting in the branches of the trees. In every tree that he could see there was a little child. And the trees were so glad to have the children back again that they had covered themselves with blossoms, and were waving their arms gently above the children's heads. The birds were flying about and twittering with delight, and the flowers were looking up through the green grass and laughing. It was a lovely scene, only in one corner it was still winter. It was the farthest corner of the garden, and in it was standing a little boy. He was so small that he could not reach up to the branches of the tree, and he was wandering all round it, crying bitterly. The poor tree was still covered with frost and snow, and the North Wind was blowing and roaring above it. 'Climb up! little boy,' said the Tree, and it bunt its branches down as low as it could; but the boy was too tiny.

And the Giant's heart melted as he looked out. 'How selfish I have been!' he said; 'now I know why the Spring would not come here. I will put that poor little boy on the top of the tree, and then I will knock down the wall, and my garden shall be the children's playground for ever and ever.' He was really very sorry for what he had done.

So he crept downstairs and opened the front door quite softly, and went out into the garden. But when the children saw him they were so frightened that they all ran away, and the garden became winter again. Only the little boy did not run, for his eyes were so full of tears that he did not see the Giant coming. And the Giant stole up behind him and took him gently in his hand, and put him up into the tree. And the tree broke at once into blossom, and the birds came and sang on it, and the little boy stretched out his two arms and flung them round the Giant's neck, and kissed him. And the other children when they saw that the Giant was not wicked any longer, came running back, and with them came the Spring. 'It is your garden now, little children,' said the Giant, and he took a great axe and knocked down the wall. And when the people were going to market at twelve o'clock they found the Giant playing with the children in the most beautiful garden they had ever seen.

All day long they played, and in the evening they came to the Giant to bid him good-bye.

'But where is your little companion?' he said: 'the boy I put into the tree.' The Giant loved him the best because he had kissed him.

'We don't know,' answered the children: 'he has gone away.'

'You must tell him to be sure and come tomorrow,' said the Giant. But the children said that they did not know where he lived, and had never seen him before; and the Giant felt very sad.

Every afternoon, when school was over, the children came and played with the Giant. But the little boy whom the Giant loved was never seen again. The Giant was very kind to all the children, yet he longed for his first little friend, and often spoke of him. 'How I would like to see him!' he used to say.

Years went over, and the Giant grew very old and feeble. He could not play about any more, so he sat in a huge armchair, and watched the children at their games, and admired his garden. 'I have many beautiful flowers,' he said; 'but the children are the most beautiful flowers of all.'

One winter morning he looked out of his window as he was dressing. He did not hate the Winter now, for he knew that it was merely the Spring asleep, and that the flowers were resting.

Suddenly he rubbed his eyes in wonder and looked and looked. It certainly was a marvellous sight. In the farthest corner of the garden was a tree quite covered with lovely white blossoms. Its branches were golden, and silver fruit hung down from them, and underneath it stood the little boy he had loved.

Downstairs ran the Giant in great joy, and out into the garden. He hastened across the grass, and came near to the child. And when he came quite close his face grew red with anger, and he said, 'Who hath[1] dared to wound thee[2]?' For on the palms of the child's hands were the prints of two nails, and the prints of two nails were on the little feet.

'Who hath dared to wound thee?' cried the Giant; 'tell me, that I may take my big sword and slay him.'

'Nay[3]!' answered the child: 'but these are the wounds of Love.'

'Who art[4] thou[5]?' said the Giant, and a strange awe fell on him, and he knelt before the little child.

And the child smiled on the Giant, and said to him, 'You let me play once in your garden, today you shall come with me to my garden, which is Paradise.'

And when the children ran in that afternoon, they found the Giant lying dead under the tree, all covered with white blossoms.

The Devoted Friend

One morning the old Water-rat put his head out of his hole. He had bright beady eyes and stiff grey whiskers, and his tail was like a long bit of black Indiarubber. The little ducks were swimming about in the pond, looking just like a lot of yellow canaries, and their mother, who was pure white with real red legs, was trying to teach them how to stand on their heads in the water.

'You will never be in the best society unless you can stand on your heads,' she kept saying to them; and every now and then she showed them how it was done. But the little ducks paid no attention to her. They were so young that they did not know what an advantage it is to be in society at all.

'What disobedient children!' cried the old Water-rat: 'they really deserve to be drowned.'

'Nothing of the kind,' answered the Duck, 'every one must make a beginning, and parents cannot be too patient.'

'Ah! I know nothing about the feelings of parents,' said the Water-rat; 'I am not a family man. In fact, I have never been married, and I never intend to be. Love is all very well in its way, but friendship is much higher. Indeed, I know of nothing in the world that is either nobler or rarer than a devoted friendship.'

'And what, pray, is your idea of the duties of a devoted friend?' asked a green Linnet, who was sitting on a willow-tree hard by, and had overheard the conversation.

'Yes, that is just what I want to know,' said the Duck; and she swam away to the end of the pond, and stood upon her head, in order to give her children a good example.

'What a silly question!' cried the Water-rat. 'I should expect my devoted friend to be devoted to me, of course.'

'And what would you do in return?' said the little bird, swinging upon a silver spray, and flapping his tiny wings.

'I don't understand you,' answered the Water-rat.

'Let me tell you a story on the subject,' said the Linnet.

'Is the story about me?' asked the Water-rat. 'If so, I will listen to it, for I am extremely fond of fiction.'

'It is applicable to you,' answered the Linnet; and he flew down, and alighting upon the bank, he told the story of The Devoted Friend.

'Once upon a time,' said the Linnet, 'there was an honest little fellow named Hans.'

'Was he very distinguished?' asked the Water-rat.

'No,' answered the Linnet, 'I don't think he was distinguished at all, except for his kind heart, and his funny, round, good-humoured face. He lived in a tiny cottage all by himself, and every day he worked in his garden. In all the country-side there was no garden so lovely as his. Sweet-Williams grew there, and Gilly-flowers, and Shepherds'-purses, and Fair-maids of France. There were damask Roses, and yellow Roses, lilac Crocuses and gold, purple Violets and white Columbine and Ladysmock, Marjoram and Wild Basil, the Cowslip and the Flower-de-luce, the Daffodil and the Clove-Pink bloomed or blossomed in their proper order as the months went by, one flower taking another flower's place, so that there were always beautiful things to look at, and pleasant odours to smell.

'Little Hans had a great many friends, but the most devoted friend of all was big Hugh the Miller. Indeed, so devoted was the rich Miller to little Hans, that he would never go by his garden without leaning over the wall and plucking a large nosegay, or a handful of sweet herbs, or filling his pockets with plums and cherries if it was the fruit season.

'"Real friends should have everything in common," the Miller used to say, and little Hans nodded and smiled, and felt very proud of having a friend with such noble ideas.

'Sometimes, indeed, the neighbours thought it strange that the rich Miller never gave little Hans anything in return, though he had a hundred sacks of flour stored away in his mill, and six milch cows, and a large flock of woolly sheep; but Hans never troubled his head about these things, and nothing gave him greater pleasure than to listen to all the wonderful things the Miller used to say about the unselfishness of true friendship.

'So little Hans worked away in his garden. During the spring, the summer, and the autumn he was very happy, but when the winter came, and he had no fruit or flowers to bring to the market, he suffered a good deal from cold and hunger, and often had to go to bed without any supper but a few dried pears or some hard nuts. In the winter, also, he was extremely lonely, as the Miller never came to see him then.

'"There is no good in my going to see little Hans as long as the snow lasts," the Miller used to say to his wife, "for when people are in trouble they should be left alone and not be bothered by visitors. That at least is my idea about friendship, and I am sure I am right. So I shall wait till the spring comes, and then I shall pay him a visit, and he will be able to give me a large basket of primroses, and that will make him so happy."

'"You are certainly very thoughtful about others," answered the Wife, as she sat in her comfortable armchair by the big pinewood fire; "very thoughtful indeed. It is quite a treat to hear you talk about friendship. I am sure the clergyman himself could not say such beautiful things as you do, though he does live in a three-storied house, and wear a gold ring on his little finger."

'"But could we not ask little Hans up here?" said the Miller's youngest son. "If poor Hans is in trouble I will give him half my porridge, and show him my white rabbits."

'"What a silly boy you are!" cried the Miller; "I really don't know what is the use of sending you to school. You seem not to learn anything. Why, if little Hans came up here, and saw our warm fire, and our good supper, and our great cask of red wine, he might get envious, and envy is a most terrible thing, and would spoil anybody's nature. I certainly will not allow Hans' nature to be spoiled. I am his best friend, and I will always watch over him, and see that he is not led into any temptations. Besides, if Hans came here, he might ask me to let him have some flour on credit, and that I could not do. Flour is one thing, and friendship is another, and they should not be confused. Why, the words are spelt differently, and mean quite different things. Everybody can see that."

'"How well you talk!" said the Miller's Wife, pouring herself out a large glass of warm ale; "really I feel quite drowsy. It is just like being in church."

'"Lots of people act well," answered the Miller; "but very few people talk well, which shows that talking is much the more difficult thing of the two, and much the finer thing also;" and he looked sternly across the table at his little son, who felt so ashamed of himself that he hung his head down, and grew quite scarlet and began to cry into his tea. However, he was so young that you must excuse him.'

'Is that the end of the story?' asked the Water-rat.

'Certainly not,' answered the Linnet, 'that is the beginning.'

'Then you are quite behind the age,' said the Water-rat. 'Every good storyteller nowadays starts with the end, and then goes on to the beginning, and concludes with the middle. That is the new method. I heard all about it the other day from a critic who was walking round the pond with a young man. He spoke of the matter at great length, and I am sure he must have been right, for he had blue spectacles and a bald head, and whenever the young man made any remark, he always answered "Pooh!" But pray go on with your story. I like the Miller immensely. I have all kinds of beautiful sentiments myself, so there is a great sympathy between us.'

'Well,' said the Linnet, hopping now on one leg and now on the other, 'as soon as the winter was over, and the primroses began to open their pale yellow stars, the Miller said to his wife that he would go down and see little Hans.

'"Why, what a good heart you have!" cried his Wife; "you are always thinking of others. And mind you take the big basket with you for the flowers."

'So the Miller tied the sails of the windmill together with a strong iron chain, and went down the hill with the basket on his arm.

'"Good morning, little Hans," said the Miller.

'"Good morning," said Hans, leaning on his spade, and smiling from ear to ear.

'"And how have you been all the winter?" said the Miller.

'"Well, really," cried Hans, "it is very good of you to ask, very good indeed. I am afraid I had rather a hard time of it, but now the spring has come, and I am quite happy, and all my flowers are doing well."

'"We often talked of you during the winter, Hans," said the Miller, "and wondered how you were getting on."

'"That was kind of you," said Hans; "I was half afraid you had forgotten me."

'"Hans, I am surprised at you," said the Miller; "friendship never forgets. That is the wonderful thing about it, but I am afraid you don't understand the poetry of life. How lovely your primroses are looking, by-the-bye!"

'"They are certainly very lovely," said Hans, "and it is a most lucky thing for me that I have so many. I am going to bring them into the market and sell them to the Burgomaster's daughter, and buy back my wheelbarrow with the money."

'"Buy back your wheelbarrow? You don't mean to say you have sold it? What a very stupid thing to do!"

'"Well, the fact is," said Hans, "that I was obliged to. You see the winter was a very hard time for me, and I really had no money at all to buy bread with. So I first sold the silver buttons off my

Sunday coat, and then I sold my silver chain, and then I sold my big pipe, and at last I sold my wheelbarrow. But I am going to buy them all back again now."

'"Hans," said the Miller, "I will give you my wheelbarrow. It is not in very good repair; indeed, one side is gone, and there is something wrong with the wheel-spokes; but in spite of that I will give it to you. I know it is very generous of me, and a great many people would think me extremely foolish for parting with it, but I am not like the rest of the world. I think that generosity is the essence of friendship, and, besides, I have got a new wheel-barrow for myself. Yes, you may set your mind at ease, I will give you my wheelbarrow."

'"Well, really, that is generous of you," said little Hans, and his funny round face glowed all over with pleasure. "I can easily put it in repair, as I have a plank of wood in the house."

'"A plank of wood!" said the Miller; "why, that is just what I want fig the roof my barn. There is a very large hole in it, and the corn will all get damp if I don't stop it up. How lucky you mentioned it! It is quite remarkable how one good action always breeds another. I have given you my wheelbarrow, and now you are going to give me your plank. Of course, the wheelbarrow is worth far more than the plank, but true friendship never notices things like that. Pray get it at once, and I will set to work at my barn this very day."

'"Certainly," cried little Hans, and he ran into the shed and dragged the plank out.

'"It is not a very big plank," said the Miller, looking at it, "and I am afraid that after I have mended my barn-roof there won't be any left for you to mend the wheelbarrow with; but, of course, that is not my fault. And now, as I have given you my wheelbarrow, I am sure you would like to give me some flowers in return. Here is the basket, and mind you fill it quite full."

'"Quite full?" said little Hans, rather sorrowfully, for it was really a very big basket, and he knew that if he filled it he would have no flowers left for the market, and he was very anxious to get his silver buttons back.

'"Well, really," answered the Miller, "as I have given you my wheelbarrow, I don't think that it is much to ask you for a few flowers. I may be wrong, but I should have thought that friendship, true friendship, was quite free from selfishness of any kind."

'"My dear friend, my best friend," cried little Hans, "you are welcome to all the flowers in my garden. I would much sooner have your good opinion than my silver buttons, any day;" and he ran and plucked all his pretty primroses, and filled the Miller's basket.

'"Good-bye, little Hans," said the Miller, and he went up the hill with the plank on his shoulder, and the big basket in his hand.

'"Good-bye," said little Hans, and he began to dig away quite merrily, he was so pleased about the wheelbarrow.

'The next day he was nailing up some honeysuckle against the porch, when he heard the Miller's voice calling to him from the road. So he jumped off the ladder, and ran down the garden, and looked over the wall.

'There was the Miller with a large sack of flour on his back.

'"Dear little Hans," said the Miller, "would you mind carrying this sack of flour for me to market?"

'"Oh, I am so sorry," said Hans, "but I am really very busy today. I have got all my creepers to nail up, and all my flowers to water, and all my grass to roll."

'"Well, really," said the Miller, "I think, that considering that I am going to give you my wheelbarrow it is rather unfriendly of you to refuse."

'"Oh, don't say that," cried little Hans, "I wouldn't be unfriendly for the whole world;" and he ran in for his cap, and trudged off with the big sack on his shoulders.

'It was a very hot day, and the road was terribly dusty, and before Hans had reached the sixth milestone he was so tired that he had to sit down and rest. However, he went on bravely, and at last he reached the market. After he had waited there for some time, he sold the sack of flour for a very good price, and then he returned home at once, for he was afraid that if he stopped too late he might meet some robbers on the way.

'"It has certainly been a hard day," said little Hans to himself as he was going to bed, "but I am glad I did not refuse the Miller, for he is my best friend and, besides, he is going to give me his wheelbarrow."

'Early the next morning the Miller came down to get the money for his sack of flour, but little Hans was so tired that he was still in bed.

'"Upon my word," said the Miller, "you are very lazy. Really, considering that I am going to give you my wheelbarrow, I think you might work harder. Idleness is a great sin, and I certainly don't like any of my friends to be idle or sluggish. You must not mind my speaking quite plainly to you. Of course I should not dream of doing so if I were not your friend. But what is the good of friendship if one cannot say exactly what one means? Anybody can say charming things and try to please and to flatter, but a true friend always says unpleasant things, and does not mind giving pain. Indeed, if he is a really true friend he prefers it, for he knows that then he is doing good."

'"I am very sorry," said little Hans, rubbing his eyes and pulling off his nightcap, "but I was so tired that I thought I would lie in bed for a little time, and listen to the birds singing. Do you know that I always work better after hearing the birds sing?"

'"Well, I am glad of that," said the Miller, clapping little Hans on the back, "for I want you to come up to the mill as soon as you are dressed and mend my barn-roof for me."

'Poor little Hans was very anxious to go and work in his garden, for his flowers had not been watered for two days, but he did not like to refuse the Miller, as he was such a good friend to him.

'"Do you think it would be unfriendly of me if I said I was busy?" he inquired in a shy and timid voice.

'"Well, really," answered the Miller, "I do not think it is much to ask of you, considering that I am going to give you my wheelbarrow; but, of course, if you refuse I will go and do it myself."

'"Oh! on no account," cried little Hans; and he jumped out of bed, and dressed himself, and went up to the barn.

'He worked there all day long, till sunset, and at sunset the Miller came to see how he was getting on.

'"Have you mended the hole in the roof yet, little Hans?" cried the Miller, in a cheery voice.

'"It is quite mended," answered little Hans, coining down the ladder.

'"Ah!" said the Miller, "there is no work so delightful as the work one does for others."

'"It is certainly a great privilege to hear you talk," answered little Hans, sitting down and wiping his forehead, "a very great privilege. But I am afraid I shall never have such beautiful ideas as you have."

'"Oh! they will come to you," said the Miller, "but you must take more pains. At present you have only the practice of friendship; some day you will have the theory also."

'"Do you really think I shall?" asked little Hans.

'"I have no doubt of it," answered the Miller, "but now that you have mended the roof, you had better go home and rest, for I want you to drive my sheep to the mountain tomorrow."

'Poor little Hans was afraid to say anything to this, and early next morning the Miller brought his sheep round to the cottage, and Hans started off with them to the mountain. It took him the whole day to get there and back; and when he returned he was so tired that he went off to sleep in his chair, and did not wake up till it was broad daylight.

'"What a delightful time I shall have in my garden!" he said, and he went to work at once.

'But somehow he was never able to look after his flowers at all, for his friend the Miller was always coming round and sending him off on long errands, or getting him to help at the mill. Little Hans was very much distressed at times, as he was afraid his flowers would think he had forgotten them, but he consoled himself by the reflection that the Miller was his best friend. "Besides," he used to say, "he is going to give me his wheelbarrow, and that is an act of pure generosity."

'So little Hans worked away for the Miller, and the Miller said all kinds of beautiful things about friendship, which Hans took down in a notebook, and used to read over at night, for he was a very good scholar.

'Now it happened that one evening little Hans was sitting by his fireside when a loud rap came at the door. It was a very wild night, and the wind was blowing and roaring round the house so terribly that at first he thought it was merely the storm. But a second rap came, and then a third, louder than any of the others.

'"It is some poor traveller," said little Hans to himself, and he ran to the door.

'There stood the Miller with a lantern in one hand and a big stick in the other.

'"Dear little Hans," cried the Miller, "I am in great trouble. My little boy has fallen off a ladder and hurt himself, and I am going for the Doctor. But he lives so far away, and it is such a bad night, that it has just occurred to me that it would be much better if you went instead of me. You know I am going to give you my wheelbarrow, and so it is only fair that you should do something for me in return."

'"Certainly," cried little Hans, "I take it quite as a compliment your coming to me, and I will start off at once. But you must lend me your lantern, as the night is so dark that I am afraid I might fall into the ditch."

'"I am very sorry," answered the Miller, "but it is my new lantern, and it would be a great loss to me if anything happened to it."

'"Well, never mind, I will do without it," cried little Hans, and he took down his great fur coat, and his warm scarlet cap, and tied a muffler round his throat, and started off.

'What a dreadful storm it was! The night was so black that little Hans could hardly see, and the wind was so strong that he could hardly stand. However, he was very courageous, and after he had been walking about three hours, he arrived at the Doctor's house, and knocked at the door.

'"Who is there?" cried the Doctor, putting his head out of his bedroom window.

'"Little Hans, Doctor."

'"What do you want, little Hans?"

'"The Miller's son has fallen from a ladder, and has hurt himself, and the Miller wants you to come at once."

'"All right!" said the Doctor; and he ordered his horse, and his big boots, and his lantern, and came downstairs, and rode off in the direction of the Miller's house, little Hans trudging behind him.

'But the storm grew worse and worse, and the rain fell in torrents, and little Hans could not see where he was going, or keep up with the horse. At last he lost his way, and wandered off on the moor, which was a very dangerous place, as it was full of deep holes, and there poor little Hans was drowned. His body was found the next day by some goatherds, floating in a great pool of water, and was brought back by them to the cottage.

'Everybody went to little Hans' funeral, as he was so popular, and the Miller was the chief mourner.

'"As I was his best friend," said the Miller, "it is only fair that I should have the best place;" so he walked at the head of the procession in a long black cloak, and every now and then he wiped his eyes with a big pocket-handkerchief.

'"Little Hans is certainly a great loss to every one," said the Blacksmith, when the funeral was over, and they were all seated comfortably in the inn, drinking spiced wine and eating sweet cakes.

'"A great loss to me at any rate," answered the Miller; "why, I had as good as given him my wheelbarrow, and now I really don't know what to do with it. It is very much in my way at home, and it is in such bad repair that I could not get anything for it if I sold it. I will certainly take care not to give away anything again. One certainly suffers for being generous."'

'Well?' and the Water-rat, after a long pause.

'Well, that is the end,' said the Linnet.

'But what became of the Miller?' asked the Water-rat.

'Oh! I really don't know,' replied the Linnet; 'and I am sure that I don't care.'

'It is quite evident that you have no sympathy in your nature,' said the Water-rat.

'I am afraid you don't quite see the moral of the story,' remarked the Linnet.

'The what?' screamed the Water-rat.

'The moral.'

'Do you mean to say that the story has a moral?'

'Certainly,' said the Linnet.

'Well, really,' said the Water-rat, in a very angry manner, 'I think you should have told me that before you began. If you had done so, I certainly would not have listened to you; in fact, I should have said "Pooh," like the critic. However, I can say it now;' so he shouted out 'Pooh,' at the top of his voice, gave a whisk with his tail, and went back into his hole.

'And how do you like the Water-rat?' asked the Duck, who came paddling up some minutes afterwards. 'He has a great many good points, but for my own part I have a mother's feelings, and I can never look at a confirmed bachelor without the tears coming into my eyes.'

'I am rather afraid that I have annoyed him,' answered the Linnet. 'The fact is that I told him a story with a moral.'

'Ah! that is always a very dangerous thing to do,' said the Duck.

And I quite agree with her.

The Remarkable Rocket

The King's son was going to be married, so there were general rejoicings. He had waited a whole year for his bride, and at last she had arrived. She was a Russian Princess, and had driven all the way from Finland in a sledge drawn by six reindeer. The sledge was shaped like a great golden swan, and between the swan's wings lay the little Princess herself. Her long ermine cloak reached right down to her feet, on her head was a tiny cap of silver tissue, and she was as pale as the Snow Palace in which she had always lived. So pale was she that as she drove through the streets all the people wondered. 'She is like a white rose!' they cried, and they threw down flowers on her from the balconies.

At the gate of the Castle the Prince was waiting to receive her. He had dreamy violet eyes, and his hair was like fine gold. When he saw her he sank upon one knee, and kissed her hand.

'Your picture was beautiful,' he murmured, 'but you are more beautiful than your picture;' and the little Princess blushed.

'She was like a white rose before,' said a young page to his neighbour, 'but she is like a red rose now;' and the whole Court was delighted.

For the next three days everybody went about saying, 'White rose, Red rose, Red rose, White rose,' and the King gave orders that the Page's salary was to be doubled. As he received no salary at all this was not of much use to him, but it was considered a great honour and was duly published in the Court Gazette.

When the three days were over the marriage was celebrated. It was a magnificent ceremony, and the bride and bridegroom walked hand in hand under a canopy of purple velvet embroidered with little pearls. Then there was a State Banquet, which lasted for five hours. The Prince and Princess sat at the top of the Great Hall and drank out of a cup of clear crystal. Only true lovers could drink out of this cup, for if false lips touched it, it grew grey dull and cloudy.

'It is quite clear that they love each other,' said the little Page, 'as clear as crystal!' and the King doubled his salary a second time.

'What an honour!' cried all the courtiers.

After the banquet there was to be a Ball. The bride and bridegroom were to dance the Rose-dance together, and the King had promised to play the flute. He played very badly, but no one had ever dared to tell him so, because he was the King. Indeed, he knew only two airs, and was never quite certain which one he was playing; but it made no matter, for, whatever he did, everybody cried out, 'Charming! charming!'

The last item on the programme was a grand display of fireworks, to be let off exactly at midnight. The little Princess had never seen a firework in her life, so the King had given orders that the Royal Pyrotechnist should be in attendance on the day of her marriage.

'What are fireworks like?' she had asked the Prince, one morning, as she was walking on the terrace.

'They are like the Aurora Borealis,' said the King, who always answered questions that were addressed to other people, 'only much more natural. I prefer them to stars myself, as you always know when they are going to appear, and they are as delightful as my own flute-playing. You must certainly see them.'

So at the end of the King's garden a great stand had been set up, and as soon as the Royal Pyrotechnist had put everything in its proper place, the fireworks began to talk to each other.

'The world is certainly very beautiful,' cried a little Squib. 'Just look at those yellow tulips. Why! if they were real crackers they could not be lovelier. I am very glad I have travelled. Travel improves the mind wonderfully, and does away with all one's prejudices.'

'The King's garden is not the world, you foolish Squib,' said a big Roman Candle; 'the world is an enormous place, and it would take you three days to see it thoroughly.'

'Any place you love is the world to you,' exclaimed the pensive Catherine Wheel, who had been attached to an old deal box in early life, and prided herself on her broken heart; 'but love is not fashionable anymore, the poets have killed it. They wrote so much about it that nobody believed them, and I am not surprised. True love suffers, and is silent. I remember myself once—But no matter now. Romance is a thing of the past.'

'Nonsense!' said the Roman Candle, 'Romance never dies. It is like the moon, and lives for ever. The bride and bridegroom, for instance, love each other very dearly. I heard all about them this morning from a brown-paper cartridge, who happened to be staying in the same drawer as myself, and he knew the latest Court news.'

But the Catherine Wheel shook her head. 'Romance is dead, Romance is dead, Romance is dead,' she murmured. She was one of those people who think that, if you say the same thing over and over a great many times, it becomes true in the end.

Suddenly, a sharp, dry cough was heard, and they all looked round.

It came from a tall, supercilious-looking Rocket, who was tied to the end of a long stick. He always coughed before he made any observations, so as to attract attention.

'Ahem! ahem!' he said, and everybody listened except the poor Catherine Wheel, who was still shaking her head, and murmuring, 'Romance is dead.'

'Order! order!' cried out a Cracker. He was something of a politician, and had always taken a prominent part in the local elections, so he knew the proper Parliamentary expressions to use.

'Quite dead,' whispered the Catherine Wheel, and she went off to sleep.

As soon as there was perfect silence, the Rocket coughed a third time and began. He spoke with a very slow, distinct voice, as if he were dictating his memoirs, and always looked over the shoulder of the person to whom he was talking. In fact, he had a most distinguished manner.

'How fortunate it is for the King's son,' he remarked, 'that he is to be married on the very day on which I am to be let off! Really, if it had not been arranged beforehand, it could not have turned out better for him; but Princes are always lucky.'

'Dear me!' said the little Squib, 'I thought it was quite the other way, and that we were to be let off in the Prince's honour.'

'It may be so with you,' he answered; 'indeed, I have no doubt that it is, but with me it is different. I am a very remarkable Rocket, and come of remarkable parents. My mother was the most celebrated Catherine Wheel of her day, and was renowned for her graceful dancing. When she made her great public appearance she spun round nineteen times before she went out, and each time that she did so she threw into the air seven pink stars. She was three feet and a half in diameter, and made of the very best gunpowder. My father was a Rocket like myself, and of French extraction. He flew so high that the people were afraid that he would never come down again. He did, though, for he was of a kindly disposition, and he made a most brilliant descent in a shower of golden rain. The newspapers wrote about his performance in very flattering terms. Indeed, the Court Gazette called him a triumph of Pylotechnic art.'

'Pyrotechnic, Pyrotechnic, you mean,' said a Bengal Light; 'I know it is Pyrotechnic, for I saw it written on my own canister.'

'Well, I said Pylotechnic,' answered the Rocket, in a severe tone of voice, and the Bengal Light felt so crushed that he began at once to bully the little squibs, in order to show that he was still a person of some importance.

'I was saying,' continued the Rocket, 'I was saying—What was I saying?'

'You were talking about yourself,' replied the Roman Candle.

'Of course; I knew I was discussing some interesting subject when I was so rudely interrupted. I hate rudeness and bad manners of every kind, for I am extremely sensitive. No one in the whole world is so sensitive as I am, I am quite sure of that.'

'What is a sensitive person?' said the Cracker to the Roman Candle.

'A person who, because he has corns himself, always treads on other people's toes,' answered the Roman Candle in a low whisper; and the Cracker nearly exploded with laughter.

'Pray, what are you laughing at?' inquired the Rocket; 'I am not laughing.'

'I am laughing because I am happy,' replied the Cracker.

'That is a very selfish reason,' said the Rocket angrily. 'What right have you to be happy? You should be thinking about others. In fact, you should be thinking about me. I am always thinking about myself, and I expect everybody else to do the same. That is what is called sympathy. It is a beautiful virtue, and I possess it in a high degree. Suppose, for instance, anything happened to me tonight, what a misfortune that would be for every one! The Prince and Princess would never be happy again, their whole married life would be spoiled; and as for the King, I know he would not get over it.

Really, when I begin to reflect on the importance of my position, I am almost moved to tears.'

'If you want to give pleasure to others,' cried the Roman Candle, 'you had better keep yourself dry.'

'Certainly,' exclaimed the Bengal Light, who was now in better spirits; 'that is only common sense.'

'Common sense, indeed!' said the Rocket indignantly; 'you forget that I am very uncommon, and very remarkable. Why, anybody can have common sense, provided that they have no imagination. But I have imagination, for I never think of things as they really are; I always think of them as being quite different.

As for keeping myself dry, there is evidently no one here who can at all appreciate an emotional nature. Fortunately for myself, I don't care. The only thing that sustains one through life is the consciousness of the immense inferiority of everybody else, and this is a feeling I have always cultivated. But none of you have any hearts. Here you are laughing and making merry just as if the Prince and Princess had not just been married.'

'Well, really,' exclaimed a small Fire-balloon, 'why not? It is a most joyful occasion, and when I soar up into the air I intend to tell the stars all about it. You will see them twinkle when I talk to them about the pretty bride.'

'Ah! what a trivial view of life!' said the Rocket; 'but it is only what I expected. There is nothing in you; you are hollow and empty. Why, perhaps the Prince and Princess may go to live in a country where there is a deep river, and perhaps they may have one only son, a little fair-haired boy with violet eyes like the Prince himself; and perhaps some day he may go out to walk with his nurse; and perhaps the nurse may go to sleep under a great elder-tree; and perhaps the little boy may fall into the deep river and be drowned. What a terrible misfortune! Poor people, to lose their only son! It is really too dreadful! I shall never get over it.'

'But they have not lost their only son,' said the Roman Candle; 'no misfortune has happened to them at all.'

'I never said that they had,' replied the Rocket; 'I said that they might. If they had lost their only son there would be no use in saying any more about the matter. I hate people who cry over spilt milk. But when I think that they might lose their only son, I certainly am very much affected.'

'You certainly are!' cried the Bengal Light. 'In fact, you are the most affected person I ever met.'

'You are the rudest person I ever met,' said the Rocket, 'and you cannot understand my friendship for the Prince.'

'Why, you don't even know him,' growled the Roman Candle.

'I never said I knew him,' answered the Rocket. 'I dare say that if I knew him I should not be his friend at all. It is a very dangerous thing to know one's friends.'

'You had really better keep yourself dry,' said the Fire-balloon. 'That is the important thing.'

'Very important for you, I have no doubt,' answered the Rocket, 'but I shall weep if I choose;' and he actually burst into real tears, which flowed down his stick like raindrops, and nearly drowned two little beetles, who were just thinking of setting up house together, and were looking for a nice he dry spot to live in.

'He must have a truly romantic nature,' said the Catherine Wheel, 'for weeps when there is nothing at all to weep about;' and she heaved a deep sigh and thought about the deal box.

But the Roman Candle and the Bengal Light were quite indignant, and kept saying, 'Humbug! humbug!' at the top of their voices. They were extremely practical, and whenever they objected to anything they called it humbug.

Then the moon rose like a wonderful silver shield; and the stars began to shine, and a sound of music came from the palace.

The Prince and Princess were leading the dance. They danced so beautifully that the tall white lilies peeped in at the window and watched them, and the great red poppies nodded their heads and beat time.

Then ten o'clock struck, and then eleven, and then twelve, and at the last stroke of midnight every one came out on the terrace, and the King sent for the Royal Pyrotechnist.

'Let the fireworks begin,' said the King; and the Royal Pyrotechnist made a low bow, and marched down to the end of the garden. He had six attendants with him, each of whom carried a lighted torch at the end of a long pole. It was certainly a magnificent display.

Whizz! Whizz! went the Catherine Wheel, as she spun round and round. Boom! Boom! went the Roman Candle. Then the Squibs danced all over the place, and the Bengal Lights made everything look scarlet. 'Good-bye,' cried the Fire-balloon, as he soared away, dropping tiny blue sparks. Bang! Bang! answered the Crackers, who were enjoying themselves immensely. Every one was a great success except the Remarkable Rocket. He was so damped with crying that he could not go off at all. The best thing in him was the gunpowder, and that was so wet with tears that it was of no use. All his poor relations, to whom he would never speak, except with a sneer, shot up into the sky like wonderful golden flowers with blossoms of fire. Huzza! Huzza! cried the Court; and the little Princess laughed with pleasure.

'I suppose they are reserving, me for some grand occasion,' said the Rocket; 'no doubt that is what it means,' and he looked more supercilious than ever.

The next day the workmen came to put everything tidy. 'This is evidently a deputation,' said the Rocket; 'I will receive them with becoming dignity:' so he put his nose in the air, and began to frown severely, as if he were thinking about some very important subject. But they took no notice of him at all till they were just going away. Then one of them caught sight of him. 'Hallo!' he cried, 'what a bad rocket!' and he threw him over the wall into the ditch.

'BAD ROCKET? BAD ROCKET?' he said, as he whirled through the air; 'impossible! GRAND ROCKET, that is what the man said. BAD and GRAND sound very much the same, indeed they often are the same;' and fell into the mud.

'It is not comfortable here,' he remarked, 'but no doubt it is some fashionable watering-place, and they have sent me away to recruit my health. My nerves are certainly very much shattered, and I require rest.'

Then a little Frog, with bright jewelled eyes, and a green mottled coat, swam up to him.

'A new arrival, I see!' said the Frog. 'Well, after all there is nothing like mud. Give me rainy weather and a ditch, and I am quite happy. Do you think it will be a wet afternoon? I am sure I hope so, but the sky is quite blue and cloudless. What a pity!'

'Ahem! ahem!' said the Rocket, and he began to cough.

'What a delightful voice you have!' cried the Frog. 'Really it is quite like a croak, and croaking is, of course, the most musical sound in the world. You will hear our glee-club this evening. We sit in the old duck-pond close by the farmer's house, and as soon as the moon rises we begin. It is so entrancing that everybody lies awake to listen to us. In fact, it was only yesterday that I heard the farmer's wife say to her mother that she could not get a wink of sleep at night on account of us. It is most gratifying to find oneself so popular.'

'Ahem! ahem!' said the Rocket angrily. He was very much annoyed that he could not get a word in.

'A delightful voice, certainly,' continued the Frog; 'I hope you will come over to the duck-pond. I am off to look for my daughters. I have six beautiful daughters, and I am so afraid the

Pike may meet them. He is a perfect monster, and would have no hesitation in breakfasting off them. Well, good-bye; I have enjoyed our conversation very much, I assure you.'

'Conversation, indeed!' said the Rocket. 'You have talked the whole time yourself. That is not conversation.'

'Somebody must listen,' answered the Frog, 'and I like to do all the talking myself. It saves time, and prevents arguments.'

'But I like arguments,' said the Rocket.

'I hope not,' said the Frog complacently. 'Arguments are extremely vulgar, for everybody in good society holds exactly the same opinions. Good-bye a second time; I see my daughters in the distance;' and the little Frog swam away.

'You are a very irritating person,' said the Rocket, 'and very ill-bred. I hate people who talk about themselves, as you do, when one wants to talk about oneself, as I do. It is what I call selfishness, and selfishness is a most detestable thing, especially to any one of my temperament, for I am well known for my sympathetic nature. In fact, you should take example by me; you could not possibly have a better model. Now that you have the chance you had better avail yourself of it, for I am going back to Court almost immediately. I am a great favourite at Court; in fact, the Prince and Princess were married yesterday in my honour. Of course, you know nothing of these matters, for you are a provincial.'

'There is no good talking to him,' said a Dragonfly, who was sitting on the top of a large brown bulrush; 'no good at all, for he has gone away.'

'Well, that is his loss, not mine,' answered the Rocket. 'I am not going to stop talking to him merely because he pays no attention. I like hearing myself talk. It is one of my greatest pleasures. I often have long conversations all by myself, and I am so clever that sometimes I don't understand a single word of what I am saying.'

'Then you should certainly lecture on Philosophy,' said the Dragon-fly, 'and he spread a pair of lovely gauze wings and soared away into the sky. 'How very silly or him not to stay here' said the Rocket. 'I am sure that he has not often got such a chance of improving his mind. However, I don't care a bit. Genius like mine is sure to be appreciated some day;' and he sank down a little deeper into the mud.

After some time a large White Duck swam up to him. She had yellow legs, and webbed feet, and was considered a great beauty on account of her waddle.

'Quack, quack, quack,' she said. 'What a curious shape you are! May I ask were you born like that, or is it the result of an accident?'

'It is quite evident that you have always lived in the country,' answered the Rocket, 'otherwise you would know who I am. However, I excuse your ignorance. It would be unfair to expect other people to be as remarkable as oneself. You will no doubt: be surprised to hear that I can fly up into the sky, and come down in a shower of golden rain.'

'I don't think much of that,' said the Duck, 'as I cannot see what use it is to any one. Now, if you could plough the fields like the ox, or draw a cart like the horse, or look after the sheep like the collie-dog, that would be something.'

'My good creature,' cried the Rocket in a very haughty tone of voice, 'I see that you belong to the lower orders. A person of my position is never useful. We have certain accomplishments, and that is more than sufficient. I have no sympathy myself with industry of any kind, least of all with such industries as you seem to recommend. Indeed, I have always been of opinion that hard work is simply the refuge of people who have nothing whatever to do.'

'Well, well,' said the Duck, who was of a very peaceful disposition, and never quarrelled with any one, 'everybody has different tastes. I hope, at any rate, that you are going to take up your residence here.'

'Oh dear no,' cried the Rocket. 'I am merely a visitor, a distinguished visitor. The fact is that I find this place rather tedious. There is neither society here, nor solitude. In fact, it is essentially suburban. I shall probably go back to Court, for I know that I am destined to make a sensation in the world.'

'I had thoughts of entering public life once myself,' remarked the Duck; 'there are so many things that need reforming. Indeed, I took the chair at a meeting some time ago, and we passed resolutions condemning everything that we did not like. However, they did not seem to have much effect. Now I go in for domesticity, and look after my family.'

'I am made for public life,' said the Rocket, 'and so are all my relations, even the humblest of them. Whenever we appear we excite great attention. I have not actually appeared myself, but when I do so it will be a magnificent sight. As for domesticity, it ages one rapidly, and distracts one's mind from higher things.'

'Ah! the higher things of life, how fine they are!' said the Duck; 'and that reminds me how hungry I feel:' and she swam away down the stream, saying, 'Quack, quack, quack.'

'Come back! come back!' screamed the Rocket, 'I have a great deal to say to you;' but the Duck paid no attention to him. 'I am glad that she has gone,' he said to himself, 'she has a decidedly middle-class mind;' and he sank a little deeper still into the mud, and began to think about the loneliness of genius, when suddenly two little boys in white smocks came running down the bank, with a kettle and some faggots.

'This must be the deputation,' said the Rocket, and he tried to look very dignified.

'Hallo!' cried one of the boys, 'look at this old stick; I wonder how it came here:' and he picked the Rocket out of the ditch.

'OLD STICK!' said the Rocket, 'impossible! GOLD STICK, that is what he said. Gold Stick is very complimentary. In fact, he mistakes me for one of the Court dignitaries!'

'Let us put it into the fire!' said the other boy, 'it will help to boil the kettle.'

So they piled the faggots together, and put the Rocket on top, and lit the fire.

'This is magnificent,' cried the Rocket, 'they are going to let me off in broad daylight, so that every one can see me.'

'We will go to sleep now,' they said, 'and when we wake up the kettle will be boiled;' and they lay down on the grass, and shut their eyes.

The Rocket was very damp, so he took a long time to burn. At last, however, the fire caught him.

'Now I am going off!' he cried, and he made himself very stiff and straight. 'I know I shall go much higher than the stars, much higher than the moon, much higher than the sun. In fact, I shall go so high that—'

Fizz! Fizz! Fizz! and he went straight up into the air.

'Delightful!' he cried, shall go on like this for ever. What a success I am!'

But nobody saw him.

Then he began to feel a curious tingling sensation all over him.

'Now I am going to explode,' he cried. 'I shall set the whole world on fire, and make such a noise that nobody will talk about anything else for a whole year.' And he certainly did explode. Bang! Bang! Bang! went the gunpowder. There was no doubt about it.

But nobody heard him, not even the two little boys, for they were sound asleep.

Then all that was left of him was the stick, and this fell down on the back of a Goose who was taking a walk by the side of the ditch.

'Good heavens!' cried the Goose. 'It is going to rain sticks;' and she rushed into the water.

'I knew I should create a great sensation,' gasped the Rocket, and he went out.

A House of Pomegranates

The Young King

It was the night before the day fixed for his coronation, and the young King was sitting alone in his beautiful chamber. His courtiers had all taken their leave of him, bowing their heads to the ground, according to the ceremonious usage of the day, and had retired to the Great Hall of the Palace, to receive a few last lessons from the Professor of Etiquette; there being some of them who had still quite natural manners, which in a courtier is, I need hardly say, a very grave offence.

The lad—for he was only a lad, being but sixteen years of age—was not sorry at their departure, and had flung himself back with a deep sigh of relief on the soft cushions of his embroidered couch, lying there, wild-eyed and open-mouthed, like a brown woodland Faun, or some young animal of the forest newly snared by the hunters.

And, indeed, it was the hunters who had found him, coming upon him almost by chance as, bare-limbed and pipe in hand, he was following the flock of the poor goatherd who had brought him up, and whose son he had always fancied himself to be. The child of the old King's only daughter by a secret marriage with one much beneath her in station—a stranger, some said, who, by the wonderful magic of his lute-playing, had made the young Princess love him; while others spoke of an artist from Rimini, to whom the Princess had shown much, perhaps too much honour, and who had suddenly disappeared from the city, leaving his work in the Cathedral unfinished—he had been, when but a week old, stolen away from his mother's side, as she slept, and given into the charge of a common peasant and his wife, who were without children of their own, and lived in a remote part of the forest, more than a day's ride from the town. Grief, or the plague, as the court physician stated, or, as some suggested, a swift Italian poison administered in a cup of spiced wine, slew, within an hour of her wakening, the white girl who had given him birth, and as the trusty messenger who bare the child across his saddle-bow stooped from his weary horse and knocked at the rude door of the goatherd's hut, the body of the Princess was being lowered into an open grave that had been dug in a deserted churchyard, beyond the city gates, a grave where it was said that another body was also lying, that of a young man of marvellous and foreign beauty, whose hands were tied behind him with a knotted cord, and whose breast was stabbed with many red wounds.

Such, at least, was the story that men whispered to each other. Certain it was that the old King, when on his death-bed, whether moved by remorse for his great sin, or merely desiring that the kingdom should not pass away from his line, had had the lad sent for, and, in the presence of the Council, kid acknowledged him as his heir.

And it seems that from the very first moment of his recognition he had shown signs of that strange passion for beauty that was destined to have so great an influence over his life. Those who accompanied him to the suite of rooms set apart for his service, often spoke of the cry of pleasure that broke from his lips when he saw the delicate raiment and rich jewels that had been prepared for him, and of the almost fierce joy with which he flung aside his rough leathern tunic and coarse sheepskin cloak. He missed, indeed, at times the freedom of the forest life, and was always apt to chafe at the tedious Court ceremonies that occupied so much of each day, but the wonderful palace—*Joyeuse*, as they called it— of which he now found himself lord, seemed to him to be a new world fresh-fashioned for his delight; and as soon as he could escape from the council-board or audience-chamber, he would run down the great staircase, with its lions of gilt bronze and its steps of bright porphyry, and wander from room to room, and from corridor to corridor, like one who was seeking to find in beauty an anodyne from pain, a sort of restoration from sickness.

Upon these journeys of discovery, as he would call them— and, indeed, they were to him real voyages through a marvellous land, he would sometimes be accompanied by the slim, fair-haired Court pages, with their floating mantles, and gay fluttering ribands; but more often he would be alone, feeling through a certain quick instinct, which was almost a divination, that the secrets of art are best learned in secret, and that Beauty, like Wisdom, loves the lonely worshipper.

Many curious stories were related about him at this period. It was said that a stout Burgomaster, who had come to deliver a florid oratorical address on behalf of the citizens of the town, had caught sight of him kneeling in real adoration before a great picture that had just been brought from Venice, and that seemed to herald the worship of some new gods. On another occasion he had been missed for several hours, and after a lengthened search had been discovered in a little chamber in one of the northern turrets of the palace gazing, as one in a trance, at a Greek gem carved with the figure of Adonis. He had been seen, so the tale ran, pressing his warm lips to the marble brow of an antique statue that had been discovered in the bed of the river on the occasion of the building of the stone bridge, and was inscribed with the name of the Bithynian slave of Hadrian. He had passed a whole night in noting the effect of the moonlight on a silver image of Endymion.

All rare and costly materials had certainly a great fascination for him, and in his eagerness to procure them he had sent away many merchants, some to traffic for amber with the rough fisher-folk of the north seas, some to Egypt to look for that curious green turquoise which is found only in the tombs of kings, and is said to possess magical properties, some to Persia for silken carpets and painted pottery, and others to India to buy gauze and stained ivory moonstones and bracelets of jade, sandal-wood and blue enamel and shawls of fine wool.

But what had occupied him most was the robe he was to wear at his coronation, the robe of tissued gold, and the ruby-studded crown, and the sceptre with its rows and rings of pearls. Indeed, it was of this that he was thinking tonight, as he lay back on his luxurious couch, watching the great pinewood log that was burning itself out on the open hearth. The designs, which were from the hands of the most famous artists of the time, had been submitted to him many months before, and he had given orders that the artificers were to toil night and day to carry them out, and that die whole world was to be searched for jewels that would be worthy of their work. He saw himself in fancy standing at the high altar of the cathedral in the fair raiment of a King, and a smile played and lingered about his boyish lips, and lit up with a bright lustre his dark woodland eyes.

After some time he rose from his seat, and leaning against the carved penthouse of the chimney, looked round at the dimly-lit room. The walls were hung with rich tapestries representing the Triumph of Beauty. A large press, inlaid with agate and lapis lazuli, filled one corner, and facing the window stood a curiously wrought cabinet with lacquer panels of powdered and mosaiced gold, on which were placed some delicate goblets of Venetian glass, and a cup of dark-veined onyx. Pale poppies were broidered on the silk coverlet of the bed, as though they had fallen from the tired hands of sleep, and tall reeds of fluted ivory bare up the velvet canopy, from which great tufts of ostrich plumes sprang, like white foam, to the pallid silver of the fretted ceiling. A laughing Narcissus in green bronze held a polished mirror above its head. On the table stood a flat bowl of amethyst.

Outside he could see the huge dome of the cathedral, looming like a bubble over the shadowy houses, and the weary sentinels pacing up and down on the misty terrace by the river. Far away, in an orchard, a nightingale was singing. A faint perfume of jasmine came through the open window. He brushed his brown curls back from his forehead, and taking up a lute, let his fingers stray across the cords. His heavy eyelids drooped, and a strange languor came over him. Never before had he felt so keenly, or with such exquisite joy, the magic and mystery of beautiful things.

When midnight sounded from the clock-tower he touched a

bell, and his pages entered and disrobed him with much ceremony, pouring rose water over his hands, and strewing flowers on his pillow. A few moments after that they had left the room, he fell asleep.

And as he slept he dreamed a dream, and this was his dream.

He thought that he was standing in a long, low attic, amidst the whir and clatter of many looms. The meagre daylight peered in through the grated windows, and showed him the gaunt figures of the weavers bending over their cases. Pale, sickly-looking children were crouched on the huge crossbeams. As the shuttles dashed through the warp they lifted up the heavy battens, and when the shuttles stopped they let the battens fall and pressed the threads together. Their faces were pinched with famine, and their thin hands shook and trembled. Some haggard women were seated at a table sewing. A horrible odour filled the place. The air was foul and heavy, and the walls dripped and streamed with damp.

The young King went over to one of the weavers, and stood by him and watched him.

And the weaver looked at him angrily and said, 'Why art thou watching me? Art thou a spy set on us by our master?'

'Who is thy[6] master?' asked the young King.

'Our master!' cried the weaver, bitterly. 'He is a man like myself. Indeed, there is but this difference between us—that he wears fine clothes while I go in rags, and that while I am weak from hunger he suffers not a little from overfeeding.'

'The land is free,' said the young King, 'and thou art no man's slave.'

'In war,' answered the weaver, 'the strong make slaves of the weak, and in peace the rich make slaves of the poor. We must work to live, and they give us such mean wages that we die. We toil for them all day long, and they heap up gold in their coffers, and our children fade away before their time, and the faces of those we love become hard and evil. We tread out the grapes, and another drinks the wine. We sow the corn, and our own board is empty. We have chains, though no eye beholds them; and we are slaves, though men call us free.'

'Is it so with all?' he asked.

'It is so with all,' answered the weaver, 'with the young as well as with the old, with the women as well as with the men, with the little children as well as with those who are stricken in years. The merchants grind us down, and we must needs do their bidding. The priest rides by and tells his beads, and no man has care of us. Through our sunless lanes creeps Poverty with her hungry eyes, and Sin with his sodden face follows close behind her. Misery wakes us in the morning, and Shame sits with us at night. But what are these things to thee? Thou art not one of us. Thy face is too happy.' And he turned away scowling, and threw the shuttle across the loom, and the young King saw that it was threaded with a thread of gold.

And a great terror seized upon him, and he said to the weaver, 'What robe is this that thou art weaving?'

'It is the robe for the coronation of the young King,' he answered; 'what is that to thee?'

And the young King gave a loud cry and woke, and lo! he was in his own chamber, and through the window he saw the great honey-coloured moon hanging in the dusky air.

And he fell asleep again and dreamed, and this was his dream.

He thought that he was lying on the deck of a huge galley that was being rowed by a hundred slaves. On a carpet by his side the master of the galley was seated. He was black as ebony, and his turban was of crimson silk. Great ear-rings of silver dragged down the thick lobes of his ears, and in his hands he had a pair of ivory scales.

The slaves were naked, but for a ragged loincloth, and each man was chained to his neighbour. The hot sun beat brightly upon them, and the negroes ran up and down the gangway and lashed them with whips of hide. They stretched out their lean arms and pulled the heavy oars through the water. The salt spray flew from the blades.

At last they reached a little bay, and began to take soundings. A light wind blew from the shore, and covered the deck and the great lateen sail with a fine red dust. Three Arabs mounted on wild asses rode out and threw spears at them. The master of the galley took a painted bow in his hand and shot one of them in the throat. He fell heavily into the surf, and his companions galloped away. A woman wrapped in a yellow veil followed slowly on a camel, looking back now and then at the dead body.

As soon as they had cast anchor and hauled down the sail, the negroes went into the hold and brought up a long rope-ladder, heavily weighted with lead. The master of the galley threw it over the side, making the ends fast to two iron stanchions. Then the negroes seized the youngest of the slaves and knocked his gyves off, and filled his nostrils and his ears with wax, and tied a big stone round his waist. He crept wearily down the ladder, and disappeared into the sea. A few bubbles rose where he sank. Some of the other slaves peered curiously over the side. At the prow of the galley sat a shark-charmer, beating monotonously upon a drum.

After some time the diver rose up out of the water, and clung panting to the ladder with a pearl in his right hand. The negroes seized it from him, and thrust him back. The slaves fell asleep over their oars.

Again and again he came up, and each time that he did so he brought with him a beautiful pearl. The master of the galley weighed them, and put them into a little bag of green leather.

The young King tried to speak, but his tongue seemed to cleave to the roof of his mouth, and his lips refused to move. The negroes chattered to each other, and began to quarrel over a string of bright beads. Two cranes flew round and round the vessel.

Then the diver came up for the last time, and the pearl that he brought with him was fairer than all the pearls of Ormuz, fir it was shaped like the full moon, and whiter than the morning star. But his face was strangely pale, and as he fell upon the deck the blood gushed from his ears and nostrils. He quivered for a little, and then he was still. The negroes shrugged their shoulders, and threw the body overboard.

And the master of the galley laughed, and, reaching out, he took the pearl, and when he saw it he pressed it to his forehead and bowed. 'It shall be,' he said, 'for the sceptre of the young King,' and he made a sign to the negroes to draw up the anchor.

And when the young King heard this he gave a great cry and woke, and through the window he saw the long grey fingers of the dawn clutching at the fading stars.

And he fell asleep again, and dreamed, and this was his dream.

He thought that he was wandering through a dim wood, hung with strange fruits and with beautiful poisonous flowers. The adders hissed at him as he went by, and the bright parrots flew screaming from branch to branch. Huge tortoises lay asleep upon the hot mud. The trees were full of apes and peacocks.

On and on he went, till he reached the outskirts of the wood, and there he saw an immense multitude of men toiling in the bed of a dried-up river. They swarmed up the crag like ants. They dug deep pits in the ground and went down into them. Some of them cleft the rocks with great axes; others grabbled in the sand. They tore up the cactus by its roots, and trampled on the scarlet blossoms. They hurried about, calling to each other, and no man was idle.

From the darkness of a cavern Death and Avarice watched them, and Death said, 'I am weary; give me a third of them and let me go.'

But Avarice shook her head. 'They are my servants,' she answered.

And Death said to her, 'What hast[7] thou in thy hand?'

'I have three grains of corn,' she answered; 'what is that to thee?'

'Give me one of them,' cried Death, 'to plant in my garden; only one of them, and I will go away.'

'I will not give thee anything,' said Avarice, and she hid her hand in the fold of her raiment.

And Death laughed, and took a cup, and dipped it into a pool of water, and out of the cup rose Ague. She passed through the great multitude, and a third of them lay dead. A cold mist followed her, and the water-snakes ran by her side.

And when Avarice saw that a third of the multitude was dead she beat her breast and wept. She beat her barren bosom, and cried aloud. 'Thou hast slain a third of my servants,' she cried, 'get thee gone. There is war in the mountains of Tartary, and the kings of each side are calling to thee. The Afghans have slain the black ox, and are marching to battle. They have beaten upon their shields with their spears, and have put on their helmets of iron. What is my valley to thee, that thou shouldst[8] tarry in it? Get thee gone, and come here no more.'

'Nay,' answered Death, 'but till thou hast given me a grain of corn I will not go.'

But Avarice shut her hand, and clenched her teeth. 'I will not give thee anything,' she muttered.

And Death laughed, and took up a black stone, and threw it into the forest, and out of a thicket of wild hemlock came Fever in a robe of flame. She passed through the multitude, and touched them, and each man that she touched died. The grass withered beneath her feet as she walked.

And Avarice shuddered, and put ashes on her head. 'Thou art cruel,' she cried; 'thou art cruel. There is famine in the walled cities of India, and the cisterns of Samarcand have run dry. There is famine in the walled cities of Egypt, and the locusts have come up from the desert. The Nile has not overflowed its banks, and the priests have nursed Isis and Osiris. Get thee gone to those who need thee, and leave me my servants.'

'Nay,' answered Death, 'but till thou hast given me a grain of corn I will not go.'

'I will not give thee anything,' said Avarice.

And Death laughed again, and he whistled through his fingers, and a woman came flying through the air. Plague was written upon her forehead, and a crowd of lean vultures wheeled round her. She covered the valley with her wings, and no man was left alive.

And Avarice fled shrieking through the forest, and Death leaped upon his red horse and galloped away, and his galloping was faster than the wind. And out of the slime at the bottom of the valley crept dragons and horrible things with scales, and the jackals came trotting along the sand, sniffing up the air with their nostrils.

And the young King wept, and said: 'Who were these men, and for what were they seeking?'

'For rubies for a king's crown,' answered one who stood behind him.

And the young King started, and, turning round, he saw a man habited a pilgrim and holding in his hand a mirror of silver.

And he grew pale, and said: 'For what king?'

And the pilgrim answered: 'Look in this mirror, and thou shalt[9] see him.'

And he looked in the mirror, and, seeing his own face, he gave a great cry and woke, and the bright sunlight was streaming into the room, and from the trees of the garden and pleasaunce the birds were singing.

And the Chamberlain and the high officers of State came in and made obeisance to him, and the pages brought him the robe of tissued gold, and set the crown and the sceptre before him.

And the Young King looked at them, and they were beautiful. More beautiful were they than aught[10] that he had ever seen. But he remembered his dreams, and he said to his lords: 'Take these things away, for I will not wear them.'

And the courtiers were amazed, and sonic of them laughed, for they thought that he was jesting.

But he spake[11] sternly to them again, and said: 'Take these things away, and hide them from me. Though it be the day of my coronation, I will not wear them. For on the loom of sorrow, and by the white hands of Pain, has this my robe been woven. There is Blood in the heart of the ruby, and Death in the heart of the pearl.' And he told them his three dreams.

And when the courtiers heard them they looked at each other and whispered, saying: 'Surely he is mad; for what is a dream but a dream, and a vision but a vision? They are not real things that one should heed them. And what have we to do with the lives of those who toil for us? Shall a man not eat bread till he has seen the sower, nor drink wine till he has talked with the vinedresser?'

And the Chamberlain spake to the young King, and said, 'My lord, I pray thee set aside these black thoughts of thine[12], and put on this fair robe, and set this crown upon thy head. For how shall the people know that thou art a king, if thou hast not a king's raiment?'

And the young King looked at him. 'Is it so, indeed?' he questioned. 'Will they not know me for a king if I have not a king's raiment?'

'They will not know thee, my lord,' cried the Chamberlain.

'I had thought that there had been men who were kinglike,' he answered, but it may be as thou sayest[13]. And yet I will not wear this robe, nor will I be crowned with this crown, but even as I came to the Palace so will I go forth from it.'

And he bade them all leave him, save one page whom he kept as his companion, a lad a year younger than himself. Him he kept for his service, and when he had bathed himself in clear water, he opened a great painted chest, and from it he took the leathern tunic and rough sheepskin coat that he had worn when he had watched on the hillside the shaggy goats of the goatherd. These he put on, and in his hand he took his rude shepherd's staff.

And the little page opened his big blue eyes in wonder, and said smiling to him, 'My lord, I see thy robe and thy sceptre, but where is thy crown?'

And the young King plucked a spray of wild briar that was climbing over the balcony, and bent it, and made a circlet of it, and set it on his own head.

'This shall be my crown,' he answered.

And thus attired he passed out of his chamber into the Great Hall, where the nobles were waiting for him.

And the nobles made merry, and some of them cried out to him, 'My lord, the people wait for their king, and thou showest[14] them a beggar,' and others were wroth and said, 'He brings shame upon our state, and is unworthy to be our master.' But he answered them not a word, but passed on, and went down the bright porphyry staircase, and out through the gates of bronze, and mounted upon his horse, and rode towards the cathedral, the little page running beside him.

And the people laughed and said, 'It is the King's fool who is riding by,' and they mocked him. And he drew rein and said, 'Nay, but I am the King.' And he told them his three dreams.

And a man came out of the crowd and spake bitterly to him, and said, 'Sir, knowest[15] thou not that out of the luxury of the rich cometh[16] the life of the poor? By your pomp we are nurtured, and your vices give us bread. To toil for a master is bitter, but to have no master to toil for is more bitter still. Thinkest[17] thou that the ravens will feed us? And what cure hast thou for these things? Wilt[18] thou say to the buyer, "Thou shalt buy for so much," and to the seller, "Thou shalt sell at this price?" I trow not. Therefore go back to thy Palace and put on thy purple and fine linen. What hast thou to do with us, and what we suffer?'

'Are not the rich and the poor brothers?' asked the young King.

'Ay,' answered the man, 'and the name of the rich brother is Cain.'

And the young King's eyes filled with tears, and he rode on through the murmurs of the people, and the little page grew afraid and left him.

And when he reached the great portal of the cathedral, the soldiers thrust their halberts out and said, 'What does thou seek here? None enters by this door but the King.'

And his face flushed with anger, and he said to them, 'I am the King,' and waved their halberts aside and passed in.

And when the old bishop saw him coming in his goatherd's dress, he rose up in wonder from his throne, and went to meet him, and said to him, 'My son, is this a king's apparel? And with what crown shall I crown thee, and what sceptre shall I place in thy hand? Surely this should be to thee a day of joy, and not a day of abasement.'

'Shall Joy wear what Grief has fashioned?' said the young King. And he told him his three dreams.

And when the Bishop had heard them knit his brows, and said, 'My son, I am an old man, and in the winter of my days, and I know that many evil things are done in the wide world. The fierce robbers come down from the mountains, and carry off the little children, and sell them to the Moors. The lions lie in wait for the caravans, and leap upon the camels. The wild boar roots up the corn in the valley, and the foxes gnaw the vines upon the hill. The pirates lay waste the sea-coast and burn the ships of the fishermen, and take their nets from them. In the salt-marshes live the lepers; they have houses of wattled reeds, and none may come nigh them. The beggars wander through the cities, and eat their food with the dogs. Canst[19] thou make these things not to be? Will thou take the leper for thy bedfellow, and set the beggar at thy board? Shall the lion do thy bidding, and the wild boar obey thee? Is not He who made misery wiser than thou art? Wherefore I praise thee not for this that thou hast done, but I bid thee ride back to the Palace and make thy face glad, and put on the raiment that beseemeth a king, and with the crown of gold I will crown thee, and the sceptre of pearl will I place in thy hand. And as for thy dreams, think no more of them. The burden of this world is too great for one man to bear, and the world's sorrow too heavy for one heart to suffer.'

'Sayest thou that in this house?' said the young King, and he strode past the Bishop, and climbed up the steps of the altar, and stood before the image of Christ. He stood before the image of Christ, and on his right hand and on his left were the marvellous vessels of gold, the chalice with the yellow wine, and the vial with the holy oil. He knelt before the image of Christ, and the great candles burned brightly by the jewelled shrine, and the smoke of the incense curled in thin blue wreaths through the dome. He bowed his head in prayer, and the priests in their stiff copes crept away from the altar.

And suddenly a wild tumult came from the street outside, and in entered the nobles with drawn swords and nodding plumes, and shields of polished steel. 'Where is this dreamer of dreams?' they cried. 'Where is this King, who is apparelled like a beggar—

this boy who brings shame upon our state? Surely we will slay him, for he is unworthy to rule over us.'

And the young King bowed his head again, and prayed, and when he had finished his prayer he rose up, and turning round he looked at them sadly.

And lo! through the painted windows came the sunlight streaming upon him, and the sunbeams wove round him a tissued robe that was fairer than the robe that had been fashioned for his pleasure. The dead staff blossomed, and bare lilies that were whiter than pearls. The dry thorn blossomed, and hare roses that were redder than rubies. Whiter than fine pearls were the lilies, and their stems were of bright silver, Redder than male rubies were the roses, and their leaves were of beaten gold.

He stood there in the raiment of a king, and the gates of the jewelled shrine flew open and from the crystal of the many-rayed monstrance shone a marvellous and mystical light. He stood there in a king's raiment, and the Glory of God filled the place, and the saints in their carven niches seemed to move. In the fair raiment of a king he stood before them, and the organ pealed out its music, and the trumpeters blew upon their trumpets, and the singing boys sang.

And the people fell upon their knees in awe, and the nobles sheathed their swords and did homage, and the Bishop's face grew pale, and his hands trembled. 'A greater than I hath crowned thee,' he cried, and he knelt before him.

And the young King came down from the high altar, and passed home through the midst of the people. But no man dared look upon his face, for it was like the Face of an angel.

The Birthday of the Infanta

It was the birthday of the Infanta. She was just twelve years of age, and the sun was shining brightly in the gardens of the palace.

Although she was a real Princess and the Infanta of Spain, she had only one birthday every year, just like the children of quite poor people, so it was naturally a matter of great importance to the whole country that she should have a really fine day for the occasion. And a really fine day it certainly was. The tall striped tulips stood straight up upon their stalks, like long rows of soldiers, and looked defiantly across the grass at the roses, and said: 'We are quite as splendid as you are now.' The purple butterflies fluttered about with gold dust on their wings, visiting each flower in turn; the little lizards crept out of the crevices of the wall, and lay basking in the white glare; and the pomegranates split and cracked with the heat, and showed their bleeding red hearts. Even the pale yellow lemons, that hung in such profusion from the mouldering trellis and along the dim arcades, seemed to have caught a richer colour from the wonderful sunlight, and the magnolia trees opened their great glove-like blossoms of folded ivory, and filled the air with a sweet heavy perfume.

The little Princess herself walked up and down the terrace with her companions, and played at hide and seek round the stone vases and the old mossgrown statues. On ordinary days she was only allowed to play with children of her own rank, so she had always to play alone, but her birthday was an exception, and the King had given orders that she was to invite any of her young friends whom she liked to come and amuse themselves with her. There was a stately grace about these slim Spanish children as they glided about, the boys with their large-plumed hats and short fluttering cloaks, the girls holding up the trains of their long brocade gowns, and shielding the sun from their eyes with huge fans of black and silver. But the Infanta was the most graceful of all, and the most tastefully attired, after the somewhat cumbrous fashion of the day. Her robe was of grey satin, the skirt and the wide puffed sleeves heavily embroidered with silver, and the stiff corset studded with rows of fine pearls. Two tiny slippers with big pink rosettes peeped out beneath her dress as she walked. Pink and pearl was her great gauze fan, and in her hair, which like an aureole of faded gold stood out stiffly round her pale little face, she had a beautiful white rose.

From a window in the palace the sad melancholy King watched them. Behind him stood his brother, Don Pedro of Aragon, whom he hated, and his confessor, the Grand Inquisitor of Granada, sat by his side. Sadder even than usual was the King, for as he looked at the Infanta bowing with childish gravity to the assembling courtiers, or laughing behind the fan at the grim Duchess of Albuquerque, who always accompanied her, he thought of the young Queen, her mother, who but a short time before—so it seemed to him—had come from the gay country of France, and had withered away in the sombre splendour of the Spanish court, dying just six months after the birth of her child, and before she had seen the almonds blossom twice in the orchard, or plucked the second year's fruit from the old gnarled fig-tree that stood in the centre of the now grass-grown courtyard. So great had been his love for her that he had not suffered even the grave to hide her from him. She had been embalmed by a Moorish physician, who in return for this service had been granted his life, which for heresy and suspicion of magical practices had been already forfeited, men said, to the Holy Office, and her body was still lying on its tapestried bier in the black marble chapel of the palace, just as the monks had borne her on that windy March day nearly twelve years before. Once every month the King, wrapped in a dark cloak and with a muffled lantern in his hand, went in and knelt by her side calling out, '*Mi reina! Mi reina!*' and sometimes breaking through the formal etiquette that in Spain governs every separate action of life, and sets limits even to the sorrow of a King, he would clutch at the pale jewelled hands in a wild agony of grief, and try to wake by his mad kisses the cold painted face.

Today he seemed to see her again, as he had seen her first at the Castle of Fontainebleau, when he was but fifteen years of age, and she still younger. They had been formally betrothed on that occasion by the Papal Nuncio in the presence of the French King and all the Court, and he had returned to the Escurial bearing with him a little ringlet of yellow hair, and the memory of two childish lips bending down to kiss his hand as he stepped into his carriage. Later on had followed the marriage, hastily performed at Burgos, a small town on the frontier between the two countries, and the grand public entry into Madrid with the customary celebration of high mass at the Church of La Atocha, and a more than usually solemn *auto-da-fé*, in which nearly three hundred heretics, amongst whom were many Englishmen, had been delivered over to the secular arm to be burned.

Certainly he had loved her madly, and to the ruin, many thought, of his country, then at war with England for the possession of the empire of the New World. He had hardly ever permitted her to be out of his sight; for her he had forgotten, or seemed to have forgotten, all grave affairs of State; and, with that terrible blindness that passion brings upon its servants, he had failed to notice that the elaborate ceremonies by which he sought to please her did but aggravate the strange malady from which she suffered. When she died he was, for a time, like one bereft of reason. Indeed, there is no doubt but that he would have formally abdicated and retired to the great Trappist monastery at Granada, of which he was already titular Prior, had he not been afraid to leave the little Infanta at the mercy of his brother, whose cruelty, even in Spain, was notorious, and who was suspected by many of having caused the Queen's death by means of a pair of poisoned gloves that he had presented to her on the occasion of her visiting his castle in Aragon. Even after the expiration of the three years of public mourning that he had ordained throughout his whole dominions by royal edict, he would never suffer his ministers to speak about any new alliance, and when the Emperor himself sent to him, and offered him the hand of the lovely Archduchess of Bohemia, his niece, in marriage, he bade the ambassadors tell their master that the King of Spain was already wedded to Sorrow, and that though she was but a barren bride he loved her better than Beauty; an answer that cost his crown the rich provinces of the Netherlands, which soon after, at the Emperor's instigation, revolted against him under the leadership of some fanatics of the Reformed Church.

His whole married life, with its fierce, fiery-coloured joys and the terrible agony of its sudden ending, seemed to come back to him today as he watched the Infanta playing on the terrace. She had all the Queen's pretty petulance of manner, the same wilful way of tossing her head, the same proud curved beautiful mouth, the same wonderful smile—*vrai sourire de France* indeed—as she glanced up now and then at the window, or stretched out her little hand for the stately Spanish gentlemen to kiss. But the shrill laughter of the children grated on his ears, and the bright pitiless sunlight mocked his sorrow, and a dull odour of strange spices such as embalmers use, seemed to taint—or was it fancy?—the clear morning air. He buried his face in his hands, and when the Infanta looked up again the curtains had been drawn, and the King had retired.

She made a little *moue* of disappointment, and shrugged her shoulders. Surely he might have stayed with her on her birthday. What did the stupid State-affairs matter? Or had he gone to that gloomy chapel, where the candles were always burning, and where she was never allowed to enter? How silly of him, when the sun was shining so brightly, and everybody was so happy! Besides, he would miss the sham bull-fight for which the trumpet was already sounding, to say nothing of the puppet-show and the other wonderful things. Her uncle and the Grand Inquisitor were much more sensible. They had come out on the terrace, and paid her nice compliments. So she tossed her pretty head, and taking Don Pedro by the hand, she walked slowly down the steps towards a long pavilion of purple silk that had been erected at the end of the garden, the other children following in strict order of precedence, those who had the longest names going first.

A procession of noble boys, fantastically dressed as *toreadors*, came out to meet her, and the young Count of Tierra-Nueva, a wonderfully handsome lad of about fourteen years of age, uncovering his head with all the grace of a born hidalgo and grandee of Spain, led her solemnly in to a little gilt and ivory chair that was placed on a raised dais above the arena. The children grouped themselves all round, fluttering their big fans and whispering to each other, and Don Pedro and the Grand Inquisitor stood laughing at the entrance. Even the Duchess—the Camerera-Mayor as she was called—a thin, hard-featured woman with a yellow ruff, did not look quite so bad-tempered as usual, and something like a chill smile flitted across her wrinkled face and twitched her thin bloodless lips.

It certainly was a marvellous bull-fight, and much nicer, the Infanta thought, than the real bull-fight that she had been brought to see at Seville, on the occasion of the visit of the Duke of Parma to her father. Some of the boys pranced about on richly-caparisoned hobby-horses brandishing long javelins with gay streamers of bright ribands attached to them; others went on foot waving their scarlet cloaks before the bull, and vaulting lightly over the barrier when he charged them; and as for the bull himself, he was just like a live bull, though he was only made of wickerwork and stretched hide, and sometimes insisted on running round the arena on his hind legs, which no live bull ever dreams of doing. He made a splendid fight of it too, and the children got so excited that they stood up upon the benches, and waved their lace handkerchiefs and cried out: *Bravo toro! Bravo toro!* just as sensibly as if they had been grown-up people. At last, however, after a prolonged combat, during which several of the hobby-horses were gored through and through, and their riders dismounted, the young Count of Tierra-Nueva brought the bull to his knees, and having obtained permission from the Infanta to give the *coup de grâce*, he plunged his wooden sword into the neck of the animal with such violence that the head came right off, and disclosed the laughing face of little Monsieur de Lorraine, the son of the French Ambassador at Madrid.

The arena was then cleared amidst much applause, and the dead hobby-horses dragged solemnly away by two Moorish pages in yellow and black liveries, and after a short interlude, during which a French posture-master performed upon the tight-rope, some Italian puppets appeared in the semi-classical tragedy of *Sophonisba* on the stage of a small theatre that had been built up for the purpose. They acted so well, and their gestures were so extremely natural, that at the close of the play the eyes of the Infanta were quite dim with tears. Indeed some of the children really cried, and had to be comforted with sweet-meats, and the Grand Inquisitor himself was so affected that he could not help saying to Don Pedro that it seemed to him intolerable that things made simply out of wood and coloured wax, and worked mechanically by wires, should be so unhappy and meet with such terrible misfortunes.

An African juggler followed, who brought in a large flat basket covered with a red cloth, and having placed it in the centre of the arena, he took from his turban a curious reed pipe, and blew through it. In a few moments the cloth began to move, and as the pipe grew shriller and shriller two green and gold snakes put out their strange wedge-shaped heads and rose slowly up, swaying to and fro with the music as a plant sways in the water. The children, however, were rather frightened at their spotted hoods and quick darting tongues, and were much more pleased when the juggler made a tiny orange-tree grow out of the sand and bear pretty white blossoms and clusters of real fruit; and when he took the fan of the little daughter of the Marquess de Las-Torres, and changed it into a blue bird that flew all round the pavilion and sang, their delight and amazement knew no bounds. The solemn minuet, too, performed by the dancing boys from the church of Nuestra Senora Del Pilar, was charming. The Infanta had never before seen this wonderful ceremony which takes place every year at Maytime in front of the high altar of the Virgin, and in her honour; and indeed none of the royal family of Spain had entered the great cathedral of Saragossa since a mad priest, supposed by many to have been in the pay of Elizabeth of England, had tried to administer a poisoned wafer to the Prince of the Asturias. So she had known only by hearsay of 'Our Lady's Dance,' as it was called, and it certainly was a beautiful sight. The boys wore old-fashioned court dresses of white velvet, and their curious three-cornered hats were fringed with silver and surmounted with huge plumes of ostrich feathers, the dazzling whiteness of their costumes, as they moved about in the sunlight, being still more accentuated by their swarthy faces and long black hair. Everybody was fascinated by the grave dignity with which they moved through the intricate figures of the dance, and by the elaborate grace of their slow gestures, and stately bows, and when they had finished their performance and doffed their great plumed hats to the Infanta, she acknowledged their reverence with much courtesy, and made a vow that she would send a large wax candle to the shrine of Our Lady of Pilar in return for the pleasure that she had given her.

A troop of handsome Egyptians—as the gipsies were termed in those days—then advanced into the arena, and sitting down cross-legs, in a circle, began to play softly upon their zithers, moving their bodies to the tune, and humming, almost below their breath, a low dreamy air. When they caught sight of Don Pedro they scowled at him, and some of them looked terrified, for only a few weeks before he had had two of their tribe hanged for sorcery in the marketplace at Seville, but the pretty Infanta charmed them as she leaned back peeping over her fan with her great blue eyes, and they felt sure that one so lovely as she was could never be cruel to anybody. So they played on very gently and just touching the cords of the zithers with their long pointed nails, and their heads began to nod as though they were falling asleep. Suddenly, with a cry so shrill that all the children were startled, and Don Pedro's hand clutched at the agate pommel of his dagger, they leapt to their feet and whirled madly round the enclosure beating their tambourines, and chaunting some wild love song in their strange guttural language. Then at another signal they all flung themselves again to the ground and lay there quite still, the dull strumming of the zithers being the only sound that broke the silence. After that they had done this several times, they disappeared for a moment and came back leading a brown shaggy bear by a chain, and carrying on their shoulders some little Barbary apes. The bear stood upon his head with the utmost gravity, and the wizened apes played all kinds of amusing tricks with two gipsy boys who seemed to be their masters, and fought with tiny swords, and fired off guns, and went through a regular soldier's drill just like the King's own bodyguard. In fact, the gipsies were a great success.

But the funniest part of the whole morning's entertainment, was undoubtedly the dancing of the little Dwarf. When he stumbled into the arena, waddling on his crooked legs and wagging his huge misshapen head from side to side, the children went off into a loud shout of and the Infanta herself laughed so much that the Camerera was obliged to remind her that although there were many precedents in Spain for a King's daughter weeping before her equals, there were none for a Princess of the blood royal making so merry before those who were her inferiors in birth. The Dwarf, however, was really quite irresistible, and even at the Spanish Court, always noted for its cultivated passion for the horrible, so fantastic a little monster had never been seen. It was his first appearance, too. He had been discovered only the day before, running wild through the forest, by two of the nobles who happened to have been hunting in a remote part of the great cork wood that surrounded the town, and had been carried off by them to the Palace as a surprise for the Infanta; his father, who was a poor charcoal burner, being but too well pleased to get rid of so ugly and useless a child. Perhaps the most musing thing about him was his complete unconsciousness of his own grotesque appearance. Indeed he seemed quite happy and full of the highest spirits. When the children laughed, he laughed as freely and as joyously as any of them, and at the close of each dance he made them each the funniest of bows, smiling and nodding at them just as if he was really one of themselves, and not a little misshapen thing that Nature, in some humorous mood, had fashioned for others to mock at. As for the Infanta, she absolutely fascinated him. He could not keep his eyes off her, and seemed to dance for her alone, and when at the close of the performance, remembering how she had seen the great ladies of the Court throw bouquets to Caffarelli, the famous Italian treble, whom the Pope had sent from his own chapel to Madrid that he might cure the King's melancholy by the sweetness of his voice, she took out of her hair the beautiful white rose, and partly for a jest and partly to tease the Camerera, threw it to him across the arena with her sweetest smile. He took the whole matter quite seriously, and pressing the flower to his rough coarse lips he put his hand upon his heart, and sank on one knee before her, grinning from ear to ear, and with his little bright eyes sparkling with pleasure.

This so upset the gravity of the Infanta that she kept on laughing long after the little Dwarf had run out of the arena, and expressed a desire to her uncle that the dance should be immediately repeated. The Camerera, however, on the plea that the sun was too hot, decided that it would be better that her Highness should return without delay to the Palace, where a wonderful feast had been already prepared for her, including a real birthday cake with her own initials worked all over it in painted sugar and a lovely silver flag waving from the top. The Infanta accordingly rose up with much dignity, and having given orders that the little dwarf was to dance again for her after the hour of siesta, and conveyed her thanks to the young Count of Tierra Nueva for his charming reception, she went back to her apartments, the children following in the same order in which they had entered.

Now when the little Dwarf heard that he was to dance a second time before the Infanta, and by her own express command, he was so proud that he ran out into the garden, kissing the white rose in an absurd ecstasy of pleasure, and making the most uncouth and clumsy gestures of delight.

The Flowers were quite indignant at his daring to intrude into their beautiful home, and when they saw him capering up and down the walks, and waving his arms above his head in such a ridiculous manner, they could not restrain their feelings any longer.

'He is really far too ugly to be allowed to play in any place where we are,' cried the Tulips.

'He should drink poppy juice, and go to sleep for a thousand years,' said the great scarlet Lilies, and they grew quite hot and angry.

'He is a perfect horror!' screamed the Cactus. 'Why, he is twisted and stumpy, and his head is completely out of proportion with his legs. Really he makes me feel prickly all over, and if he comes near me I will sting him with my thorns.'

'And he has actually got one of my best blooms,' exclaimed the White Rose Tree. 'I gave it to the Infanta this morning myself, as a birthday present, and he has stolen it from her.' And she called out: 'Thief, thief, thief' at the top of her voice.

Even the red Geraniums, who did not usually give themselves airs, and were known to have a great many poor relations themselves, curled up in digust when they saw him, and when the Violets meekly remarked that though he was certainly extremely plain, still he could not help it, they retorted with a good deal of justice that that was his chief defect, and that there was no reason why one should admire a person because he was incurable; and, indeed, some of the Violets themselves felt that the ugliness of the little Dwarf was almost ostentatious, and that he would have shown much better taste if he had looked sad, or at least pensive, instead of jumping about merrily, and throwing himself into such grotesque and silly attitudes.

As for the old Sundial, who was an extremely remarkable individual, and had told the time of day to no less a person than the Emperor Charles V. himself, he was so taken aback by the little Dwarf's appearance, that he almost forgot to mark two whole minutes with his long shadowy finger, and could not help saying to the great milk white Peacock, who was sunning herself on the balustrade, that every one knew that the children of Kings were Kings, and that the children of charcoal burners were charcoal burners, and that it was absurd to pretend that it wasn't so; a statement with which the Peacock entirely agreed, and indeed screamed out, 'Certainly, certainly,' in such a loud, harsh voice, that the goldfish who lived in the basin of the cool splashing fountain put their heads out oldie water, and asked the huge stone Tritons what on earth was the matter.

But somehow the Birds liked him. They had seen him often in the forest, dancing about like an elf after the eddying leaves, or crouched up in the hollow of some old oak tree, sharing his nuts with the squirrels. They did not mind his being ugly a bit. Why, even the nightingale herself, who sang so sweetly in the orange groves at night that sometimes the Moon leaned down to listen, was not much to look at after all; and, besides, he had been kind to them, and during that terribly bitter winter, when there were no berries on the trees, and the ground was as hard as iron, and the wolves had come down to the very gates of the city to look for food, he had never once forgotten them, hut had always given them crumbs out of his little hunch of black bread, and divided with them whatever poor breakfast he had.

So they flew round and round him, just touching his cheek with their wings as they passed, and chattered to each other, and the little Dwarf was so pleased that he could not help showing them the beautiful white rose, and telling them that the Infanta herself had given it to him because she loved him.

They did not understand a single word of what he was saying, but that made no matter, for they put their heads on one side, and looked wise, which is quite as good as understanding a thing, and very much easier.

The Lizards also took an immense fancy to him, and when he grew tired of running about and flung himself down on the grass to rest, they played and romped all over him, and tried to amuse him in the best way they could. 'Every one cannot be as beautiful as a lizard,' they cried; 'that would be too much to expect. And, though it sounds absurd to say so, he is really not so ugly after all, provided, of course, that one shuts one's eyes, and does not look at him.' The Lizards were extremely philosophical by nature, and often sat thinking for hours and hours together, when there was nothing else to do, or when the weather was too rainy for them to go out.

The Flowers, however, were excessively annoyed at their behaviour, and at the behaviour of the birds. 'It only shows,' they said, 'what a vulgarising effect this incessant rushing and flying about has. Well-bred people always stay exactly in the same place as we do. No one ever saw us hopping up and down the walks, or galloping madly through the grass after dragonflies. When we do want change of air, we send for the gardener, and he carries us to another bed. This is dignified, and as it should be. But birds and lizards have no sense of repose, and indeed birds have not even a permanent address. They are mere vagrants like the gipsies, and should be treated in exactly the same manner.' So they put their noses in the air, and looked very haughty, and were quite delighted when after some time they saw the little Dwarf scramble up from the grass, and make his way across the terrace to the Palace.

'He should certainly be kept indoors for the rest of his natural life,' they said. 'Look at his hunched back, and his crooked legs,' and they began to titter.

But the little Dwarf knew nothing of all this. He liked the birds and the lizards immensely, and thought that the flowers were the most marvellous things in the whole world, except of course the Infanta, but then she had given him the beautiful white rose, and she loved him, and that made a great difference. How he wished that he had gone back with her! She would have put him on her right hand, and smiled at him, and he would have never left her side, but would have made her his playmate, and taught her all kinds of delightful tricks. For though he had never been in a palace before, he knew a great many wonderful things. He could make little cages out of rushes for the grasshoppers to sing in, and fashion the long jointed bamboo into the pipe that Pan loves to hear. He knew the cry of every bird, and could call the starlings from the tree top, or the heron from the mere. He knew the trail of every animal, and could track the hare by its delicate footprints, and the boar by the trampled leaves. All the wild dances he knew, the mad dance in red raiment with the autumn, the light dance in blue sandals over the corn, the dance with white snow wreaths in winter, and the blossom dance, through the orchards in spring. He knew where the wood pigeons built their nests, and once when a fowler had snared the parent birds, he had brought up the young ones himself, and had built a little dovecot for them in the cleft of a pollard elm. They were quite tame, and used to feed out of his hands every morning. She would like them, and the rabbits that scurried about in the long fern, and the jays with their steely feathers and black bills, and the hedgehogs that could curl themselves up into prickly balls, and the great wise tortoises that crawled slowly about, shaking their heads and nibbling at the young leaves. Yes, she must certainly come to the forest and play with him. He would give her his own little bed, and would watch outside the window till dawn, to see that the wild horned cattle did not harm her, nor the gaunt wolves creep too near the hut. And at dawn he would tap at the shutters and wake her, and they would go out and dance together all the day long. It was really not a bit lonely in the forest. Sometimes a Bishop rode through on his white mule, reading out of a painted book. Sometimes in their green velvet caps, and their jerkins of tanned deerskin, the falconers passed by, with hooded hawks on their wrists. At vintage time came the grape treaders, with purple hands and feet, wreathed with glossy ivy and carrying dripping skins of wine; and the charcoal burners sat round their huge braziers at night, watching the dry logs charring slowly in the fire, and roasting chestnuts in the ashes, and the robbers came out of their caves and made merry with them. Once, too, he had seen a beautiful procession winding up the long dusty road to Toledo. The monks went in front singing sweetly, and carrying bright banners and crosses of gold, and then, in silver armour, with matchlocks and pikes, came the soldiers, and in their midst walked three barefooted men, in strange yellow dresses painted all over with wonderful figures, and carrying lighted candles in their hands. Certainly there was a great deal to look at in the forest, and when she was tired he would find a soft bank of moss for her, or carry her in his arms, for he was very strong, though he knew that he was not tall. He would make her a necklace of red bryony berries, that would be quite as pretty as the white berries that she wore on her dress, and when she was tired of them, she could throw them away, and he would find her others. He would bring her acorn cups and dew drenched anemones, and tiny glow worms to be stars in the pale gold of her hair.

But where was she? He asked the white rose, and it made him no answer. The whole palace seemed asleep, and even where the shutters had not been closed, heavy curtains had been drawn across the windows to keep out the glare. He wandered all round looking for some place through which he might gain an entrance, and at last he caught sight of a little private door that was lying open. He slipped through, and found himself in a splendid hall, far more splendid he feared, than the forest, for there was so much more gilding everywhere, and even the floor was made of great coloured stones, fitted together into a sort of geometrical pattern. But the little Infanta was not there, only some wonderful white statues that looked down on him from their jasper pedestals, with sad blank eyes and strangely smiling lips.

At the end of the hall hung a richly embroidered curtain of black velvet, powdered with suns and stars, the King's favourite devices, and broidered on the colour he loved best. Perhaps she was hiding behind that? He would try at any rate.

So he stole quietly across, and drew it aside. No; there was only another room, though a prettier room, he thought, than the one he had just left. The walls were hung with a many-figured green arras of needle wrought tapestry representing a hunt, the work of some Flemish artists who had spent more than seven years in its composition. It had once been the chamber of *Jean le Fou*, as he was called, that mad King who was so enamoured of the chase, that he had often tried in his delirium to mount the huge rearing horses, and to drag down the stag on which the great hounds were leaping, sounding his hunting horn, and stabbing with his dagger at the pale flying deer. It was now used as the council room, and on the centre table were lying the red portfolios of the ministers, stamped with the gold tulips of Spain, and with the arms and emblems of the house of Hapsburg.

The little Dwarf looked in wonder all round him, and was half afraid to go on. The strange silent horsemen that galloped so swiftly through the long glades without making any noise, seemed to him like those terrible phantoms of whom he had heard the charcoal burners speaking—the Comprachos, who hunt only at night, and if they meet a man, turn him into a hind, and chase him. But he thought of the pretty Infanta, and took courage. He wanted to find her alone, and to tell her that he too loved her. Perhaps she was in the room beyond.

He ran across the soft Moorish carpets, and opened the door. No! She was not here either. The room was quite empty.

It was a throne room, used for the reception of foreign ambassadors, when the King, which of late had not been often, consented to give them a personal audience; the same room in which, many years before, envoys had appeared from England to make arrangements for the marriage of their Queen, then one of the Catholic sovereigns of Europe, with the Emperor's eldest son. The hangings were of gilt Cordovan leather, and a heavy gilt chandelier with branches for three hundred wax lights hung down from the black and white ceiling. Underneath a great canopy of gold cloth, on which the lions and towers of Castile were broidered in seed pearls, stood the throne itself, covered with a rich pall of black velvet studded with silver tulips and elaborately fringed with silver and pearls. On the second step of the throne was placed the kneeling stool of the Infanta, with its cushion of cloth of silver tissue, and below that again, and beyond the limit of the canopy, stood the chair for the Papal Nuncio, who alone had the right to be seated in the King's presence on the occasion of any public ceremonial, and whose Cardinal's hat, with its tangled scarlet tassels, lay on a purple *tabouret* in front. On the wall, facing the throne, hung a life-sized portrait of Charles V. in hunting dress, with a great mastiff by his side, and a picture of Philip II. receiving the homage of the Netherlands, occupied the centre of the other wall. Between the windows stood a black ebony cabinet, inlaid with plates of ivory, on which the figures from Holbein's Dance of Death had been graved—by the hand, some said, of that famous master himself.

But the little Dwarf cared nothing for all this magnificence. He would not have given his rose for all the pearls on the canopy, nor one white pearl of his rose for the throne itself. What he wanted was to see the Infanta before she went down to the pavilion, and to ask her to come away with him when he had finished his dance. Here, in the Palace, the air was close and heavy, but in the forest the wind blew free, and the sunlight with wandering hands of gold moved the tremulous leaves aside. There were flowers, too, in the forest, not so splendid, perhaps, as the flowers in the garden, but more sweetly scented for all that; hyacinths in early spring that flooded with waving purple the cool glens, and grassy knolls; yellow primroses that nestled in little clumps round the gnarled roots of the oak trees; bright celandine, and blue speedwell, and irises lilac and gold. There were grey catkins on the hazels, and the foxgloves drooped with the weight of their dappled bee-haunted cells. The chestnut had its spires of white stars, and the hawthorn its pallid moons of beauty. Yes; surely she would come if he could only find her! She would come with him to the fair forest, and all day long he would dance for her delight. A smile lit up his eyes at the thought, and he passed into the next room.

Of all the rooms this was the brightest and the most beautiful. The walls were covered with a pink-flowered Lucca damask, patterned with birds and dotted with dainty blossoms of silver; the furniture was of massive silver, festooned with florid wreaths, and swinging Cupids; in front of the two large fireplaces stood great screens broidered with parrots and peacocks, and the floor, which was of sea-green oynx, seemed to stretch far away into the distance. Nor was he alone. Standing under the shadow of the doorway, at the extreme end of the room, he saw a little figure watching him. His heart trembled, a cry of joy broke from his lips, and he moved out into the sunlight. As he did so, the figure moved out also, and he saw it plainly.

The Infanta! It was a monster, the most grotesque monster he had ever beheld. Not properly shaped as all other people were, but hunchbacked, and crooked-limbed, with huge lolling head and mane of black hair. The little Dwarf frowned, and the monster frowned also. He laughed, and it laughed with him, and held its hands to its sides, just as he himself was doing. He made it a mocking bow, and it returned him a low reverence. He went towards it, and it came to meet him, copying each step that he made, and stopping when he stopped himself. He shouted with amusement, and ran forward, and reached out his hand, and the hand of the monster touched his, and it was as cold as ice. He grew afraid, and moved his hand across, and the monster's hand followed it quickly. He tried to press on, but something smooth and hard stopped him. The face of the monster was now close to his own, and seemed full of terror. He brushed his hair off his eyes. It imitated him. He struck at it, and it returned blow for blow. He loathed it, and it made hideous faces at him. He drew back, and it retreated.

What is it? He thought for a moment, and looked round at the rest of the room. It was strange, but everything seemed to have its double in this invisible wall of clear water. Yes, picture for picture was repeated, and couch for couch. The sleeping Faun that lay in the alcove by the doorway had its twin brother that slumbered, and the silver Venus that stood in the sunlight held out her arms to a Venus as lovely as herself.

Was it Echo? He had called to her once in the valley, and she had answered him word for word. Could she mock the eye, as she mocked the voice? Could she make a mimic world just like the real world? Could the shadows of things have colour and life and movement? Could it be that—?

He started, and taking from his breast the beautiful white rose, he turned round, and kissed it. The monster had a rose of its own, petal for petal the same! It kissed it with like kisses, and pressed it to its heart with horrible gestures.

When the truth dawned upon him, he gave a wild cry of despair, and fell sobbing to the ground. So it was he who was misshapen and hunchbacked, foul to look at and grotesque. He himself was the monster, and it was at him that all the children had been laughing, and the little Princess who he had thought loved him she, too, had been merely mocking at his ugliness, and making merry over his twisted limbs. Why had they not left him in the forest, where there was no mirror to tell him how loathsome he was? Why had his father not killed him, rather than sell him to his shame? The hot tears poured down his cheeks, and he tore the white rose to pieces. The sprawling monster did the same, and scattered the faint petals in the air. It grovelled on the ground, and, when he looked at it, it watched him with a face drawn with pain. He crept away, lest he should see it, and covered his eyes with his hands. He crawled, like some wounded thing, into the shadow, and lay there moaning.

And at that moment the Infanta herself came in with her companions through the open window, and when they saw the ugly little Dwarf lying on the ground and beating the floor with his clenched hands, in the most fantastic and exaggerated manner, they went off into shouts of happy laughter, and stood all round him and watched him.

'His dancing was funny,' said the Infanta; 'but his acting is funnier still. Indeed, he is almost as good as the puppets, only, of course, not quite so natural.' And she fluttered her big fan and applauded.

But the little Dwarf never looked up, and his sobs grew fainter and fainter, and suddenly he gave a curious gasp, and clutched his side. And then he fell back again, and lay quite still.

'That is capital,' said the Infanta, after a pause; 'but now you must dance for me.'

'Yes,' cried all the children, 'you must get up and dance, for you are as clever as the Barbary apes, and much more ridiculous.'

But the little Dwarf made no answer.

And the Infanta stamped her foot, and called out to her uncle, who was walking on the terrace with the Chamberlain, reading some despatches that had just arrived from Mexico, where the Holy Office had recently been established. 'My funny little Dwarf is sulking,' she cried, 'you must wake him up, and tell him to dance for me.'

They smiled at each other, and sauntered in, and Don Pedro stooped down, and slapped the Dwarf on the cheek with his embroidered glove. 'You must dance,' he said, '*petit monstre*. You must dance. The Infanta of Spain and the Indies wishes to be amused.'

But the little Dwarf never moved.

'A whipping master should be sent for,' said Don Pedro wearily, and he went back to the terrace. But the Chamberlain looked grave, and he knelt beside the little Dwarf, and put his hand upon his heart. And after a few moments he shrugged his shoulders, and rose up, and having made a low bow to the Infanta, he said—

'*Mi bella Princesa*, your funny little Dwarf will never dance again. It is a pity, for he is so ugly that he might have made the King smile.'

'But why will he not dance again?' asked the Infanta, laughing.

'Because his heart is broken,' answered the Chamberlain.

And the Infanta frowned, and her dainty rose-leaf lips curled in pretty disdain. 'For the future let those who come to play with me have no hearts,' she cried, and she ran out into the garden.

The Fisherman and his Soul

Every evening the young Fisherman went out upon the sea, and threw his nets into the water.

When the wind blew from the land he caught nothing, or but little at best, for it was a bitter and black-winged wind, and rough waves rose up to meet it. But when the wind blew to the shore, the fish came in from the deep, and swam into the meshes of his nets, and he took them to the market place and sold them.

Every evening he went out upon the sea, and one evening the net was so heavy that hardly could he draw it into the boat. And he laughed, and said to himself, 'Surely I have caught all the fish that swim, or snared some dull monster that will be a marvel to men, or some thing of horror that the great Queen will desire,' and putting forth all his strength, he tugged at the coarse ropes till, like lines of blue enamel round a vase of bronze, the long veins rose up on his arms. He tugged at the thin ropes, and nearer and nearer came the circle of flat corks, and the net rose at last to the top of the water.

But no fish at all was in it, nor any monster or thing of horror, but only a little Mermaid lying fast asleep.

Her hair was as a wet fleece of gold, and each separate hair as a thread of fine gold in a cup of glass. Her body was as white ivory, and her tail was of silver and pearl. Silver and pearl was her tail, and the green weeds of the sea coiled round it; and like seashells were her ears, and her lips were like sea coral. The cold waves dashed over her cold breasts, and the salt glistened upon her eyelids.

So beautiful was she that when the young Fisherman saw her he was filled with wonder, and he put out his hand and drew the net close to him, and leaning over the side he clasped her in his arms. And when he touched her, she gave a cry like a startled seagull, and woke, and looked at him in terror with her mauve-amethyst eyes, and struggled that she might escape. But he held her tightly to him, and would not suffer her to depart.

And when she saw that she could in no way escape from him, she began to weep, and said, 'I pray thee let me go, for I am the only daughter of a King, and my father is aged and alone.'

But the young Fisherman answered, 'I will not let thee go save thou makest[20] me a promise that whenever I call thee, thou wilt come and sing to me, for the fish delight to listen to the song of the Sea-folk and so shall my nets be full.'

'Wilt thou in very truth let me go, if I promise thee this?' cried the Mermaid.

'In very truth I will let thee go,' said the young Fisherman.

So she made him the promise he desired, and sware it by the oath of the Sea-folk. And he loosened his arms from about her, and she sank down into the water, trembling with a strange fear.

Every evening the young Fisherman went out upon the sea,

and called to the Mermaid, and she rose out of the water and sang to him. Round and round her swam the dolphins, and the wild gulls wheeled above her head.

And she sang a marvellous song. For she sang of the Sea-folk who drive their flocks from cave to cave, and carry the little calves on their shoulders; of the Tritons who have long green beards, and hairy breasts, and blow through twisted conchs when the King passes by; of the palace of the King which is all of amber, with a roof of clear emerald, and a pavement of bright pearl; and of the gardens of the sea where the great filigrane fans of coral wave all day long, and the fish dart about like silver birds, and the anemones cling to the rocks, and the pinks bourgeon in the ribbed yellow sand. She sang of the big whales that come down from the north seas and have sharp icicles hanging to their fins; of the Sirens who tell of such wonderful things that the merchants have to stop their ears with wax lest they should hear them, and leap into the water and be drowned; of the sunken galleys with their tall masts, and the frozen sailors clinging to the rigging, and the mackerel swimming in and out of the open portholes; of the little barnacles who are great travellers, and cling to the keels of the ships and go round and round the world; and of the cuttlefish who live in the sides of the cliffs and stretch out their long black arms, and can make night come when they will it. She sang of the nautilus who has a boat of her own that is carved out of an opal and steered with a silken sail; of the happy Mermen who play upon harps and can charm the great Kraken to sleep; of the little children who catch hold of the slippery porpoises and ride laughing upon their backs; of the Mermaids who lie in the white foam and hold out their arms to the mariners; and of the sea lions with their curved tusks, and the sea horses with their floating manes.

And as she sang, all the tunny fish came in from the deep to listen to her, and the young Fishermen threw his nets round them and caught them, and others he took with a spear. And when his boat was well-laden, the Mermaid would sink down into the sea, smiling at him. Yet would she never come near him that he might touch her. Oftentimes he called to her and prayed of her, but she would not; and when he sought to seize her she dived into the water as a seal might dive, nor did he see her again that day. And each day the sound of her voice became sweeter to his ears. So sweet was her voice that he forgot his nets and his cunning, and had no care of his craft. Vermilion-finned and with eyes of bossy gold, the tunnies went by in shoals, but he heeded them not. His spear lay by his side unused, and his baskets of plaited osier were empty. With lips parted, and eyes dim with wonder, he sat idle in his boat and listened, listening till the sea mists crept round him and the wandering moon stained his brown limbs with silver.

And one evening he called to her, and said: 'Little Mermaid, little Mermaid, I love thee. Take me for thy bridegroom for I love thee.' But the Mermaid shook her head. 'Thou hast a human Soul,' she answered. 'If only thou wouldst[21] send away thy Soul, then could I love thee.'

And the young Fisherman said to himself, 'Of what use is my soul to me? I cannot see it. I may not touch it. I do not know it. Surely I will send it away from me, and much gladness shall be mine.' And a cry of joy broke from his lips, and standing up in the painted boat, he held out his arms to the Mermaid. 'I will send my Soul away,' he cried, 'and you shall be my bride, and I will be thy bridegroom, and in the depth of the sea we will dwell together, and all that thou hast sung of thou shalt show me, and all that thou desirest[22] I will do, nor shall our lives be divided.'

And the little Mermaid laughed for pleasure and hid her face in her hands.

'But how shall I send my Soul from me?' cried the young Fisherman. 'Tell me how I may do it, and lo! it shall be done.'

'Alas! I know not,' said the little Mermaid: 'the Sea-folk have no souls.' And she sank down into the deep, looking wistfully at him.

Now early on the next morning, before the sun was the span of a man's hand above the hill, the young Fisherman went to the house of the Priest and knocked three times at the door. The novice looked out through the wicket, and when he saw who it was, he drew back the latch and said to him, 'Enter.'

And the young Fisherman passed in, and knelt down on the sweet-smelling rushes on the floor, and cried to the Priest who was reading out of the Holy Book and said to him, 'Father, I am in love with one of the Sea-folk, and my Soul hindereth me from having my desire. Tell me how I can send my Soul away from me, for in truth I have no need of it. Of what value is my soul to me? I cannot see it. I may not touch it. I do not know it.'

And the Priest beat his breast, and answered, 'Alack, alack, thou art mad, or hast eaten of some poisonous herb, for the Soul is the noblest part of man, and was given to us by God that we should nobly use it. There is no thing more precious than a human soul, nor any earthly thing that can be weighed with it. It is worth all the gold that is in the world, and is more precious than the rubies of the kings. Therefore, my son, think not any more of this matter, for it is a sin that may not be forgiven. And as for the Sea-folk, they are lost, and they who would traffic with them are lost also. They are the beasts of the field that know not good from evil, and for them the Lord has not died.'

The young Fisherman's eyes filled with tears when he heard the bitter words of the Priest, and he rose up from his knees and said to him, 'Father, the Fauns live in the forest and are glad, and on the rocks sit the Mermen with their harps of red gold. Let me be as they are, I beseech thee, for their days are as the days of flowers. And as for my Soul, what doth[23] my Soul profit me, if it stand between me and the thing that I love?'

'The love of the body is vile,' cried the Priest, knitting his brows, 'and vile and evil are the pagan things God suffers to wander through His world. Accursed be the Fauns of the woodland, and accursed be the singers of the sea! I have heard them at night-time, and they have sought to lure me from my beads. They tap at the window and laugh. They whisper into my ears the tale of their perilous joys. They tempt me with temptations, and when pray they make mouths at me. They are lost, I tell thee, they are lost. For them there is no heaven nor hell, and in neither shall they praise God's name.'

'Father,' cried the young Fisherman, 'thou knowest not what thou sayest. Once in my net I snared the daughter of a King. She is fairer than the morning star, and whiter than the moon. For her body I would give my soul, and for her love I would surrender heaven. Tell me what I ask of thee, and let me go in peace.'

'Away! Away!' cried the Priest: 'thy leman is lost, and thou shalt be lost with her.' And he gave him no blessing, but drove him from his door.

And the young Fisherman went down into the market place,

and he walked slowly, and with bowed head, as one who is in sorrow.

And when the merchants saw him coming, they began to whisper to each other, and one of them came forth to meet him, and called him by name, and said to him, 'What hast thou to sell?'

'I will sell thee my Soul,' he answered: 'I pray thee buy it off me, for I am weary of it. Of what use is my Soul to me? I cannot see it. I may not touch it. I do not know it.'

But the merchants mocked at him, and said, 'Of what use is a man's soul to us? It is not worth a clipped piece of silver. Sell us thy body for a slave, and we will clothe thee in sea purple, and put a ring upon thy finger, and make thee the minion of the great Queen. But talk not of the Soul, for to us it is nought, nor has it any value for our service.'

And the young Fisherman said to himself: 'How strange a thing this is! The Priest telleth[24] me that the Soul is worth all the gold in the world, and the merchants say that it is not worth a clipped piece of silver.' And he passed out of the market place, and went down to the shore of the sea, and began to ponder on what he should do.

And at noon he remembered how one of his companions, who was a gatherer of samphire, had told him of a certain young Witch who dwelt in a cave at the head of the bay and was very cunning in her witcheries. And he set to and ran, so eager was he to get rid of his soul, and a cloud of dust followed him as he sped round the sand of the shore. By the itching of her palm the young Witch knew his coming, and she laughed and let down her red hair. With her red hair falling around her, she stood at the opening of the cave, and in her hand she had a spray of wild hemlock that was blossoming.

'What d'ye lack? What d'ye lack?' she cried, as he came panting up the steep, and bent down before her. 'Fish for thy net, when the wind is foul? I have a little reed pipe, and when I blow on it the mullet come sailing into the bay. But it has a price, pretty boy, it has a price. What d'ye lack? What d'ye lack? A storm to wreck the ships, and wash the chests of rich treasure ashore? I have more storms than the wind has, for I serve one who is stronger than the wind, and with a sieve and a pail of water. I can send the great galleys to the bottom of the sea. But I have a price, pretty boy, I have a price. What d'ye lack? What d'ye lack? I know a flower that grows in the valley, none knows it but I. It has purple leaves, and a star in its heart, and its juice is as white as milk. Shouldst thou touch with this flower the hard lips of the Queen, she would follow thee all over the world. Out of the bed of the King she would rise, and over the whole world she would follow thee. And it has a price, pretty boy, it has a price. What d'ye lack? What d'ye lack? I can pound a toad in a mortar, and make broth of it, and stir the broth with a dead man's hand. Sprinkle it on thine enemy while he sleeps, and he will turn into a black viper, and his own mother will slay him. With a wheel I can draw the Moon from heaven, and in a crystal I can show thee Death. What d'ye lack? What d'ye lack? Tell me thy desire, and I will give it thee, and thou shalt pay me a price, pretty boy, thou shalt pay me a price.'

'My desire is but for a little thing,' said the young Fisherman, 'yet hath the Priest been wroth with me, and driven me forth. It is but for a little thing, and the merchants have mocked at me, and denied me. Therefore am I come to thee, though men call thee evil, and whatever be thy price I shall pay it.'

'What wouldst thou?' asked the Witch, coming near to him.

'I would send my Soul away from me,' answered the young Fisherman.

The Witch grew pale, and shuddered, and hid her face in her blue mantle. 'Pretty boy, pretty boy,' she muttered, 'that is a terrible thing to do.'

He tossed his brown curls and laughed. 'My Soul is nought to me,' he answered. 'I cannot see it. I may not touch it. I do not know it.'

'What wilt thou give me if I tell thee?' asked the Witch, looking down at him with her beautiful eyes.

'Five pieces of gold,' he said, 'and my nets, and the wattled house where I live, and the painted boat in which I sail. Only tell me how to get rid of my Soul, and I will give thee all that I possess.'

She laughed mockingly at him, and struck him with the spray of hemlock. 'I can turn the autumn leaves into gold,' she answered, 'and I can weave the pale moonbeams into silver if I will it. He whom I serve is richer than all the kings of this world, and has their dominions.'

'What then shall I give thee,' he cried, 'if thy price be neither gold nor silver?'

The Witch stroked his hair with her thin white hand. 'Thou must dance with me, pretty boy,' she murmured, and she smiled at him as she spoke.

'Nought but that?' cried the young Fisherman in wonder, and he rose to his feet.

'Nought but that,' she answered, and she smiled at him again. 'Then at sunset in some secret place we shall dance together,' he said, 'and after that we have danced thou shalt tell me the thing which I desire to know.'

She shook her head. 'When the moon is full, when the moon is full,' she muttered. Then she peered all round, and listened. A blue bird rose screaming from its nest and circled over the dunes, and three spotted birds rustled through the coarse grey grass and whistled to each other. There was no other sound save the sound of a wave fretting the smooth pebbles below. So she reached out her hand, and drew him near to her and put her dry lips close to his ear.

'Tonight thou must come to the top of the mountain,' she whispered. 'It is a Sabbath, and fie will be there.'

The young Fisherman started and looked at her, and she showed her white teeth and laughed. 'Who is He of whom thou speakest[25]?' he asked.

'It matters not,' she answered. 'Go thou tonight, and stand under the branches of the hornbeam, and wait for my coming. If a black dog run towards thee, strike it with a rod of willow, and it will go away. If an owl speak to thee, make it no answer. When the moon is full I shall be with thee, and we will dance together on the grass.'

'But wilt thou swear to me to tell me how I may send my Soul from me?' he made question.

She moved out into the sunlight, and through her red hair rippled the wind. 'By the hoofs of the goat I swear it,' she made answer.

'Thou art the best of the witches,' cried the young Fisherman, 'and I will surely dance with thee tonight on the top of the mountain. I would indeed that thou hadst[26] asked of me either gold or silver. But such as thy price is thou shalt have it, for it is but a little thing.' And he doffed his cap to her, and bent his head low, and ran back to the town filled with a great joy.

And the Witch watched him as he went, and when he had passed from her sight she entered her cave, and having taken a mirror from a box of carved cedarwood, she set it up on a frame, and burned vervain on lighted charcoal before it, and peered through the coils of the smoke. And after a time she clenched her hands in anger. 'He should have been mine,' she muttered, 'I am as fair as she is.'

And that evening, when the moon had risen, the young Fisherman climbed up to the top of the mountain, and stood under the branches of the hornbeam. Like a targe of polished metal the round sea lay at his feet, and the shadows of the fishing boats moved in the little bay. A great owl, with yellow sulphurous eyes, called to him by his name, but he made it no answer. A black dog ran towards him and snarled. He struck it with a rod of willow, and it went away whining.

At midnight the witches came flying through the air like bats. 'Phew!' they cried, as they lit upon the ground, 'there is some one here we know not!' and they sniffed about, and chattered to each other, and made signs. Last of all came the young Witch, with her red hair streaming in the wind. She wore a dress of gold tissue embroidered with peacocks' eyes, and a little cap of green velvet was on her head.

'Where is he, where is he?' shrieked the witches when they saw her, but she only laughed, and ran to the hornbeam, and taking the Fisherman by the hand she led him out into the moonlight and began to dance.

Round and round they whirled, and the young Witch jumped so high that he could see the scarlet heels of her shoes. Then right across the dancers came the sound of the galloping of a horse, but no horse was to be seen, and he felt afraid.

'Faster,' cried the Witch, and she threw her arms about his neck, and her breath was hot upon his face. 'Faster, faster!' she cried, and the earth seemed to spin beneath his feet, and his brain grew troubled, and a great terror fell on him, as of some evil thing that was watching him, and at last he became aware that under the shadow of a rock there was a figure that had not been there before.

It was a man dressed in a suit of black velvet, cut in the Spanish fashion. His face was strangely pale, but his lips were like a proud red flower. He seemed weary, and was leaning back toying in a listless manner with the pommel of his dagger. On the grass beside him lay a plumed hat, and a pair of riding gloves gauntleted with gilt lace, and sewn with seed pearls wrought into a curious device. A short cloak lined with sables hung from his shoulder, and his delicate white hands were gemmed with rings. Heavy eyelids drooped over his eyes.

The young Fisherman watched him, as one snared in a spell. At last their eyes met, and wherever he danced it seemed to him that the eyes of the man were upon him. He heard the Witch laugh, and caught her by the waist, and whirled her madly round and round.

Suddenly a dog bayed in the wood, and the dancers stopped, and going up two by two, knelt down, and kissed the man's hands. As they did so, a little smile touched his proud lips, as a bird's wing touches the water and makes it laugh. But there was disdain in it. He kept looking at the young Fisherman.

'Come! let us worship,' whispered the Witch, and she led him up, and a great desire to do as she besought him seized on him, and he followed her. But when he came close, and without knowing why he did it, he made on his breast the sign of the Cross, and called upon the holy name.

No sooner had he done so than the witches screamed like hawks and flew away, and the pallid face that had been watching him twitched with a spasm of pain. The man went over to a little wood, and whistled. A jennet with silver trappings came running to meet him. As he leapt upon the saddle he turned round, and looked at the young Fisherman sadly.

And the Witch with the red hair tried to fly away also, but the Fisherman caught her by her wrists, and held her fast.

'Loose me,' she cried, 'and let me go. For thou hast named what should not be named, and shown the sign that may not be looked at.'

'Nay,' he answered, 'but I will not let thee go till thou hast told me the secret.'

'What secret?' said the Witch, wrestling with him like a wild cat, and biting her foam-flecked lips.

'Thou knowest,' he made answer.

Her grass-green eyes grew dim with tears, and she said to the Fisherman, 'Ask me anything but that!'

He laughed, and held her all the more tightly.

And when she saw that she could not free herself, she whispered to him, 'Surely I am as fair as the daughter of the sea, and as comely as those that dwell in the blue waters,' and she fawned on him and put her face close to his.

But he thrust her back frowning, and said to her, 'If thou

keepest[27] not the promise that thou madest[28] to me I will slay thee for a false witch.'

She grew grey as a blossom of the Judas tree, and shuddered. 'Be it so,' she muttered. 'It is thy Soul and not mine. Do with it as thou wilt.' And she took from her girdle a little knife that had a handle of green viper's skin, and gave it to him.

'What shall this serve me?' he asked of her, wondering.

She was silent for a few moments, and a look of terror came over her face. Then she brushed her hair back from her forehead, and smiling strangely she said to him, 'What men call the shadow of the body is not the shadow of the body, but is the body of the Soul. Stand on the seashore with thy back to the moon, and cut away from around thy feet thy shadow, which is thy Soul's body, and bid thy soul leave thee, and it will do so.'

The Young Fisherman trembled. 'Is this true?' he murmured.

'It is true, and I would that I had not told thee of it,' she cried, and she clung to his knees weeping.

He put her from him and left her in the rank grass, and going to the edge of the mountain he placed the knife in his belt and began to climb down.

And his Soul that was within him called out to him and said, 'Lo! I have dwelt with thee for all these years, and have been thy servant. Send me not away from thee now, for what evil have I done thee?'

And the young Fisherman laughed. 'Thou hast done me no evil, but I have no need of thee,' he answered. 'The world is wide, and there is Heaven also, and Hell, and that dim twilight house that lies between. Go wherever thou wilt, but trouble me not, for my love is calling to me.'

And his Soul besought him piteously, but he heeded it not, but leapt from crag to crag, being surefooted as a wild goat, and at last he reached the level ground and the yellow shore of the sea.

Bronze-limbed and well-knit, like a statue wrought by a Grecian, he stood on the sand with his back to the moon, and out of the foam came white arms that beckoned to him, and out of the waves rose dim forms that did him homage. Before him lay his shadow, which was the body of his Soul, and behind him hung the moon in the honey-coloured air.

And his Soul said to him, 'If indeed thou must drive me from thee, send me not forth without a heart. The world is cruel, give me thy heart to take with me.'

He tossed his head and smiled. 'With what should I love my love if I gave thee my heart?' he cried.

'Nay, but be merciful,' said his Soul: 'give me thy heart, for the world is very cruel, and I am afraid.'

'My heart is my love's,' he answered, 'therefore tarry not, but get thee gone.'

'Should I not love also?' asked his Soul.

'Get thee gone, for I have no need of thee,' cried the young Fisherman, and he took the little knife with its handle of green viper's skin, and cut away his shadow from around his feet, and rose up and stood before him, and looked at him, and it was even as himself.

He crept back, and thrust the knife into his belt, and a feeling of awe came over him. 'Get thee gone,' he murmured, 'and let me see thy face no more.'

'Nay, but we must meet again,' said the Soul. Its voice was low and flute-like, and its lips hardly moved while it spake.

'How shall me meet?' cried the young Fisherman. 'Thou wilt not follow me into the depths of the sea?'

'Once every year I will come to this place, and call to thee,' said the Soul. 'It may be that thou wilt have need of me.'

'What need should I have of thee?' cried the young Fisherman, 'but be it as thou wilt,' and he plunged into the water, and the Tritons blew their horns, and the little Mermaid rose up to meet him, and put her arms around his neck and kissed him on the mouth.

And the Soul stood on the lonely beach and watched them. And when they had sunk down into the sea, it went weeping away over the marshes.

And after a year was over the Soul came down to the shore of the sea and called to the young Fisherman, and he rose out of the deep, and said, 'Why dost[29] thou call to me?

And the Soul answered, 'Come nearer, that I may speak with thee, for I have seen marvellous things.'

So he came nearer, and couched in the shallow water, and leaned his head upon his hand and listened.

And the Soul said to him, 'When I left thee I turned my face to the East and journeyed. From the East cometh everything that is wise. Six days I journeyed, and on the morning of the seventh day I came to a hill that is in the country of the Tartars. I sat down under the shade of a tamarisk tree to shelter myself from the sun. The land was dry and burnt up with the heat. The people went to and fro over the plain like flies crawling upon a disk of polished copper.

'When it was noon a cloud of red dust rose up from the flat rim of the land. When the Tartars saw it, they strung their painted bows, and having leapt upon their little horses they galloped to meet it. The women fled screaming to the waggons, and hid themselves behind the felt curtains.

'At twilight the Tartars returned, but five of them were missing, and of those that came back not a few had been wounded. They harnessed their horses to the waggons and drove hastily away. Three jackals came out of a cave and peered after them. Then they sniffed up the air with their nostrils, and trotted off in the opposite direction.

'When the moon rose I saw a campfire burning on the plain, and went towards it. A company of merchants were seated round it on carpets. Their camels were picketed behind them, and the negroes who were their servants were pitching tents of tanned skin upon the sand, and making a high wall of the prickly pear.

'As I came near them, the chief of the merchants rose up and drew his sword and asked me my business.

'I answered that I was a Prince in my own land, and that I had escaped from the Tartars, who had sought to make me their slave. The chief smiled, and showed me five heads fixed upon long reeds of bamboo.

'Then he asked me who was the prophet of God, and I answered him Mohammed.

'When he heard the name of the false prophet, he bowed and took me by the hand, and placed me by his side. A negro brought me some mare's milk in a wooden dish, and a piece of lamb's flesh roasted.

'At daybreak we started on our journey. I rode on a red-haired camel by the side of the chief, and a runner ran before us carrying a spear. The men of war were on either hand, and the mules followed with the merchandise. There were forty camels in the caravan, and the mules were twice forty in number.

'We went from the country of the Tartars into the country of those who curse the Moon. We saw the Gryphons guarding their gold on the white rocks, and the scaled Dragons sleeping in their caves. As we passed over the mountains we held our breath lest the snows might fall on us, and each man tied a veil of gauze before his eyes. As we passed through the valleys the Pygmies shot arrows at us from the hollows of the trees, and at night-time we heard the wild men beating on their drums. When we came to the Tower of Apes we set fruits before them, and they did not harm us. When we came to the Tower of Serpents we gave them warm milk in bowls of brass, and they let us go by. Three times in our journey we came to the banks of the Oxus. We crossed it on rafts of wood with great bladders of blown hide. The river horses raged against us and sought to slay us. When the camels saw them they trembled.

'The kings of each city levied tolls on us, but would not suffer us to enter their gates. They threw us bread over the walls, little maizecakes baked in honey and cakes of fine flour filled with dates. For every hundred baskets we gave them a bead of amber.

'When the dwellers in the villages saw us coming, they poisoned the wells and fled to the hill summits. We fought with the Magadae who are born old, and grow younger and younger every year, and die when they are little children; and with the Laktroi who say that they are the sons of tigers, and paint themselves yellow and black; and with the Aurantes who bury their dead on the tops of trees, and themselves live in dark caverns lest the Sun, who is their god, should slay them; and with the Krimnians who worship a crocodile, and give it earrings of green grass, and feed it with butter and fresh fowls; and with the Agazonbae, who are dog-faced; and with the Sibans, who have horses' feet, and run more swiftly than horses. A third of our company died in battle, and a third died of want. The rest murmured against me, and said that I had brought them an evil fortune. I took a horned adder from beneath a stone and let it sting me. When they saw that I did not sicken they grew afraid.

'In the fourth month we reached the city of Illel. It was night-time when we came to the grove that is outside the walls, and the air was sultry, for the Moon was travelling in Scorpion. We took the ripe pomegranates from the trees, and brake them, and drank their sweet juices. Then we lay down on our carpets and waited for the dawn.

'And at dawn we rose and knocked at the gate of the city. It was wrought out of red bronze, and carved with sea-dragons and dragons that have wings. The guards looked down from the battlements and asked us our business. The interpreter of the caravan answered that we had come from the island of Syria with much merchandise. They took hostages, and told us that they would open the gate to us at noon, and bade us tarry till then.

'When it was noon they opened the gate, and as we entered in the people came crowding out of the houses to look at us, and a crier went round the city crying through a shell. We stood in the market place, and the negroes uncorded the bales of figured cloths and opened the carved chests of sycamore. And when they had ended their task, the merchants set forth their strange wares, the waxed linen from Egypt, and the painted linen from the country of the Ethiops, the purple sponges from Tyre and the blue hangings from Sidon, the cups of cold amber and the fine vessels of glass and the curious vessels of burnt clay. From the roof of a house a company of women watched us. One of them wore a mask of gilded leather.

'And on the first day the priests came and bartered with us, and on the second day came the nobles, and on the third day came the craftsmen and the slaves. And this is their custom with all merchants as long as they tarry in the city.

'And we tarried for a moon, and when the moon was waning, I wearied and wandered away through the streets of the city and came to the garden of its god. The priests in their yellow robes moved silently through the green trees, and on a pavement of black marble stood the rose-red house in which the god had his dwelling. Its doors were of powdered lacquer, and bulls and peacocks were wrought on them in raised and polished gold. The tilted roof was of sea-green porcelain and the jutting eaves were festooned with little bells. When the white doves flew past, they struck the bells with their wings and made them tinkle.

'In front of the temple was a pool of clear water paved with veined onyx. I lay down beside it, and with my pale fingers I touched the broad leaves. One of the priests came towards me and stood behind me. He had sandals on his feet, one of soft serpent skin and the other of birds' plumage. On his head was a mitre of black felt decorated with silver crescents. Seven yellows were woven into his robe, and his frizzed hair was stained with antimony.

'And after a little while he spake to me, and asked me my desire.

'I told him that my desire was to see the god.

'"The god is hunting," said the priest, looking strangely at me with his small slanting eyes.

'"Tell me in what forest, and I will ride with him," I answered.

'He combed out the soft fringes of his tunic with his long pointed nails. "The god is asleep," he murmured.

'"Tell me on what couch, and I will watch by him," I answered.

'"If the wine be sweet, I will drink it with him, and if it be bitter I will drink it with him also," was my answer.

'"The god is at the feast," he cried.

'He bowed his head in wonder, and, taking me by the hand, he raised me op, and led me into the temple.

'And in the first chamber I saw an idol seated on a throne of jasper bordered with great orient pearls. It was carved out of ebony, and in stature was of the stature of a man. On its forehead was a ruby, and thick oil dripped from its hair on to its thighs. Its feet were red with the blood of a newly-slain kid, and its loins girt with a copper belt that was studded with seven beryls.

'And I said to the priest, "Is this the god?" And he answered me, "This is the god."

'"Show me the god," I cried, "or I will surely slay thee." And I touched his hand, and it became withered.

'And the priest besought me, saving, "Let my lord heal his servant, and I will show him the god."

'So I breathed with my breath upon his hand, and it became whole again, and he trembled and led me into the second chamber, and I saw an idol standing on a lotus of jade hung with great emeralds. It was carved out of ivory, and in stature was twice the stature of a man. On its forehead was a chrysolite, and its breasts were smeared with myrrh and cinnamon. In one hand it held a crooked sceptre of jade, and in the other a round crystal. It wore buskins of brass, and its thick neck was circled with a circle of selenites.

'And I said to the priest, "Is this the god?" And he answered me, "This is the god."

"Show me the god," I cried, "or I will surely slay thee." And I touched his eyes, and they became blind.

'And the priest besought me, saying, "Let my lord heal his servant, and I will show him the god."

'So I breathed with my breath upon his eyes, and the sight came back to them, and he trembled again, and led me into the third chamber, and lo! there was no idol in it, nor image of any kind, but only a mirror of round metal set on an altar of stone.

'And I said to the priest, "Where is the god?"

'And he answered me: "There is no god but this mirror that thou seest[30], for this is the Mirror of Wisdom. And it reflecteth[31] all things that are in heaven and on earth, save only the face of him who looketh[32] into it. This it reflecteth not, so that he who looketh into it may be wise. Many other mirrors are there, but they are mirrors of Opinion. This only is the Mirror of Wisdom. And they who possess this mirror know everything, nor is there anything hidden from them. And they who possess it not have not Wisdom. Therefore is it the god, and we worship it." And I looked into the mirror, and it was even as he had said to me.

'And I did a strange thing, but what I did matters not, for in a valley that is but a day's journey from this place have I hidden the Mirror of Wisdom. Do but suffer me to enter into thee again and be thy servant, and thou shalt be wiser than all the wise men, and Wisdom shall be thine. Suffer me to enter into thee, and none will be as wise as thou.

But the young Fisherman laughed. 'Love is better than Wisdom,' he cried, 'and the little Mermaid loves me.'

'Nay, but there is nothing better than Wisdom,' said the Soul.

'Love is better,' answered the young Fisherman, and he plunged into the deep, and the Soul went weeping away over the marshes.

And after the second year was over, the Soul came down to the shore of the sea, and called to the young Fisherman and he rose out of the deep and said, 'Why dost thou call to me?'

And the Soul answered, 'Come nearer, that I may speak with thee, for I have seen marvellous things.'

So he came nearer, and couched in the shallow water, and leaned his head upon his hand and listened.

And the Soul said to him, 'When I left thee, I turned my face to the South and journeyed. From the South cometh everything that is precious. Six days I journeyed along the highways that lead to the city of Ashter, along the dusty red-dyed highways by which the pilgrims are wont to go did I journey, and on the morning of the seventh day I lifted up my eyes, and lo! the city lay at my feet, for it is in a valley.

'There are nine gates to this city, and in front of each gate stands a bronze horse that neighs when the Bedouins come down from the mountains. The walls are cased with copper, and the watchtowers on the wall are roofed with brass. In every tower stands an archer with a bow in his hand. At sunrise he strikes with an arrow on a gong, and at sunset he blows through a horn of horn.

'When I sought to enter, the guards stopped me and asked of

me who I was. I made answer that I was a Dervish and on my way to the city of Mecca, where there was a green veil on which the Koran was embroidered in silver letters by the hands of the angels. They were filled with wonder, and entreated me to pass in.

'Inside it is even as a bazaar. Surely thou shouldst have been with me. Across the narrow streets the gay lanterns of paper flutter like large butterflies. When the wind blows over the roofs they rise and fall as painted bubbles do. In front of their booths sit the merchants on silken carpets. They have straight black beards, and their turbans are covered with golden sequins, and long strings of amber and carved peach stones glide through their cool fingers. Some of them sell galbanum and nard, and curious perfumes from the islands of the Indian Sea, and the thick oil of red roses, and myrrh and little nail-shaped cloves. When one stops to speak to them, they throw pinches of frankincense upon a charcoal brazier and make the air sweet. I saw a Syrian who held in his hands a thin rod like a reed. Grey threads of smoke came from it, and its odour as it burned was as the odour of the pink almond in spring. Others sell silver bracelets embossed all over with creamy blue turquoise stones, and anklets of brass wire fringed with little pearls, and tigers' claws set in gold, and the claws of that gilt cat, the leopard, set in gold also, and earrings of pierced emerald, and finger-rings of hollowed jade. From the tea houses comes the sound of the guitar, and the opium smokers, with their white smiling faces look out at the passers-by.

'Of a truth thou shouldst have been with me. The wine-sellers elbow their way through the crowd with great black skins on their shoulders. Most of them sell the wine of Schiraz, which is as sweet as honey. They serve it in little metal cups and strew rose leaves upon it. In the market place stand the fruitsellers, who sell all kinds of fruit: ripe figs, with their bruised purple flesh, melons, smelling of musk and yellow as topazes, citrons and rose apples and clusters of white grapes, round red-gold oranges, and oval lemons of green gold. Once I saw an elephant go by. Its trunk was painted with vermilion and turmeric, and over its ears it had a net of crimson silk cord. It stopped opposite one of the booths and began eating the oranges, and the man only laughed. Thou canst not think how strange a people they are. When they are glad they go to the bird-sellers and buy of them a caged bird, and set it free that their joy may be greater, and when they are sad they scourge themselves with thorns that their sorrow may not grow less.

'One evening I met some negroes carrying a heavy palanquin through the bazaar. It was made of gilded bamboo, and the poles were of vermilion lacquer studded with brass peacocks. Across the windows hung thin curtains of muslin embroidered with beetles' wings and with tiny seed pearls, and as it passed by a pale-faced Circassian looked out and smiled at me. I followed behind, and the negroes hurried their steps and scowled. But I did not care. l felt a great curiosity come over me.

'At last they stopped at a square white house. There were no windows to it, only a little door like the door of a tomb. They set down the palanquin and knocked three times with a copper hammer. An Armenian in a caftan of green leather peered through the wicket, and when he saw them he opened, and spread a carpet on the ground, and the woman stepped out. As she went in, she turned round and smiled at me again. I had never seen any one so pale.

'When the moon rose I returned to the same place and sought

for the house, but it was no longer there. When I saw that, I knew who the woman was, and wherefore she had smiled at me.

'Certainly thou shouldst have been with me. On the feast of the New Moon the young Emperor came forth from his palace and went into the mosque to pray. His hair and beard were dyed with rose leaves, and his cheeks were powdered with a fine gold dust. The palms of his feet and hands were yellow with saffron.

'At sunrise he went forth from his palace in a robe of silver, and at sunset he returned to it again in a robe of gold. The people flung themselves on the ground and hid their faces, but I would not do so. I stood by the stall of a seller of dates and waited. When the Emperor saw me, he raised his painted eyebrows and stopped. I stood quite still, and made him no obeisance. The people marvelled at my boldness, and counselled me to flee from the city. I paid no heed to them, but went and sat with the sellers of strange gods, who by reason of their craft are abominated. When I told them what I had done, each of them gave me a god and prayed me to leave them.

'That night, as I lay on a cushion in the tea house that is in the Street of Pomegranates, the guards of the Emperor entered and led me to the palace. As I went in they closed each door behind me, and put a chain across it. Inside was a great court with an arcade running all round. The walls were of white alabaster, set here and there with blue and green tiles. The pillars were of green marble, and the pavement of a kind of peach-blossom marble. I had never seen anything like it before.

'As I passed across the court two veiled women looked down from a balcony and cursed me. The guards hastened on, and the butts of the lances rang upon the polished floor. They opened a gate of wrought ivory, and I found myself in a watered garden of seven terraces. It was planted with tulip cups and moon flowers, and silver-studded aloes. Like a slim reed of crystal a fountain hung in the dusky air. The cypress trees were like burnt-out torches. From one of them a nightingale was singing.

'At the end of the garden stood a little pavilion. As we approached it two eunuchs came out to meet us. Their fat bodies swayed as they walked, and they glanced curiously at me with their yellow-lidded eyes. One of them drew aside the captain of the guard, and in a low voice whispered to him. The other kept munching scented pastilles, which he took with an affected gesture out of an oval box of lilac enamel.

'After a few moments the captain of the guard dismissed the soldiers. They went back to the palace, the eunuchs following slowly behind and plucking the sweet mulberries from the trees as they passed. Once the elder of the two turned round, and smiled at me with an evil smile.

'Then the captain of the guard motioned me towards the entrance of the pavilion. I walked on without trembling, and drawing the heavy curtain aside I entered in.

'The young Emperor was stretched on a couch of dyed lion skins, and a gerfalcon perched upon his wrist. Behind him stood a brass-turbaned Nubian, naked down to the waist, and with heavy earrings in his split ears. On a table by the side of the couch lay a mighty scimitar of steel.

'When the Emperor saw me he frowned, and said to me, "What is thy name? Knowest thou not that I am Emperor of this city?" But I made him no answer.

'He pointed with his finger at the scimitar, and the Nubian

seized it, and rushing forward struck at me with great violence. The blade whizzed through me, and did me no hurt. The man fell sprawling on the floor, and when he rose up his teeth chattered with terror and he hid himself behind the couch.

'The Emperor leapt to his feet, and taking a lance from a stand of arms, he threw it at me. I caught it in its flight, and brake the shaft into two pieces. He shot at me with an arrow, but I held up my hands and it stopped in mid-air. Then he drew a dagger from a belt of white leather, and stabbed the Nubian in the throat lest the slave should tell of his dishonour. The man writhed like a trampled snake, and a red foam bubbled from his lips.

'As soon as he was dead the Emperor turned to me, and when he had wiped away the bright sweat from his brow with a little napkin of purfled and purple silk, he said to me, "Art thou a prophet, that I may not harm thee, or the son of a prophet, that I can do thee no hurt? I pray thee leave my city tonight, for while thou art in it I am no longer its lord."

'And I answered him, "I will go for half of thy treasure. Give me half of thy treasure, and I will go away."

'He took me by the hand, and led me out into the garden. When the captain of the guard saw me, he wondered. When the eunuchs saw me, their knees shook and they fell upon the ground in fear.

'There is a chamber in the palace that has eight walls of red porphyry, and a brass-scaled ceiling hung with lamps. The Emperor touched one of the walls and it opened, and we passed down a corridor that was lit with many torches. In niches upon each side stood great wine jars filled to the brim with silver pieces. When we reached the centre of the corridor the Emperor spoke the word that may not be spoken, and a granite door swung back on a secret spring, and he put his hands before his face lest his eyes should be dazzled.

'Thou couldst[33] not believe how marvellous a place it was. There were huge tortoise shells full of pearls, and hollowed moonstones of great size piled up with red rubies. The gold was stored in coffers of elephant hide, and the gold dust in leather bottles. There were opals and sapphires, the former in cups of crystal, and the latter in cups of jade. Round green emeralds were ranged in order upon thin plates of ivory, and in one corner were silk bags filled, some with turquoise stones, and others with beryls. The ivory horns were heaped with purple amethysts, and the horns of brass with chalcedonies and sards. The pillars, which were of cedar, were hung with strings of yellow lynx stones. In the flat oval shields there were carbuncles, both wine-coloured and coloured like grass. And yet I have told thee but a tithe of what was there.

'And when the Emperor had taken away his hands from before his face he said to me: "This is my house of treasure, and half that is in it is thine, even as I promised to thee. And I will give thee camels and camel drivers, and they shall do thy bidding and take thy share of the treasure to whatever part of the world thou desirest to go. And the thing shall be done tonight, for I would not that the Sun, who is my father, should see that there is in my city a man whom I cannot slay."

'But I answered him, "The gold that is here is thine, and the silver also is thine, and thine are the precious jewels and the things of price. As for me, I have no need of these. Nor shall I take aught from thee but that little ring that thou wearest[34] on the finger of thy hand.'

'And the Emperor frowned. "It is but a ring of lead" he cried, "nor has it any value. Therefore take thy half of the treasure and go from my city."

'"Nay," I answered, "but I will take nought but that leaden ring, for I know what is written within it, and for what purpose."

'And the Emperor trembled, and besought me and said, "Take all the treasure and go from my city. The half that is mine shall be thine also."

'And I did a strange thing, but what I did matters not, for in a cave that is but a day's journey from this place have I hidden the Ring of Riches. It is but a day's journey from this place, and it waits for thy corning. He who has this Ring is richer than all the kings of the world. Come therefore and take it, and the world's riches shall be thine.'

But the young Fisherman laughed. 'Love is better than Riches,' he cried, 'and the little Mermaid loves me.'

'Nay, but there is nothing better than Riches,' said the Soul.

'Love is better,' answered the young Fisherman, and he plunged into the deep, and the Soul went weeping away over the marshes.

And after the third year was over, the Soul came down to the shore of the sea, and called to the young Fisherman, and he rose out of the deep and said, 'Why dost thou call to me?'

And the Soul answered, 'Come nearer, that I may speak with thee, for I have seen marvellous things.'

So he came nearer, and couched in the shallow water, and leaned upon his hand and listened.

And the Soul said to him, 'In a city that I know of there is an inn that standeth by a river. I sat there with sailors who drank of two different-coloured wines, and ate bread made of barley, and little salt fish served in bay leaves with vinegar. And as we sat and made merry, there entered to us an old man bearing a leathern carpet and a lute that had two horns of amber. And when he had laid out the carpet on the floor, he struck with a quill on the wire strings of his lute, and a girl whose face was veiled ran in and began to dance before us. Her face was veiled with a veil of gauze, but her feet were naked. Naked were her feet, and they moved over the carpet like little white pigeons. Never have I seen anything so marvellous, and the city in which she dances is but a day's journey from this place.

'Now when the young Fisherman heard the words of his Soul, he remembered that the little Mermaid had no feet and could not dance. And a great desire came over him, and he said to himself, 'It is but a day's journey, and I can return to my love,' and he laughed and stood up in the shallow water, and strode towards the shore.

And when he had reached the dry shore he laughed again, and held out his arms to his Soul. And his Soul gave a great cry of joy and ran to meet him, and entered into him, and the young Fisherman saw stretched before him upon the sand that shadow of the body that is the body of the Soul.

And his Soul said to him, 'Let us not tarry, but get hence at once, for the Sea-gods are jealous, and have monsters that do their bidding.'

So they made haste, and all that night they journeyed beneath the moon, and all the next day they journeyed beneath the sun, and on the evening of the day they came to a city.

And the young Fisherman said to his Soul, 'Is this the city in which she dances of whom thou didst[35] speak to me?'

And his Soul answered him, 'It is not this city, but another. Nevertheless let us enter in.'

So they entered in and passed through the streets, and as they passed through the Street of the Jewellers the young Fisherman saw a fair silver cup set forth in a booth. And his Soul said to him, 'Take that silver cup and hide it.'

So he took the cup and hid it in the fold of his tunic, and they went hurriedly out of the city.

And after that they had gone a league from the city, the young Fisherman frowned, and flung the cup away, and said to his Soul, 'Why didst thou tell me to take this cup and hide it, for it was an evil thing to do?'

But his Soul answered him, 'Be at peace, be at peace.'

And on the evening of the second day they came to a city, and the young Fisherman said to his Soul, 'Is this the city in which she dances of whom thou didst speak to me?'

And his Soul answered him, 'It is not this city, but another. Nevertheless let us enter in.'

So they entered in, and passed through the streets, and as they passed through the Street of the Sellers of Sandals, the young Fisherman saw a child standing by a jar of water. And his Soul said to him, 'Smite that child.' So he smote the child till it wept, and when he had done this they went hurriedly out of the city.

And after that they had gone a league from the city the young Fisherman grew wroth, and said to his Soul, 'Why didst thou tell me to smite the child, for it was an evil thing to do?'

But his Soul answered him, 'Be at peace, be at peace.'

And on the evening of the third day they came to a city, and the young Fisherman said to his Soul, 'Is this the city in which she dances of whom thou didst speak to me?'

And his Soul answered him, 'It may be that it is in this city, therefore let us enter in.'

So they entered in and passed through the streets, but nowhere could the young Fisherman find the river or the inn that stood by its side. And the people of the city looked curiously at him, and he grew afraid and said to his Soul, 'Let us go hence, for she who dances with white feet is not here.'

But his Soul answered, 'Nay, but let us tarry, for the night is dark and there will be robbers on the way.'

So he sat him down in the market place and rested, and after a time there went by a hooded merchant who had a cloak of cloth of Tartary, and bare a lantern of pierced horn at the end of a jointed reed. And the merchant said to him, 'Why does thou sit in the market place, seeing that the booths are closed and the bales corded?'

And the young Fisherman answered him, 'I can find no inn in this city, nor have I any kinsman who might give me shelter.'

'Are we not all kinsmen?' said the merchant. 'And did not one God make us? Therefore come with me, for I have a guest chamber.'

So the young Fisherman rose up and followed the merchant to his house. And when he had passed through a garden of pomegranates and entered into the house, the merchant brought him rose water in a copper dish that he might wash his hands, and ripe melons that he might quench his thirst, and set a bowl of rice and a piece of roasted kid before him.

And after that he had finished, the merchant led him to the

guest chamber, and bade him sleep and be at rest. And the young Fisherman gave him thanks, and kissed the ring that was on his hand, and flung himself down on the carpets of dyed goat's hair. And when he had covered himself with a covering of black lamb's wool he fell asleep.

And three hours before dawn, and while it was still night, his Soul waked him and said to him, 'Rise up and go to the room of the merchant, even to the room in which he sleepeth[36], and slay him, and take from him his gold, for we have need of it.'

And the young Fisherman rose up and crept towards the room of the merchant, and over the feet of the merchant there was lying a curved sword, and the tray by the side of the merchant held nine purses of gold. And he reached out his hand and touched the sword, and when he touched it the merchant started and awoke, and leaping up seized himself the sword and cried to the Young Fisherman, 'Dost thou return evil for good, and pay with the shedding of blood for the kindness that I have shown thee?'

And his Soul said to the young Fisherman, 'Strike him,' and he struck him so that he swooned, and he seized then the nine purses of gold, and fled hastily through the garden of pomegranates, and set his face to the star that is the star of morning.

And when they had gone a league from the city, the young Fisherman beat his breast, and said to his Soul, 'Why didst thou bid me slay the merchant and take his gold? Surely thou art evil.'

But his Soul answered him, 'Be at peace, be at peace.'

'Nay,' cried the young Fisherman, 'I may not be at peace, for all that thou hast made me to do I hate. Thee also I hate, and I bid thee tell me wherefore thou hast wrought with me in this wise.'

And his Soul answered him, 'When thou didst send me forth

into the world thou gavest[37] me no heart, so I learned to do all these things and love them.'

'What sayest thou?' murmured the young Fisherman.

'Thou knowest,' answered his Soul, 'thou knowest it well. Hast thou forgotten that thou gavest me no heart? I trow not. And so trouble not thyself[38] nor me, but be at peace, for there is no pain that thou shalt not give away, nor any pleasure that thou shalt not receive.'

And when the young Fisherman heard these words he trembled and said to his Soul, 'Nay, but thou art evil, and hast made me forget my love, and hast tempted me with temptations, and hast set my feet in the ways of sins.'

And his Soul answered him, 'Thou hast not forgotten that when thou didst send me forth into the world thou gavest me no heart. Come, let us go to another city, and make merry, for we have nine purses of gold.'

But the young Fisherman took the nine purses of gold, and flung them down, and trampled on them.

'Nay,' he cried, 'but I will have nought to do with thee, nor will I journey with thee anywhere, but even as I sent thee away before, so will I send thee away now, for thou hast wrought me no good.' And he turned his back to the moon, and with the little knife that had the handle of green viper's skin he strove to cut from his feet that shadow of the body which is the body of the Soul.

Yet his Soul stirred not from him, nor paid heed to his command, but said to him, 'The spell that the Witch told thee avails thee no more, for I may not leave thee, nor mayest[39] thou drive me forth. Once in his life may a man send his Soul away, but he who receiveth[40] back his Soul must keep it with him for ever, and this is his punishment and his reward.'

And the young Fisherman grew pale and clenched his hands and cried, 'She was a false Witch in that she told me not that.'

'Nay', answered his Soul, 'but she was true to Him she worships, and whose servant she will be ever.'

And when the young Fisherman knew that he could no longer get rid of his Soul, and that it was an evil Soul, and would abide with him always, he fell upon the ground weeping bitterly.

And when it was day, the young Fisherman rose up and said to his Soul, 'I will bind my hands that I may not do thy bidding, and close my lips that I may not speak thy words, and I will return to the place where she whom I love has her dwelling. Even to the sea will I return, and to the little bay where she is wont to sing, and I will call to her and tell her the evil I have done and the evil thou hast wrought on me.'

And his Soul tempted him and said, 'Who is thy love, that thou shouldst return to her? The world has many fairer than she is. There are the dancing girls of Samaris who dance in the manner of all kinds of birds and beasts. Their feet are painted with henna, and in their hands they have little copper bells. They laugh while they dance, and their laughter is as clear as the laughter of water. Come with me and I will show them to thee. For what is this trouble of thine about the things of sin? Is that which is pleasant to eat not made for the eater? Is there poison in that which is sweet to drink? Trouble not thyself, but come with me to another city. There is a little city hard by in which there is a garden of tulip trees. And there dwell in this comely garden white peacocks and peacocks that have blue breasts. Their tails when they spread them to the sun are like disks of ivory and like gilt disks. And she who feeds them dances for pleasure, and sometimes she dances on her hands and at other times she dances with her feet. Her eyes are coloured with stibium, and her nostrils are shaped like the wings of a swallow. From a hook in one of her nostrils hangs a flower that is carved out of a pearl. She laughs while she dances, and the silver rings that are about her ankles tinkle like bells of silver. And so trouble not thyself any more, but come with me to this city.'

But the young Fisherman answered not his Soul, but closed his lips with the seal of silence and with a tight cord bound his hands, and journeyed back to the place from which he had come, even to the little bay where his love had been wont to sing. And ever did his Soul tempt him by the way, but he made it no answer, nor would he do any of the wickedness that it sought to make him do, so great was the power of the love that was within him.

And when he had reached the shore of the sea, he loosed the cord from his hands, and took the seal of silence from his lips, and called to the little Mermaid. But she came not to his call, though he called to her all day long and besought her.

And his Soul mocked him and said, 'Surely thou hast but little joy out of thy love. Thou art as one who in time of death pours water into a broken vessel. Thou gavest away what thou hast, and nought is given to thee in return. It were better for thee to come with me, for I know where the Valley of Pleasure lies, and what things are wrought there.'

But the young Fisherman answered not his Soul, but in a cleft of rock he built himself a house of wattles, and abode there for the space of a year. And every morning he called to the Mermaid, and every noon he called to her again, and at night-time he spake her name. Yet never did she rise out of the sea to meet him, nor in any place of the sea could he find her though he sought for her in the caves and in the green water, in the pools of the tide and in the wells that are at the bottom of the deep.

And ever did his Soul tempt him with evil, and whisper of terrible things. Yet did it not prevail against him, so great was the power of his love.

And after the year was over, the Soul thought within himself, 'I have tempted my master with evil, and his love is stronger than I am. I will tempt him now with good, and it may be that he will come with me.'

So he spake to the young Fisherman and said, 'I have told thee of the joy of the world, and thou hast turned a deaf ear to me. Suffer me now to tell thee of the world's pain, and it may be that thou wilt hearken. For of a truth pain is the Lord of this world, nor is there any one who escapes from its net. There be some who lack raiment, and others who lack bread. There be widows who sit in purple, and widows who sit in rags. To and fro over the fens go the lepers, and they are cruel to each other. The beggars go up and down on the highways, and their wallets are empty. Through the streets of the cities walks Famine, and the Plague sits at their gates. Come, let us go forth and mend these things, and make them not to be. Wherefore shouldst thou tarry here calling to thy love, seeing she comes not to thy call? And what is love, that thou shouldst set this high store upon it?'

But the young Fisherman answered it nought, so great was the power of his love. And every morning he called to the Mermaid, and every noon he called to her again, and at night-time he spake her name. Yet never did she rise out of the sea to meet him, nor in any place of the sea could he find her, though he sought for her in the rivers of the sea, and in the valleys that are under the waves, in the sea that the night makes purple, and in the sea that the dawn leaves grey.

And after the second year was over, the Soul said to the young Fisherman at night-time, and as he sat in the wattled house alone, 'Lo! now I have tempted thee with evil, and I have tempted thee with good, and thy love is stronger than I am. Wherefore will I tempt thee no longer, but I pray thee to suffer me to enter thy heart, that I may be one with thee even as before.'

'Surely thou mayest enter,' said the young Fisherman, 'for in the days when with no heart thou didst go through the world thou must have much suffered'

'Alas!' cried his Soul, 'I can find no place of entrance, so compassed about with love is this heart of thine.'

'Yet I would that I could help thee,' said the young Fisherman.

And as he spake there came a great cry of mourning from the sea, even the cry that men hear when one of the Sea-folk is dead. And the young Fisherman leapt up, and left his wattled house, and ran down to the shore. And the black waves came hurrying to the shore, bearing with them a burden that was whiter than silver. White as the surf it was, and like a flower it tossed on the waves. And the surf took it from the waves, and the foam took it from the surf, and the shore received it, and lying at his feet the young Fisherman saw the body of the little Mermaid. Dead at his feet it was lying.

Weeping as one smitten with pain he flung himself down beside it, and he kissed the cold red of the mouth, and toyed with the wet amber of the hair. He flung himself down beside it on the sand, weeping as one trembling with joy, and in his brown arms he held it to his breast. Cold were the lips, yet he kissed them. Salt was the honey of the hair, yet he tasted it with a bitter joy. He kissed the closed eyelids, and the wild spray that lay upon their cups was less salt than his tears.

And to the dead thing he made confession. Into the shells of its ears he poured the harsh wine of his tale. He put the little hands round his neck, and with his fingers he touched the thin reed of the throat. Bitter, bitter was his joy, and full of strange gladness was his pain.

The black sea came nearer, and the white foam moaned like a leper. With white claws of foam the sea grabbled at the shore. From the palace of the Sea-King came the cry of mourning again, and far out upon the sea the great Tritons blew hoarsely upon their horns.

'Flee away,' said his Soul, 'for ever doth the sea come nigher, and if thou tarriest it will slay thee. Flee away, for I am afraid, seeing that thy heart is closed against me by reason of the greatness of thy love. Flee away to a place of safety. Surely thou wilt not send me without a heart into another world?'

But the young Fisherman listened not to his Soul, but called on the little Mermaid and said, 'Love is better than wisdom, and more precious than riches, and fairer than the feet of the daughters of men. The fires cannot destroy it, nor can the waters quench it. I called on thee at dawn, and thou didst come to my call. The moon heard thy name, yet hadst thou no heed of me. For evilly had I left thee, and to my own hurt had I wandered away. Yet ever did thy love abide with me, and ever was it strong, nor did aught prevail against it, though I have looked upon evil and looked upon good.

And now that thou art dead, surely I will die with thee also.'

And his Soul besought him to depart, but he would not, so great was his love. And the sea came nearer, and sought to cover him with its waves, and when he knew that the end was at hand he kissed with mad lips the cold lips of the Mermaid, and the heart that was within him brake. And as through the fullness of his love his heart did break, the Soul found an entrance and entered in, and was one with him even as before. And the sea covered the young Fisherman with its waves.

And in the morning the Priest went forth to bless the sea, for it had been troubled. And with him went the monks and the musicians, and the candle bearers, and the swingers of censers, and a great company.

And when the Priest reached the shore he saw the young Fisherman lying drowned in the surf, and clasped in his arms was the body of the little Mermaid. And he drew back frowning, and having made the sign of the Cross, he cried aloud and said, 'I will not bless the sea nor anything that is in it. Accursed be the Sea-folk, and accursed be all they who traffic with them. And as for him who for love's sake forsook God, and so lieth[41] here with his leman slain by God's judgment, take up his body and the body of his leman, and bury them in the corner of the Field of the Fullers, and set no mark above them, nor sign of any kind, that none may know the place of their resting. For accursed were they in their lives, and accursed shall they be in their deaths also.'

And the people did as he commanded them, and in the corner of the Field of the Fullers, where no sweet herbs grew, they dug a deep pit, and laid the dead things within it.

And when the third year was over, and on a day that was a

holy day, the Priest went up to the chapel, that he might show to the people the wounds of the Lord, and speak to them about the wrath of God.

And when he had robed himself with his robes, and entered in and bowed himself before the altar, he saw that the altar was covered with strange flowers that never had been seen before. Strange were they to look at, and of curious beauty, and their beauty troubled him, and their odour was sweet in his nostrils, and he felt glad, and understood not why he was glad. And after that he had opened the tabernacle, and incensed the monstrance that was in it, and shown the fair wafer to the people, and hid it again behind the veil of veils, he began to speak to the people, desiring to speak to them of the wrath of God. But the beauty of the white flowers troubled him, and their odour was sweet in his nostrils, and there came another word into his lips, and he spake not of the wrath of God, but of the God whose name is Love. And why he so spake, he knew not.

And when he had finished his word the people wept, and the Priest went back to his sacristy, and his eyes were full of tears. And the deacons came in and began to unrobe him, and took from him the alb and the girdle, the maniple and the stole. And he stood as one in a dream.

And after that they had unrobed him, he looked at them and said, 'What are the flowers that stand on the altar, and whence do they come?'

And they answered him, 'What flowers they are we cannot tell, but they come from the corner of the Fullers' Field.' And the Priest trembled, and returned to his own house and prayed.

And in the morning, while it was still dawn, he went forth

with the monks and the musicians, and the candle bearers and the swingers of censers, and a great company, and came to the shore of the sea, and blessed the sea, and all the wild things that are in it. The Fauns also he blessed, and the little things that dance in the woodland, and the bright-eyed things that peer through the leaves. All the things in God's world he blessed, and the people were filled with joy and wonder. Yet never again in the corner of the Fullers' Field grew flowers of any kind, but the field remained barren even as before. Nor came the Sea-folk into the bay as they had been wont to do, for they went to another part of the sea.

The Star-Child

Once upon a time two poor Woodcutters were making their way home through a great pine forest. It was winter, and a night of bitter cold. The snow lay thick upon the ground, and upon the branches of the trees: the frost kept snapping the little twigs on either side of them, as they passed: and when they came to the Mountain Torrent she was hanging motionless in air, for the Ice-King had kissed her.

So cold was it that even the animals and the birds did not know what to make of it.

'Ugh!' snarled the Wolf, as he limped through the brushwood with his tail between his legs, 'this is perfectly monstrous weather. Why doesn't the Government look to it?'

'Weet! weet! weet!' twittered the green Linnets, 'the old Earth is dead, and they have laid her out in her white shroud.'

'The Earth is going to be married, and this is her bridal dress,' whispered the Turtle doves to each other. Their little pink feet were quite frost-bitten, but they felt that it was their duty to take a romantic view of the situation.

'Nonsense!' growled the Wolf. 'I tell you that it is all the fault of the Government, and if you don't believe me I shall eat you.' The Wolf had a thoroughly practical mind, and was never at a loss for a good argument.

'Well, for my own part,' said the Woodpecker, who was a born philosopher, 'I don't care an atomic theory for explanations. If a thing is so, it is so, and at present it is terribly cold.'

Terribly cold it certainly was. The little Squirrels, who lived inside the tall fir tree, kept rubbing each other's noses to keep themselves warm, and the Rabbits curled themselves up in their holes, and did not venture even to look out of doors. The only people who seemed to enjoy it were the great horned Owls. Their feathers were quite stiff with rime, but they did not mind, and they rolled their large yellow eyes, and called out to each other across the forest, 'Tu-whit! Tu-whoo! Tu-whit! Tu-whoo! what delightful weather we are having!'

On and on went the two Woodcutters, blowing lustily upon their fingers, and stamping with their huge iron-shod boots upon the caked snow. Once they sank into a deep drift, and came out as white as millers are, when the stones are grinding; and once they slipped on the hard smooth ice where the marsh water was frozen, and their faggots fell out of their bundles, and they had to pick them up and bind them together again; and once they thought that they had lost their way, and a great terror seized on them, for they knew that the Snow is cruel to those who sleep in her arms. But they put their trust in the good Saint Martin, who watches over all travellers, and retraced their steps, and went warily, and at last they reached the outskirts of the forest, and saw, far down in the valley beneath them, the lights of the village in which they dwelt.

So overjoyed were they at their deliverance that they laughed aloud, and the Earth seemed to them like a flower of silver, and the Moon like a flower of gold.

Yet, after that they had laughed they became sad, for they remembered their poverty, and one of them said to the other, 'Why did we make merry, seeing that life is for the rich, and not for such as we are? Better that we had died of cold in the forest, or that some wild beast had fallen upon us and slain us.'

'Truly,' answered his companion, 'much is given to some, and little is given to others. Injustice has parcelled out the world, nor is there equal division of aught save of sorrow.'

But as they were bewailing their misery to each other this strange thing happened. There fell from heaven a very bright and beautiful star. It slipped down the side of the sky, passing by the other stars in its course, and, as they watched it wondering, it seemed to them to sink behind a clump of willow trees that stood hard by a little sheepfold no more than a stone's-throw away.

'Why! there is a crock of gold for whoever finds it,' they cried, and they set to and ran, so eager were they for the gold.

And one of them ran faster than his mate, and outstripped him, and forced his way through the willows, and came out on the other side, and lo! there was indeed a thing of gold lying on the white snow. So he hastened towards it, and stooping down placed his hands upon it, and it was a cloak of golden tissue, curiously wrought with stars, and wrapped in many folds. And he cried out to his comrade that he had found the treasure that had fallen from the sky, and when his comrade had come up, they sat them down in the snow, and loosened the folds of the cloak that they might divide the pieces of gold. But, alas! no gold was in it, nor silver, nor, indeed, treasure of any kind, but only a little child who was asleep.

And one of them said to the other: 'This is a bitter ending to our hope, nor have we any good fortune, for what cloth a child profit to a man? Let us leave it here, and go our way, seeing that we are poor men, and have children of our own whose bread we may not give to another.'

But his companion answered him: 'Nay, but it were an evil thing to leave the child to perish here in the snow, and though I am as poor as thou art, and have many mouths to feed, and but little in the pot, yet will I bring it home with me, and my wife shall have care of it,'

So very tenderly he took up the child, and wrapped the cloak around it to shield it from the harsh cold, and made his way down the hill to the village, his comrade marvelling much at his foolishness and softness of heart.

And when they came to the village, his comrade said to him, 'Thou hast the child, therefore give me the cloak, for it is meet that we should share.'

But he answered him: 'Nay, for the cloak is neither mine nor thine, but the child's only,' and he bade him Godspeed, and went to his own house and knocked.

And when his wife opened the door and saw that her husband had returned safe to her, she put her arms round his neck and kissed him, and took from his back the bundle of faggots, and brushed the snow off his boots, and bade him come in.

But he said to her, 'I have found something in the forest, and I have brought it to thee to have care of it,' and he stirred not from the threshold.

'What is it?' she cried. 'Show it to me, for the house is bare, and we have need of many things.' And he threw the cloak back, and showed her the sleeping child.

'Alack, goodman!' she murmured, 'have we not children enough of our own, that thou must needs bring a changeling to sit by the hearth? And who knows if it will not bring us bad fortune? And how shall we tend it?' And she was wroth against him.

'Nay, but it is a Star-Child,' he answered; and he told her the strange manner of the finding of it.

But she would not be appeased, but mocked at him, and spoke angrily, and cried; 'Our children lack bread, and shall we feed the child of another? Who is there who careth[42] for us? And who giveth us food?'

'Nay, but God careth for the sparrows even, and feedeth them,' he answered.

'Do not the sparrows die of hunger in the winter?' she asked. 'And is it not winter now?' And the man answered nothing, but stirred not from the threshold.

And a bitter wind from the forest came in through the open door, and made her tremble, and she shivered, and said to him: 'Wilt thou not close the door? There cometh a bitter wind into the house, and I am cold.'

'Into a house where a heart is hard cometh there not always a bitter wind?' he asked. And the woman answered him nothing, but crept closer to the fire.

And after a time she turned round and looked at him, and her eyes were full of tears. And he came in swiftly, and placed the child in her arms, and she kissed it, and laid it in a little bed where the youngest of their own children was lying. And on the morrow the

Woodcutter took the curious cloak of gold and placed it in a great chest, and a chain of amber that was round the child's neck his wife took and set it in the chest also.

So the Star-Child was brought up with the children of the Woodcutter, and sat at the same board with them, and was their playmate. And every year he became more beautiful to look at, so that all those who dwelt in the village were filled with wonder, for, while they were swarthy and black-haired, he was white and delicate as sawn ivory, and his curls were like the rings of the daffodil. His lips, also, were like the petals of a red flower, and his eyes were like violets by a river of pure water, and his body like the narcissus of a field where the mower comes not.

Yet did his beauty work him evil. For he grew proud, and cruel, and selfish. The children of the Woodcutter, and the other children of the village, he despised, saying that they were of mean parentage, while he was noble, being sprung from a Star, and he made himself master over them, and called them his servants. No pity had he for the poor, or for those who were blind or maimed or in any way afflicted, but would cast stones at them and drive them forth on to the highway, and bid them beg their bread elsewhere, so that none save the outlaws came twice to that village to ask for alms. Indeed, he was as one enamoured of beauty, and would mock at the weakly and ill-favoured, and make jest of them; and himself he loved, and in summer, when the winds were still, he would lie by the well in the priest's orchard and look down at the marvel of his own face, and laugh for the pleasure he had in his fairness.

Often did the Woodcutter and his wife chide him, and say: 'We did not deal with thee as thou dealest[43] with those who are left desolate, and have none to succour them. Wherefore are thou so cruel to all who need pity?'

Often did the old priest send for him, and seek to teach him the love of living things, saying to him: 'The fly is thy brother. Do it no harm. The wild birds that roam through the forest have their freedom. Snare them not for thy pleasure. God made the blind worm and the mole, and each has its place. Who art thou to bring pain into God's world? Even the cattle of the field praise Him.'

But the Star-Child heeded not their words, but would frown and flout, and go back to his companions, and lead them. And his companions followed him, for he was fair, and fleet of foot, and could dance, and pipe, and make music. And wherever the Star-Child led them they followed, and whatever the Star-Child bade them do, that did they.

And when he pierced with a sharp reed the dim eyes of the mole, they laughed, and when he cast stones at the leper they laughed also. And in all things he ruled them, and they became hard of heart even as he was.

Now there passed one day through the village a poor beggar-woman. Her garments were torn and ragged, and her feet were bleeding from the rough road on which she had travelled, and she was in very evil plight. And being weary she sat her down under a chestnut tree to rest.

But when the Star-Child saw her, he said to his companions, 'See! There sitteth[44] a foul beggar-woman under that fair and green-leaved tree. Come, let us drive her hence, for she is ugly and ill-favoured.'

So he came near and threw stones at her, and mocked her, and she looked at him with terror in her eyes, nor did she move her gaze from him. And when the Woodcutter, who was cleaving logs in a haggard hard by, saw what the Star-Child was doing, he ran up and rebuked him, and said to him: 'Surely thou art hard of heart and knowest not mercy, for what evil has this poor woman done to thee that thou shouldst treat her in this wise?'

And the Star-Child grew red with anger, and stamped his foot upon the ground, and said, 'Who art thou to question me what I do? I am no son of thine to do thy bidding.'

'Thou speakest truly,' answered the Woodcutter, 'yet did I show thee pity when I found thee in the forest.'

And when the woman heard these words she gave a loud cry and fell into a swoon. And the Woodcutter carried her to his own house, and his wife had care of her, and when she rose up from the swoon into which she had fallen, they set meat and drink before her, and bade her have comfort.

But she would neither eat nor drink, but said to the Woodcutter, 'Didst thou not say that the child was found in the forest? And was it not ten years from this day?'

And the Woodcutter answered, 'Yea, it was in the forest that I found him, and it is ten years from this day.'

'And what signs didst thou find with him?' she cried. 'Bare he not upon his neck a chain of amber? Was not round him a cloak of gold tissue broidered with stars?'

'Truly,' answered the Woodcutter, 'it was even as thou sayest.' And he took the cloak and the amber chain from the chest where they lay, and showed them to her.

And when she saw them she wept for joy, and said, 'He is my little son whom I lost in the forest. I pray thee send for him quickly, for in search of him have I wandered over the whole world.'

So the Woodcutter and his wife went out and called to the Star-Child, and said to him, 'Go into the house, and there shalt thou find thy mother, who is waiting for thee.'

So he ran in, filled with wonder and great gladness. But when he saw her who was waiting there, he laughed scornfully and said, 'Why, where is my mother? For I see none here but this vile beggar-woman.'

And the woman answered him, 'I am thy mother.'

'Thou art mad to say so,' cried the Star-Child angrily. 'I am no son of thine, for thou art a beggar, and ugly, and in rags. Therefore get thee hence, and let me see thy foul face no more.'

'Nay, but thou art indeed my little son, whom I bare in the forest,' she cried, and she fell on her knees, and held out her arms to him. 'The robbers stole thee from me, and left thee to die,' she murmured, 'but I recognised thee when I saw thee, and the signs also have I recognised, the cloak of golden tissue and the amber chain. Therefore, I pray thee come with me, for over the whole world have I wandered in search of thee. Come with me, my son, for I have need of thy love.'

But the Star-Child stirred not from his place, but shut the doors of his heart against her, nor was there any sound heard save the sound of the woman weeping for pain.

And at last he spoke to her, and his voice was hard and bitter. 'If in very truth thou art my mother,' he said, 'it had been better hadst thou stayed away, and not come here to bring me to shame, seeing that I thought I was the child of some Star, and not a beggar's child, as thou tellest me that I am. Therefore get thee hence, and let me see thee no more.

'Alas my son,' she cried, 'wilt thou not kiss me before I go? For I have suffered much to find thee.'

'Nay,' said the Star-Child, 'but thou art too foul to look at, and rather would I kiss the adder or the toad than thee.'

So the woman rose up, and went away into the forest weeping bitterly, and when the Star-Child saw that she had gone, he was glad, and ran back to his playmates that he might play with them.

But when they beheld him coming, they mocked him and said, 'Why, thou art as foul as the toad, and as loathsome as the adder. Get thee hence, for we will not suffer thee to play with us,' and they drave him out of the garden.

And the Star-Child frowned and said to himself, 'What is this that they say to me? I will go to the well of water and look into it, and it shall tell me of my beauty.'

So he went to the well of water and looked into it, and lo! his face was as the face of a toad, and his body was scaled like an adder. And he flung himself down on the grass and wept, and said to himself, 'Surely this has come upon me by reason of my sin. For I have denied my mother, and driven her away, and been proud, and cruel to her. Wherefore I will go and seek her through the whole world, nor will I rest till I have found her.'

And there came to him the little daughter of the Woodcutter, and she put her hand upon his shoulder and said, 'What doth it matter if thou hast lost thy comeliness? Stay with us, and I will not mock at thee.'

And he said to her, 'Nay, but I have been cruel to my mother, and as a punishment has this evil been sent to me. Wherefore I must go hence, and wander through the world till I find her, and she give me forgiveness.'

So he ran away into the forest and called out to his mother to come to him, but there was no answer. All day long he called to her, and when the sun set he lay down to sleep on a bed of leaves, and the birds and the animals fled from him, for they remembered his cruelty, and he was alone save for the toad that watched him, and the slow adder that crawled past.

And in the morning he rose up, and plucked some bitter berries from the trees and ate them, and took his way through the great wood, weeping sorely. And of everything that he met he made inquiry if perchance they had seen his mother.

He said to the Mole, 'Thou canst go beneath the earth. Tell me, is my mother there?'

And the Mole answered, 'Thou hast blinded mine eyes. How should I know?'

He said to the Linnet, 'Thou canst fly over the tops of the tall trees, and canst see the whole world. Tell me, canst thou see my mother?'

And the Linnet answered, 'Thou hast clipt my wings for thy pleasure. How should I fly?'

And to the little Squirrel who lived in the fir tree, and was lonely, he said, 'Where is my mother?'

And the Squirrel answered, 'Thou hast slain mine. Dost thou seek to slay thine also?'

And the Star-Child wept and bowed his head, and prayed forgiveness of God's things, and went on through the forest, seeking for the beggar-woman. And on the third day he came to the other side of the forest and went down into the plain.

And when he passed through the villages the children mocked him, and threw stones at him, and the carlots would not suffer him even to sleep in the byres lest he might bring mildew on the stored corn, so foul was he to look at, and their hired men drave him away, and there was none who had pity on him. Nor could he hear anywhere of the beggar-woman who was his mother, though for the space of three years he wandered over the world, and often seemed to see her on the road in front of him, and would call to her, and run after her till the sharp flints made his feet to bleed. But overtake her he could not, and those who dwelt by the way did ever deny that they had seen her, or any like to her, and they made sport of his sorrow.

For the space of three years he wandered over the world, and in the world there was neither love nor loving-kindness nor charity for him, but it was even such a world as he had made for himself in the days of his great pride.

And one evening he came to the gate of a strong-walled city that stood by a river, and, weary and footsore though he was, he made to enter in. But the soldiers who stood on guard dropped their halberts across the entrance, and said roughly to him, 'What is thy business in the city?'

'I am seeking for my mother,' he answered, 'and I pray ye to suffer me to pass, for it may be that she is in this city.'

But they mocked at him, and one of them wagged a black beard, and set down his shield and cried, 'Of a truth, thy mother will not be merry when she sees thee, for thou art more ill-favoured than the toad of the marsh, or the adder that crawls in the fen. Get thee gone. Get thee gone. Thy mother dwells not in this city.'

And another, who held a yellow banner in his hand, said to him, 'Who is thy mother, and wherefore art thou seeking for her?'

And he answered, 'My mother is a beggar even as I am, and I have treated her evilly, and I pray ye to suffer me to pass that she may give rue her forgiveness, if it be that she tarrieth in this city.' But they would not, and pricked him with their spears.

And, as he turned away weeping, one whose armour was inlaid with gilt flowers, and on whose helmet couched a lion that had wings, came up and made inquiry of the soldiers who it was who had sought entrance. And they said to him, 'It is a beggar and the child of a beggar, and we have driven him away.'

'Nay,' he cried, laughing, 'but we will sell the foul thing for a slave, and his price shall be the price of a bowl of sweet wine.'

And an old and evil-visaged man who was passing by called out, and said, 'I will buy him for that price,' and, when he had paid the price, he took the Star-Child by the hand and led him into the city.

And after that they had gone through many streets they came to a little door that was set in a wall that was covered with a pomegranate tree. And the old man touched the door with a ring of graved jasper and it opened, and they went down five steps of brass into a garden filled with black poppies and green jars of burnt clay. And the old man took then from his turban a scarf of figured silk, and bound with it the eyes of the Star-Child, and drave in front of him. And when the scarf was taken off his eyes, the Star-Child found himself in a dungeon, that was lit by a lantern of horn.

And the old man set before him some mouldy bread on a trencher and said, 'Eat,' and some brackish water in a cup and said, 'Drink,' and when he had eaten and drunk, the old man went out, locking the door behind him and fastening it with an iron chain.

And on the morrow the old man, who was indeed the subtlest of the magicians of Libya and had learned his art from one who dwelt in the tombs of the Nile, came in to him and frowned at him, and said, 'In a wood that is nigh to the gate of this city of Giaours there are three pieces of gold. One is of white gold, and another is of yellow gold, and the gold of the third one is red. Today thou shalt bring me the piece of white gold, and if thou bringest it not back, I will beat thee with a hundred stripes. Get thee away quickly, and at sunset I will be waiting for thee at the door of the garden. See that thou bringest[45] the white gold, or it shall go ill with thee, for thou art my slave, and I have bought thee for the price of a bowl of sweet wine.' And he bound the eyes of the Star-Child with the scarf of figured silk, and led him through the house, and through the garden of poppies, and up the five steps of brass. And having opened the little door with his ring he set him in the street.

And the Star-Child went out of the gate of the city, and came to the wood of which the Magician had spoken to him.

Now this wood was very fair to look at from without, and seemed full of singing birds and of sweet-scented flowers, and the Star-Child entered it gladly. Yet did its beauty profit him little, for wherever he went harsh briars and thorns shot up from the ground and encompassed him, and evil nettles stung him, and the thistle pierced him with her daggers, so that he was in sore distress. Nor could he anywhere find the piece of white gold of which the Magician had spoken, though he sought for it from morn to noon, and from noon to sunset. And at sunset he set his face towards home, weeping bitterly, for he knew what fate was in store for him. But when he had reached the outskirts of the wood, he heard from a thicket a cry as of some one in pain. And forgetting his own sorrow he ran back to the place, and saw there a little Hare caught in a trap that some hunter had set for it.

And the Star-Child had pity on it, and released it, and said to it, 'I am myself but a slave, yet may I give thee thy freedom.'

And the Hare answered him, and said: 'Surely thou hast given me freedom, and what shall I give thee in return?'

And the Star-Child said to it, 'I am seeking for a piece of white gold, nor can I any where find it, and if I bring it not to my master he will beat me.'

'Come thou with me,' said the Hare, 'and I will lead thee to it, for I know where it is hidden, and for what purpose.'

So the Star-Child went with the Hare, and lo! in the cleft of a great oak tree he saw the piece of white gold that he was seeking. And he was filled with joy, and seized it, and said to the Hare, 'The service that I did to thee thou hast rendered back again many times over, and the kindness that I thee hast repaid a hundred-fold.'

'Nay,' answered the Hare, 'but as thou dealt with me, so I did deal with thee,' and it ran away swiftly, and the Star-Child went towards the city.

Now at the gate of the city there was seated one who was a leper. Over his face hung a cowl of grey linen, and through the eyelets his eyes gleamed like red coals. And when he saw the Star-Child coming, he struck upon a wooden bowl, and clattered his bell, and called out to him, and said, 'Give me a piece of money, or I must die of hunger. For they have thrust me out of the city, and there is no one who has pity on me.'

'Alas!' cried the Star-Child, 'I have but one piece of money in my wallet, and if I bring it not to my master he will beat me, for I am his slave.'

But the leper entreated him, and prayed of him, till the Star-Child had pity, and gave him the piece of white gold.

And when he came to the Magician's house, the Magician opened to him, and brought him in, and said to him, 'Hast thou the piece of white gold?' And the Star-Child answered, 'I have it not.' So the Magician fell upon him, and beat him, and set before him an empty trencher, and said, 'Eat,' and an empty cup, and said, 'Drink,' and flung him again into the dungeon.

And on the morrow the Magician came to him, and said, 'If today thou bringest me not the piece of yellow gold, I will surely keep thee as my slave, and give thee three hundred stripes.'

So the Star-Child went to the wood, and all day long he searched for the piece of yellow gold, but nowhere could he find it. And at sunset he sat him down and began to weep, and as he was weeping there came to him the little Hare that he had rescued from the trap.

And the Hare said to him, 'Why art thou weeping? And what dost thou seek in the wood?'

And the Star-Child answered, 'I am seeking for a piece of yellow gold that is hidden here, and if I find it not my master will beat me, and keep me as a slave.'

'Follow me,' cried the Hare, and it ran through the wood till it came to a pool of water. And at the bottom of the pool the piece of yellow gold was lying.

'How shall I thank thee?' said the Star-Child, 'for lo! this is the second time that you have succoured me.'

'Nay, but thou hadst pity on me first,' said the Hare, and it ran away swiftly.

And the Star-Child took the piece of yellow gold, and put it in his wallet, and hurried to the city. But the leper saw him coming, and ran to meet him, and knelt down and cried, 'Give me a piece of money or I shall die of hunger.'

And the Star-Child said to him, 'I have in my wallet but one piece of yellow gold, and if I bring it not to my master he will beat me and keep me as his slave.'

But the leper entreated him sore, so that the Star-Child had pity on him, and gave him the piece of the yellow gold.

And when he came to the Magician's house, the Magician opened to him, and brought him in, and said to him, 'Hast thou the piece of yellow gold?' And the Star-Child said to him, 'I have not.' So the Magician fell upon him, and beat him, and loaded him with chains, and cast him again into the dungeon.

And on the morrow the Magician came to him, and said, 'If today thou bringest me the piece of red gold I will set thee free, but if thou bringest it not I will surely slay thee.'

So the Star-Child went to the wood, and all day long he searched for the piece of red gold, but nowhere could he find it. And at evening he sat him down and wept, and as he was weeping there came to him the little Hare.

And the Hare said to him, 'The piece of red gold that thou seekest is in the cavern that is behind thee. Therefore weep no more but be glad.'

'How shall I reward thee?' cried the Star-Child, 'for lo! this is the third time thou hast succoured me.'

'Nay, but thou hadst pity on me first,' said the Hare, and it ran away swiftly.

And the Star-Child entered the cavern, and in its farthest corner he found the piece of red gold. So he put it in his wallet, and hurried to the city. And the leper seeing him coming, stood in the centre of the road, and cried out, and said to him, 'Give me the piece of red money, or I must die,' and the Star-Child had pity on him again, and gave him the piece of red gold, saying 'Thy need is greater than mine.' Yet his heart was heavy, for he knew what evil fate awaited him.

But lo! as he passed through the gate of the city, the guards bowed down and made obeisance to him, saying, 'How beautiful is our lord!' and a crowd of citizens followed him, and cried out, 'Surely there is none so beautiful in the whole world!' so that the Star-Child wept, and said to himself, 'They are mocking me, and making light of my misery.' And so large was the concourse of the people, that he lost the threads of his way, and found himself at last in a great square, in which there was a palace of a King.

And the gate of the palace opened, and the priests and the high officers of the city ran forth to meet him, and they abased themselves before him, and said, 'Thou art our lord for whom we have been waiting, and the son of our King.'

And the Star-Child answered them and said, 'I am no king's son, but the child of a poor beggar-woman. And how say ye that I am beautiful, for I know that I am evil to look at?'

Then he, whose armour was inlaid with gilt flowers, and on whose helmet crouched a lion that had wings, held up a shield, and cried, 'How saith my lord that he is not beautiful?'

And the Star-Child looked, and lo! his face was even as it had been, and his comeliness had come back to him, and he saw that in his eyes which he had not seen there before.

And the priests and the high officers knelt down and said to him, 'It was prophesied of old that on this day should come he who was to rule over us. Therefore, let our lord take this crown and this sceptre, and be in his justice and mercy our King over us.'

But he said to them, 'I am not worthy, for I have denied the mother who bare me, nor may I rest till I have found her, and known her forgiveness. Therefore, let me go, for I must wander again over the world, and may not tarry here, though ye bring me the crown and the sceptre.' And as he spake he turned his face from them towards the street that led to the gate of the city, and lo! amongst the crowd that pressed round the soldiers, he saw the beggar-woman who was his mother, and at her side stood the leper, who had sat by the road.

And a cry of joy broke from his lips, and he ran over, and kneeling down he kissed the wounds on his mother's feet, and wet them with his tears. He bowed his head in the dust, and sobbing, as one whose heart might break, he said to her: 'Mother, I denied thee in the hour of my pride. Accept me in the hour of my humility. Mother, I gave thee hatred. Do thou give me love. Mother, I rejected thee. Receive thy child now.' But the beggar-woman answered him not a word.

And he reached out his hands, and clasped the white feet of the leper, and said to him: 'Thrice did I give thee of my mercy. Bid my mother speak to me one.' But the leper answered him not a word.

And he sobbed again and said: 'Mother, my suffering is greater than I can bear. Give me thy forgiveness, and let me go back to the forest.' And the beggar-woman put her hand on his head, and said to him, 'Rise,' and the leper put his hand on his head, and said to him, 'Rise,' also.

And he rose up from his feet, and looked at them, and lo! they were a King and a Queen.

And the Queen said to him, 'This is thy father whom thou hast succoured.'

And the King said, 'This is thy mother whose feet thou hast washed with thy tears.'

And they fell on his neck and kissed him, and brought him into the palace and clothed him in fair raiment, and set the crown upon his head, and the sceptre in his hand, and over the city that stood by the river he ruled, and was its lord. Much justice and mercy did he show to all, and the evil Magician he banished, and to the Woodcutter and his wife he sent many rich gifts, and to their children he gave high honour. Nor would he suffer any to be cruel to bird or beast, but taught love and loving-kindness and charity, and to the poor he gave bread, and to the naked he gave raiment, and there was peace and plenty in the land.

Yet ruled he not long, so great had been his suffering, and so bitter the fire of his testing, for after the space of three years he died. And he who came after him ruled evilly.

Notes

1 have	10 anything	19 can	28 made	37 gave
2 you	11 spoke	20 make	29 do	38 yourself
3 no	12 yours	21 would	30 see	39 may
4 are	13 say	22 desire	31 reflects	40 receives
5 you	14 show	23 does	32 looks	41 lies
6 your	15 know	24 tells	33 could	42 cares
7 have	16 comes	25 speak	34 wear	43 deal
8 should	17 think	26 had	35 did	44 sits
9 shall	18 will	27 keep	36 sleeps	45 bring

快樂王子

快樂王子

快樂王子的像在一根高圓柱上面，高高地聳立在城市的上空。他滿身貼着薄薄的純金葉子，一對藍寶石做成他的眼睛，一隻大的紅寶石嵌在他的劍柄上，燦爛地發着紅光。

他的確得到一般人的稱讚。一個市參議員為了表示自己有藝術的欣賞力，說過："他像風信標那樣漂亮，"不過他又害怕別人會把他看作一個不務實際的人（其實他並不是不務實際的），便加上一句："只是他不及風信標那樣有用。"

"為甚麼你不能像快樂王子那樣呢？"一位聰明的母親對她那個哭着要月亮的孩子說，"快樂王子連做夢也沒想到會哭着要東西。"

"我真高興世界上究竟還有一個人是很快樂的，"一個失意的人望着這座非常出色的像喃喃地說。

"他很像一個天使，"孤兒院的孩子們說，他們正從大教堂出來，披着光亮奪目的猩紅色斗篷，束着潔白的遮胸。

"你們怎麼知道？"數學先生說，"你們從沒有見過一位天使。"

"啊！可是我們在夢裏見過的，"孩子們答道。數學先生皺起眉頭，板着面孔，因為他不贊成小孩子做夢。

某一個夜晚一隻小燕子飛過城市的上空。他的朋友們六個星期以前就到埃及去了，但是他還留在後面，因為他戀着那根最美麗的蘆葦。他還是在早春遇見她的，那時他正沿着河順流飛去，追一隻黃色飛蛾，她的細腰很引起他的注意，他便站住同她談起話來。"我可以愛你嗎？"燕子説，他素來就有馬上談到本題的脾氣。蘆葦對他深深地彎一下腰，他便在她的身邊不停地飛來飛去，用他的翅子[2] 點水，做出許多銀色的漣漪，這便是他求愛的表示，他就這樣地過了一整個夏天。

"這樣的戀愛太可笑了，"別的燕子呢喃地説，"她沒有錢，而且親戚太多，"的確河邊長滿了蘆葦，到處都是。後來秋天來了，他們都飛走了。

他們走了以後，他覺得寂寞，討厭起他的愛人來了。他説："她不講話，我又害怕她是一個蕩婦，因為她老是跟風調情。"這倒是真的，風一吹，蘆葦就行着最動人的屈膝禮。他又説："我相信她是慣於家居的，可是我喜歡旅行，那麼我的妻子也應該喜歡旅行才成。"

"你願意跟我走嗎？"他最後忍不住了問她道，然而蘆葦搖搖頭，她非常依戀家。

"原來你從前是跟我尋開心的，"他叫道。"我現在到金字塔那邊去了。再會吧！"他飛走了。

他飛了一個整天，晚上他到了這個城市。"我在甚麼地方過夜呢？"他説，"我希望城裏已經給我預備了住處。"

隨後他看見了立在高圓柱上面的那座像。他說："我就在這兒³過夜吧，這倒是一個空氣新鮮的好地點。"他便飛下來，恰好停在快樂王子的兩隻腳中間。

"我找到一個金的睡房了，"他向四周看了一下，輕輕地對自己說，他打算睡覺了，但是他剛剛把頭放到他的翅膀下面去的時候，忽然大大的一滴水落到他的身上來。"多麼奇怪的事！"他叫起來，"天上沒有一片雲，星星非常明亮，可是下起雨來了。北歐的天氣真可怕。蘆葦素來喜歡雨，不過那只是她的自私。"

接着又落下了一滴。

"要是一座像不能夠遮雨，那麼它又有甚麼用處？"他說，"我應該找一個好的煙囱去，"他決定飛開了。

但是他還沒有張開翅膀，第三滴水又落了下來，他仰起頭去看，他看見——啊！他看見了甚麼呢？

快樂王子的眼裏裝滿了淚水，淚珠沿着他的黃金的臉頰流下來。他的臉在月光裏顯得這麼美，叫小燕子的心裏也充滿了憐憫。

"你是誰？"他問道。

"我是快樂王子。"

"那麼你為甚麼哭呢？"燕子又問，"你看，你把我一身都打濕了。"

"從前我活着，有一顆人心的時候，"王子慢慢地答道，"我並不知道眼淚是甚麼東西，因為我那個時候住在無愁宮裏，悲哀是不能夠進去的。白天有人陪我在花園裏玩，晚上我又在大廳裏領頭跳舞。花園的四周圍着一道高牆，我就從沒有想到去問人牆外是甚麼樣的景象，我眼前的一切都是非常美的。我的臣子都稱我作快樂王子，不錯，如果歡娛可以算作快樂，我就的確是快樂的了。我這樣地活着，我也這樣地死去。我死了，他們就把我放在這兒，而且立得這麼高，讓我看得見我這個城市的一切醜惡和窮苦，我的心雖然是鉛做的，我也忍不住哭了。"

"怎麼，他並不是純金的？"燕子輕輕地對自己說，他非常講究禮貌，不肯高聲談論別人的私事。

"遠遠的，"王子用一種低微的、音樂似的聲音說下去。"遠遠的，在一條小街上有一所窮人住的房子。一扇窗開着，我看見窗內有一個婦人坐在桌子旁邊。她的臉很瘦，又帶病容。她的一雙手粗糙、發紅，指頭上滿是針眼，因為她是一個裁縫。她正在一件緞子衣服上繡花，繡的是西番蓮，預備給皇后的最可愛的宮女在下一次宮中舞會裏穿的。在這屋子的角落裏，她的小孩躺在牀上生病。他發熱，嚷着要橙子吃。他母親沒有別的東西給他，只有河水，所以他在哭。燕子，燕子，小燕子，你肯把我劍柄上的紅寶石取下來給她送去嗎？我的腳釘牢在這個像座上，我動不了。"

"朋友們在埃及等我，"燕子說。"他們正在尼羅河上飛來飛去，同大朵的蓮花談話。他們不久就要到偉大的國王的墳墓裏去睡眠了。那個國王自己也就睡在那裏他的彩色的棺材裏。他的身子是用黃布緊緊裹着的，而且還用了香料來保存它。一串淺綠色翡翠做成的鏈子繫在他的頸項上，他的一隻手就像是乾枯的落葉。"

"燕子，燕子，小燕子，"王子要求說，"你難道不肯陪我過一夜，做一回我的信差麼？那個孩子渴得太厲害了，他母親太苦惱了。"

"我並不喜歡小孩，"燕子回答道，"我還記得上一個夏天，我停在河上的時候，有兩個粗野的小孩，就是磨坊主人的兒子，他們常常丟石頭打我。不消説他們是打不中的；我們燕子飛得極快，不會給他們打中，而且我還是出身於一個以敏捷出名的家庭，更不用害怕。不過這究竟是一種不客氣的表示。"

然而快樂王子的面容顯得那樣地憂愁，叫小燕子的心也軟下來了。他便説："這裏冷得很，不過我願意陪你過一夜，我高興做你的信差。"

"小燕子，謝謝你，"王子説。

燕子便從王子的劍柄上啄下了那塊大紅寶石，銜着它飛起來，飛過櫛比的屋頂，向遠處飛去了。

他飛過大教堂的塔頂，看見那裏的大理石的天使雕像。他飛過王宮，聽見了跳舞的聲音。一個美貌的少女同她的情人正走到露台上來。"你看，星星多麼好，愛的魔力多麼大！"他對她説。"我希望我的衣服早點送來，趕得上大跳舞會，"她接着説道，"我叫人在上面繡了西番蓮花；可是那些女裁縫太懶了。"

他飛過河面，看見掛在船桅上的無數的燈籠，他又飛過猶太村，看見一些年老的猶太人在那裏做生意講價錢，把錢放在銅天平上面稱着。最後他到了那所窮人的屋子，朝裏面看去，小孩正發着熱在牀上翻來覆去，母親已經睡熟，因為她太疲倦了。他跳進窗裏，把紅寶石放在桌上，就放在婦人的頂針旁邊。過後他又輕輕地繞着牀飛了一陣，用翅子扇着小孩的前額。"我覺得多麼涼，"孩子説，"我一定好起來了。"他便沉沉地睡去了，他睡得很甜。

燕子回到快樂王子那裏，把他做過的事講給王子聽。他又說：「這倒是很奇怪的事，雖然天氣這麼冷，我卻覺得很暖和。」

「那是因為你做了一件好事，」王子說。小燕子開始想起來，過後他睡着了。他有這樣的一種習慣，只要一用思想，就會打瞌睡的。

天亮以後他飛下河去洗了一個澡。一位禽學教授走過橋上，看見了，便說：「真是一件少有的事，冬天裏會有燕子！」他便寫了一封講這件事的長信送給本地報紙發表。每個人都引用這封信，儘管信裏有那麼多他們不能了解的句子。

「今晚上我要到埃及去，」燕子說，他想到前途，心裏非常高興。他把城裏所有的公共紀念物都參觀過了，並且還在教堂的尖頂上坐了好一陣。不管他到甚麼地方，麻雀們都吱吱叫着，而且互相說：「這是一位多麼顯貴的生客！」因此他玩得非常高興。

月亮上升的時候，他飛回到快樂王子那裏。他問道：「你在埃及有甚麼事要我辦嗎？我就要動身了。」

「燕子，燕子，小燕子，」王子說，「你不肯陪我再過一夜麼？」

「朋友們在埃及等我，」燕子回答道。「明天他們便要飛往尼羅河上游到第二瀑布去，在那兒[4]河馬睡在紙草中間，門農神坐在花崗石寶座上面。他整夜守着星星，到曉星發光的時候，他發出一聲歡樂的叫喊，然後便沉默了。正午時分，成群的黃獅走下河邊來飲水。他們有和綠柱玉一樣的眼睛，他們的吼叫比瀑布的吼聲還要響亮。」

「燕子，燕子，小燕子，」王子說，「遠遠的，在城的那一邊，我看見一個年輕人住在頂樓裏面。他埋着頭在一張堆滿稿紙的書桌上寫字，手邊一個大玻璃杯裏放着一束枯萎的紫羅蘭。他的頭髮是棕色的，亂蓬蓬的，他的嘴唇像石榴一樣地紅，他還有一對朦朧的大眼睛。他在寫一個戲，預備寫成給戲院經理送去，可是他太冷了，不能夠再寫一個字。爐子裏沒有火，他又餓得頭昏眼花了。"

"我願意陪你再待[5]一夜，"燕子説，他的確有好心腸。"你要我也給他送一塊紅寶石去嗎？"

"唉！我現在沒有紅寶石了，"王子説，"我就只剩下一對眼睛。它們是用珍奇的藍寶石做成的，這對藍寶石還是一千年前在印度出產的，請你取出一顆來給他送去。他會把它賣給珠寶商，換錢來買食物、買木柴，好寫完他的戲。"

"我親愛的王子，我不能夠這樣做，"燕子説着哭起來了。

"燕子，燕子，小燕子，"王子説，"你就照我吩咐你的話做罷。"

燕子便取出王子的一隻眼睛，往學生的頂樓飛去了。屋頂上有一個洞，要進去是很容易的，他便從洞裏飛了進去。那個年輕人兩隻手托着臉頰，沒有聽見燕子的撲翅聲，等到他抬起頭來，卻看見那顆美麗的藍寶石在枯萎的紫羅蘭上面了。

"現在開始有人賞識我了，"他叫道；"這是某一個欽佩我的人送來的。我現在可以寫完我的戲了，"他露出很快樂的樣子。

第二天燕子又飛到港口去。他坐在一隻大船的桅杆上，望着水手們用粗繩把大箱子拖出船艙來。每隻箱子上來的時候，他們就叫着："杭唷[6]！……""我要到埃及去了！"燕子嚷道，可是沒有人注意他，等到月亮上升的時候，他又回到快樂王子那裏去。

"我是來向你告別的，"他叫道。

"燕子，燕子，小燕子，"王子說，"你不肯陪我再過一夜麼？"

"這是冬天了，"燕子答道，"寒冷的雪就快要到這兒來了，這時候在埃及，太陽照在濃綠的棕櫚樹上，很暖和，鱷魚躺在泥沼裏，懶洋洋地朝四面看。朋友們正在巴伯克的太陽神廟裏築巢，那些淡紅的和雪白的鴿子在旁邊望着，一面在講情話。親愛的王子，我一定要離開你了，不過我決不會忘記你，來年春天我要給你帶回來兩粒美麗的寶石，償還你給了別人的那兩顆。我帶來的紅寶石會比一朵紅玫瑰更紅，藍寶石會比大海更藍。"

"就在這下面的廣場上，站着一個賣火柴的女孩，"王子說。"她把她的火柴都掉在溝裏了，它們全完了。要是她不帶點錢回家，她的父親會打她的，她現在正哭着。她沒有鞋、沒有襪，小小的頭上沒有一頂帽子。你把我另一隻眼睛也取下來，拿去給她，那麼她的父親便不會打她了。"

"我願意陪你再過一夜，"燕子說，"我卻不能夠取下你的眼睛。那個時候你就要變成瞎子了。"

"燕子，燕子，小燕子，"王子說，"你就照我吩咐你的話做罷。"

他便取下王子的另一隻眼睛，帶着它飛到下面去。他飛過賣火柴女孩的面前，把寶石輕輕放在她的手掌心裏。"這是一塊多麼可愛的玻璃！"小女孩叫起來；她一面笑着跑回家去。

燕子又回到王子那兒。他說："你現在眼睛瞎了，我要永遠跟你在一塊兒[7]。"

"不，小燕子，"這個可憐的王子說，"你應該到埃及去。"

"我要永遠陪伴你，"燕子説，他就在王子的腳下睡了。

第二天他整天坐在王子的肩上，給王子講起他在那些奇怪的國土上見到的種種事情。他講起那些紅色的朱鷺，牠們排成長行站在尼羅河岸上，用牠們的長嘴捕捉金魚。他講起斯芬克斯，它活得跟世界一樣久，住在沙漠裏面，知道一切的事情。他講起那些商人，他們手裏捏着琥珀唸珠，慢慢地跟着他們的駱駝走路；他講起月山的王，他黑得像烏木，崇拜一塊大的水晶。他講起那條大綠蛇，牠睡在棕櫚樹上，有二十個僧侶拿蜜糕餵牠；他講起那些侏儒，他們把扁平的大樹葉當作小舟，載他們渡過大湖，又常常同蝴蝶發生戰爭。

"親愛的小燕子，"王子説，"你給我講了種種奇特的事情，可是最奇特的還是那許多男男女女的苦難。再沒有比貧窮更不可思議的了。小燕子，你就在我這個城的上空飛一轉罷，你告訴我你在這個城裏見到些甚麼事情。"

燕子便在這個大城的上空飛着，他看見有錢人在他們的漂亮的住宅裏作樂，乞丐們坐在大門外捱凍。他飛進陰暗的小巷裏，看見那些飢餓的小孩伸出蒼白的瘦臉沒精打采地望着污穢的街道。在一道橋的橋洞下面躺着兩個小孩，他們緊緊地摟在一起，想使身體得到一點溫暖。"我們真餓啊！"他們説。"你們不要躺在這兒，"看守人吼道，他們只好站起來走進雨中去了。

他便回去把看見的景象告訴了王子。

"我滿身貼着純金，"王子説，"你給我把它一片一片地拿掉，拿去送給那些窮人，活着的人總以為金子能夠使他們幸福。"

燕子把純金一片一片地啄了下來，最後快樂王子就變成灰暗難看的了。他又把純金一片一片地拿去送給那些窮人。小孩們的臉頰上現出了紅色，他們在街上玩着，大聲笑着。"我們現在有麵包了，"他們這樣叫道。

隨後雪來了，嚴寒也到了。街道彷彿是用銀子築成的，它們是那麼亮，那麼光輝，長長的冰柱像水晶的短劍似的懸掛在簷前，每個行人都穿着皮衣，小孩們也戴上紅帽子溜冰取樂。

可憐小燕子卻一天比一天地更覺得冷了，可是他仍然不肯離開王子，他太愛王子了。他只有趁着麵包師不注意的時候，在麵包店門口啄一點麵包屑吃，而且拍着翅膀來取暖。

但是最後他知道自己快要死了。他就只有一點氣力，夠他再飛到王子的肩上去一趟。"親愛的王子，再見罷！"他喃喃地說，"你肯讓我親你的手嗎？"

"小燕子，我很高興你到底要到埃及去了，"王子說，"你在這兒住得太久了，不過你應該親我的嘴唇，因為我愛你。"

"我現在不是到埃及去，"燕子說。"我是到死之家去的。聽說死是睡的兄弟，不是嗎？"

他吻了快樂王子的嘴唇，然後跌在王子的腳下，死了。

那個時候在這座像的內部忽然起了一個奇怪的爆裂聲，好像有甚麼東西破碎了似的。事實是王子的那顆鉛心已經裂成兩半了。這的確是一個極可怕的嚴寒天氣。

第二天大清早市參議員們陪着市長在下面廣場上散步。他們走過圓柱的時候，市長仰起頭看快樂王子的像。"啊，快樂王子多麼難看！"他說。

"的確很難看！"市參議員們齊聲叫起來，他們平日總是附和市長的意見的，這時大家便走上去細看。

"他劍柄上的紅寶石掉了，眼睛也沒有了，他也不再是黃金的了，"市長說；"講句老實話，他比一個討飯的好不了多少！"

"比一個討飯的好不了多少，"市參議員們說。

"他腳下還有一隻死鳥！"市長又說，"我們的確應該發一個佈告，禁止鳥死在這個地方。"書記員立刻把這個建議記錄下來。

以後他們就把快樂王子的像拆下來了。大學的美術教授説："他既然不再是美麗的，那麼不再是有用的了。"

他們把這座像放在爐裏熔化，市長便召集一個會來決定金屬的用途。"自然，我們應該另外鑄一座像，"他說，"那麼就鑄我的像吧。"

"不，還是鑄我的像，"每個市參議員都這樣説，他們爭吵起來。我後來聽見人談起他們，據說他們還在爭吵。

"真是一件古怪的事，"鑄造廠的監工說。"這塊破裂的鉛心在爐裏熔化不了。我們一定得把它扔掉。"他們便把它扔在一個垃圾堆上，那隻死燕子也躺在那裏。

"把這個城裏兩件最珍貴的東西給我拿來，"上帝對他的一個天使說；天使便把鉛心和死鳥帶到上帝面前。

"你選得不錯，"上帝說，"因為我可以讓這隻小鳥永遠在我天堂的園子裏歌唱，讓快樂王子住在我的金城裏讚美我。"

夜鶯與薔薇

"**她**說過只要我送給她一朵紅薔薇，她就同我跳舞，"年輕的學生大聲説，"可是我的花園裏，連一朵紅薔薇也沒有。"

夜鶯在她的常青橡樹上的巢裏聽見了他的話，她從綠葉叢中向外張望，非常驚訝。

"找遍我整個花園都找不到一朵紅薔薇，"他帶哭説，他美麗的眼睛裏充滿了淚水。"唉，想不到幸福就繫在這麼細小的事情上面！我讀過了那班聰明人寫的東西，一切學問的秘密我都知道了，可是因為少了一朵紅薔薇，我的生活就變成很不幸的了。"

"現在到底找到一個忠實的情人了，"夜鶯自語道。"我雖然不認識他，可是我每夜都在歌頌他。我一夜又一夜地把他的故事講給星星聽，現在我親眼看見他了。他的頭髮黑得像盛開的風信子，他的嘴唇就像他想望的薔薇那樣紅。可是熱情使他的臉變得像一塊失色的象牙，憂愁已經印上他的眉梢了。"

"王子明晚要開跳舞會，"年輕的學生喃喃説，"我所愛的人要去赴會。要是我帶一朵紅薔薇去送她，她便會同我跳舞到天亮。要是我送她一朵紅薔薇，我便可以摟着她，讓她的頭靠在我肩上，她的手捏在我手裏。可是我的園子裏並沒有紅薔薇，我就不得不寂寞地枯坐在那兒，她會走過我面前不理我。她不理睬我，我的心就要碎了。"

"這的確是一個忠實的情人，"夜鶯說。"我所歌唱的，正是使他受苦的東西。在我是快樂的東西，在他卻成了痛苦。愛情真是一件了不起的東西。它比綠寶石更寶貴，比貓眼石更值價。用珠寶也買不到它。它不是陳列在市場上的，它不是可以從商人那兒買到的，也不能稱輕重拿來換錢。"

"樂師們會坐在他們的廊廂裏，"年輕的學生說，"彈奏他們的弦樂器，我心愛的人會跟着豎琴和小提琴的聲音跳舞。她會跳得那麼輕快，好像她的腳就沒有挨着地板似的，那些穿漂亮衣服的朝臣會團團地圍住她。可是她不會同我跳舞，因為我沒有紅薔薇帶給她，"於是他撲倒在草地上，雙手蒙住臉哭起來。

"他為甚麼哭？"一條小小的綠蜥蜴豎起尾巴跑過學生面前，這樣問道。

"的確，為的甚麼[8]？"一隻蝴蝶說，他正跟着一線日光飛舞。

"的確，為的甚麼？"一朵雛菊溫和地對他的鄰人小聲說。

"他為了一朵紅薔薇在哭！"夜鶯答道。

"為了一朵紅薔薇！"他們嚷起來，"多麼可笑！"小蜥蜴素來愛譏誚人，他大聲笑了。

然而夜鶯了解學生的煩惱，她默默地坐在橡樹枝上，想着愛情的不可思議。

突然她張開她的棕色翅膀，往空中飛去。她像影子似地穿過樹林，又像影子似地飛過了花園。

在草地的中央有一棵美麗的薔薇樹，她看見了那棵樹，便飛過去，棲在它的一根小枝上。

"給我一朵紅薔薇，"她大聲說，"我要給你唱我最好聽的歌。"

可是這棵樹搖搖它的頭。

"我的薔薇是白的，"它回答，"像海裏浪花那樣白，比山頂的積雪更白。你去找我那個長在舊日晷儀旁邊的兄弟吧，也許他會把你要的東西給你。"

夜鶯便飛到那棵生長在日晷儀旁邊的薔薇樹上去。

"給我一朵紅薔薇，"她大聲說，"我要給你唱我最好聽的歌。"

可是這棵樹搖搖它的頭。

"我的薔薇是黃的，"它答道，"就像坐在琥珀寶座上的美人魚的頭髮那樣黃，比刈草人帶着鐮刀到來以前在草地上開花的水仙更黃。去找我那個長在學生窗下的兄弟吧，也許他會把你要的東西給你。"

夜鶯便飛到那棵長在學生窗下的薔薇樹上去。

"給我一朵紅薔薇，"她大聲說，"我要給你唱我最好聽的歌。"

可是這棵樹搖搖它的頭。

"我的薔薇是紅的，"它答道，"像鴿子腳那樣紅，比在海洋洞窟中扇動的珊瑚大扇更紅。可是冬天已經凍僵了我的血管，霜已經凍枯了我的花苞，風雨已經打折了我的樹枝，我今年不會再開花了。"

"我只要一朵紅薔薇，"夜鶯叫道。"只是一朵紅薔薇！我還有甚麼辦法可以得到它嗎？"

"有一個辦法，"樹答道；"只是那太可怕了，我不敢對你説。"

"告訴我吧，"夜鶯説，"我不怕。"

"要是你想要一朵紅薔薇，"樹説，"你一定要在月光底下用音樂造成它，並且用你的心血染紅它。你一定要拿你的胸脯抵住我的一根刺來給我唱歌。你一定要給我唱一個整夜，那根刺一定要刺穿你的心。你的鮮血也一定要流進我的血管裏來變成我的血。"

"拿死來換一朵紅薔薇，代價太大了，"夜鶯大聲説，"生命對每個人都是很寶貴的。坐在綠樹上望着太陽駕着他的金馬車，月亮駕着她的珍珠馬車出來，是一件多快樂的事。山楂的氣味是香的，躲藏在山谷裏的桔梗同在山頭開花的石楠也是香的。可是愛情勝過生命，而且一隻鳥的心怎麼能跟一個人的心相比呢？"

她便張開她的棕色翅膀飛起來，飛到空中去了。她像影子似地掠過花園，又像影子似地穿過了樹叢。

年輕的學生仍然躺在草地上，跟她先前離開他的時候一樣，他那美麗眼睛裏的淚水還不曾乾去。

"你要快樂啊，"夜鶯大聲説，"你要快樂啊，你就會得到你那朵紅薔薇的。我要在月光底下用音樂造成它，拿我的心血把它染紅。我只要求你做一件事來報答我，就是你要做一個忠實的情人，因為不管哲學是怎樣地聰明，愛情卻比她更聰明，不管權力是怎樣地偉大，愛情卻比他更偉大。愛情的翅膀是像火焰一樣的顏色，他的身體也是像火焰一樣的顏色。他的嘴唇像蜜一樣甜；他的氣息香得跟乳香一樣。"

學生在草地上仰起頭來，並且側着耳朵傾聽，可是他不懂夜鶯在對他講些甚麼，因為他只知道那些寫在書本上的事情。

可是橡樹懂得，他覺得難過，因為他很喜歡這隻在他枝上做窠的小夜鶯。

"給我唱個最後的歌吧，"他輕輕地說；"你死了，我會覺得很寂寞。"

夜鶯便唱歌給橡樹聽，她的聲音好像銀罐子裏沸騰着的水聲一樣。

她唱完歌，學生便站起來，從他的衣袋裏拿出一個筆記本和一支鉛筆。

"她長得好看，"他對自己說，便穿過樹叢走開了——"這是不能否認的；可是她有情感嗎？我想她大概沒有。事實上她跟大多數的藝術家一樣；她只有外表的東西，沒有一點真誠。她不會為着別人犧牲她自己。她只關心音樂，每個人都知道藝術是自私的。不過我還得承認她的聲音裏也有些美麗的調子。只可惜它們完全沒有意義，也沒有一點實際的好處。"他走進屋子，躺在他那張小牀上，又想起他的愛人，過一會，他便睡熟了。

等着月亮升到天空的時候，夜鶯便飛到薔薇樹上來；拿她的胸脯抵住薔薇刺。她把胸脯抵住刺整整唱了一夜，清澈的冷月也俯下頭來靜靜聽着，她整整唱了一夜，薔薇刺也就刺進她的胸膛，越刺越深，她的鮮血也越來越少了。

她起初唱着一對小兒女心裏的愛情。在薔薇樹最高的枝上開出了一朵奇異的薔薇，歌一首一首地唱下去，花瓣也跟着一片一片地開放了。花起初是淺白的，就像罩在河上的霧，淺白色像晨光的腳，銀白色像黎明的翅膀。最高枝上開花的那朵薔薇，就像一朵在銀鏡中映出的薔薇花影，就像一朵在水池中映出的薔薇花影。

可是樹叫夜鶯把刺抵得更緊一點。"靠緊些，小夜鶯，"樹大聲說，"不然，薔薇還沒有完成，白天就來了。"

夜鶯便把薔薇刺抵得更緊，她的歌聲也越來越響亮了，因為她正唱着一對成年男女心靈中的熱情。

一層嬌嫩的紅暈染上了薔薇花瓣，就跟新郎吻着新娘的時候，他臉上泛起的紅暈一樣。可是刺還沒有達到夜鶯的心，所以薔薇的心還是白的，因為只有夜鶯的心血才可以把薔薇的心染紅。

樹叫夜鶯把刺抵得更緊一點。"靠緊些，小夜鶯，"樹大聲說，"不然，薔薇還沒有完成，白天就來了。"

夜鶯便把薔薇刺抵得更緊，刺到了她的心。一陣劇痛散佈到她全身。她痛得越厲害，越厲害，她的歌聲也唱得越激昂，越激昂，因為她唱到了由死來完成的愛，在墳墓裏永遠不朽的愛。

這朵奇異的薔薇變成了深紅色，就像東方天空的朝霞。花瓣的外圈是深紅的，花心紅得像一塊紅玉。

可是夜鶯的歌聲漸漸地弱了，她的小翅膀撲起來，一層薄翳罩上了她的眼睛。她的歌聲越來越低，她覺得喉嚨被甚麼東西堵住了。

於是她唱出了最後的歌聲。明月聽見它，居然忘記落下去，卻只顧在天空徘徊。紅薔薇聽見它，便帶了深的喜悅顫抖起來，張開花瓣去迎接清晨的涼氣。回聲把它帶到山中她的紫洞裏去，將酣睡的牧童從好夢中喚醒。它又飄過河畔蘆葦叢中，蘆葦又把它的消息給大海帶去。

"看啊，看啊！"樹叫起來，"現在薔薇完成了。"可是夜鶯並不回答，因為她已經死在長得高高的青草叢中了，心上還帶着那根薔薇刺。

正午學生打開窗往外看。

「啊，真是很好的運氣啊！」他嚷起來；「這兒有一朵紅薔薇！我一輩子沒有見過一朵這樣的薔薇。它真美，我相信它有一個長的拉丁名字。」他彎下身子到窗外去摘了它。

於是他戴上帽子，拿着紅薔薇，跑到教授家中去。

教授的女兒坐在門口，正在紡車上繞纏青絲，她的小狗躺在她的腳邊。

「你説過要是我送你一朵紅薔薇，你就會跟我跳舞，」學生大聲説。「這兒有一朵全世界中最紅的薔薇。你今晚上就把它帶在你貼心的地方，我們一塊兒跳舞的時候，它會對你説，我多麼愛你。」

可是少女皺着眉頭。

「我怕它跟我的衣服配不上，」她答道，「而且御前大臣的姪兒送了我一些上等珠寶，誰都知道珠寶比花更值錢。」

「好吧，我老老實實告訴你，你是忘恩負義的，」學生帶怒地説；他把花丟到街上去，花剛巧落進路溝，一個車輪在它身上碾了過去。

「忘恩負義！」少女説。「我老實對你説，你太不懂禮貌了；而且你究竟是甚麼人？你不過是一個學生。唔，我不相信你會像御前大臣的姪兒那樣鞋子上釘着銀釦子，」她站起來走進屋裏去了。

「愛情是多無聊的東西，」學生一邊走，一邊説。「它的用處比不上邏輯的一半。因為它甚麼都不能證明，它總是告訴人一些不會有的事，並且總是教人相信一些並不是實有的事。總之，它是完全不實際的，並且在我們這個時代，甚麼都得講實際，我還是回到哲學上去，還是去研究形而上學吧。」

他便回到他的屋子裏，拿出一本滿是灰塵的大書讀起來。

自私的巨人

每天下午，孩子們放學以後，總喜歡到巨人的花園裏去玩。

這是一個可愛的大花園，園裏長滿了柔嫩的青草。草叢中到處露出星星似的美麗花朵；還有十二棵桃樹，在春天開出淡紅色和珍珠色的鮮花，在秋天結着豐富的果子。小鳥們坐在樹枝上唱出悦耳的歌聲，牠們唱得那麼動聽，孩子們都停止了遊戲來聽牠們。"我們在這兒多快樂！"孩子們互相歡叫。

有一天巨人回來了。他原先離家去看他的朋友，就是那個康華爾地方的吃人鬼，在那裏一住便是七年。七年過完了，他已經把他要說的話說盡了（因為他談話的才能是有限的），他便決定回他自己的府邸去。他到了家，看見小孩們正在花園裏玩。

"你們在這兒做甚麼？"他粗暴地叫道，小孩們都跑開了。

"我自己的花園就是我自己的花園，"巨人說，"這是隨便甚麼人都懂得的，除了我自己以外，我不准任何人在裏面玩。"所以他就在花園的四周築了一道高牆，掛起一塊佈告牌來。

> 不准擅入
>
> 違者重懲

他是一個非常自私的巨人。

那些可憐的小孩們現在沒有玩的地方了。他們只好勉強在街上玩，可是街道灰塵多，到處都是堅硬的石子，他們不喜歡這個地方。他們放學以後常常在高牆外面轉來轉去，並且談論牆內的美麗的花園。"我們從前在那兒是多麼快活啊，"他們都這樣說。

春天來了，鄉下到處都開着小花，到處都是小鳥歌唱。單單在巨人的花園裏卻仍舊是冬天的氣象。鳥兒[9]不肯在他的花園裏唱歌，因為那裏再沒有小孩的蹤跡，樹木也忘了開花。偶爾有一朵美麗的花從草間伸出頭來，可是它看見那塊佈告牌，禁不住十分憐惜那些不幸的孩子，它馬上就縮回在地裏，又去睡覺了。覺得高興的只有雪和霜兩位。她們嚷道："春天把這個花園忘記了，所以我們一年到頭都可以住在這兒。"雪用她的白色大氅蓋着草，霜把所有的樹枝塗成了銀色。她們還請北風來同住，他果然來了。他身上裹着皮衣，整天在園子裏四處叫吼，把煙囪管帽也吹倒了。他說："這是一個適意的地方，我們一定要請雹來玩一趟。"於是雹來了。他每天總要在這府邸屋頂上鬧三個鐘頭，把瓦片弄壞了大半才停止。然後他又在花園裏繞着圈子用力跑。他穿一身的灰色，他的氣息就像冰一樣。

"我不懂為甚麼春天來得這樣遲，"巨人坐在窗前，望着窗外他那寒冷的、雪白的花園，自言自語，"我盼望天氣不久就會變好。"

可是春天始終沒有來，夏天也沒有來。秋天給每個花園帶來金色果實，但巨人的花園卻甚麼也沒有得到。"他太自私了，"秋天這樣說。因此冬天永遠留在那裏，還有北風，還有雹，還有霜，還有雪，他們快樂地在樹叢中跳舞。

一天早晨巨人醒在牀上，他忽然聽見了動人的音樂。這音樂非常好聽，他以為一定是國王的樂隊在他的門外走過。其實這只是一隻小小的梅花雀在他的窗外唱歌，但是他很久沒有聽見一隻小鳥在他的園子裏歌唱了，所以他會覺得這是全世界中最美的音樂。這時雹也停止在他的頭上跳舞，北風也不叫吼，一股甜香透過開着的窗來到他的鼻端。"我相信春天到底來了，"巨人說，他便跳下牀去看窗外。

他看見了甚麼呢？

他看見一個非常奇怪的景象。孩子們從牆上一個小洞爬進園子裏來，他們都坐在樹枝上面，他在每一棵樹上都可以見到一個小孩。樹木看見孩子們回來十分高興，便都用花朵把自己裝飾起來，還在孩子們的頭上輕輕地舞動胳膊。鳥兒們快樂地四處飛舞歌唱，花兒[10] 們也從綠草中間伸出頭來看，而且大笑了。這的確是很可愛的景象。只有在一個角落裏冬天仍然留着，這是園子裏最遠的角落，一個小孩正站在那裏。他太小了，他的手還挨不到樹枝，他就在樹旁轉來轉去，哭得很厲害。這株可憐的樹仍然滿身蓋着霜和雪，北風還在樹頂上吹，叫。"快爬上來！小孩，"樹對孩子說，一面盡可能地把枝子垂下去，然而孩子還是太小了。

巨人看見窗外這個情景，他的心也軟了。他對自己說："我是多麼自私啊！現在我明白為甚麼春天不肯到這兒來了。我要把那個可憐的小孩放到樹頂上去，隨後我要把牆毀掉，把我的花園永遠永遠變作孩子們的遊戲場。"他的確為着他從前的舉動感到十分後悔。

他輕輕地走下樓，靜悄悄地打開前門，走進院子裏去。但是孩子們看見他，非常害怕，他們立刻逃走了，花園裏又現出冬天的景象。只有那個最小的孩子沒有跑開，因為他的眼裏充滿了淚水，使他看不見巨人走過來。巨人偷偷地走到他後面，輕輕地抱起他，放到樹枝上去。這棵樹馬上開花了，鳥兒們也飛來在枝上歌唱，小孩伸出他的兩隻胳膊，抱住巨人的頸項，跟他接吻。別的小孩看見巨人不再像先前那樣兇狠了，便都跑回來。春天也就跟着小孩們來了。巨人對他們說："孩子們，花園現在是你們的了，"他拿出一把大斧，砍倒了圍牆。中午人們趕集，經過這裏，他們看見巨人和小孩們一塊兒在他們從未見過的這樣美的花園裏面玩。

巨人和小孩們玩了一整天，天黑了，小孩們便來向巨人告別。

"可是你們那個小朋友在哪兒[11]？我是說那個由我放到樹上去的孩子。"巨人最愛那個小孩，因為那個小孩吻過他。

"我們不知道，他已經走了，"小孩們回答。

"你們不要忘記告訴他，叫他明天一定要到這兒來，"巨人囑咐道，但是小孩們說他們不知道他住在甚麼地方，而且他們以前從沒有見過他；巨人覺得很不快活。

每天下午小孩們放學以後，便來找巨人一塊兒玩。可是巨人喜歡的那個小孩卻再也看不見了。巨人對待所有的小孩都很和氣，可是他非常想念他的第一個小朋友，並且時常講起他。"我多麼想看見他啊！"他時常這樣説。

許多年過去了，巨人也很老了。他不能夠再跟小孩們一塊兒玩，因此他便坐在一把大的扶手椅上看小孩們玩各種遊戲，同時也欣賞他自己的花園。他説："我有許多美麗的花，可是孩子們卻是最美麗的花。"

一個冬天的早晨，他起牀穿衣的時候，把眼睛掉向窗外望。他現在不恨冬天了，因為他知道這不過是春天在睡眠，花在休息罷了。

他突然驚訝地揉他的眼睛，並且向窗外看了再看。這的確是一個很奇妙的景象。園子的最遠的一個角裏有一棵樹，枝上開滿了可愛的白花。樹枝完全是黃金的，枝上低垂着纍纍的銀果，在這棵樹下就站着他所愛的那個小孩。

巨人很歡喜地跑下樓，進了花園。他急急忙忙地跑過草地，到小孩身邊去。等他挨近小孩的時候，他的臉帶着憤怒脹紅了，他問道："誰敢傷害了你？"因為小孩的兩隻手掌心上現出兩個釘痕，在他兩隻小腳的腳背上也有兩個釘痕。

"誰敢傷害了你？我立刻拿我的大刀去殺死他，"巨人叫道。

"不！"小孩答道，"這是愛的傷痕啊。"

"那麼你是誰？"巨人説，他突然起了一種奇怪的敬畏的感覺，便在小孩面前跪下來。

小孩向着巨人微笑了，對他説："你有一回讓我在你的園子裏玩過，今天我要帶你到我的園子裏去，那就是天堂啊。"

那天下午小孩們跑進園子來的時候，他們看見巨人躺在一棵樹下，他已經死了，滿身蓋着白花。

忠實的朋友

有天早晨一隻老河鼠從他的洞裏伸出頭來。他有明亮的小眼睛和堅硬的灰色頰鬚,他的尾巴好像是一條長長的黑橡皮。小鴨們在池塘裏游來游去,看起來真像一群黃色的金絲雀,他們的母親全身純白,配上一對真正的紅腿,她正在教他們怎樣在水中倒立。

"你們要是不會倒立,就永不會有跟上等人來往的機會,"她不斷地對他們說,並且她時常做給他們看,怎樣才可以倒立起來。可是小鴨們並不注意她。他們太年輕了,完全不知道跟上等人來往的好處。

"多麼不聽話的孩子!"老河鼠嚷道,"他們實在應當淹死。"

"不是的,"母鴨答道,"開頭不容易,對誰都是一樣,做父母的要有耐心才好。"

"啊!我一點也不懂做父母的情感,"河鼠說。"我不是個有家室的人。其實,我從沒有結過婚,也決不想結婚。愛情就它本身來說也很不錯,可是友誼卻比它高尚得多。老實說,我不知道在世界上還有甚麼比忠實的友誼更高貴、更難得的東西。"

"那麼請問，你以為一個忠實的朋友究竟有些甚麼樣的義務？"一隻綠色梅花雀坐在近旁一棵柳樹上面，聽見他們的談話便插嘴問道。

"對啊，我也就是想知道這一點，"母鴨說，她便游到池子[12]的那一頭去，倒立起來，給她的孩子們做一個好榜樣。

"你問得多傻！"河鼠大聲說。"自然啊，我希望我的忠實的朋友對我忠實。"

"那麼你又怎樣報答呢？"小鳥說，他拍起他的小翅膀，跳上了一根銀色的丫枝。

"我不明白你的意思，"河鼠答道。

"我給你講一個這方面的故事吧，"梅花雀說。

"這是跟我有關的故事嗎？"河鼠問道，"要是那樣的話，我倒高興聽，因為我很喜歡小說。"

"這個故事也可以用到你身上，"梅花雀答道，他飛下來，站在河岸上，開始講着"忠實的朋友"的故事。

"從前，"梅花雀說道，"有一個非常老實的小傢伙名叫漢斯。"

"他很出名嗎？"河鼠問道。

"不，"梅花雀答道，"我一點兒[13]也不覺得他出名，不過他的心腸好，而且有一張很滑稽的、和善的圓臉，那倒是很多人知道的。他一個人住在一間小茅屋裏，每天在他的園子裏工作。在他那一帶地方沒有一個花園像他的那樣可愛的。那兒有美洲石竹，有紫羅蘭，有薺，有法國的松雪草。有淡紅色薔薇，有黃薔薇，有番紅花，有金色、紫色和白色的菫菜。耬斗菜和碎米薺，牛膝草和野蘭香，蓮香花和鳶尾，黃水仙和丁香都按照季節依次開花，一種花剛謝了，另一種花又跟着開放，園中永遠看得見美麗的東西，永遠聞得到好聞的香氣。

"小漢斯有許多朋友，不過裏面最忠實的卻要算磨麵師大修。的確這個有錢的磨麵師對小漢斯是極忠實的，他每次走過小漢斯的花園一定要靠在籬笆上折一大束花，或者拔一把香草，要是在有果子的季節，他一定要拿梅子和櫻桃裝滿他的衣袋。

"磨麵師常常對小漢斯說：'真朋友應當共用一切，'小漢斯聽着，點頭微笑，他覺得自己有一個思想這麼高超的朋友，是很可驕傲的事。

"的確，有時候鄰居們也覺得奇怪：那個有錢的磨麵師儘管有一百袋麵粉存在他的磨坊裏，又有六頭奶牛和一大群綿羊，他卻從沒有給過小漢斯一點東西；不過小漢斯始終沒有想過那些，而且磨麵師常常對他講些關於真正友誼的不自私的事情，在他，再沒有甚麼比聽他朋友講那些奇妙事情更使他高興的了。

"小漢斯就這樣一直在他的園子裏勞動着。在春、夏、秋三季裏他很快樂，可是冬天一來，他沒有果子或者鮮花帶到市場去賣，他就得大大地捱餓受凍，常常連晚飯也吃不上，只吃一兩個乾梨或者硬核桃就上牀睡覺了。在冬天他還很寂寞，因為磨麵師在那些時候從沒有來看過他。

"磨麵師常常對他妻子說：'雪還沒有化的時候，我去看小漢斯，是沒有好處的，因為人在困難時候，應該讓他安靜，不應當有客人去打擾他。這至少是我對於友誼的看法，我相信我是對的。所以我要等到春天來，才去探望他，那時他便可以送我一大

籃櫻草，這會使他非常高興。'

　　"他的妻子正坐在壁爐旁一把舒適的圈手椅上，對着一爐旺柴火，便叫道：'你為着別人想得很周到，的確很周到。聽你談起友誼，真叫人滿意。我相信連牧師本人也講不出這樣美麗的事，哪怕他住在一所三層的樓房裏，小手指上還戴了一個金戒指。'

　　"這時磨麵師的最小的兒子在旁邊插嘴說：'可是我們不能請小漢斯到這兒來嗎？要是可憐的漢斯有困難的話，我願意把我的粥分一半給他，我還要給他看我的小白兔。'

　　"磨麵師聽見這話便嚷起來：'你這孩子多傻！我真不明白送你上學唸書有甚麼用。你好像甚麼都沒有學到，你聽我說，要是小漢斯到了我們這兒，看見我們的一爐旺火，看見我們的好的飲食和大桶的紅酒，他說不定會妒忌的，妒忌是件最可怕的事，它會損害人的天性。我決不願意叫漢斯的天性給損害了。我是他最好的朋友，我要永遠照管，並且留心他不要受到任何的誘惑。而且，要是漢斯到了這兒，他也許會要求我賒欠點麵粉給他，這是我辦不到的事。麵粉是一件事，友誼又是一件事，不能夠混在一塊兒。你看，這兩個詞兒[14] 唸起來聲音差得很遠，意思也完全不同。每個人都看得出來。'

　　"磨麵師的妻子給自己斟了一大杯溫熱的麥酒，一面稱讚道：'你說得多好！真的我在打瞌睡了。真正像在禮拜堂裏聽講一樣。'

　　"磨麵師答道：'做得好的人多，可是說得好的人卻很少，可見兩者之中還是說話更難，而且也更漂亮。'他用嚴厲的眼光望着坐在桌子那面的小兒子，那個孩子十分不好意思，低下頭，滿臉通紅，眼淚偷偷地掉到他的茶杯裏去了。然而，他年紀還這麼小，你們得原諒他啊。"

"這是故事的收場嗎？"河鼠問道。

"當然不是，"梅花雀答道，"這是開頭啊。"

"那麼你太落伍了，"河鼠說。"現在會講故事的人都是從收場講起，然後講到開頭，最後才是中段，這是新方法。前些時候我聽見一個批評家講起這些話，那天他正同一個年輕人在池塘邊散步。他談起這個問題發了長篇大論，我相信他說得不錯，因為他頭頂全禿了，鼻樑上架着一副藍眼鏡，並且只要年輕人一講話，他就回答一聲'呸！'不過請你還是把你的故事講下去吧。我很喜歡那個磨麵師。我自己也有一大堆美麗的情感，所以我非常同情他。"

"好的，"梅花雀說，他時而用這隻腿跳，時而又用那隻腿跳，"等到冬天一過去，櫻草開出淺黃色的星花來的時候，磨麵師馬上對他妻子說，他想下山去探望小漢斯。

"他的妻子大聲稱讚道：'啊，你心腸多好啊！你總是想着別人。你千萬不要忘記把大籃子帶去裝花回來。'

"磨麵師便用一根結實的鐵鏈把風車的翅子縛在一塊兒，又將籃子掛在他的胳膊上走下山去。

"磨麵師見着小漢斯便招呼道：'早安，小漢斯。'

"漢斯把身子支在他的鐵鏟上，滿面笑容地回答：'早安。'

"磨麵師問道：'這一個冬天你過得怎樣？'

"漢斯大聲說：'啊，承你問起這個，你實在太好了，你真是太好了。過去我倒有過一點兒困難，可是春天已經來了，我真快樂，我所有的花全開得很好。'

"磨麵師說：'這個冬天我們常常講起你，我們常常擔心你怎樣地在過日子。'

"漢斯說：'你太厚道了，我倒有點害怕你已經把我忘記了。'

"磨麵師說：'漢斯，你這個想法真叫人驚奇，友誼絕不會使人忘記。這就是友誼的了不起的地方，不過我想你也許不懂生活的詩意。還有，啊，你的櫻草多好看！'

"漢斯答道：'它們的確很好看，並且我今年運氣真好，會有這麼多的櫻草，我要把它們帶到市上去，賣給市長小姐，得到錢來贖回我的小車。'

"磨麵師說：'贖回你的小車？你是說你已經把小車賣掉了嗎？這多傻啊！'

"漢斯說：'啊，我不得不這樣做。你知道冬天對我是個很艱難的時期，我真的沒有一個錢買麵包。所以我最初賣掉我禮拜天穿的衣服上的銀鈕釦，隨後賣掉我的銀鏈子，後來又賣掉我的大煙斗，最後賣掉我的小車。可是我現在就要把它們全贖回來。'

"磨麵師說：'漢斯，我願意把我的小車給你。它不算十分完好；的確，它有一邊是落了，輪條也有點毛病；可是不管這個，我還是要把它送給你。我知道，我是非常慷慨的，並且很多人都會認為我送掉它是件很傻的舉動，可是我跟一般人不同。我以為慷慨就是友誼的精華，並且我還給自己留着一輛新的小車。不錯，你大可以放心，我會把我的小車給你。'

"小漢斯一張滑稽有趣的圓臉上充滿了喜色，他說：'啊，你真慷慨。我可以毫不費力地把它修好，因為我屋裏有一塊木板。'

"磨麵師說：'一塊木板！啊，我正想找塊木板來補我的倉頂。我倉頂上有個大洞，要是我不塞住它，穀子都會受潮的。幸好你提起了它！一件好事常常引起另一件來，這句話真不錯。我已經把我的小車給了你，現在你要把你的木板給我了。不用説，小車比木板貴得多，可是真正的友誼從來不留心這樣的事情。請你馬上把木板拿來，我今天就要動手修我的倉。'

"小漢斯大聲説：'我馬上去，'他跑進他的小茅屋，把木板拖了出來。

"磨麵師望着木板，一面説：'這塊木板並不很大，我擔心我用來補了我的倉頂以後就沒有留給你補小車的了；不過，這當然不是我的錯。並且我既然把我的小車給了你，我相信你一定高興給我一些花作報答。籃子在這兒，請你給我裝得滿滿的。'

"小漢斯接着籃子，帶點煩惱地説：'裝得滿滿的嗎？'因為這個籃子實在很大，他知道要是他把它裝滿，就沒有花留下來拿到市上去賣了，可是他很想把他的銀鈕釦贖回來。

"磨麵師答道：'當然啊，我既然把我的小車給了你，我覺得向你討一點花，也不為過。我也許錯了，可是我總以為友誼，真正的友誼是不帶一點兒私心的。'

"小漢斯大聲嚷起來：'我親愛的朋友，我最好的朋友，所有我園子裏的花全聽你自由使用。我寧願早得到你的看重，至於我那銀鈕釦隨便哪天都成，'他便跑去，把他園裏所有的美麗的櫻草全摘下來，裝滿了磨麵師的籃子。

"磨麵師説：'小漢斯，再見，'他把木板扛在肩頭，大籃子拿在手裏上山去了。

"小漢斯説：'再見，'他又很高興地繼續挖起土來，那輛小車太使他滿意了。

"第二天，他正把忍冬釘在門廊上的時候，聽見磨麵師的聲音在大路上喚他。他便從梯子上跳下來，跑到花園裏去，向牆外張望。

"磨麵師站在那兒，背上扛着一大袋麵粉。

"磨麵師說：'親愛的小漢斯，你肯替我把這袋麵粉扛到市上去嗎？'

"漢斯說：'啊，真對不起，不過我今天實在很忙。我得把我那些藤子全釘起來，把我那些花全澆了水，把我那些草全剪平。'

"磨麵師說：'好，你說得不錯，不過我就要把我的小車送給你了，你還拒絕我，我覺得你未免不講交情。'

"小漢斯大聲說：'啊，你不要這樣說，我無論如何，不會不講交情；'他便跑進屋去拿了帽子，然後出去接過了那一大袋麵粉，扛在他的肩頭，動身往市上去了。

"這是一個大熱天，路上塵土多得可怕，漢斯還不曾走到第六個里程石，他就累得沒有辦法，不得不坐下來休息了。可是他又勇敢地繼續向前走去，後來他到了市場。他在市上等了一忽兒[15]，便把那袋麵粉賣出去了，賣價很高，他得到錢立刻回家去，因為他害怕，要是他在市場上耽擱久了，說不定會在路上遇見強盜的。

"晚上小漢斯上牀睡覺的時候，他對自己說：'今天實在是很吃力，不過我倒高興我並沒有拒絕磨麵師，因為他是我最好的朋友，並且他就要把他的小車送給我。'

"第二天大清早磨麵師就下山來拿賣麵粉的錢，可是小漢斯太疲倦了，他還睡在牀上。

"磨麵師說：'說老實話，你太懶了。我就要把我的小車給你，你應當更勤快點才像話。懶惰是一件大罪。我當然不喜歡我有個偷懶朋友。你一定不會怪我跟你很坦白地直說。自然啊，我要不是你的朋友，我決不會這樣做的。可是如果一個人不能把自己的意思直說出來，那麼還用得着友誼幹嗎？隨便甚麼人都可以說漂亮話，討好人，巴結人，可是一個真心朋友卻總是說些不中聽的話，並且不惜給人苦吃。的確，一個真正的真心朋友是高興這樣做的，因為他知道他是在做好事。'

"小漢斯揉着他的眼睛，脫下他的睡帽來，一面說：'請你原諒，我實在太累了，我還想在牀上躺一忽兒，聽聽小鳥兒唱歌。你知道我聽過小鳥兒唱歌以後做事情總是更有精神嗎？'

"磨麵師拍着小漢斯的背說：'好，我聽見很高興，因為我要你穿好衣服馬上就到我磨坊來，給我補穀倉頂。'

"可憐的小漢斯很想就到他自己的園子裏去工作，因為他的花已經有兩天沒有澆水了，可是磨麵師是他一個極好的朋友，他不願意拒絕他。

"他便用一種半羞慚半害怕的聲調問道：'如果我說我很忙，你會以為我不講交情嗎？'

"磨麵師答道：'是啊，我並不覺得我對你要求得太多，既然我要把我的小車送給你；不過要是你不肯，我就自己動手做。'

"小漢斯連忙叫起來：'啊，絕不可以；'他從牀上跳下來，穿好衣服，走到穀倉那兒去了。

"他在那兒做了一整天，一直做到黃昏，黃昏時分磨麵師來看他究竟做得怎樣了。

"磨麵師快樂地叫起來：'小漢斯，你把屋頂上的洞補好了嗎？'

"小漢斯從梯子上爬下來，答道：'完全補好了。'

"磨麵師說：'啊，世界上再沒有比替別人做事情更快樂的了。'

"小漢斯坐下來，揩着額上的汗答道：'聽你談話，的確是大的光榮，極大的光榮，可是我害怕我永遠不會有你這樣的美麗的思想。'

"磨麵師說：'啊，你慢慢兒[16] 就會有的，不過你得再努力些。現在你才只做到友誼的實行；將來有一天你也會有理論的。'

"小漢斯便問：'你真的以為我會嗎？'

"磨麵師答道：'我一點兒也不懷疑，不過現在你既然補好了屋頂，你最好就回家去休息，因為我明天還要你把我的羊趕到山上去。'

"可憐的小漢斯對這件事情連一句話也害怕說，第二天大清早磨麵師便把他的羊趕到茅屋外面來了，漢斯只好帶牠們上山去。這樣的來回一趟就花了他整天的功夫；他回到家的時候，人疲倦得要命，就坐在椅子上睡着了，一直睡到大天亮。

"他對自己說：'我今天在園子裏一定多快活啊，'他馬上就去工作了。

"然而他還是永遠不能夠照料他的花，因為他的朋友磨麵師仍舊常常跑來麻煩他，派他去出長差，不然就叫他到磨坊裏去幫忙。小漢斯有時也很痛苦，他害怕他的花會以為他已經忘記了它們，不過他還用這樣的一個想法來安慰自己，就是，磨麵師是他最好的朋友。他常常對自己說：'況且他就要把他的小車給我，那完全是一種慷慨的行為。'

"小漢斯就這樣不斷地替磨麵師做事，磨麵師也不斷地對他講起種種關於友誼的美麗的事情，漢斯把那些話全記在一本筆記本上，晚上常常拿出來讀，因為他是一個非常好學的人。

"有一天晚上小漢斯正坐在家裏烤火，忽然聽見響亮的敲門聲。這個夜裏天氣很壞，風一直在房屋四周怒吼，狂吹，他起初還以為這只是風暴聲。可是第二下敲門聲又響起來了，隨後又是第三下，比前兩下聲音更大。

"小漢斯對自己説：'這是一個窮苦的出門人，'他便跑去開門。

"門前站着磨麵師，一隻手提一個燈籠，另一隻手拿一根手杖。

"磨麵師看見他，便叫起來：'親愛的小漢斯，我碰到很不幸的事情了。我的小兒子從梯子上跌下來受了傷，我現在去請醫生。可是醫生住在很遠的地方，今晚上天氣又是這麼壞，我剛才忽然想起，要是你替我跑一趟，那倒好得多。你知道我就要把我的小車給你，所以你應該替我做點事情來報答，這是很公平的。'

"小漢斯大聲説：'當然啊，你跑來找我，我覺得非常榮幸，我馬上就動身。不過你得把你的燈籠借給我，因為夜裏黑得很，我害怕我會跌到溝裏去。'

"磨麵師卻答道：'對不起，這是我的新燈籠，要是它出了毛病，對我是一個不小的損失。'

"小漢斯大聲説：'好，不要緊，我不用它了，'他把他那件寬大的皮衣和那頂暖和的紅色便帽取下來穿戴好，又纏了一根圍巾在頸項上，便動身了。

"這真是一個可怕的夜！天很黑，小漢斯伸手看不見自己的指頭，風颳得很厲害，他幾乎站不穩了。可是他非常勇敢，他大約走了三個鐘頭以後，居然走到了醫生的家，他敲着門。

"'誰呀？'醫生從他寢室的窗裏伸出頭來，大聲問道。

"他說：'醫生，我是小漢斯。'

"醫生又問：'小漢斯，你來做甚麼？'

"他答道：'磨麵師的兒子從梯子上跌下來受了傷，磨麵師要你馬上就去。'

"醫生說：'很好，'他便叫人備馬，又穿好靴子，拿了燈籠，走下樓來，騎着馬，朝着磨麵師家的方向走去，小漢斯吃力地跟在馬後。

"可是風暴越來越厲害，雨下得像河流一樣，小漢斯看不清路，也趕不上馬了。後來他迷了道，就在一片沼地上面轉來轉去，那是一塊很危險的地方，因為到處都是很深的洞穴，可憐的小漢斯就淹死在這兒了。第二天他的屍首被幾個牧羊人找到了，正浮在一個大池塘的水面上，他們把他抬回他的茅屋裏去。

"小漢斯下葬的時候，大家都去參加，因為他平日很得人心，喪主便是磨麵師。

"磨麵師說：'我既然是他最好的朋友，那麼理應由我佔最好的地位，'所以他便走在行列的最前頭，穿一件黑色長袍，時時用一塊大的手帕揩眼睛。

"葬禮完畢，送葬的人都舒舒服服地坐在客棧裏面，喝香料酒，吃甜點心，鐵匠忽然說：'小漢斯的死對每個人的確都是一個大損失。'

"磨麵師答道：'無論如何對我是個大損失，我差不多已經把我的小車給他了，我現在真不知道拿它來做甚麼好。它放在我家裏對我很不方便，它破爛得沒有辦法，我又不能拿它賣錢。我以後一定要當心不再把任何東西送人，人常常吃慷慨的虧。'"

"又怎樣呢？"過了好一忽兒河鼠說。

"怎樣，我的故事講完啦，"梅花雀說。

"可是磨麵師的結果怎樣呢？"河鼠問道。

"啊！老實說我並不知道，"梅花雀答道，"我相信我不會關心這個。"

"顯然你天性裏面並沒有同情，"河鼠說。

"我害怕你還不大明白這個故事裏面含的教訓，"梅花雀說。

"你說甚麼？"河鼠嚷道。

"教訓。"

"你是說這個故事裏面有一種教訓嗎？"

"當然啊，"梅花雀說。

"好吧，"河鼠很生氣地說，"我覺得你講故事以前，就應當先告訴我那個。要是你那樣做了，我一定不會聽你的；說實在話，我應當像批評家那樣說一聲'呸'。不過我現在還可以說。"所以他拚命地叫出了一聲'呸'，又拿尾巴掃了一下，便回到他的洞裏去了。

"你喜不喜歡河鼠？"過了幾分鐘母鴨用腳拍着水浮上水面來了，她向梅花雀問道。"他有很多的優點，不過拿我來說，我有一般的母親的情感，看見決心不結婚的人，總要掉眼淚的。"

"我害怕我把他得罪了，"梅花雀說。"因為我對他講了一個帶教訓的故事。"

"啊喲！這倒常常是一件很危險的事。"母鴨說。

我完全同意她的話。

了不起的火箭

國王的兒子要結婚了，國內準備着普遍的慶祝，王子等他的新娘整整等了一年，後來她畢竟來了。她是一位俄國公主，坐着六匹馴鹿拉的雪車從芬蘭一路趕來的。雪車的形狀很像一隻金色大天鵝，小公主就坐在天鵝的兩隻翅膀中間。她那件銀鼠皮的長外套一直蓋到她的腳，她頭上戴了一頂銀線小帽，她的臉色蒼白得就像她平時住的雪宮的顏色。她是那麼蒼白，所以她的雪車經過街中的時候，百姓們都感到驚奇。"她像一朵白薔薇！"他們嚷道，他們從露台上朝着她丟下花來。

王子在宮城門口等着迎接她。他有一對愛夢想的青紫色眼睛，和純金一般的頭髮。他看見她來，便跪下一隻腿，吻她的手。

"你的照相很美，"他喃喃地説，"可是你本人比照相還要美，"小公主臉紅起來。

"她先前像一朵白薔薇，可是現在她像一朵紅薔薇了，"一個年輕的侍從對他的朋友説，整個宮裏的人聽見了都很高興。

這以後的三天裏面人人都説着："白薔薇，紅薔薇，紅薔薇，白薔薇。"國王便下令把那個侍從的薪金增加一倍。其實他根本就沒有薪金,加薪的命令對他並沒有甚麼用處,不過這是一種大的榮譽,並且照例地在《宮報》上公佈了。

過了這三天,婚禮便舉行了。這是一個隆重的儀式,一對新人在一幅繡着小珍珠的紫天鵝絨華蓋下面手拉手地走着。隨後又舉行盛大的宴會,一共繼續了五個鐘頭。王子同公主坐在大殿的首位,用一個透明的水晶杯子喝酒。據說只有真誠的愛人才能夠用這個杯子喝酒,要是虛假的愛情的嘴唇一挨到杯子,杯子馬上就會變成灰暗無光而混濁了。

"他們分明互相愛着,就跟水晶一樣地潔白!"那個小侍從又說,國王第二次下令給他加薪。"多大的光榮啊!"朝臣們全這樣地嚷着。

大宴後又舉行跳舞會。新娘和新郎應當一塊兒跳薔薇舞,國王答應吹笛子。他吹得很壞,可是沒有人敢當面對他說,因為他是國王。事實上他只知道兩個調子,並且他從來就不能確定他吹的是哪個調子,可是這也沒有甚麼關係,因為不管他吹甚麼,大家都一樣高聲叫起來:"好極了!好極了!"

秩序單上最後一個節目是大放煙火,燃放的時間規定在當天的午夜。小公主一輩子沒有見過煙火,因此國王下令在她結婚那一天要皇家花炮手到場伺候。

"煙火是甚麼樣子?"小公主有天早晨在露台上散步的時候,這樣問過王子。

"它們就像極光,"國王說,他素來喜歡插嘴替別人回答問話,"不過它們更自然得多。拿我自己來說,我喜歡它們,不喜歡星星，因為你永遠知道它們甚麼時候要出現，它們跟我自己吹笛子一樣地有趣味。你一定得看看它們。"

在御花園的盡頭已經搭起了一座高台，等着皇家花炮手把一切安排好以後，煙火們就交談起來。

"世界的確很美，"一個小爆竹大聲説。"你只看那些黃色的鬱金香，嘿！假使它們是真的炮仗，它們也不會比現在更好看的。我很高興我旅行過了。旅行很能增長見識，並且會消除一個人的一切成見。"

"國王的花園並不是世界啊，你這傻爆竹，"一個大的羅馬花筒説；"世界是個很大的地方，你要看遍世界，得花三天的功夫。"

"不論甚麼地方，只要你愛它，它就是你的世界，"一個多思慮的輪轉炮嚷道，她年輕時候愛過一個舊的杉木匣子，常常以她的失戀自誇，"不過愛情不再是時髦的了，它已經給詩人們殺死了。他們寫了那麼多談愛情的東西，弄得沒有人相信了，我覺得這是毫不足怪的。真的愛情是痛苦的，而且還是沉默的。我記得我自己從前——可是現在沒有甚麼關係了。羅曼司是過時的東西了。"

"胡説！"羅馬花筒説，"羅曼司是永不會死的。它就跟月亮一樣，永遠活着。例如，新娘和新郎就是那麼熱烈地互相愛着。今早晨有個棕色紙做的火藥筒把他們的事情詳細地對我説了，他知道最近的宮廷新聞，他剛巧跟我同住在一個抽屜裏頭。"

可是輪轉炮搖着頭，喃喃説："羅曼司已經死了，羅曼司已經死了，羅曼司已經死了。"她是這樣一種人，她認為，要是你把一件事情翻來覆去地説許多次，到頭來假的事情也會變成真的了。

突然聽見一聲尖的乾咳，他們都掉頭朝四面張望。

咳嗽的是一個高高的、樣子傲慢的火箭，他給綁在一根長棍子的頭上。他每次要説話，總得先咳一兩聲嗽，來引起人們注意。

"啊哼！啊哼！"他説，大家都側耳靜聽，只有那個可憐的輪轉炮仍舊搖着她的頭喃喃説："羅曼司已經死了。"

"守秩序！守秩序！"一個炮仗叫起來。他是政客一流的人物，在地方選舉裏面他總是很出風頭，所以他會使用議會裏的習慣用語。

"死絕了，"輪轉炮低聲説，她去睡了。

等着四周完全靜下來的時候，火箭又第三次咳嗽而且説起話來了。他説話聲音很慢，而且很清楚，好像他在讀他的論文讓人記錄似的，他從不正眼看聽話的人。他的確有一副堂堂的儀表。

"國王的兒子運氣多好，"他説，"他的婚期就定在我燃放的那天。真的，即或這是預先安排好了的，對他也不能夠再有更好的結果了；不過王子們總是很幸運的。"

"啊，奇怪！"小爆竹説，"我的想法完全相反，我以為我們是燃放來恭賀王子的。"

"對你們可能是這樣，"他答道，"的確，我相信是這樣，可是對我情形就兩樣了，我是一個很了不起的火箭，我出身在一個了不起的人家。我母親是她那個時代最著名的輪轉炮，她以舞姿優美出名。每當她公開登場的時候，她總要旋轉十九次才出去。她每轉一次就要拋出七顆粉紅色的星到空中去。她的直徑有三英尺半，她是用最好的火藥做成的。我的父親跟我一樣是火箭，他生在法國。他飛得那麼高，人都以為他不會再下來了。然而他還是下來了，因為他心地很好，並且他變作一陣金雨非常光輝堂皇地落下來。報紙上用了非常恭維的字句記載他的表演。的確，《宮報》上稱他為化炮術的一大成功。"

"花炮，你是說花炮吧，"旁邊一個藍色煙火說，"我知道是花炮，因為我看見我自己的匣子上寫得有這樣的字。"

"唔，我說'化炮'，"火箭用了莊嚴的聲調說，藍色煙火覺得自己給火箭壓倒了，心裏不舒服，馬上就去欺侮旁邊那些小爆竹，為的表示他仍舊是一個有點重要的人。

"我在說，"火箭繼續說下去，"我在說——我在說甚麼呢？"

"你在講你自己，"羅馬花筒答道。

"不錯；我知道我正在討論一個有趣味的題目就讓人很無禮地打岔了。我討厭一切粗魯無禮的舉動，因為我非常敏感。全世界上沒有一個人像我這樣敏感的，我十分相信。"

"甚麼是一個敏感的人？"炮仗問羅馬花筒道。

"一個人因為自己生雞眼，就老是去踏別人的腳指頭，他就是敏感的人，"羅馬花筒低聲答道；炮仗差不多要笑破肚皮了。

"請問你笑甚麼？"火箭問道，"我並不在笑。"

"我笑，因為我高興，"炮仗答道。

"這個理由太自私了，"火箭生氣地說。"你有甚麼權利高興？你得想到別人。事實上你得想到我。我常常想到我自己，我希望每個別的人都想到我。這就是所謂同情。這是一個美麗的德性，我倒有很多很多。譬如，假設今晚上我出了甚麼事，那麼對每個人都會是多大的不幸！王子和公主永遠不會再高興了，他們整個的結婚生活都給毀了，至於國王呢，我知道他一定受不了這個。

真的，我一想起我自己地位的重要來，我差不多感動得流眼淚了。"

"要是你想使別人快樂。你最好不要流眼淚弄濕你的身子，"羅馬花筒大聲說。

"的確，"藍色煙火現在興致好多了，他接嘴嚷道，"這只是極普通的常識。"

"不錯，常識！"火箭憤怒地說，"你忘了我是很不尋常，很了不起的。唔，不論誰，只要是沒有想像力的人，就可以有常識。可是我有想像力，因為我從不照着事物的真相去想它們；我老是把它們當作完全不同的東西來想。至於說不要流眼淚，很明顯，這裏沒有一個人能夠欣賞多情善感的天性的。幸而我自己並不介意。只有想着任何人都比我差得很多，只有靠着這個念頭，一個人才能夠活下去，我平日培養的就是這樣一種感覺。你們全是沒有心腸的。你只顧在笑，開玩笑，好像王子同公主剛才並沒有結婚似的。"

"嗯，不錯，"一個小火球嚷道，"為甚麼不可以呢？這是椿大喜事，我飛到天空裏的時候，我要把這一切對星星詳說。我跟它們講起美麗的公主的時候，你會看見它們眼睛發亮。"

"啊！多麼平凡的人生觀！"火箭說，"不過這正如我所料。你心裏甚麼都沒有；你是空空洞洞的。就說，也許王子同公主會住在一個有河的地方，那是一條很深的河，也許他們會有一個獨生子，那個小孩就跟王子一樣有一頭金髮和一對青紫色的眼睛；也許有一天他會跟他的保姆一塊兒出去散步；也許保姆會在一棵大的接骨木樹下睡着了，也許小孩會跌進那條深的河裏淹死了。

多麼可怕的災禍！可憐的人，他們要失掉他們的獨生子了！的確太駭人了！我永遠忘不了它。”

“可是他們並沒有失掉他們的獨生子呢，”羅馬花筒説，“他們根本就沒有遇到甚麼災禍。”

“我並沒有説他們已經失掉了他們的獨生子，”火箭答道，“我是説他們可能失掉。要是他們已經失掉了他們的獨生子，那還用得着我來多講。我就恨那班事後追悔的人。可是一想到他們可能失掉他們的獨生子，我就非常難過。”

“虛偽？你的確是的！”藍色煙火大聲説。“你實在是我所見過的最虛偽的人。”

“你是我所見過的最無禮的人，”火箭説，“你不能了解我跟王子的友情。”

“唔？你連他都不認識呢，”羅馬花筒吼道。

“我從來沒有説過我認識他，”火箭回答道。“我敢説，要是我認識他，我就不會做他的朋友了。要認識自己的朋友，那是一件很危險的事。”

“的確你還是不要流眼淚好，”火球説，“這倒是要緊的事。”

“我相信，對你倒是很要緊的，”火箭答道，“但是我要哭就哭，”他真的流出了眼淚來，淚水像雨點似地流下他的棍子，兩個小甲蟲正打算一塊兒安家，要找一塊乾燥的地方住進去，差一點被這淚水淹死了。

“他一定有一種真正浪漫的天性，”輪轉炮説，“因為並沒有一點值得哭的事情，他會哭得那麼傷心。”她發出一聲長歎，又想起了杉木匣子來了。

可是羅馬花筒和藍色煙火非常不高興，他們不停地大聲叫着：“騙人！騙人！”他們素來是很實際的，無論甚麼，只要是他們不贊成的，他們就説是“騙人”。

明月像一面很出色的銀盾似的升了起來，星星開始閃光，從宮中傳出來樂聲。

王子同公主這對新人開舞。他們跳得非常美，連那些亭亭玉立的白蓮花也靠窗偷看他們的舞姿，大朵的紅罌粟花不住地點他們的頭，敲拍子。

十點鐘敲了，十一點鐘敲了，現在敲十二點鐘，十二點的最後一下剛敲過，所有的人都走到露台上來，國王便派人叫來皇家花炮手。

“放煙火吧，”國王吩咐道；皇家花炮手深深地一鞠躬，便走下露台，到花園的盡頭去。他帶了六個隨從人員，每人拿一根竹竿，竿頭綁了一段點燃的火把。

這的確是一個壯觀的場面。

呼呼！呼呼！輪轉炮走了，她一路旋轉着。轟隆！轟隆！羅馬花筒走了。然後爆竹們到處跳舞，藍色煙火使得每樣東西都帶着深紅色。“再見，”火球嚷着就飛向天空去，撒下了不少藍色小火星來，砰！砰！炮仗們回應道，他們非常快活。每個都很成功，就除了那個了不起的火箭。他哭得一身都濕透了，他完全不能燃放了。他身上最好的東西便是火藥，火藥被眼淚浸濕，哪裏還有甚麼用處。所有他的窮親戚們，他平日間不屑對他們講話，偶爾講一兩句話總要帶一聲冷笑，現在他們都飛上天空去了，就像一些開放火紅花朵的出色的金花。“好呀！好呀！”宮裏的人全叫起來；小公主高興地笑了。

"我想，他們一定把我留到舉行大典的時候用，"火箭說，"一定就是這個意思，"他做出比以前更傲慢的樣子。

第二天工人們來收拾園子。"這明明是個代表團，"火箭說，"我要帶着相當的尊嚴來接見他們，"所以他擺出昂然得意的神氣，莊嚴地皺起眉頭來，好像在思索一個很重要的問題似的。可是他們一點也不注意他。他們正要走開，忽然其中一個人看見了他。"喂，"那個人大聲説，"一個多麼壞的火箭！"便把他丟到牆外，落進陰溝裏去了。

"壞火箭，壞火箭？"他在空中旋轉翻過牆頭的時候一面自言自語，"不可能！大火箭，那個人是這樣説的。'壞'和'大'，説起來聲音簡直是一樣，的確常常是一樣的，"他落進爛泥裏去了。

"這兒並不舒服，"他說，"不過這一定是個時髦的礦泉浴場，他們送我來休養，讓我恢復健康的。我的神經的確受了很大的損害，我需要休息。"

隨後一隻小蛙（他有一對嵌寶石的發光的眼睛和一件綠色斑點的上衣）向着火箭泅水過來了。

"原來是個新來的！"蛙説。"啊，畢竟再也找不出像爛泥那樣好的東西。我只要有落雨天和一條溝，我就很幸福了。你看下午會落雨嗎？我倒真希望落雨，可是天很藍，一片雲也沒有。多可惜！"

"啊哼！啊哼！"火箭説，他咳起嗽來。

"你的聲音多有趣！"蛙大聲説。"真的它很像蛙叫，蛙叫自然是世界上最富音樂性的聲音。今晚上我們有個合唱會，你可以聽聽。我們在農人房屋旁邊那個老鴨池裏面，等到月亮一升起來，我們就開始。這實在好聽極了，每個人都睜着眼躺在牀上聽我們唱，事實上我昨天還聽見農人妻子對她母親說，她因為我們的緣故，夜裏一點兒也睡不好覺。看見自己這麼受歡迎，的確是一件最快活的事。"

"啊哼！啊哼！"火箭生氣地説。他看見自己連一句話也插不進去，非常不高興。

"的確，悦耳的聲音，"蛙繼續説，"我希望你會到鴨池那邊來。我現在去找我的女兒。我有六個漂亮的女兒，我很怕梭魚會碰到她們。他真是個怪物，他會毫不遲疑地拿她們當早飯吃。好吧，再見；説真話，我們這番談話使我滿意極了。"

"談話，不錯！"火箭説。"完全是你一個人在講話。這並不是談話。"

"總得有人聽，"蛙説，"我就喜歡我自己一個人講話。這節省時間，並且免掉爭論。"

"可是我喜歡爭論，"火箭説。

"我不希望這樣，"蛙得意地説。"爭論太粗野了，因為在好的社會裏，大家的意見都是一樣的。再説一次，再見吧；我看見我的女兒們在遠處了，"小蛙便泅着水走開了。

"你是個很討厭的人，"火箭説，"教養很差。我就恨你們這一類人：像我這樣，人家明明想講講自己，你卻喋喋不休地拚命講你的事。這就是我所謂的自私，自私是最叫人討厭的，尤其是對於像我這樣的人，因為我是以富有同情心出名的。事實上你應當學學我，你的確不能再找一個更好的榜樣了。你既然有這個機會，就得好好地利用它，因為我差一點兒馬上就要回到宮裏去了。我是宮裏很得寵的人；事實上昨天王子和公主就為了祝賀我而舉行婚禮。自然你對這些事一點兒也不會知道，因為你是一個鄉下人。"

"你跟他講話，沒有甚麼好處，"一隻蜻蜓接嘴說，他正坐在一棵大的棕色菖蒲的頂上，"完全沒有好處，因為他已經走開了。"

"那麼這是他的損失，並不是我的，"火箭答道。"我並不單單因為他不注意聽我就不跟他講下去。我喜歡聽我自己講話。這是我一個最大的快樂。我常常獨自一個談很久的話，我太聰明啦，有時候我講的話我自己一句也不懂。"

"那麼你的確應當去講哲學，"蜻蜓說，他展開一對可愛的紗翼飛到天空去了。

"他不留在這兒多傻！"火箭說。"我相信他並不常有這種進修的機會。不過我倒一點兒也不在乎。像我這樣的天才總有一天會給人賞識的，"他在爛泥裏又陷進去一點兒。

過了一忽兒一隻大白鴨向他游了過來。她有一對黃腿和一雙蹼腳，而且因為她走路搖擺的姿勢被人當作一個絕世美人。

"嘎，嘎，嘎，"她說。"你形狀多古怪！我可以問一句，你是生下來這樣的，還是遇到甚麼意外事弄成這樣的？"

"很顯然你是一直住在鄉下，"火箭答道，"不然你一定知道我是誰。不過我原諒你的無知。要想別人跟我自己一樣了不起，未免不公平。要是我告訴你我能夠飛到天空中去，再落着一大股金雨下來，你一定會吃驚的。"

"我並不看重這個，"鴨子說，"因為我看不出它對甚麼人有益處。要是你能夠像牛一樣地耕田，像馬一樣地拉車，像守羊狗一樣地看羊，那才算一回事。"

"我的好人啊，"火箭用了很傲慢的聲調嚷道，"我現在明白你是下等人了。像我這樣身份的人永遠不會有用處。我們有一點才學，那就很夠了。我對任何一種勤勞都沒有好感，尤其對你好像在稱讚的那些勤勞我更不贊成。的確我始終認為苦工不過是這班無事可做的人的退路。"

"好的，好的，"鴨子說，她素來性情平和，從不同任何人爭吵，"各人有各人的趣味。我想，無論如何，你要在這住下來吧。"

"啊，不會，"火箭大聲說，"我只是一位客人，一位尊貴的客人。事實是我覺得這個地方有點討厭。這兒既無交際，又不安靜，事實上，這本來就是郊外。我大概要回到宮裏去，因為我知道我是命中注定要轟動世界的。"

"我自己從前也曾想過服務社會，"鴨子說，"社會上需要改革的事情太多了，前不久我做過一次會議的主席，我們通過決議反對一切我們所不喜歡的東西。然而那些決議好像並沒有多大的效果。現在我專心料理家事，照管我的家庭。"

"我是生來做大事的，"火箭說，"我所有的親戚全是這樣，連那些最卑賤的也是一樣的。不管甚麼時候，只要我們一出場，我們就引起廣大的注意。實在說我自己還沒有出場，不過等我出場，那一定是一個壯觀。至於家事，它會使人老得更快，使人分心，忘掉更高尚的事。"

"呀！人生更高尚的事，它們多麼好啊！"鴨子説，"這使我想起來我多麼餓，"她向着下游泅水走了，一路上還説着："嘎，嘎，嘎。"

"回來！回來！"火箭用力叫道，"我有許多話跟你説，"可是鴨子並不理他。"我倒高興她走了，"他對自己説，"她的心思實在太平凡了，"他在爛泥裏又陷得更深一點，他想起天才的寂寞來，忽然有兩個穿白色粗外衣的小男孩提着水壺抱着柴塊跑到岸邊來。

"這一定是代表團了，"火箭説，他極力做出莊嚴的樣子。

"喂！"一個孩子嚷道，"看這根舊棍子！我不明白它怎麼會到這兒來。"他把火箭從溝裏拾起。

"舊棍子！"火箭説，"不可能！金棍子，他説的就是這個，金棍子，金杖，這是很有禮貌的話。事實上他把我錯認做朝中大官了！"

"我們把它放進火裏去吧！"另一個孩子説，"它會幫忙把水燒開的。"

他們便把柴堆在一塊兒，再將火箭放在頂上，燃起火來。

"這可了不得，"火箭嚷道，"他們要在青天白日裏燃放我，讓每個人都看得見。"

"我們現在要睡覺了，"孩子們説，"等我們醒來，水就會燒開了。"他們便在草地上躺下來，閉上了眼睛。

火箭很潮濕，所以過了許久才燃得起來。最後他終於着火了。

"現在我要燃放了！"他嚷道，他把身子挺得很直、很硬。"我知道我要飛得比星星更高，比月亮更高，比太陽更高。事實上我要飛得那麼高——"

嘶嘶！嘶嘶！嘶嘶！他一直升到天空中去了。"真有趣！"他叫道，"我要像這樣飛個不停。我多麼成功！"可是沒有一個人看見他。

這時他覺得全身起了一種奇怪的刺痛的感覺。

"現在我要爆炸了，"他嚷起來。"我要轟動全世界，我要那麼出風頭，使得以後一年裏面沒有一個人再談論別的事情。"他的確爆炸了。砰！砰！砰！火藥燃了。那是毫無可疑的。

可是沒有人聽見他，連那兩個小孩也沒有，因為他們睡熟了。

現在他就只剩下棍子了，這根棍子落在一隻正在溝邊散步的鵝背上。

"天呀！"鵝叫起來。"要落棍子雨了。"她便跳進水裏去。

"我知道我要大出風頭的。"火箭喘息地說，他滅了。

石榴之家

少年國王

在加冕日前一天晚上，少年國王一個人坐在他那漂亮的房間裏。他的朝臣們都按照當時的規矩鞠躬到地行了禮，退出去，到宮內大殿中，向禮儀先生再學幾遍宮廷禮節，因為他們中間有幾位還不諳熟朝禮，朝臣而不熟悉朝禮，不用說，這是大不敬的事。

這個孩子（因為他還只是一個孩子，今年才十六歲）看見他們全走開了並不覺得難過，他暢快地吐出一口長氣，把身子往後一靠，靠在他那繡花長椅的軟墊上，他躺在那兒，睜大眼睛張着嘴，活像一位褐色的森林的牧神，或者一隻剛被獵人捉住的小野獸。

的確是獵人把他找到的，他們差不多偶然地碰到了他，那時候他光着腳，手裏拿着笛子，正跟在那個把他養大的窮牧羊人的羊群後面，他始終認為自己是那個人的兒子。其實他的母親是老王的獨養女兒，她偷偷地跟一個地位比她差得多的男人結了婚生下他來。（有人說那個男人是一個外地人，會一種很出色的吹笛的魔術，叫年輕的公主愛上了他；又有人說，那是一個里米尼的美術家，公主很看重他，也許太看重他了，後來他突然離開了這個地方，連大禮拜堂的壁畫都沒有完成。）孩子出世只有一個星期，在他母親睡着的時候，就讓人把他從她身邊偷走了，交給一對普通的農家夫婦去照管。這對夫婦自己沒有孩子，住在遠僻的樹林裏，從城裏騎馬去，有一天多的路。生他的那個顏色蒼白的少女醒過來不到一個鐘頭就死了，她究竟是讓悲哀殺死的呢，還是像御醫所宣佈的，染了時疫死去，抑或照某一些人隱隱約約地說的，喝了放在香料酒裏的意大利急性毒藥致死呢，這就沒有人知道了。一個忠心的公差騎着馬把孩子搭在鞍轎上帶着走，在他從倦馬上彎下身子去叩牧人茅屋的門的時候，公主的屍體正讓人放進一個開着的墓穴，這個墓穴是在城外一個荒涼的墳地裏面，據說墓穴裏還有一具屍首，是一個非常漂亮的外國男子，他雙手被繩子反縛在背後，胸膛上滿是帶血的傷痕。

至少人們偷偷地互相傳述的故事就是這樣的內容。有一件事倒是確實的：老王臨死的時候，不知是因為懺悔自己的大罪過，還是單單為了不讓他的國土從他的嫡系落到別人的手裏，他差人去把那個孩子找了來，並且當着內閣大臣們的面承認孩子是他的繼承人。

孩子剛剛被指定作繼承人以後，好像立刻就表現出那種奇怪的愛美的熱情來，這熱情注定了對他的一生有非常大的影響。那些把他送到給他預備好的房間去的人常常講起，他看見留給他穿戴的華美衣服和貴重珠寶，就發出了快樂的叫聲，並且他又是多麼高興地脫下他身上穿的粗皮衣和粗羊皮外套。有時候他的確也想念他從前那種悠遊自在的山林生活，繁重的宮廷禮節佔去了他一天那麼多的時間，這常常使他感到厭煩，可是這座富麗堂皇的宮殿（人們稱它作"歡樂宮"，他現在是它的主人了），對他彷彿是一個為了滿足他的快樂剛造出來的新世界；只要他能夠從會議席上或引見室裏逃出來，他總是立刻跑下那道裝飾着鍍金的銅獅和亮雲斑石級的大樓梯，從一間屋子走到另一間屋子，從一條走廊走到另一條走廊，好像一個人要在美裏面找出一副止痛的藥，一種治病的仙方似的。

他把這稱為探險旅行，事實上在他看來這真是漫遊奇境，有時候還有幾個披着斗篷垂着漂亮的飄帶的金髮長身的內侍陪伴他；不過在更多的時候，他總是一個人，他從一種差不多等於先知預見的敏捷的本能上覺得藝術的秘密最好在暗中求得，美同智慧一樣，都喜歡孤寂的崇拜者。

在這個時期中流傳着不少關於他的古怪的故事。據説有位胖胖的市長代表全城市民來説一大篇堂皇的效忠的話，曾經看見他非常恭敬地跪在一幅剛從威尼斯送來的畫面前，那幅大畫好像有崇拜新神的意思。又有一次他失蹤了幾個鐘頭，人們到處找尋，後來才在宮內北部小塔中一個小房間裏找到了他，他正在出神地望着一塊雕刻着阿多尼斯像的希臘寶石。又傳説，有人看見他拿他的暖熱的嘴唇去吻一座大理石古雕像的前額，那座石像是人們修建石橋的時候在河牀中挖出來的，像上還刻着哈得良的俾斯尼亞奴隸的名字。他還花了整夜的功夫去觀察月光照在一座恩狄米昂的銀像上是怎樣的景象。

凡是稀有的和值錢的東西對他的確都有很大的魔力，他非常迫切地想得到這些東西，便派了許多商人出去，有的去向北海的漁民買琥珀，有的到埃及去找尋只有在帝王陵墓中才找得到的神奇的綠玉，據説那種綠玉具有魔術的效力，有的去波斯收集絲絨的氈毯和着色的陶器，還有一些人便到印度去買輕紗和染色的象牙，月長石和翡翠手鐲，檀香，藍色琺瑯器和細毛披肩。

可是最費他心思的卻是他在加冕時候穿的袍子，那件金線織的袍子，那頂嵌滿紅寶石的王冠和那根垂着珍珠串的節杖。的確他今晚靠在豪華的長沙發椅上望着大段的松柴在壁爐中漸漸燒盡的時候，心裏所想的正是這個。它們都是由當時最出名的美術家設計的，圖樣在許多個月前就進呈給他看過了，他還下過命令要工匠們不分晝夜地趕工，照圖樣做出來，並且要人到處去搜求那些配得上他們的手藝的珠寶，就是找遍全世界他也不在乎。他在想像中看見他自己穿着華貴的王袍站在大禮拜堂中高高的祭壇上，他的孩子的嘴唇上現出了微笑，他那雙深黑的森林人的眼睛也燦爛地發光了。

過了一忽兒他站起來，身子靠着壁爐的雕花庇簷，把這間燈光陰暗的屋子四處望了一下。牆上掛着表現美的勝利的華貴壁衣。一個嵌鑲瑪瑙和琉璃的大櫥把一個角落填滿了，面對窗戶立着一個非常精巧的櫃子，它那些漆格子都是灑着金粉和鑲金的，上面放了幾個精緻的威尼斯玻璃酒杯和一個黑紋瑪瑙的杯子。綢子牀單上繡着淺色的罌粟花，它們像是從睡着的倦手裏掉下來的；有凹槽的長象牙柱撐起天鵝絨的華蓋，大簇的鴕鳥毛像白泡沫似地從那裏伸向天花板上的灰白色銀浮雕。一個青銅的那喀索斯滿臉笑容，兩手伸出頭上，高高地捧着一面光亮的鏡子。桌上放了一個紫水晶盆。

窗外，現出禮拜堂的大圓頂，像一個大氣泡，隱約地露在一大片陰暗的房屋上面，疲乏的哨兵在夜霧籠罩的河邊台地上踱來踱去。遠遠地在一座果樹園裏有一隻夜鶯在唱歌。素馨花的淡香從開着的窗送進來。他把他的棕色鬈髮從前額向後掠回去，然後拿起一隻琵琶，信手漫彈着。他的沉重的眼皮往下垂，他感到一種奇怪的倦意。他從沒有像這樣強烈地或者像這麼快樂地感覺到美的東西的魔力與神秘。

鐘樓敲午夜鐘的時候，他打一下鈴，內侍們進來了，他們按照繁重的禮節給他脫去衣服，在他手上灑了玫瑰香水，又在他的枕頭上撒了些鮮花。他們退去後不多久，他就睡着了。

他睡着了，做了一個夢，他的夢是這樣的：

他覺得自己站在一間又長又矮的頂樓裏面，周圍是許多織布機的旋轉聲和拍擊聲。微弱的陽光從格子窗外射進來，給他照出俯在織架上面的織工們的憔悴的身形。一些帶病容的蒼白的小孩蹲在大的橫樑上。梭子急急穿過經線的時候，他們便把沉重的夾板拿起，梭子一停下來，他們又放下夾板，把線壓在一起。他們的臉上帶着被飢餓蹂躪的痕跡，他們的手不住地震搖、顫抖。幾個瘦弱的婦人坐在一張桌子前面縫紉。這個地方充滿了可怕的臭氣。空氣不乾淨，又氣悶，牆壁潮濕，還在滴水。

少年國王走到一個織工的面前，站在他身邊，望着他工作。

那個織工帶怒地看他，説道：“你為甚麼守着我？你是不是我們主人派來偵查我們的偵探？”

“你們的主人是誰？”少年國王問道。

“我們的主人！”那個織工痛苦地大聲説。“他是一個跟我一樣的人。的確我跟他中間就只有這一個小小的區別——他穿漂亮衣服，我卻總是穿破衣裳，我餓壞了身體，他卻飽得不舒服。"

"這是一個自由國家，"少年國王說，"你不是任何人的奴隸。"

"打仗的時候，強者強迫弱者做奴隸，"織工答道，"和平的時候，有錢人強迫窮人做奴隸。我們不得不做工來養活自己，可是他們只給我們那樣少的工錢，我們簡直活不了。我們整天給他們做苦工，他們箱子裏金子裝滿了，我們的兒女不到成年就夭折了，我們所愛的人的臉色也變得兇惡難看了。我們的腳踏出了葡萄汁，卻讓別人來喝葡萄酒。我們種了穀子，我們的飯桌卻是空的。我們都戴着鏈子，雖然鏈子是肉眼看不見的；我們都是奴隸，不管人們說我們怎樣自由。"

"所有的人都是這樣的嗎？"國王問道。

"所有的人都是這樣，"織工答道，"不論是年輕人或是老年人，不論是女或是男，不論是小孩或是老頭兒都是一樣。商人剝削我們，我們只好聽他們的話，教士騎着馬從我們身邊走過，只顧數他的唸珠，並沒有人關心我們。貧窮張着一雙飢餓的眼睛溜過我們那些見不到陽光的小巷，它後面緊緊跟着那個酒糟面孔的罪惡。早晨來喚醒我們的是慘苦，晚上跟我們待在一塊兒的是恥辱。不過這些事跟你有甚麼相干？你不是我們一夥的人。看你這張臉，你太快樂了。"他不高興地掉開頭，把梭子投過織機，少年國王看見梭子上面繫的是金線。

他大吃一驚，便問織工道："你織的是甚麼袍子？"

"這是小王加冕時穿的袍子，"他答道，"它跟你有甚麼相干？"

少年國王大叫一聲，便醒過來了。啊！他是在他自己的屋子裏面，穿過窗戶他看見蜜色的大月亮掛在朦朧的天空。

他又睡着了，做夢了，他的夢是這樣的：

他覺得自己躺在一隻大船的甲板上，一百個奴隸正在給這隻船盪槳。船長就坐在他旁邊一幅毯子上。這個人黑得像烏木，包着一張紅綢頭巾。厚厚的耳朵肉上垂着一對大的銀耳墜，他手裏拿着象牙的天平。

奴隸們除了一塊破爛的腰布外，全身再沒有穿別的；每個人都和他的鄰人鎖在一塊兒。炎熱的太陽直射到他們身上，一些黑人在過道上跑來跑去，拿皮鞭亂打他們。他們伸出乾瘦的膀子扳動沉重的槳。鹹水從槳上濺起來。

最後他們到了一個小小的海灣，開始測量水深。從岸上吹來一陣微風，給甲板和大三角帆都罩上一層細細的紅沙。三個阿拉伯人騎着野驢跑近，把長槍對着他們投過來。船長拿起一隻畫弓，一箭射在一個阿拉伯人的咽喉上。那個人重甸甸地跌進岸邊的激浪中去，他那兩個同伴騎着驢飛跑開了。一個蒙黃面紗的女人騎着一匹駱駝，慢慢地跟在後面，她不時回過頭來看那死屍。

黑人們拋了錨、收了帆以後，馬上就走進底艙去，拿出一架長的繩梯來，梯上縛了鉛，增加不少梯身的重量。船長將繩梯丟進海裏，只把梯頭拴在兩根鐵柱上面。隨後黑人們抓住一個年紀最輕的奴隸，敲去他的腳鐐，在他鼻孔和耳朵孔裏塗滿蠟，還在他的腰間縛上一塊大石頭。他疲倦地爬下繩梯，隱在海水裏去了。在他沉下去的地方，水面上浮起了幾個氣泡。有幾個奴隸好奇地望着海面。一個趕鯊魚的人坐在船頭，單調地擊着鼓。

過了一忽，潛水人升到水面上來了，他喘着氣，左手抓緊梯子，右手拿着一顆珍珠。黑人們從他手裏搶過珍珠來，又把他丟進海裏去。奴隸們俯在槳上睡着了。

他又上來好幾次，每次他上來的時候，他都帶來一顆美麗的珍珠。船長把珍珠一一地稱過，全放在一隻綠皮小袋裏面。

少年國王想說話，可是他的舌頭好像黏在他的上腭上面，他的嘴唇也不會動了。黑人們不停地談話，他們為了一串亮珠子吵起來。兩隻白鶴繞着船飛來飛去。

潛水人最後一次浮上水面來，這次他帶來的珠子比所有奧馬茲的珍珠都美，因為它圓得像一輪滿月，並且比晨星還要白。可是他的臉白得出奇，他一倒在甲板上，耳朵和鼻孔裏立刻冒出血來。他略略顫抖了一下，便不動了。黑人們聳了聳肩頭，把他的身體丟到海裏去了。

船長笑了，他伸出手來拿起那顆珠子，他看了看它，便把它按到他的前額上，俯下頭行了一個禮。"它應當用來裝飾小王的節杖，"他說，就打個手勢叫黑人起錨。

少年國王聽到這句話，他大叫一聲，便醒過來了，穿過窗戶，他看見黎明的灰色長指頭正在摘取垂滅的星星。

他又睡着了，做夢了，他的夢是這樣的：

他覺得他正走過一個陰暗的樹林，樹上懸垂着奇異的果子和美麗而有毒的花朵。他經過的時候，毒蛇向他嘶嘶地叫着，彩色鸚鵡帶着尖叫聲飛過樹叢。大龜在熱的泥水中昏睡。林中到處都是猴子和孔雀。

他繼續向前走着，走到樹林口便站住了，他看見一大群人在一條乾了的河牀上做工。他們像螞蟻似地擠在崖上。他們在地上挖了些深坑，自己下到坑裏去。有的人拿着大斧在劈岩石；有的人在沙裏掏摸。他們連根拔起仙人掌，又隨意踐踏紅花。他們你叫我、我喊你地忙來忙去，並沒有一個偷懶的人。

死和貪慾躲在一個石洞的陰處守着他們，死說：“我厭煩啦，把他們分給我三分之一，讓我走吧。”

可是貪慾搖頭不肯。她答道：“他們是我的傭人。”

死對她說：“你手裏是甚麼東西？”

“我有三粒穀子，”她回答，“這跟你有甚麼相干？”

“給我一粒，”死說，“來種在我的園子裏；只要一粒，我就會走開的。”

“我甚麼也不給你，”貪慾說，她把她的手藏在她的衣服褶子裏面。

死笑了，他拿出一個杯子，把它浸在水池裏，於是從杯中出來了瘧疾。瘧疾走過人叢中，三分之一的人倒下來死了。她後面起了一陣冷霧，無數的水蛇在她旁邊跑竄。

貪慾看見人死了三分之一，便捶胸大哭。她捶着她那乾瘦的胸膛，哭得很傷心。“你殺死了我三分之一的傭人，”她哭道，“你去吧。韃靼人的山中正有戰爭，雙方的國王都在喚你去。阿富汗人殺了黑牛，正開去參戰。他們用他們的長矛打他們的盾牌，並且戴上了鐵盔。我這山谷跟你有甚麼相干，你為甚麼留在這兒不走呢？你去吧，不要再到這兒來了。”

“不，”死答道，“你不給我一粒穀子，我就不走。”

可是貪慾捏緊了手，牙齒也閉得緊緊的。“我甚麼也不給你，”她喃喃地說。

死笑了，他在地上撿起一塊黑石子，擲進樹林中去，從野松叢中走出來熱病，穿着一件火焰的袍子。她走過人叢中，隨意挨着人們，凡是被她挨到的人都倒下死了。她的腳踏過草上，草也枯了。

貪慾顫抖起來，把灰抹到頭上。"你太殘忍了，"她說，"你太殘忍了。在印度各大城內正發生饑荒，撒馬耳罕的蓄水池已經乾了。在埃及各大城內正發生饑荒，蝗蟲已經從沙漠飛來了。尼羅河水並沒有漲上岸來，僧侶們埋怨着伊西斯和奧西里斯。你到那些需要你的人那兒去吧，不要弄我的傭人。"

"不，"死答道，"你不給我一粒穀子，我就不走。"

"我甚麼也不給你，"貪慾說。

死不說了，他舉起手在指縫間吹起哨子，一個女人在空中飛來。她額上寫着"瘟疫"二字，一群瘦老鷹在她周圍盤旋。她的翅膀罩住了整個山谷，所有的人全死了。

貪慾哭叫着穿過樹林逃走了，死跳上他的紅馬騎着走了，他的馬跑得比風還快。從谷底黏泥中爬出來龍和有鱗的怪物，一群胡狼在沙上跑着，仰起鼻孔大聲吸氣。

少年國王哭了，他說："這些人是誰呢？他們在找尋甚麼東西？"

"他們找尋國王王冠上面嵌的紅寶石，"站在他背後的一個人答道。

少年國王吃了一驚，他轉過身子，看見了一個香客打扮的人，手裏捧着一面銀鏡。

他臉色發白，又問："哪一個國王？"

香客答道："看這面鏡子吧，你就會看見他。"

他看那面鏡子，卻見到他自己的臉孔，他大叫一聲，便醒了，明亮的陽光流進屋子裏來，窗外，花園和別苑的樹上，鳥群正在唱歌。

御前大臣和文武官員進來向他行禮，內侍們給他捧來金線的王袍，又把王冠和節杖放在他面前。

少年國王望着那些東西，它們非常美。它們比他以前見過的任何東西都更美。可是他記起了自己的夢，便對他的大臣們說："把這些東西拿開，我不要穿它們。"

朝臣們大吃一驚，有的人笑了，他們以為他是在開玩笑。

可是他又嚴肅地對他們說："把這些東西拿開，把它們藏起來，不給我看見。雖然是我加冕的日子，我也不穿戴它們。因為我這件袍子是在憂愁的織機上用痛苦的白手織成的。紅寶石的心上有的是血，珍珠的心上有的是死。"他把他的三個夢都對他們講了。

朝臣們聽了他這三個夢以後，他們面面相覷，低聲交談說："他一定瘋了；因為夢不過是一個夢，幻覺也不過是幻覺吧。它們並不是真的，值不得我們去注意。並且那些替我們做工的人的生命跟我們有甚麼相干呢？難道一個人沒有見過播種人就不應該吃麵包，沒有跟葡萄園丁談過話就不應該喝酒嗎？"

御前大臣向少年國王進言道："陛下，我求您把這些陰鬱的思想丟開，穿起這件漂亮的袍子，戴起這頂王冠。因為要是您沒有一件王袍，百姓怎麼知道您是國王呢？"

少年國王望着他。"真的是這樣嗎？"他問道。"要是我沒有一件王袍，他們會認不出我是國王嗎？"

"他們會認不出的，陛下，"御前大臣大聲說。

"我從前還以為真有帶帝王相的人，"少年國王答道，"可是也許倒是你說的不錯。不過我還是不穿這件袍子，也不戴這頂王冠，我進宮來的時候是怎樣打扮，現在也就怎樣打扮着出宮去。"

他吩咐他們全退出，只留下一個內侍，那是一個比他小一歲的孩子。他留下這孩子來伺候他。他在清潔的水裏洗了澡，打開一口大的漆上顏色的箱子，拿出他在山腰給牧人看羊時候穿的皮衣和粗羊皮外套。他把它們穿在身上，他手裏拿着他那根牧人杖。

那個小內侍驚奇地圓睜着一雙大的藍眼睛，含笑對他說："陛下，我看見您的王袍和節杖，可是您的王冠在哪兒呢？"

少年國王隨手折下一枝爬在露台上面的荊棘，把它折彎，做成一個圓圈，放在他自己的頭上。"這就是我的王冠。"他答道。

他這樣打扮好了，就走出他的屋子到大殿上去，貴族們正在那兒等候他。

貴族們拿他取笑，有的對他叫起來："陛下，百姓們等着看他們的國王，您卻扮一個乞丐給他們看。"有的動了怒說："他丟了我們國家的臉，不配做我們的主子。"可是他一個字也不回答，便走了過去，他走下亮雲斑石的樓梯，出了銅門，上了馬，到禮拜堂去，小內侍在他旁邊跑着。

百姓們笑着，嚷着："國王的弄臣騎馬走過了！"他們一路嘲笑他。

他勒住馬韁說："不，我就是國王。"他便把他的三個夢對他們講了。

人叢中走出一個男人來，他痛苦地對少年國王說："皇上，您不知道窮人的生活是從富人的奢華中來的嗎？我們就是靠您的闊綽來活命的，您的惡習給我們麵包吃。給一個嚴厲的主子做工固然苦，可是找不到一個要我們做工的主子卻更苦。您以為烏鴉會養活我們嗎？您對這些事又有甚麼補救辦法？您會對買東西的人說：'你得出這麼多錢買下'，又對賣的人說：'你得照這樣價錢賣出'嗎？我不相信。所以您還是回到您的宮裏去，穿上您的紫袍、細衣吧。您跟我們同我們的痛苦有甚麼關係呢？"

"富人和窮人不是弟兄嗎？"少年國王問道。

"是的，"那個人答道，"那個闊兄長的名字叫該隱。"少年國王的眼裏充滿了淚水，他策着馬在百姓們的喃喃怨聲中緩緩前進，那個小內侍害怕起來，便走開了。

他走到禮拜堂的大門口，兵士們橫着他們的戟攔住他說："你在這兒找甚麼！這道門只有國王才能進來。"

他氣紅了臉，對他們說："我就是國王，"他把他們的戟揮開，走進去了。

老主教看見他穿一身牧羊人衣服走進來，便驚訝地從寶座上站起來，走去迎接他，對他說："孩子，這是國王的衣服嗎？那麼我拿甚麼王冠給你加冕呢？我拿甚麼節杖放在你手中呢？事實上這在你應該是一個最快樂的日子，不是一個屈辱的日子。"

"那麼快樂應當穿愁苦做的衣服嗎？"少年國王說。他把他的三個夢對主教講了。

主教聽完了他的夢，便皺着眉頭說："孩子，我是一個老人，已經臨到我的晚年了，我知道這個廣大的世界上有過許多壞事情。兇惡的土匪從山上跑下來綁走一些小孩，拿去賣給摩爾人。獅子躺着等候商隊走過，抓駱駝吃。野豬挖起山溝裏的穀子，狐狸咬了山上的葡萄藤。海盜洗劫了海岸，焚燒漁船，搶走漁網。

痲瘋病人住在鹽澤裏，用蘆葦稈子造房屋，沒有人可以走近他們。乞丐們流落街頭，到處漂泊，跟狗一塊兒吃飯。你能夠叫這些事情不發生嗎？你會跟痲瘋病人同牀睡眠，讓乞丐跟你一塊兒進餐嗎？你會叫獅子聽你的吩咐，野豬服從你的意志嗎？難道那位造出貧苦來的他不比你聰明？因此我並不讚美你所做的事情，我卻要你回到你的宮裏去，做出快樂的面容，穿上適合國王身份的衣服，我要拿金王冠來給你加冕，我要把珍珠的節杖放在你手中。至於你那些夢，不要再去想它們。現世的擔子太重了，不是一個人擔得起的，人世的煩惱也太大了，不是一顆心受得了的。"

"你在這個地方講這種話嗎？"少年國王説，他大步走過主教面前，登上祭壇的台階，立在基督的像前。

他立在基督像前，在他右手邊和在他左手邊有着燦爛的金盆，盛黃酒的聖餐杯和裝聖油的瓶子。他跪在基督像前，珠寶裝飾的神座旁邊蠟燭燃得十分明亮，香的煙雲盤成青色細圈在圓頂下繚繞。他垂着頭祈禱，那些穿着硬法衣的教士都下了祭壇讓開了。

突然從外面街上傳來一陣吵鬧聲，羽纓顫搖的貴族們拿着出鞘的劍和發光的鋼盾牌進來了，"那個做夢的人在哪兒？"他們叫着。"那個打扮得像乞丐的國王——那個給我們國家丟臉的孩子在哪兒？我們一定要殺死他，因為他不配統治我們。"

少年國王又埋下他的頭祈禱，他禱告完畢便站起來，他轉過身子憂愁地望着他們。

看啊！太陽穿過彩色玻璃窗照在他身上，日光在他四周織成一件金袍，比那件照他的意思做成的王袍還要好看。那根枯死的杖開花了，開着比珍珠還要白的百合花。乾枯的荊棘也開花了，開着比紅寶石還要紅的玫瑰花。百合花比最好的珍珠更白，梗子是亮銀的。玫瑰花比上等紅寶石更紅，葉子是金葉做的。

他穿着國王的衣服站在那兒，珠寶裝飾的神龕打開了，從光輝燦爛的"聖餅台"的水晶上射出一種非凡的神奇的光。他穿着國王的服裝站在那兒，這個地方充滿了上帝的榮光，連那些雕刻的壁龕中的聖徒們也好像在動了。他穿着華貴的王袍立在他們面前，風琴奏出樂調來，喇叭手吹起他們的喇叭，唱歌的孩子們唱着歌。

百姓們敬畏地跪了下來，貴族們把寶劍插回劍鞘，向他行着敬禮，主教臉色發白，他的手顫抖着。"比我偉大的已經給你加冕了。"他大聲說，跪倒在國王的面前。

少年國王從高高的祭壇上走下來，穿過人叢回宮去。沒有一個人敢看他的臉，因為這跟天使的面容極相似。

西班牙公主的生日

這是西班牙公主的生日。她剛滿十二歲，這天御花園裏陽光十分燦爛。

她雖是一個真正的公主，一位西班牙公主，可是她跟窮人的小孩完全一樣，每年只有一個生日，因此全國的人自然把這看作一件非常重要的事，就是她的生日應該是一個很好的晴天。那天的確是一個很好的晴天。高高的有條紋的鬱金香挺直地立在花莖上，像是長列的士兵，它們傲慢地望着草地那一頭的薔薇花，一面說："我們現在完全跟你們一樣漂亮了。"紫色蝴蝶帶着兩翅的金粉在各處翻飛，輪流拜訪群花；小蜥蜴從牆壁縫隙中爬出來，曬太陽；石榴受了熱裂開，露出它們帶血的紅心。連鏤花的棚架上，沿着陰暗的拱廊，懸垂着的纍纍的淡黃色檸檬，也似乎從這特別好的日光裏，得到一種更鮮明的顏色，玉蘭樹也打開了它們那些閉着的象牙的球形花苞，使得空氣中充滿了濃郁的甜香。

小公主本人同她的遊伴們在陽台上走來走去，繞着石瓶和長了青苔的古石像玩捉迷藏的遊戲。在平日公主只可以和那些跟她身份相同的小孩玩，因此她總是一個人玩，沒有誰來陪伴她。可是她生日這一天卻是一個例外，國王下了命令，她在這天可以邀請她所喜歡的任何小朋友進宮來跟她一塊兒玩。這班身材細長的西班牙小孩走起路來，姿勢非常優美，男的頭上戴着裝飾了大羽毛的帽子，身上披着飄動的短外衣，女的提着錦緞長衣的後裾，用黑、銀兩色的巨扇給她們的眼睛遮住太陽。公主卻是他們中間最優雅的，而且她打扮得最雅緻，還是依照當時流行的一種相當繁重的式樣。她的衣服是灰色緞子做的，衣裾和脹得很大的袖子上繡滿了銀花，硬的胸衣上裝飾了幾排上等珍珠。她走動的時候衣服下面露出一雙配着淺紅色大薔薇花的小拖鞋。她那把大紗扇是淡紅色和珍珠色的，她的頭髮像一圈褪色黃金的光環圍繞着她那張蒼白的小臉，頭髮上戴了一朵美麗的白薔薇。

那位愁悶不快的國王從宮中一扇窗裏望着這群小孩。他所憎厭的兄弟，阿拉貢的唐·彼德洛，立在他背後，他的懺悔師，格拉那達的大宗教裁判官，坐在他的身邊。這時候國王比往常更加愁悶，因為他望着小公主帶了一種小孩的認真樣子向她面前那群小朝臣俯身答禮，或者向那個時常跟她在一塊兒的面目可憎的阿布奎基公爵夫人用扇子掩着臉嬌笑的時候，他不由得想起了她的母親，他覺得好像還是不久以前的事情，那位年輕的王后從歡樂的法國來到西班牙，在西班牙宮廷那種陰鬱的華貴生活中憔悴死去，留下一個半歲的女孩，她來不及看見園子裏的杏樹二度開花，也沒有能在院子中央那棵多節的老無花果樹上採摘第二年的果實，院子裏現在已經長滿雜草了。他對她的愛是這樣地大，所以他不肯把她埋在墳墓裏讓他見不到她的面。他叫一個摩爾族的醫生用香料保存了她的屍首，這個醫生因為信邪教和行魔術的嫌疑據說已經被宗教裁判所判了死刑，國王為了他這件工作便赦免了他。她的身體現在還睡在宮中黑大理石的禮拜堂內張着帷幔的屍架上，跟將近十二年前那個起風的三月天裏僧侶們把她抬到那裏去的時候完全一樣。一個月裏總有一次，國王用一件黑大氅裹住身子，手裏提一個掩住光的燈籠走進這個禮拜堂，跪在她的旁邊喚着："我的王后！我的王后！有時他甚至不顧禮節（在西班牙個人任何行為都得受禮節的拘束，連國王的悲哀也得受它的限制），在悲痛突然發作的時候抓住她那隻戴珠寶的沒有血色的手，狂吻她那冰冷的化粧過的臉，想把她喚醒。

今天他好像又看見她了，就像他在楓丹白露宮裏第一次看見她那樣，他那時只有十五歲，她更年輕。他們就在那個時候正式訂婚，由羅馬教皇的使節主持典禮，法國國王和全體朝臣都在場參加。以後他便帶着一小圈黃頭髮回到他的西班牙王宮去了，他進馬車的時候，兩片孩子氣的嘴唇埋下來吻她的手，這回憶伴着他回國。婚禮後來在蒲爾哥斯（法西兩國邊境上一個西班牙小城）匆促地舉行了，隨後回到京城馬德里，才公開舉行盛大的慶祝，依着舊例在拉·阿多奇亞教堂裏做一次大彌撒，並且舉行一次比平常更莊嚴的判處異教徒火刑的典禮，把將近三百個異教徒（裏面有不少的英國人）交給刑吏燒死在火柱上。

他的確瘋狂地愛着她，他的國家當時正為了爭奪新世界的帝國和英國作戰，許多人認為就是他的這種愛使他的國家戰敗了的。他幾乎不能夠跟她離開片刻；為了她，他忘記了或者似乎忘記了一切國家大事；激情使他盲目到這樣可怕的地步，他竟然看不出來他為了使她高興苦心想出的那些繁重禮節，反而加重了她那個奇怪的病症。她死後，有一個時期他好像發了狂一樣。並且要不是他害怕他退位後小公主會受到他那個以殘酷著稱的兄弟的虐待，他一定會正式遜位到格拉那達的特拉卜教派大寺院中修道去，他已經是那個寺院的名譽院長了。他的兄弟的殘酷就是在西班牙也是很出名的，許多人還疑心他毒死了王后，說是王后到他的阿拉貢宮堡中訪問的時候，他送了她一雙有毒的手套。為了紀念死去的王后，國王曾通令全國服喪三年，甚至在三年期滿之後他還不許大臣們向他提續弦的事，後來皇帝本人出面要把姪女波希米亞郡主（一位可愛的郡主）嫁給他，他卻吩咐使臣們對他們的皇帝說，西班牙國王已經同"悲哀"結了婚，雖然她只是一個不會生育的新娘，他卻愛她比愛"美麗"更多。他這個答覆便使他的王國失去了尼德蘭的富裕省份。那些省份不久就在皇帝的鼓動下，由少數改革教派的狂信者領導，發動了反對他的叛亂。

今天他望着公主在園子裏陽台上遊戲的時候，他全部的結婚生活似乎在他眼前重現了，他又經歷了一次他結婚生活中那些強烈的、火熱的歡樂和因這生活的突然結束所引起的可怕的痛苦。死去的王后所有的一切動人的傲慢態度，小公主都有，她也有她母親那種任性的擺頭的樣子，她母親那張驕傲的美麗的彎彎的嘴，她母親那種非常漂亮的微笑（的確是所謂"真正法國的微笑"）；她偶爾仰起頭來看這堵窗，或者伸出她的小手給西班牙顯貴們親的時候，他看到了這種微笑。可是小孩們的尖銳的笑聲刺着他的耳朵，明媚而無情的陽光嘲弄着他的悲哀，連清爽的早晨空氣也被一種古怪香料（就像人用來保存屍首使它不會腐爛的那種香料）的沉滯的香味弄髒了——或者這只是他的幻想吧？他把臉埋在兩隻手裏。等到小公主再抬起頭看窗戶的時候，窗簾已經垂了下來，國王走開了。

她稍稍噘起嘴做出失望的樣子，又聳了聳肩。今天是她的生日，他實在應該陪她。那些愚蠢的國事有甚麼要緊呢？或者他是到那個陰沉的禮拜堂去了吧？那個地方是不許她進去的，她知道那兒永遠燃着蠟燭。他多傻，太陽這樣亮，大家都這樣高興，他卻一個人躲在那兒！並且假鬥牛戲的號聲已經響起來了，他會錯過它的，更不必說傀儡戲和別的出色的遊藝了。她的叔父和大宗教裁判官倒更近人情。他們到了陽台上來給她道喜。所以她搖擺着她那美麗的頭，拉着唐・彼德洛的手，慢慢兒走下了石級，朝着一座搭在園子盡頭的長長的紫綢帳篷走去，別的小孩們嚴格地依着次序跟在她後面：誰的姓名最長，就在最前頭。

一隊化裝為鬥牛士的貴族男孩們走出來迎接她，年輕的新地伯爵（一個非常漂亮的十四歲光景的孩子）帶着西班牙貴冑世家的全部優雅態度向她脫帽致敬，莊重地引她進去，走到場內高台上一把鑲金的小象牙椅前面。女孩們圍成一個圈子在四周坐下，一面揮着她們的大扇子低聲交談。唐・彼德洛和大宗教裁判官帶笑地立在場子的入口。連那位公爵夫人（一個臉色嚴厲的瘦女人，還戴着一圈黃色縐領，人們叫她做“侍從女官長”）今天也不像往常那樣地板着面孔了，一個冷淡的微笑在她的起皺紋的臉上掠過，使她那消瘦的沒有血色的嘴唇抽動起來。

這的確是一場了不起的鬥牛戲，而且照小公主看來，比真的鬥牛戲還好（那次帕馬公爵來訪問她父親的時候，她在塞維爾被人帶去看過真的鬥牛戲）。一些男孩騎着披了華貴馬衣的木馬在場子裏跑，他們揮動着長槍，槍上掛了用顏色鮮明的絲帶做的漂亮的長幡，另一些男孩徒步走着，在"牛"面前舞動他們的猩紅色大氅，要是"牛"向他們進攻，他們便輕輕地跳過了柵欄，至於"牛"呢，雖然它不過是用柳枝細工和張開的牛皮做成的，它卻跟一條活牛完全一樣，只是有時候它單用後腿繞着場子跑，這卻是活牛從沒有夢想到的了。它鬥得也很不錯，女孩們興奮得不得了，她們竟然在長凳上站起來，揮舞她們的花邊手帕，大聲叫着："好呀！好呀！"她們好像跟成人一樣地懂事。這場戰鬥故意拖長下去，有幾匹木馬被戳穿了，騎馬的人也下了馬來，最後那個年輕的新地伯爵把"牛"弄得跪在地上，他央求小公主允許他下那"致命的一擊"，他得着她的許可，便將他的木劍刺進那個畜生的頸子裏去，他用力太猛，一下就把牛頭砍掉了，小羅南先生的笑臉露了出來，那是法國駐馬德里大使的兒子。

在眾人長久拍掌歡呼聲中，場子收拾乾淨了，兩個摩爾族的侍役穿着黃黑兩色的制服莊嚴地拖走了木馬的屍首，又來一段短短的插曲：一個法國走繩師做了一次走繩的表演，然後在一個特地建築來演傀儡戲的小劇院的舞台上由意大利傀儡戲班演出了半古典的悲劇《莎福尼士巴》。傀儡們演得很好，它們的動作非常自然，戲演完公主的眼裏已經充滿淚水了。有幾個女孩真的哭了起來，得拿糖果去安慰她們，連大宗教裁判官也很受感動，他忍不住對唐·彼德洛說，像這種用木頭和染色的蠟做成，並且由提線機械地調動着的東西居然會這樣地不快樂，又會遇到這麼可怕的惡運，他覺得實在太難過了。

接着是一個非洲變戲法人的表演。他提了一個大而扁平的籃子進來，籃子上面覆着一塊紅布，他把籃子放在場子的中央，從他的包頭帕下拿出一根奇怪的蘆管吹起來。過了一會兒，布開始動了，蘆管聲來愈來愈尖，兩條金綠兩色的蛇從布下面伸出牠們古怪的楔形的頭，慢慢地舉起來，跟着音樂擺來擺去，就像一棵植物在水中搖動一樣。小孩們看見牠們有斑點的頭頂和吐出來很快的舌頭，倒有點害怕，不過後來看見變戲法人在沙地上種出一棵小小的橙子樹，開出美麗的白花，並且結了一簇真的果子，他們卻很高興了；最後變戲法人拿起拉斯‧多列士侯爵小女兒的扇子，把它變成一隻青鳥在帳篷裏飛來飛去，唱着歌，這時孩子們很高興又很驚愕。還有畢拉爾聖母院禮拜堂的跳舞班男孩們表演的莊嚴的“梅呂哀舞”也是很動人的。這個盛典每年五月裏要在聖母的主祭壇前舉行一次，來禮拜聖母，可是小公主以前從沒有見過；並且自從一個瘋教士（許多人認為他是被英國伊麗莎白女王收買了的）企圖用一塊有毒的聖餅謀害阿斯都里亞王以後，的確就沒有一位西班牙王族進過薩拉戈薩的大教堂。因此她只聽見別人傳說“聖母舞”怎樣怎樣（那種舞就叫做“聖母舞”）。這確實很好看，跳舞的男孩們都穿着白色天鵝絨的舊式宮裝，他們的奇特的三角帽上垂着銀的穗子，帽頂上飾着大的鴕鳥毛，他們在日光裏邁着舞步的時候，他們那身炫目的白衣裳襯着他們的帶黑色的皮膚和黑色的長髮越顯得燦爛奪目。他們在這錯雜的跳舞中自始至終都帶着莊重尊嚴的神情，他們的徐緩的舞步和動作有一種極考究的優雅，他們的鞠躬也是很氣派的，所有的人都被這一切迷住了。最後他們表演完畢，脫下他們的羽毛大帽向小公主致敬，她非常客氣地答禮，並且答應送一支大蠟燭到畢拉爾聖母的神壇上去，報答聖母賜給她的快樂。

於是一群漂亮的埃及人（當時一般人稱吉卜賽人為埃及人）走進場子裏來，他們圍成一個圈子，盤着腿坐下，輕輕地彈起他們的弦琴，他們的身子跟着琴調擺動，並且差不多叫人聽不見地低聲哼着一支輕柔的調子。他們看見唐‧彼德洛，便對他皺起眉頭來，有的人還露出驚恐的樣子，因為才只幾個星期以前他們有兩個同胞被唐‧彼德洛用了行妖術的罪名絞死在塞維爾的市場上。不過小公主把身子向後靠着，她一對大的藍眼睛從扇子上頭望着他們的時候，她的美麗把他們迷住了，他們相信像她這樣可愛的人決不能對別人殘酷的。因此他們很文靜地彈着弦琴，他們的長而尖的指甲剛剛挨到琴弦，他們的頭開始點着，好像他們在打瞌睡似的。突然間他們發出一聲非常尖銳的叫聲，小孩們全吃了一驚，唐‧彼德洛的手連忙握住他短劍的瑪瑙劍柄，以為發生了甚麼變故，原來那些彈琴的人跳了起來，瘋狂地繞着場子旋轉，一面敲手鼓，一面用他們那種古怪的帶喉音的語言唱熱烈的情歌。後來響起了另一聲信號，他們全體又撲到地上去，就靜靜地躺在那兒，真是靜得很，整個場子裏就只有一陣單調的琴聲。他們這樣做了幾次之後就不見了，過了一忽兒，又用鏈子牽了一隻毛茸茸的褐色大熊回來，他們的肩頭上還坐了幾個小巴巴利猴子。熊非常嚴肅地倒立起來，那些枯瘦的猴子跟兩個吉卜賽小孩（他們好像是猴子的主人）玩着各種有趣的把戲，比劍，放槍，並且做完像國王的禁衛軍那樣的正規兵的操練。吉卜賽人的表演的確是很成功的。

然而整個早晨的遊藝節目中最有趣的倒還是小矮人的跳舞。小矮人搖搖晃晃地移動那雙彎曲的腿，擺動他那個畸形的大頭，連跌帶滾地跑進場子裏來的時候，小孩們高興得大聲歡呼起來，小公主也禁不住放聲大笑。因此那位"侍從女官"不得不提醒她說，一位國王的女兒在一些跟她同等的人面前哭，這樣的事在西班牙雖有不少的先例，可是卻不曾見過一位皇族公主在一班身份比她低下的人面前這樣高興的。然而矮人的魔力太大了，真正是無法抗拒的，西班牙宮廷素來以培養恐怖的嗜好著稱，卻也從沒有見過一個這麼怪相的小怪物。並且他還是第一次出場。他是剛剛在昨天被人發現的。兩個貴族在環城的大軟木樹林的最遠的一段打獵，他正在林子[17]裏亂跑，他們遇見了他，便把他帶進宮裏來，打算給小公主一番驚喜；矮人的父親是個貧窮的燒炭夫，看見有人肯收養這個極醜陋又毫無用處的孩子，倒是求之不得。關於矮人的最有趣的事也許就是他一點也不覺得自己難看。的確他好像很快樂，而且很有精神似的，孩子們笑的時候，他也笑，而且笑得跟他們中間任何人一樣隨便，一樣快樂；每次跳舞完畢，他都要給他們每個人鞠個最滑稽的躬，對他們點頭微笑，就好像他真的是跟他們同類的人，並不是大自然懷着作弄的心思特地造出來給別人戲弄的一個畸形小東西。至於小公主呢，他完全被她迷住了。他不能夠把眼睛從她身上拿開，他好像專為她一個人跳舞似的。等他表演完畢，小公主記起來從前有一次教皇把他自己禮拜堂裏唱歌的意大利著名最高音歌者加法奈利派到馬德里來，用他美好的歌喉治療西班牙國王的愁悶，那個時候她親眼看見宮廷貴婦們向加法奈利投擲花束，她便從她頭髮上取下那朵美麗的白薔薇，一半開玩笑，一半戲弄那個"侍從女官"，她帶着最甜蜜的微笑，把花丟到場子裏去給他；他把事情看得十分認真，拿起花按在他粗糙的嘴唇上，一手拊着心跪在她面前，嘴張得大大的，一對小小的亮眼睛射出喜悅的光輝。

小公主更沒有辦法保持她的莊嚴了，小矮人跑出場子以後許久她還在笑，並且對她的叔父表示她希望這種跳舞馬上再來一次。然而那位"侍從女官"說是太陽太大了，公主殿下應當立刻回宮去，宮裏已經為她預備了盛宴，有一個生日大蛋糕，上面用彩色的糖做出她名字的縮寫字母，還有一面可愛的小銀旗在上面飄舞。小公主便很尊嚴地站起來，吩咐小矮人在午睡時間以後再表演跳舞給她看，又道謝年輕的新地伯爵今天這番殷勤的招待，然後回宮去了。小孩們仍舊依照先前進來時候的次序跟着走出。

小矮人聽說叫他在公主面前再表演一次跳舞，而且是公主自己特別吩咐的，他十分得意，便跑進花園裏去，他高興得忘記了自己，居然接連不斷地吻着白薔薇，做出些最笨拙、最難看的快樂的動作。

花看見他居然大膽闖進他們美麗的家裏來，非常不高興，他們看到他在花徑裏跳來跳去，那麼可笑地舉起兩手不住地揮舞，他們再也忍耐不下去了。

"他實在太難看了，不應當讓他到我們在的任何地方來玩，"鬱金香嚷道。

"他應當喝罌粟汁睡一千年才成，"大的紅百合花說，他們氣得不得了。

"他是個十足可怕的東西！"仙人掌叫道。"他身子矮胖，又扭歪得不成形，他的頭大得跟腿完全不成比例。他的確使我看着不舒服，要是他走近我身邊，我就要拿我的刺去刺他。"

"他倒的確得到了我一朵最漂亮的花！"白薔薇樹大聲説。"我今早晨親自送給公主，作為生日的禮物，他從公主那裏把它偷走了。"於是她拚命地叫起來："賊，賊，賊！"

連平日不大裝腔作勢的紅風露草（他們自己也有不少的窮親戚，這是盡人皆知的事）看見小矮人也憎厭地盤起身子；紫羅蘭在旁邊謙虛地説小矮人的確很難看，可是他自己也沒有辦法，風露草立刻做出很公平的樣子反駁道，那是他主要的短處，而且沒有理由因為一個人有不治的病症就應當恭維他；其實有一些紫羅蘭也覺得小矮人的醜陋大半是他自己故意做出來的，並且要是他帶着愁容，或者至少帶着沉思的神情，不要像這樣快樂地跳來跳去，做出種種古怪的傻樣子，那麼他看起來也要順眼一點。

至於老日晷儀呢，他是一位很著名的人物，他從前還親自向查理五世皇帝陛下報告過時刻，他看見小矮人，大吃一驚，他幾乎忘記用他那帶影子的長指頭指出整整兩分鐘了，他忍不住對那位在欄杆上曬太陽的乳白色大孔雀表示意見説，誰都知道，國王的孩子也是國王，燒炭夫的孩子也是燒炭夫，沒法希望事情不是這樣；孔雀完全贊成他這種説法，並且的確叫起來："不錯，不錯。"她聲音那樣大，那樣粗，連住在清涼的噴泉的池子裏的金魚們也從水裏伸出頭來，向那些石頭雕的大海神探問世間發生了甚麼事情。

可是鳥卻喜歡他。他們常常看見他在林子裏玩，有時像妖精似地追逐在空中旋轉的落葉跳舞，有時蹲在一棵老橡樹的洞孔裏，把他的硬殼果分給松鼠們吃。他們一點也不介意他的醜陋。

是啊，夜鶯晚上在橙子林裏唱歌唱得那麼甜，明月有時候也俯下身子來聽她唱，連她也並不是那麼好看的。並且小矮人過去對待鳥都很仁慈，譬如在那個可怕的嚴冬，樹上再沒有果子了，土地又像鐵一樣地硬，狼群居然跑到城門口來找食物，他也不曾忘記他們，他常常把他的小塊黑麵包揉成屑給他們吃，不管他自己的早餐怎樣壞，他總要分一些給他們。

所以他們現在繞着他飛來飛去，他們飛過他頭上的時候便用翅膀輕輕挨一下他的臉頰，他們吱吱喳喳地交談，小矮人非常高興，他忍不住把那朵美麗的白薔薇拿給他們看，並且告訴他們，這是公主親自給他的，因為她愛他。

他講的話他們連一個字也不懂，可是並沒有關係，因為他們把頭偏在一邊，做出很明白的神氣，這跟真正了解是一樣地好，並且更容易得多。

蜥蜴也很喜歡他，他跑倦了躺倒在草地上休息的時候，他們在他周身爬着，玩着，竭力使他高興。他們大聲説："不是每個人都可以像蜥蜴那樣地漂亮。那是過份的要求了。並且説起來雖然有點不近情理，但事實卻是這樣，要是我們閉上眼睛不看他，他倒也並不太難看。"蜥蜴生就是一種完全哲學家的氣質，在他們無事可做或者雨水太多他們不能外出的時候，他們常常坐着沉思幾個鐘頭。

然而他們這種舉動和鳥兒的舉動，都使花非常擔心。花説："顯而易見，這樣不停地跳跳蹦蹦，會有一種很壞的影響，有教養的人總是像我們這樣規規矩矩地待在一個地方。從沒有人看見我們在花徑裏跳來跳去，或者瘋狂地穿過草叢追逐蜻蜓。要是我們想換換空氣，我們就去找了園丁來，他便把我們搬到另一個花壇上去。這是很尊嚴的，而且應當是這樣。可是鳥和蜥蜴卻不懂休息，並且鳥連一個固定的地址也沒有。他們不過是跟吉卜賽人一樣的流浪人，實在應當受到對那種人的待遇。"他們便昂起頭，做出高貴的神氣，過了一忽兒他們看見小矮人從草地上爬起來，穿過陽台往宮裏走去，他們非常高興。

"他應當一輩子都關在房裏，"他們說。"看他的駝背同他的彎腿，"他們吃吃地笑起來。

可是小矮人對這些一點也不知道，他很喜歡鳥和蜥蜴，他以為花是全世界中最好的東西，自然要除開小公主，但是小公主已經給了他一朵美麗的白薔薇，她愛他，那就大有區別了。他多麼希望他同她一塊兒回到林子裏去！她會讓他坐在她右手邊，對他微笑，他永遠不離開她身邊，他要她做他的遊伴，教給她各種有趣的把戲。因為雖然他以前從沒有進過王宮，他也知道許多了不起的事情。他能夠用燈心草做出小籠子，關住蚱蜢叫牠在裏面唱歌，又能把細長的竹管做成笛子，吹起調子來連牧神也愛聽。他懂得每隻鳥的叫聲，他能夠從樹梢喚下歐椋鳥，從小湖裏喚起蒼鷺。他認識每頭獸的腳跡，能夠憑着輕微的腳印追趕野兔，靠着大熊踐踏過的樹葉追蹤大熊。風的各種跳舞他都知道，秋天穿着紅衣的狂舞，穿着藍草鞋在穀上的輕舞，冬天戴着白的雪冠的跳舞，春天果園中的花舞。他知道斑鳩在甚麼地方做窩[18]，有一次捕鳥人把老鳩捉去了，他便親自擔負起養育幼鳥的責任；他在一棵剪去頂枝的榆樹的洞孔裏為牠們造了一個小小的鳩舍。牠們很馴，已經習慣了每天早晨在他手上吃東西。她會喜歡牠們，還有在長鳳尾草叢中竄來竄去的兔子，有着硬羽毛和黑嘴的鳥，能夠蜷縮成帶刺圓球的刺蝟，以及搖擺着頭、輕輕咬着嫩葉、慢慢地爬着的大智龜，她都會喜歡的。是的，她一定要到林子裏來跟他一塊兒玩。他會把他的小牀讓給她，自己在窗外守着她直到天亮，不要叫長角的野獸傷害她，也不讓面目猙獰的豺狼走近茅屋來。天亮後他會輕輕敲着窗板，喚醒她，他們會一塊兒出去，跳舞跳一個整天。林子裏的確一點兒也不寂寞。有時一個主教騎着他的白騾子走過，手裏還拿着一本有圖的書在讀。有時一些飼鷹人戴着他們的綠絨便帽，穿着他們的熟鹿皮短上衣走過去，手腕上站着蒙了頭的鷹。在葡萄收穫期中，採葡萄做酒的人來了，滿手滿腳都是紫色，頭上戴着新鮮常春藤編的花冠，拿着還在滴葡萄酒的皮酒袋；燒炭人晚上圍了大火盆坐着，望着乾柴在火中慢慢燃燒，把栗子埋在熱灰中烘着，強盜們從山洞裏出來跟他們一塊兒作樂。還有一回，他看見一個美麗的行列在長而多塵土的去托雷多的路上蜿蜒地前進。僧侶走在前頭，口裏唱着好聽的歌，手裏拿着顏色鮮明的旗子和金十字架，隨後跟着穿銀盔甲執火繩槍與長矛的兵士，在這隊兵士中間還有三個赤腳的人，身穿古怪的黃袍，袍上繪滿了奇怪的像，手中拿着點燃的蠟燭。的確林子裏有好多值得看的東西，要是她倦了，他便會找一個長滿青苔的淺灘給她休息，或者就抱着她走，因為他雖然知道自己長得並不高，他卻是很強壯的。他會用一種蔓草的紅果給她做一串項鏈，這種紅果子一定會跟她裝飾在衣服上面的白果子一樣美，要是她看厭了它們，她可以把它們丟開，他會給她另外找一些來。他會給她找些皂斗和露水浸透了的秋牡丹，還有螢火蟲可以做她淡金色頭髮中間的星星。

可是她在甚麼地方呢？他問白薔薇，白薔薇不回答他。整個王宮好像都睡着了，就是在百葉窗沒有關上的地方，窗上也放下了厚厚的窗帷來遮住陽光。他到處轉來轉去，想找個進門地方，後來他看見一道小小的便門開着。他便溜了進去，原來這是一個漂亮的廳子，他覺得它比樹林漂亮得多，到處都是金光燦爛的，地板是用五色的大石頭砌的，安放得十分平正，沒有一點歪斜，簡直跟一個整塊一樣。可是公主並不在那兒，只有幾個非常漂亮的白石像從他們的綠玉像座上，埋下憂愁而茫然的眼睛望着他，他們的嘴唇上露出奇怪的微笑。

在廳子的盡頭掛着一幅繡得很華麗的黑天鵝絨的帷幔，上面點綴了一些太陽和星星，這是國王最得意的設計，並且繡的是他最愛的顏色。也許她藏在那後面吧？無論如何他要過去看一下。

因此他便悄悄地走過去，把帷幔拉開了。不，那兒不過是另一個房間，只是他覺得它比他剛才離開的那間屋子好看多了。牆上的綠色掛毯，繡着一幅行獵圖，畫中人物很多，是幾個佛蘭德斯美術家花了七年以上的時間完成的。這房間以前是“傻約翰”（那個瘋王的綽號）的寢室，那個瘋王太喜歡打獵了，他在精神錯亂的時候還常常想騎上畫中那些揚起前蹄的大馬，拖開那隻大群獵狗正在圍攻的公鹿，吹起行獵的號角，用他的短劍刺一隻奔逃的母鹿。現在房間改作為會議室了，在屋中央那張桌子上放着國務大臣們的紅色文書夾，上面印着西班牙的國徽金鬱金香和哈布斯堡的紋章和標識。

小矮人驚奇地看着四周，他有點害怕再往前走了。那些奇怪的沉默的騎馬人那麼輕捷地馳過樹林中一段長長的草地，連一點聲音也沒有，他覺得他們好像是他聽見燒炭夫們講過的那種可怕的鬼怪"康卜拉卻"，他們只在夜間出來打獵，要是碰到一個人，他們就使他變成赤鹿，然後來獵他。可是小矮人想起了美麗的公主，膽子又大起來了。他盼望他找到她一個人在屋子裏，他要告訴她，他也愛她。也許她就在隔壁那間屋子裏。

他跑過柔軟的摩爾地毯，打開了門。不！她也不在那兒。屋子空得很。

這是一間御殿，用來接見外國使臣的，要是國王同意親自接見他們（這樣的事近來少有了），就叫他們到這裏來；許多年以前，英國專使到西班牙來安排他們的女王（她是當時歐洲天主教君主之一）同皇帝的長子結婚，就在這間屋子晉見國王。屋裏掛的帷幔都是用鍍了金的西班牙皮做的，黑白二色的天花板下面垂着一個很重的鍍金的燭架，架上可以插三百支蠟燭。一個金布大華蓋上面用小粒珍珠繡成了獅子和加斯的爾的塔，華蓋下便安放了國王的寶座，是用一塊華貴的黑天鵝絨罩衣蓋着的，罩衣上到處都是銀色的鬱金香，並且很精巧地配着銀和珍珠的穗子。在寶座的第二級上面放着公主用的跪凳，墊子是用銀線布做成的，在跪凳下面，放着教皇使節的椅子，但已經出了華蓋的界線了，只有教皇使節才有權在舉行任何公開典禮的時候當着國王的面坐着，並且把他那主教的禮帽（帽上有纏結着的深紅色帽纓）放在前面一個紫色小幾上。牆上正對着寶座掛了一幅查理五世的獵裝像，跟活人一樣大小，身邊還站着一隻獒犬，另一面牆壁的正中掛着一幅腓力二世受尼德蘭各省朝貢時的畫像。在兩堵窗戶的中間放着一個烏木櫥，上面嵌了一些象牙碟子，碟子上刻着霍爾的"死的跳舞"中的人物，據說還是這位大師親手雕刻的。

　　然而小矮人對這一切莊嚴堂皇的景象一點也不注意。他不肯拿他的薔薇花來換華蓋上的全部珍珠，也不肯犧牲一片白花瓣來換那寶座。他所想望的，只是在公主到帳篷去以前見她一面，要求她等他跳舞完畢以後，跟他一塊兒走。在這兒宮裏空氣是很鬱悶的，可是在林子裏風自由自在地吹着，日光用飄動不停的金手撥開顫抖的樹葉。林子裏也有花，也許不及這花園裏的花漂亮，可是它們更香；早春有風信子在清涼的幽谷中和草覆的小丘上泛起一片紫浪；還有黃色櫻草一小簇一小簇地叢生在多節的橡樹根的四周；更有顏色鮮明的白屈菜，藍色的威靈仙，紫紅和金色的鳶尾。榛樹上有灰色的柔荑花，頂針花上面懸垂着有斑點的、蜜蜂常住的小房，累得它身子都彎了。栗樹有它的白色星的尖塔，山楂有它的蒼白的美麗的月亮。是的，只要他能夠找到她，她一定會跟他去的！她會跟他一塊兒到那美好的樹林裏去，他要跳舞一整天給她看，使她快樂。他這樣一想，眼睛上便露出微笑了，他走進隔壁屋子裏去。

　　在所有的屋子裏面這一間算是最亮，最美麗的。牆壁上蒙着淺紅色花的意大利花緞，緞上有鳥的圖樣，還點綴了很好看的銀花；傢具是用大塊銀子做的，上面裝飾着鮮花的花彩和轉動的小愛神；兩個大壁爐前面都放了繡着鸚鵡和孔雀的屏風，地板是海綠色的條紋瑪瑙，望過去，就彷彿沒有邊際似的。並且房裏不只他一個人。屋子的另一頭，門蔭下，有一個小小的人形正在望他。他的心顫抖起來，他的嘴唇裏發出一聲快樂的叫喚，他便走出這間屋子到日光裏去。他這樣做的時候，那個人形也跟着他往外走，他現在看清楚那個東西了。

公主！不，這是一個怪物，他所見過的最難看的怪物。它並不像常人那樣身材端正，它駝背，拐腳，還有一個搖搖晃晃的大腦袋，和一頭鬃毛似的黑髮。小矮人皺眉頭，怪物也皺眉頭。他笑，它也跟着他笑，他把兩手放在腰間，它也把兩手放在腰間。他嘲弄地給它鞠一個躬，它也同樣地還一個禮。他向着它走去，它也走過來迎他。它每一步都摹仿他，他站住時它也站住。他感到有趣地叫起來，跑上前去，伸出他的手，怪物的手挨着他的手，它的手像冰一樣地冷。他害怕起來，把手伸過去，怪物的手也很快地伸過來了。他想再向前推去，可是有甚麼光滑、堅硬的東西擋住了他。怪物的臉現在跟他自己的臉挨得很近了，那臉上彷彿充滿了恐怖似的。他把垂下的頭髮從眼睛上抹開。它也模仿他。他動手打它，它也還手打，並且是一下還一下的。他做出厭惡的樣子，它也對他做怪相。他退回來，它也跟着退開了。

它是甚麼東西呢？他想了一忽兒，並且掉轉頭看了看屋子裏其餘的地方。真奇怪，每樣東西在這堵看不見的清水牆上都有一個跟它完全一樣的副本。是的，這兒一幅圖像，牆上也有同樣的一幅圖像，那兒一張榻，牆上也有同樣的一張榻。那個躺在門口壁龕中的酣睡的牧神也有一個孿生兄弟在睡着，那個立在日光裏的銀美神也向着一個跟她一樣可愛的美神伸出兩隻胳膊來。

難道這又是"回聲"嗎？他有一次在山谷中喚過她（指回聲），她一個字一個字照樣地回答。難道她能夠摹仿眼睛像她模仿聲音那樣？難道她能夠造出一個跟真實世界完全一樣的假世界？難道物件的影子能夠有顏色、生命和動作嗎？難道這能夠是？——

他吃了一驚，便從懷裏拿出那朵美麗的白薔薇來，掉轉身子吻着花。那個怪物也有一朵薔薇，花瓣跟他的薔薇完全一樣！它也在吻花，而且吻法也是一樣，它一樣地把花按在它的胸上，做出可怕的動作。

當他明白了真相的時候，他發出一聲絕望的狂叫，倒在地上嗚嗚地哭起來。原來那個畸形怪狀、駝背的醜八怪就是他。他自己就是那個怪物！所有的小孩都在笑他，他原以為小公主在愛他，其實她也不過是在嘲笑他的醜陋，拿他的拐腳開心。為甚麼他們不讓他待在樹林裏面呢？那兒沒有鏡子告訴他，他生得多醜陋。為甚麼他父親不殺死他卻賣他出去丟醜呢？熱淚流下了他的臉頰，他把白薔薇撕碎了。那個爬在地上的怪物也照樣做了，把殘花瓣朝空中亂丟。它在地上爬行；他朝它看，它那張帶了痛苦皺着的臉也在望他。他害怕再看見它，便爬開了，還用兩隻手蒙住眼睛。他像一隻受傷的動物似地爬進陰影裏去，就躺在那兒呻吟。

就在這一刻小公主本人帶着她的一群遊伴從開着的落地窗進來了，他們看見醜陋的小矮人躺在地上，捏緊拳頭打着地板，樣子極古怪，極誇張，他們高興得大笑起來，便圍在他四周望着他。

"他的跳舞很有趣，"公主說，"可是他演戲更有趣。的確他差不多跟木偶人一樣地好，不過不用說他還不夠自然。"她搖着她的大扇子，喝采。

可是小矮人並不抬起頭來看一眼，他的抽泣聲漸漸地減弱，突然他發出一陣奇怪的哮喘，把手在身上亂抓。隨後他又倒下去，一點兒也不動了。

"這好極了，"公主停了一忽兒說，"可是現在你得給我跳舞了。"

　　"是啊，"小孩們齊聲叫起來，"你得站起來跳舞，因為你跟巴巴利猴子一樣聰明，你卻比牠們更可笑。"

　　可是小矮人一聲也不回答。

　　小公主頓着腳，喚她叔父，她叔父正跟御前大臣一塊兒在陽台上散步，讀着剛從墨西哥（宗教裁判所最近已經在那地方成立了）來的緊要公文。她大聲對她叔父說："我這個有趣的小矮人生氣了，您得叫他起來，要他跳舞給我看。"

　　他們兩個人對望着笑了笑，慢慢地走了進來，唐·彼德洛俯下身去，用他的繡花手套打小矮人的臉頰。他說："你得跳舞啊，小怪物。你得跳舞啊。西班牙和東印度群島的公主要娛樂啊。"

　　可是小矮人連動也不動一下。

　　"應該找個掌鞭者來敲他一頓，"唐·彼德洛厭煩地說，他便回到陽台上去了。可是御前大臣面帶莊容，跪在小矮人的身旁，把一隻手按在小矮人的心上。過了一忽兒，他聳了聳肩頭，站起來，向着公主深深地鞠了一躬，說道：

　　"我美麗的公主，您那個有趣的小矮人永不會跳舞了。真可惜，他是這麼醜陋，他一定會使國王陛下發笑的。"

　　"可是他為甚麼不再跳舞呢？"公主帶笑問道。

　　"因為他的心碎了，"御前大臣答道。

　　公主皺着眉頭，她那可愛的薔薇葉的嘴唇瞧不起地朝上動了一下。"以後凡是來陪我玩的人都要沒有心的才成。"她大聲說，就跑出屋子到花園裏去了。

打魚人和他的靈魂

每天晚上年輕的打魚人出海打魚，撒下他的網到水裏去。

遇到風從陸地上吹來的時候，他便捉不到魚，或者最多捉到一丁點兒，因為那是一種厲害的有黑翅膀的風，而且巨浪湧了起來迎接它。然而要是風向岸上吹的時候，魚便從水底浮起，游到他的網裏去，他捉住了牠們拿到市場上去賣。

每天晚上他出海打魚，有一晚，他拽網時網重得不得了，他差一點兒沒法把網拖到船上來。他笑了，他對自己説："我一定把所有的遊魚全捉到了，不然就是甚麼討厭的怪物進了網，那個東西在一般人看來也許是一種珍奇的異物，再不然就是偉大的女王喜歡玩的一種可怕的東西。"他便用盡力氣拉粗繩，直拉到他兩隻胳膊上長長的血管暴起來，就跟盤繞在一個銅花瓶上面的藍釉條紋一樣。他又用力拉細繩，那個扁平軟木浮子的圈兒[19]越來越近，最後網就升到水面上來了。

可是裏面一尾魚都沒有，也沒有怪物，也沒有可怕的東西，只有一個小小的人魚躺在網中酣睡。

她的頭髮像是一簇簇打濕了的金羊毛，而每一根細髮都像放在玻璃杯中的細金線，她的身體像白的象牙，她的尾巴是銀和珍珠的顏色。銀和珍珠顏色的便是她的尾巴，碧綠的海草纏在它上面；她的耳朵像貝殼，她的嘴唇像珊瑚。冰涼的波浪打着她冰涼的胸膛，海鹽在她眼皮上閃光。

她實在太美了，那個年輕的打魚人一眼看到她，就充滿了驚訝、讚歎，他伸出手，將網拉到自己身邊，埋下身子，把她抱在懷裏。他挨到她的時候，她像一隻受了驚的海鷗似地叫出聲來就醒了，她用她那紫水晶一般的眼睛驚恐地看他，一面掙扎着，想逃出來。可是他把她抱得緊緊的，不肯放開她。

她看見自己實在無法逃走了，便哭起來，一面說："我求你放我走，因為我是一位國王的獨養女，我父親上了年紀，而且只有一個人。"

可是年輕的打魚人答道："我不放你走，除非你答應我不論在甚麼時候，只要我喚你，你就來唱歌給我聽，因為魚喜歡聽人魚的歌聲，那麼我的網就會裝滿了。"

"要是我答應了你這個，你真的放我走嗎？"人魚大聲說。

"我真的放你走，"年輕的打魚人說。

她照他所想望的答應了，並且用了人魚的誓言賭了咒。他鬆開兩隻胳膊，她帶着一種奇怪的恐懼渾身抖着，沉到水裏去了。

每天晚上年輕的打魚人出海打魚，他喚人魚，她便從水中升起，給他唱歌。海豚成群地遊到她四周來。野鷗們在她的頭上盤旋。

她唱一首很出色的歌。因為她唱的是人魚們的事情：他們把他們的家畜從一個洞裏趕到另一個洞裏去，將小牛扛在他們的肩頭；她又唱到半人半魚的海神，他們生着綠色的長鬍，露着多毛的胸膛，每逢國王經過的時候他們便吹起螺旋形的海螺；她又唱到國王的宮殿，那是完全用琥珀造成的，碧綠的綠寶石蓋的屋頂，發光的珍珠鋪的地；又唱到海的花園，園中有許多精緻的珊瑚大扇整天在扇動，魚群像銀鳥似地遊來滑去，秋牡丹扒在岩石上，淺紅的石竹在隆起的黃沙中出芽。她又唱到從北海下來的大鯨魚，牠們的鰭上還掛着尖利的冰柱；又唱到會講故事的海中妖女，她們講得那麼好，叫過往的客商不得不用蠟塞住兩耳，為的是怕聽見她們的故事，會跳進海裏淹死；又唱到有高桅杆的沉船，凍僵的水手們抱住了索具，青花魚穿過開着的艙門遊來遊去；又唱到那些小螺螄，牠們都是大旅行家，牠們黏在船的龍骨上周遊了世界；又唱到住在崖邊的烏賊魚，牠們伸出牠們黑黑的長臂，牠們可以隨意使黑夜降臨。她又唱到鸚鵡螺，她有自己的貓眼石刻出來的小舟，靠着一張綢帆航行；又唱到那些彈豎琴的快樂的雄人魚，他們能夠把大海怪催睡；又唱到一些小孩子，他們捉住光滑的海豚，笑着騎在牠們的背上；又唱到那些美人魚，她們躺在白泡沫中，向水手們伸出胳膊來；又唱到生着彎曲長牙的海獅，和長着飄動的鬃毛的海馬。

她這樣唱着的時候，所有的金槍魚都從水深處浮上來聽她的歌聲，年輕的打魚人在牠們的四周撒下網捉住了牠們，不在網中的那些又被他用漁叉擒住了。他的船上載滿了魚，小人魚就對他微微一笑，沉到海裏去了。

然而她從來不肯走近他，讓他挨到她的身子。他常常喚她，求她，可是她不答應；要是他想去捉住她，她立刻就跳進水裏去了，快得像海豹一樣，並且那一整天他就再也看不到她了。她的歌聲在他的耳裏聽來一天比一天更好聽。她的聲音是那麼美好，他聽得連他的網和他的本領都忘記了，他也不去管他的行業了。金槍魚成群地游過他面前，朱紅色的鰭和凸起的金眼非常顯明，可是他並沒有注意牠們。他的漁叉擱在旁邊不用了，他那柳條編的籃子也是空空的。他張着嘴，驚異地瞪着眼，呆呆地坐在他的船上傾聽，一直聽到海霧在他四周升起，浪遊的明月將他的褐色的四肢染上銀白。

一天晚上他喚她，並且對她說："小人魚，小人魚，我愛你。讓我做你的新郎吧，因為我愛你。"

可是人魚搖搖她的頭。"你有一個人的靈魂，"她答道。"要是你肯送走你的靈魂，我才能夠愛你。"

年輕的打魚人便對自己說："我的靈魂對我有甚麼用處呢？我不能夠看見它。我不可以觸摸它。我又不認識它。我一定要把它送走，那麼我就會得到很大的快樂了。"於是他發出一聲快樂的叫喊，就在漆着彩色的船上立起來，向人魚伸出他的胳膊。"我要送走我的靈魂，"他大聲說，"你就會做我的新娘，我要做你的新郎，我們要一塊兒住在海底下，凡是你所歌唱過的你都引我去看，你願望的事我都要做，我們一輩子永不分離。"

小人魚快樂地笑出聲來，她把臉藏在了手中。

"可是我怎樣把我的靈魂送走呢？"年輕的打魚人大聲說。"告訴我要怎樣才辦得到，是啊，我一定會照辦的。"

"啊呀！我不知道啊，"小人魚說，"我們人魚族是沒有靈魂的。"她帶着沉思的樣子望望他,就沉下去了。

第二天大清早,太陽從山頭升起還不到一掌高,年輕的打魚人就走到神父的家裏去,叩了三下門。

門徒從門洞中往外面看,看見是他,便拉開了門閂,對他說:"進來。"

年輕的打魚人進去了,他跪在地板上鋪的清香的燈心草上,向着那位正在誦讀聖書的神父大聲喊着說:"神父啊,我愛上一個人魚了,我的靈魂在阻攔我,不讓我隨心所慾。請告訴我,要怎樣才能夠送走我的靈魂,因為我實在用不着它。我的靈魂對我有甚麼價值呢?我不能夠看見它。我不可以觸摸它。我又不認識它。"

神父打着自己的胸膛,回答道:"唉,唉,你瘋了,再不然你就吃了甚麼毒草了,因為靈魂是人的最高貴的一部分,它是上帝賜給我們的,我們應當把它用到高貴的地方。世間再沒有比人的靈魂更寶貴的東西,任何地上的東西都不能跟它相比。把全世界的黃金集在一塊兒,才有它那樣的價值,它比國王們的紅寶石貴重得多。所以,我的孩子,不要再想這件事,因為這是一椿不可饒恕的罪過啊。至於人魚,他們是無可救藥的,甚麼人跟他們交往,也會是無可救藥的。他們就跟那些不分善惡的野獸一樣,主並不是為着他們死的啊。"

青年漁人聽了神父這番不入耳的嚴厲的話,眼裏充滿了淚水,他站起來,對神父說:"神父啊,牧神住在樹林裏,他們很快樂,雄人魚坐在岩石上彈紅金的豎琴,他們也很快樂。我求您,讓我也像他們那樣吧,因為他們過的日子就跟花的日子一樣。至於我的靈魂,要是我的靈魂在跟我所愛的東西中間作梗,那麼它對我還有甚麼好處呢？"

"肉體的愛是淫邪的，"神父皺着眉頭大聲說，"上帝聽任在他的世界中出現的那些邪教的東西都是邪惡的。林中的牧神是該詛咒的，海裏的歌者也是該詛咒的！我在夜晚聽見過她們的聲音，她們想引誘我拋開我的晚課經。她們敲我的窗，大聲笑。她們在我的耳邊悄聲地講她們那些有毒的歡樂的故事。她們用種種的誘惑來誘惑我，我要禱告的時候，她們卻跑來揶揄我。她們是無可救藥的，我告訴你，她們是無可救藥的了。對於她們既沒有天堂，也沒有地獄，更不會讓她們到天堂或地獄裏面去讚美上帝的名字。"

"神父啊，"年輕的打魚人叫喊道，"您不知道您說的甚麼。有一天我下網捉住了一位國王的女兒。她比晨星還要美，比月亮還要白。為了她的肉體我甘願捨掉我的靈魂，為了她的愛我甘願放棄天國。我求您的事，請您告訴我吧，讓我平安地走回去。"

"去！去！"神父叫道，"你的情婦是無可救藥的了，你也會跟着她弄到無可救藥的地步。"神父不給他祝福，卻把他趕出門去。

年輕的打魚人從神父那裏出來便走到市場去，他走得很慢，埋着頭，好像有甚麼憂愁似的。

商人們看見他走來，便低聲交談，其中一個人走到他面前，喚他的名字，對他說："你要賣甚麼東西？"

"我要把我的靈魂賣給您，"他答道，"我求您把它給我買去吧，因為我討厭它。我的靈魂對我有甚麼用處呢？我不能夠看見它。我不可以觸摸它。我也不認識它。"

可是商人們拿他開玩笑，對他說："人的靈魂對我們有甚麼用處？它連半個破銀元也不值。把你的身體賣給我們做奴隸吧，我們給你穿上海紫色的衣服，在你手指頭上戴一個戒指，把你拿去給偉大的女王做弄臣。可是不要再提你的靈魂，因為它對我們毫無用處，而且一文不值。"

年輕的打魚人便對自己說：

"這是一件多麼奇怪的事！神父對我說，靈魂的價值比得上全世界的黃金，商人們卻說它不值半邊破銀元。"

他出了市場走下海邊去，他坐在那裏沉思他究竟應該怎樣做。

到了正午他記起來他一個同伴（那是一個採集傘形草的）曾經對他講過，有一個年輕的女巫，住在海灣頭一個洞窟裏，她的巫術十分高明。他便站起來跑去找她，他非常着急地要弄掉他的靈魂，他沿了海邊沙灘跑着，在他後面揚起一股塵霧。那個年輕的女巫由於自己手掌發癢知道他走來了，她笑着，把她一頭紅髮散開來。她站在洞口等他，她的紅頭髮長長地垂在她四周，她手裏拿着一枝正在開花的野毒芹。

他氣咻咻地跑上懸崖來向她俯身行禮的時候，她大聲問道："你缺少甚麼呢？你缺少甚麼呢？你是要在逆風的時候魚進你的網來麼？我有一支小蘆管，只要我吹起它來，鯔魚就會游進海灣裏來的。可是這有個代價，漂亮的孩子，這有個代價。你缺少甚麼呢？你缺少甚麼呢？你是要風暴打翻船，好把珠寶箱子給沖到岸上來麼？我有的風暴比風有的還多，因為我所伺候的主人比風更有力，用一個篩子和一桶水我就能夠把大船送到海底去。可是我要個代價，漂亮的孩子，我要個代價。你缺少甚麼呢？你缺少甚麼呢？我知道有株花生在山谷裏，就只有我一個人知道它。它的葉子是紫色的，有一顆星長在花心，它的汁像牛奶一樣的白。要是你用花去挨王后的堅貞的嘴唇，她就會跟隨你走到天涯海角。她會從國王的牀上起來，跟着你走遍全世界。但這有個代價，漂亮的孩子，這有個代價。你缺少甚麼呢？你缺少甚麼呢？我能夠把蟾蜍拿來在研缽中搗碎，將粉末做成羹，用一隻死人的手去攪拌它。等你的仇人睡着的時候，把羹灑在他身上，他就會變成一條黑黑的毒蛇，他自己的母親會將他殺死。我能夠用一個輪子把月亮從天上拉下來，我可以拿一塊水晶讓你在那裏面看見死。你缺少甚麼呢？你缺少甚麼呢？告訴我你要甚麼，我就會把它給你，你得償給我一個代價，漂亮的孩子，你得償給我一個代價。"

"我要的只是一件小事，"年輕的打魚人説，"然而神父卻跟我生氣，把我趕出來。這只是一件小事，商人們都拿我開玩笑，拒絕了我。所以我才來找你，不管人們都説你是壞人，並且不論你要的代價是甚麼，我要付給你。"

"那麼你要做甚麼事呢？"女巫走到他跟前，問他。

"我要送走我的靈魂，"年輕的打魚人答道。

女巫的臉色馬上發白，她渾身發抖，把她的臉藏在她的青色大氅裏邊。"漂亮的孩子，漂亮的孩子，"她喃喃地説，"那是一椿可怕的事情啊。"

他搖了搖他的棕色鬈髮，笑起來。他回答道，"我的靈魂對我毫無用處。我不能夠看見它。我不可以觸摸它。我也不認識它。"

"要是我告訴了你，那麼你給我甚麼呢？"女巫用她那美麗的眼睛望着他，問道。

"五個金元，"他説，"還有我的網，我住的樹條編的房子，我用的那隻漆着彩色的船，只要你告訴我怎樣去掉我的靈魂，我就把我所有的東西全給你。"

她嘲弄地笑他，又拿她手裏那枝毒芹去打他。"我能夠把秋天的樹葉變成黃金，"她答道，"只要我肯，我就能把蒼白的月光織成銀子。我所伺候的主人比世界上一切的國王都闊，他的領土有他們全體的那麼大。"

他叫起來："倘使你的代價既不是金子，又不是銀子，那麼我得給你甚麼呢？"

女巫用她那纖細的白手撫摸他的頭髮。"你一定得跟我一塊兒跳舞，漂亮的孩子，"她喃喃地說，一面對他微笑。

"就只有那樣嗎？"年輕的打魚人驚奇地大聲說，他站了起來。

"就只有那樣，"她答道，她又向他微笑。

他說："那麼等到太陽落下去的時候，我們就找一個秘密地方一塊兒跳舞，跳過舞，你就得告訴我，我要知道的那件事。"

她搖她的頭。"等到月亮圓的時候，等到月亮圓的時候，"她喃喃地說。隨後她向四周張望一下，又側耳傾聽一忽兒。一隻青鳥唧唧地叫着從巢裏飛起來，在沙丘上空打圈子，三隻有斑點的小鳥在灰色的野草叢中跳着，發出沙沙的聲響，牠們在低聲講話。此外就只有海浪在沖洗下邊光滑石子的聲音。她便伸出她的手，拉他到她身邊來，把她的乾嘴唇放在他耳邊。她低聲說：

"今天晚上你一定得到山頭來。今天是安息日，'他'要來的。"

年輕的打魚人吃了一驚，他望着她，她露出她的白牙齒笑着。"你說的'他'是甚麼人？"

"你不用管，"她答道。"今晚上你去站在鵝耳櫪樹下等着我來。要是有隻黑狗向着你跑來，你用一枝柳條去打牠，牠就會跑開的。要是有隻貓頭鷹跟你講話，你不要答牠。等到月亮圓的時候，我就會跟你在一塊兒，我們在草地上一塊兒跳舞。"

"可是你肯對我發誓，你一定告訴我，怎樣送走我的靈魂嗎？"他發問道。

她走到大太陽下面去，風微微吹動她的紅頭髮。"我拿山羊蹄子來起誓，"她答道。

"你是女巫裏面最好的，"年輕的打魚人大聲說，"我今晚上一定要跟你在山頭上跳舞。說實話，我倒願意你向我要金要銀呢。不過你要的代價既然是這樣，你就會得到的，因為這只是一件小事。"他向她脫帽，深深地點一個頭，滿心歡喜地跑回城裏去了。

女巫目送着他的背影，等到他不見了的時候她才回到她的洞裏去，她從一個雕花的杉木匣子裏面拿出一面鏡子來放在架上，在架子面前一塊燃紅的木炭上燒起馬鞭草來，於是從煙圈中去望鏡子。過了一忽兒她氣憤地捏緊拳頭。"他應當是我的，"她喃喃地說，"我跟她一樣地好看。"

那天晚上，月亮升起以後，年輕的打魚人便爬到山頂上去，站在鵝耳櫪樹枝下面。圓形的海像一面磨光的金屬的盾似地橫在他的腳下，在小海灣中移動着漁船的影子。一隻大貓頭鷹長着一對硫磺般的黃眼睛，在喚他的名字，可是他並不答應。一條[20] 黑狗向着他跑來，對他狂叫。他用一枝柳條去打牠，狗汪汪地哀號着走開了。

到了半夜女巫們蝙蝠似地從空中飛來了。她們落到地上的時候，馬上叫起來：“呸！這兒有個生人！”她們用鼻子到處嗅着，彼此交談着，又做着暗號。最後那個年輕的女巫來了，她的紅頭髮在空中飄動。她穿一件金線衣裳，上面繡了許多孔雀的眼睛，一頂綠色天鵝絨的小帽戴在她的頭上。

女巫們看見她的時候，她們尖聲叫起來：“他在哪兒？他在哪兒？”但她只是笑了笑，她跑到鵝耳櫪樹那兒，拉起打魚人的手，把他帶到月光裏，開始跳起舞來。

他們不停地轉來轉去，年輕的女巫跳得那麼高，他可以看見她那對深紅色的鞋跟。於是一陣馬蹄聲迎着跳舞的人們衝過來，這是一匹馬快跑的聲音，可是他看不見馬，他害怕起來了。

“更要快，”年輕女巫叫道，她把胳膊挽在他的頸項上，她的氣息熱熱地挨到他的臉。“更要快，更要快！”她叫道，地好像在他的腳下旋轉起來，他覺得頭暈，他忽然感到一種大的恐懼，彷彿有甚麼兇惡的東西在望着他似的，後來他看見在一塊岩石的陰影下面有一個人，可是先前並沒有人在那個地方。

那是一個男人，穿一身黑天鵝絨衣服，是照西班牙樣式剪裁的。他的臉色蒼白得很古怪，可是他的嘴唇卻像一朵驕傲的紅花。他好像很疲倦，身子向後靠着，沒精打采地玩弄着他的短劍的劍柄。在他身旁草地上放着一頂裝飾着羽毛的帽子，還有一副騎馬的手套，鑲着金邊，並且縫了珍珠在上面，設計非常巧妙。一件黑貂皮裏子的短上衣掛在他的肩上，他一雙纖細潔白的手上戴滿了指環，重重的眼皮垂在他的眼睛上。

年輕的打魚人呆呆地望着他，就好像中了魔法似的。後來他們兩個人的眼睛對上了，不管他跳舞到甚麼地方去，他總覺得那個人的眼睛在盯着他。他聽見年輕的女巫在笑，便摟緊了她的腰，帶着她瘋狂地旋轉。

忽然間一條狗在樹林裏叫起來，跳舞的人全停止了，她們兩個兩個地走過去，跪下，吻那個人的手。她們這樣做的時候，小小的微笑便挨到他的驕傲的嘴唇，就像一隻小鳥的翅膀挨着水，使得水發笑一樣。可是他的微笑中含得有輕蔑的意味。他還是不停地望着年輕的打魚人。

"來！我們也去禮拜去，"年輕的女巫悄聲説，她拉着他過去。他忽然有了一個強烈的慾望，願意去做她求他做的事，他便跟着她過去。可是等他走近的時候，他自己也不知道為了甚麼緣故，他在胸上畫了一個十字，並且喚了聖名。

他剛剛這樣做了，女巫們立刻像老鷹似地尖叫起來，飛走了，而那張老是望着他的蒼白臉孔上也起了痛苦的痙攣，那個人走到一個小樹林去，吹起口哨。一匹戴着銀轡頭的小馬跑來接他。他跳上了馬鞍，還回轉頭來憂愁地望望年輕的打魚人。

那個紅頭髮的女巫也想飛走，可是打魚人捉住她的手腕，緊緊地捏着。

"放開我，"她叫道，"讓我走吧。因為你説了不應該説的名字，做了我們不可以看的記號。"

"不，"他答道，"除非你把秘密告訴我，我就不放你走。"

"甚麼秘密呢？"女巫説，她像一頭野貓似地跟他掙扎，一面咬着她那在冒泡沫的嘴唇。

"你知道的，"他回答。

她那草綠色的眼睛被淚水弄暗了，她對打魚人說："你向我要甚麼都可以，只是不要提這個。"

他笑着，把她捏得更緊了。

她看見她跑不掉了，便悄悄地對他說："實在說，我跟海的女兒一樣地好看，我跟那些住在碧海裏的姑娘一樣地漂亮，"她說着便向他獻媚，把她的臉挨在他的臉上。

可是他皺着眉頭把她推開，對她說："要是你不遵守你給我的諾言，我就要把你當做一個假的女巫殺死。"

她的臉立刻變成灰色，像一朵洋蘇木的花一樣，渾身戰抖起來。"好，就那樣吧，"她喃喃地說。"這是你的靈魂，又不是我的。你高興怎樣就怎樣辦吧。"她從她的腰帶裏拿出一把有着綠蛇皮刀柄的小刀來，給了他。

"這東西對我有甚麼用處呢？"他驚奇地向她道。

她沉默了一忽兒，臉上現出了恐怖的表情。隨後她把她垂下的頭髮從前額抹上去，她帶着古怪的微笑對他說："人們所謂身體的影子，並不是身體的影子，卻是靈魂的身體。你把背朝着月亮站在海灘上，從你雙腳的四周切開你的影子，那就是說你的靈魂的身體，你再叫你的靈魂離開你，它就會照你的話做的。"

年輕的打魚人打起顫來。"這是真的嗎？"他低聲說。

"這是真的，我倒寧願不曾告訴你啊，"她大聲說，就抱住他的雙膝哭起來。

他推開她，讓她留在繁茂的草叢中，他把小刀放在腰帶裏，走到了山邊，便爬下去。

他的靈魂在他的身體內喚他，對他說："喂！我跟你同住了這許多年，又做了你的傭人。現在不要把我趕走吧，我對你做過甚麼壞事呢？"

年輕的打魚人笑起來，他答道："你並沒有對我做過甚麼壞事，不過我現在用不着你了。世界大得很，有天堂、也有地獄，還有在這兩者之間的那所昏暗不明的房子。你高興去哪裏就去哪裏，可是不要來麻煩我，因為我的愛人現在在喚我。"

他的靈魂向他苦苦地哀求，但是他並不理它，他只顧一個岩一個岩地跳過去，腳步輕快得像一頭野山羊，最後他到了平地，到了黃沙的海灘。

他站在沙灘上，背朝着月亮，他有着青銅色的四肢和結實的身材，看起來就跟一座希臘人雕塑的像一樣，從海的泡沫裏伸出好些隻雪白的胳膊來招呼他，從海的波浪中站出好些個朦朧的人形來對他行禮。在他的前面躺着他的影子，那就是他的靈魂的身體，在他的後面蜂蜜色的空中掛着一輪明月。

他的靈魂對他說："倘使你真要趕走我的話，你一定得在我走之前給我一顆心。這個世界是殘酷的，把你的心給我一塊兒上路吧。"

他搖搖頭微笑。"要是我把我的心給了你，我拿甚麼去愛我的愛人呢？"他大聲說。

"你存點好心吧，"他的靈魂說，"把你的心給我，這個世界太殘酷了，我害怕。"

"我的心是屬於我的愛人的，"他答道，"你不要耽擱了，走你的！"

"難道我就不應該愛嗎？"他的靈魂問道。

"走你的，因為我用不着你了，"年輕的打魚人不耐煩地叫起來，他拿出那把帶綠蛇皮刀柄的小刀從他雙腳的四周把他的影子切開了，影子站起來就立在他面前，望着他，它的相貌跟他完全一樣。

他向後退，把小刀插進他的腰帶裏去，他感到了恐懼。"走你的，"他喃喃地説，"不要讓我再看見你的臉。"

"不，我們一定要再見的，"靈魂説。它的聲音很低，又好像笛聲一樣，它説話的時候，它的嘴唇彷彿就沒有動似的。

"我們怎麼會再見呢？"年輕的打魚人大聲説。"你不會跟着我到海底下去吧？"

"我每年要到這兒來一次，來喚你，"靈魂説。"也許你會用得着我。"

"我用你來做甚麼呢？"年輕的打魚人大聲説，"不過隨你的便吧，"他説完就鑽進水裏去了，那些半人半魚的海神吹起他們的號角，小人魚便浮上來迎他，伸出她的兩隻胳膊抱住他的頸項，吻他的嘴。

靈魂站在寂寞的海灘上，望着他們。等他們沉到海裏去了以後，它就哭哭啼啼地穿過沼地走了。

一年過完了，靈魂回到海邊來，喚着年輕的打魚人，他從海底浮上來，對它説："你喚我做甚麼？"

靈魂回答道："走近一點，我好跟你講話，因為我看見了好些奇奇怪怪的東西。"

他便走近一點，蹲在淺水裏，用手托着頭靜靜地聽着。

靈魂對他説："我離開你以後，便轉過臉向東方旅行。一切聰明的事物都是從東方來的。我走了六天，在第七天的早晨我到了一座小山下面，那是韃靼人國境內的山。我坐在一棵檉柳樹的蔭下躲避太陽。地是乾的，而且熱得燙人。人們在平原上不斷地來來往往，就像蒼蠅在打磨得很光的銅盤子上面爬來爬去一樣。

"在正午時候，地平線上揚起一股紅沙塵的雲煙來。韃靼人看見了，便張起他們的畫弓，跳上他們的小馬，朝着那兒跑去。女人們尖聲叫着跳進大車裏，躲藏在毛簾子後邊。

"到了黃昏時候，韃靼人回來了，可是他們中間少了五個人，就是回來的人裏面受傷的也不少。他們把馬套在大車上，急急忙忙地趕着車子走了。三隻胡狼從洞裏出來，在後面望着他們。牠們用鼻孔吸了幾口氣，便朝相反的方向走開了。

"在月亮升起來的時候，我看見平原上燃起了營火，便朝那兒走去。一群商人圍着火坐在氈上。他們的駱駝拴在他們後面的椿上，服侍他們的黑奴們正在沙地上搭起熟皮帳篷，還用霸王樹做了高高的圍牆。

"我走近他們的時候，商人中間的頭領站起來，抽出他的刀，問我來幹[21]甚麼。

"我回答說：我是我自己國裏的一個王子，韃靼人要拿我做他們的奴隸，我逃了出來。頭領微微笑了，他指給我看掛在長竹竿上的五個頭顱。

"然後他又問我誰是上帝的先知，我回答他說穆罕默德。

"他聽見了假先知的名字，便深深地鞠躬，拿起我的手，叫我坐在他的身邊。一個黑奴拿木盆盛了一點馬奶給我送來，還拿來一塊烤小羊肉。

"天剛剛亮，我們便動身了。我騎在一匹紅毛駱駝上，在頭領的旁邊慢慢地走着，一個‘跑前站的’擎着一根長槍跑在我們前面。戰士們在兩邊走，騾子馱着商貨跟在後面。這個商隊裏一共有四十匹駱駝，騾子的數目卻有兩個四十。

"我們從韃靼人的國土走進了詛咒月亮的人的國境。我們看見鷹獅在白岩石上看守牠們的黃金，有鱗甲的龍在牠們的洞穴裏酣睡。我們走過山上的時候，大家都不敢吐氣，恐怕雪會落在我們的身上，各人的眼睛上都綁了一條紗帕。我們穿過山谷的時候，矮人們躲在大樹窟窿裏用箭射我們，夜晚我們還聽見野人擂鼓。我們到猴塔的時候，我們在猴子面前放了些果子，牠們便沒有傷害我們。我們到蛇塔的時候，我們用銅碗盛了熱牛奶給蛇喝，蛇便放我們平安地過去。我們在路上有三次到過奧古薩斯河岸邊。我們坐在拴着吹脹了的大皮口袋的木筏上渡過河去。河馬氣沖沖地朝着我們，牠們想把我們弄死。駱駝看見牠們，就打顫。

"每個城的王都向我們徵收過境稅，卻不許我們走進他們的城門。他們從城牆上丟下麵包來給我們，還有小的蜂蜜玉麥糕和大棗餡的細麵餅。每一百個籃子的東西換我們一顆琥珀珠子。

"鄉村裏的人看見我們走近，就在井裏放下毒藥，自己逃到山頂去了。我們同馬加代人打了仗，那種人生下來是老人，卻一年比一年地越長越年輕，長到小孩的時候就死了；我們又同拉克土伊人打了仗，那種人說自己是老虎的兒子，把渾身塗成黃黑兩種顏色；又同奧南特人打了仗，那種人把死人埋在樹頂上，自己卻住在黑洞裏，為的是害怕太陽（那是他們的神）會殺死他們；又同克林尼安人打了仗，那種人崇拜一隻鱷魚，給牠戴上了綠玻璃

耳環，還拿牛油和鮮雞去餵牠；又同長着狗臉的阿加中拜人打了
仗；又同長着馬腳的西班人打了仗，他們跑得比馬還快。我們商
隊裏有三分之一的人戰死了，另外三分之一的人餓死了。剩下的
人都抱怨我，説我給他們帶來了厄運。我從一塊石頭底下捉到一
條有角的毒蛇，讓牠剌我。他們看見我沒有病痛，都害怕了。

"在第四個月，我們到了伊勒爾城。我們走到城外小樹林的
時候，已經是夜晚了，空氣十分悶熱，因為月亮到天蠍宮裏旅行
去了。我們從樹上摘下熟了的石榴，剖開它們喝它們的甜汁。然
後我們躺在氈上等待天明。

"天一亮，我們就站起來，叩城門。城門是用紅銅鑄的，上面
刻着海龍和飛龍。守城人從城垛上看下來，問我們來幹甚麼。商
隊的通譯人説，我們是從敍利亞帶了許多商貨來做生意的。他們
向我們要了幾個人質，然後告訴我們，正午給我們開城門，叫我
們等到那個時候。

"正午他們果然開了城門，我們走進去的時候，人們成群地從
房屋裏跑出來看我們，一個市集通告人吹着海螺到城內各處去通
知。我們站在市場上，黑奴們解開花布包，打開雕花的楓木箱。
等他們做完了他們的事情，商人們便擺出他們的珍奇的貨物來，
有埃及的塗蠟的麻布，有衣索比亞國內來的花布，有推羅的紫色
海綿，有西頓的藍色帷幔，有冰涼的琥珀杯子，有上等的玻璃器
和珍奇的陶器。某一處房屋的屋頂上有一群女人埋下眼光望着我
們。其中有一位戴着一副鍍金的皮面具。

"第一天是僧侶們來跟我們交易，第二天是貴族，第三天是匠
人同奴隸。凡是商人耽擱在這個城裏的時候，他們對待商人的規

矩總是這樣。

"我們在這兒耽擱了一個月，月缺的時候，我覺得無聊，便在城內各處街上閒蕩，我走到了本城神的花園裏面。僧侶們披着黃袍默默地穿過綠樹叢中，在黑色大理石鋪砌的地上有一座玫瑰紅的神廟。門是上過金漆的，上面凸出來燦爛的金鑄的公牛和孔雀。房頂是用海綠色瓷瓦蓋的，伸出的屋簷上掛着小鈴子。每當白鴿飛過的時候，牠們用翅膀打着鈴，叫鈴子叮噹地響起來。

"廟前有一個條紋瑪瑙修的淨水池。我躺在池子旁邊，用我的蒼白的手指摩着那些寬大的樹葉。一個僧侶朝着我走來，站在我背後。他腳上穿着草鞋，一隻是軟蛇皮做的，另一隻用鳥的羽毛做成。他頭上戴一頂黑氈的僧帽，帽上裝飾了一些銀的新月。他的袍子上繡着七道黃色，他鬈曲的頭髮上抹着銻粉。

"過了一忽兒他便跟我講起話來，他問我要甚麼。

"我告訴他我要拜見神。

"僧侶用他那對小小的斜眼睛奇怪地望着我，他說：'神在打獵。'

"我答道：'告訴我，在哪一個林子裏，我要陪他一塊兒跑馬。'

"他用他那又長又尖的指甲理順袍子邊上細軟的流蘇。他喃喃地說：'神在睡覺。'

"我答道：'告訴我，在哪一張牀上，我要去守護他。'

"他大聲說：'神在開宴會。'

"我回答：'倘使酒是甜的，我要和他同飲，倘使酒是苦的，我也要和他同飲。'

"他驚奇地埋下頭，拉着我的手，把我拉起來，領我進廟裏去。

"在第一間屋子裏我看見一尊偶像坐在用東方大明珠鑲邊的碧玉寶座上。這尊偶像是用烏木雕成的，身材跟常人的一樣大小。前額上有一塊紅寶石，濃的油從它的頭髮上滴下來，一直滴到腿上。它的雙腳用新殺的小山羊的血染得鮮紅，腰間束着一根銅帶，帶上嵌了七顆綠柱玉。

"我對那個僧侶説：'這就是神嗎？'他回答我：'這就是神。'

"我大聲喊道：'引我去見神，不然我一定要殺死你。'我摸他的手，他的手立刻就乾癟了。

"僧侶哀求我説：'請主人把他的僕人治好吧，我就要引他見神去。'

"我便吹一口氣到他那隻手上，他的手又長好了，他渾身發顫，就把我領到第二間屋子裏去，我看見一尊偶像立在一朵翡翠的蓮花上面，蓮花四周懸垂了好些大的綠寶石。這尊偶像是用象牙雕成的，身材比常人的大過一倍。前額上有一塊黃玉，胸前塗着沒藥和肉桂末。它一隻手拿着一根彎彎的翡翠王節，另一隻手裏捏着一塊圓圓的水晶。腳上穿的是黃銅的靴子，在它的粗的頸項上套了個透明石膏的圈子。

"我對那個僧侶説：'這就是神嗎？'他回答我説：'這就是神。'

"我大聲喊道：'引我去見神，不然我一定要殺死你。'我摸他的眼睛，他兩隻眼睛都瞎了。

"僧侶哀求我説：'請主人把他的僕人治好吧，我就要引他見神去。'

"我便吹一口氣到他的眼睛上，他那兩隻眼睛立刻就看見了，他又渾身發顫，把我引進第三間屋子，啊！這間屋子裏面並沒有偶像，也沒有任何種類的畫像，就只有一面圓圓的金屬鏡子放在一個石頭祭壇上。

"我對僧侶說：'神在哪兒？'

"他回答我道：'我們並沒有神，就只有您看見的一面鏡子，因為這是"智慧鏡"。它把天上地下的一切的東西都反映出來，只有那個向鏡子裏面看的人的臉它才不反映。它不反映這個，所以向鏡子裏面看的人就可能是聰明的。世間有許多別的鏡子，不過那都是"意見鏡"。只有這個才是"智慧鏡"。有這面鏡子的人甚麼事都知道，沒有一件事情能夠瞞過他。沒有這面鏡子的人就沒有"智慧"。因此它便是神，我們都拜它。'我聽了這番話，朝鏡子裏一看，果然跟他對我說的一樣。

"我做了一件奇怪的事，不過我做的也算不了甚麼，因為我把'智慧鏡'藏了起來，藏在離這個地方一天路程的一個山谷裏面。我只求你允許我再進到你身體裏去，做你的僕人，那麼你就會比一切聰明的人都更聰明，'智慧'也就屬於你的了。我求你允許我進你的身體裏去，那麼你就是世界上最聰明的人了。"

可是年輕的打魚人笑了。"愛比'智慧'好，"他大聲說，"而且小魚人愛我。"

"不，世界上並沒有比'智慧'更好的東西，"靈魂說。

"愛更好，"年輕的打魚人答道，他便沉到海底去了，靈魂哭哭啼啼地穿過沼地走了。

第二年過完了，靈魂又回到海邊來，喚着年輕的打魚人，他從海底浮上來，對它說：“你喚我做甚麼？”

靈魂回答道：“走近一點，我好跟你講話，因為我看見好些奇奇怪怪的東西。”

他便走近一點，蹲在淺水裏，用手托着頭靜靜地聽着。

靈魂對他說：“我離開你以後，我就轉過臉向南方旅行。一切寶貴的東西都是從南方來的。我順着上愛席脫城的大路走了六天，我順着進香人平常走的塵土飛揚的紅色大道走着，第七天的早晨我抬起眼睛，看啊！城就在我的腳下，因為它在山谷裏面。

“這座城有九道門，每一道城門前立着一匹青銅馬，每當貝都因人從山上下來的時候，九匹馬便齊聲長嘶。城牆用銅皮包鑲着，城牆上的守望塔是用黃銅作屋頂的。每一個守望塔中站着一個手裏拿弓的射手。日出的時候他用一根箭敲銅鑼，日落的時候他吹號角。

“我想進城去，守城人攔住我問我是甚麼人。我回答說我是一個回教的僧侶，要到麥加城去，那兒有一幅綠色帳幔，幔上有天使們用銀字繡成的《古蘭經》。他們聽見我的話，充滿了驚奇，便請我進城去。

“城裏就好像是一個商場。你的確應當跟我一塊兒去的。華麗的紙燈籠像許多隻大蝴蝶似地在那些窄狹的街上飄舞。風吹過屋頂的時候，它們一起一落，好像是一些五顏六色的肥皂泡。商人們坐在他們的貨攤前的絲毯上。他們長着筆直的黑鬍子，他們的頭帕用金幣作裝飾，長串的琥珀和刻花桃核在他們的冰涼的手指中間滑來滑去。他們裏面有的人賣楓脂香和甘松香，還有從印度海的島嶼上來的珍奇的香水，濃濃的紅玫瑰油，沒藥和小釘形的丁香。要是有人站住跟他們談話，他們便把一撮一撮的乳香投在炭火盆裏，使四周的空氣變香。我看見一個敘利亞人手裏拿着一根像蘆葦似的細棒。棒頭上升起灰色的煙絲，棒燃着的時候氣味就跟春天裏淡紅扁桃的氣味一樣。有的人賣着上面鑲滿了乳藍色土耳其玉的銀手鐲，和用銅絲串的小珍珠踝環，還有鑲了金座子的老虎爪，和金黃貓（就是豹子）的腳爪，也是鑲了金座子的，還有穿了眼的綠寶石耳環，和中間空的翡翠戒指。從茶館裏傳出來的六弦琴的聲音，抽鴉片煙的人帶了他們蒼白的笑顏望着行人。

"你實在應當跟我一塊兒去的。賣酒的人肩頭扛着黑色大皮簍，在人群中用肘拐擠開路。他們大半都賣'西拉茲酒'，那種酒甜得像蜂蜜一樣。他們用金屬杯子盛着酒賣給顧客，再把玫瑰花瓣鋪在上面。市場裏站着賣水果的，他們賣着各色各樣的水果，熟透的無花果帶着受傷的紫色鮮肉，甜瓜像麝香一般的香，像黃玉一般的黃。香櫞，番石榴，一球一球的白葡萄，圓圓的金紅橘子，橢圓的金綠檸檬。有一次我看見一匹大象走過。牠身上塗着銀朱和薑黃，牠耳朵上戴了個朱紅絲線網子。牠在一個貨攤前面站住，吃起橘子來，那個賣水果的人只是笑着。你想不到他們是多麼古怪的一種民族。他們高興的時候他們到賣鳥人那兒去買一隻養在籠裏的鳥，開籠把鳥放走，這樣他們可以更高興一點；他們不快活的時候，他們用荊棘鞭打他們自己，免得他們的憂愁消滅。

"一天傍晚我遇見幾個黑人抬着一乘沉重的轎子走過商場。轎子是用鍍金的竹子做的，轎杆漆成了朱紅色，上面裝飾着黃銅的孔雀。轎窗上掛着薄薄的紗簾，窗簾上繡着些甲蟲翅膀和小粒珍珠，轎子走過的時候一個臉色蒼白的塞加西亞女人從轎裏往外望，對着我微笑。我跟在後面，黑人們便加快腳步，皺起眉頭來。可是我並不去管它。我覺得我讓一種大的好奇心抓住了。

"最後他們在一所四方形的白屋前面停下來。這所房屋沒有窗戶，就只有一道墓門似的小門。他們放下轎子，用一個銅錘敲了三下門。一個穿綠皮長袍的亞美尼亞人從門洞裏往外張望一下，他看見他們，便把門打開了，還鋪了一張毯子在地上。那個女人走出轎來。她進門去的時候，還回過頭來，再對我一笑。我從沒有見過像這樣蒼白的人。

"月亮出來的時候，我回到那個地方去，找尋那所房屋，可是房屋已經沒有了。我看見這情形，我便知道那個女人是誰，而且為甚麼她向我微笑。

"你確實應當跟我一塊兒去。在'新月節'，年輕的皇帝從他的宮裏出來到廟裏去禱告。他的頭髮和鬍鬚都是用玫瑰花瓣染紅的，他的臉頰上擦了極細的金粉。他的手掌和腳心都用番紅花染成了黃色。

"日出的時候他穿着銀袍從宮裏出來，日落的時候他穿着金袍回去。百姓們都跪在地上把臉藏起來，可是我不這樣做。我站在一個賣棗子的貨攤旁邊等待着。皇帝看見了我，便揚起他那畫過的眉毛，站住了。我靜靜地直立在那兒，也不向他跪拜。百姓們對我的大膽都表示驚訝，都勸我逃出城去。我不理他們。我卻走到那些出賣外教神像的人那兒去，跟那班人坐在一塊兒，那班人由於他們的行業在這兒是受到人們厭惡的。我告訴他們我做過了甚麼事情，他們每個人都給我一個神像，請我離開他們。

　　"當天夜晚我正躺在石榴街那家茶館裏的墊子上面，皇帝的衛士便走進來，把我帶到宮裏去。等我進去以後，他們一道門一道門接連地關上了，並且加了鎖。裏面有一個大院子，四面環繞着一帶拱廊。牆是用白色雪花石膏做的，有些地方嵌着藍色和綠色的花磚。柱子是綠色大理石的，鋪地的是一種桃花色的大理石。我從沒有見過像這樣的東西。

　　"我跨過院子的時候，有兩個戴面紗的女人從露台上望下來，一面在咒罵我。衛士們急急地走着，他們的矛頭在擦磨得光亮的地板上不停地發響。他們打開了一道精緻的象牙門，我便走進一個有七個花壇的帶水的花園了。園裏種的是鬱金香，牛眼菊，銀色點點的蘆薈。一股噴泉在陰暗的空中懸垂着彷彿一根細長的水晶棒。柏樹就像燃過了的火把。在一棵柏樹上有一隻夜鶯在唱歌。

　　"花園的盡頭有一座小小的亭子。我們走近那兒，兩個太監出來迎接我們。他們走起路來，肥胖的身子一直在顫搖，他們用那黃色眼皮的眼睛好奇地望着我。其中的一位把衛士長拉在一邊，小聲在他耳邊說了一些話。另一位太監裝腔作勢地從一個淡紫色琺瑯的橢圓形盒子中拿出些香錠來細嚼着。

　　"過了一忽兒衛士長把衛士們遣散了。衛士們便回到宮裏去，兩個太監慢慢地跟在後面，他們一邊走，一邊從樹上摘下甜的桑果來吃。有一回那個年紀較大的太監回過頭來，懷着惡意地對我微笑。

　　"然後衛士長向我示意，要我走進亭子裏去。我毫不膽怯地走上前，拉起那幅重重的簾子進去了。

"年輕的皇帝躺在染了色的獅皮榻上，手腕上棲着一隻白隼。在他背後站着一個頭戴銅帽的努比亞人，腰以上完全裸着，兩隻穿了洞的耳朵上掛着一副沉重的耳環。榻旁邊一張桌子上放了一把彎彎的大鋼刀。

"皇帝看見我，便皺起眉頭對我説：'你叫甚麼名字？你不知道我是這座城的皇帝嗎？'可是我不回答他。

"他用手指頭指着鋼刀，那個努比亞人拿起它來往前一衝，對着我的身子用力砍下去，刀鋒颼颼地從我身上穿過，但是我沒有受到一點傷。那個人撲倒在地上，他再立起來的時候，他嚇得牙齒直打顫，躲到榻後面去了。

"皇帝馬上跳起來，從武器架上拿起一根長矛，向我擲過來。我接住了它，把矛杆折成兩段。他又用箭射我，可是我舉起手，箭就在半空中停住了。他隨後從一根白皮帶裏抽出一把短劍，刺進努比亞人的咽喉，他害怕努比亞人會説出他丟臉的事情。那個人像一條給人踐踏了的蛇似地把身子猛扭幾下，從他的嘴唇裏冒出紅色的泡沫來。

"那個人一死，皇帝又轉向着我，用一方鑲花邊的紫綢小巾揩去了額上一顆顆亮晃晃的汗珠，對我説：'你是一個我不應當傷害的先知呢，還是一個我不能加害的先知的兒子？我求你今晚上離開我這座城，因為有你在這裏，我就不再是一城之主了。'

"我回答他道：'把你的財寶分我一半，我就走。把你的財寶分一半給我，我就走開。'

"他拿起我的手，把我引進花園裏去。衛士長看見我，他吃了一驚。太監們看見我，他們的膝頭打起顫來，他們嚇得跪倒在地上。

"宮裏有一間屋子，有着八面牆壁，都是紅雲斑石造的，天花板上包了一層銅皮，懸着一些燈。皇帝伸手去摸某一面牆，那面牆就開了，我們走了進去，裏面是一條長廊，廊上燃了許多支火炬。廊兩旁都是壁龕，每個龕裏放着大酒缸，缸裏銀元裝得滿滿的。我們到了走廊中央的一段，皇帝說了句平時不可以說的話，一道裝得有暗彈簧的花崗石門馬上彈開了，他用手遮住他的臉，恐怕會弄花他的眼睛。

"你不會相信這是個多麼奇妙的地方。大的龜殼裏滿滿的裝着珍珠，中間空的大型月長石內堆滿了紅寶石。黃金藏在象皮箱中，金粉盛在皮酒瓶內。還有貓眼石和青玉，貓眼石放在水晶杯裏，青玉盛在翡翠杯內。圓圓的綠柱玉整整齊齊地排列在薄薄的象牙碟子上面，一個角落裏堆着些綢口袋，有的袋裏裝滿綠松石，有的袋裏滿是綠玉。象牙角杯中滿滿堆着紫玉英，黃銅角杯中滿滿堆着玉髓和紅玉髓。杉木柱子上掛着成串的黃山貓石。扁平的橢圓形盾牌上堆着紅玉，有的像葡萄酒的顏色，有的卻跟草的顏色一樣。我對你說了這許多，還不過是那兒有的十分之一呢。

"皇帝把手從臉上拿開，他對我說：'這是我的寶庫，這裏面有的東西一半歸你，就照我答應你的那樣辦。我還要送給你駱駝和趕駱駝的人，他們會聽你的吩咐，把你那份財寶帶到你想去的任何地方。這件事情今晚上就要辦好，因為我不願意讓太陽（那是我的父親）看見我的城裏有一個我不能殺死的人。'

"可是我答道：'這兒的黃金是你的，白銀也是你的，貴重的珠寶和值錢的東西都是你的。至於我呢，這些東西我一點兒也用不着。你的東西我甚麼也不要，我只要你手指上戴的那個小指

環。’

　　"皇帝皺起了眉頭。他喊着説：‘這不過是一個鉛指環，它沒有一點兒價值。所以還是請你帶着你那一半財寶離開我這座城吧。’

　　"我答道：‘不，我甚麼都不要，就只要那個鉛指環，因為我知道指環裏面寫得有甚麼，而且那有甚麼用處。’

　　"皇帝渾身打顫，向我哀求，他説：‘你把所有的財寶全拿去，快離開我這座城吧。我那一半現在也歸你。’

　　"我做了一件奇怪的事，不過我做的也算不了甚麼，因為我把‘財富指環’藏起來，藏在離這個地方一天路程的一個洞裏面。離這個地方只有一天的路程，它等着你去呢。誰得到這個指環，他就比世界上所有的國王都有錢。所以請你來把它拿去，那麼世界上的財富就是你的了。"

　　可是年輕的打魚人笑了。"愛比‘財富’好，"他大聲説，"而且小人魚愛我。"

　　"不，世界上並沒有比‘財富’更好的東西，"靈魂説。

　　"愛更好，"年輕的打魚人答道，他便沉到海底去了，靈魂哭哭啼啼地穿過沼地走了。

　　第三年過完了，靈魂又回到海邊來，喚着年輕的打魚人，他從海底浮上來對它説："你喚我做甚麼？"

　　靈魂回答道："走近一點，我好跟你講話，因為我看見了好些奇奇怪怪的東西。"

　　他便走近一點，蹲在淺水裏，用手托着頭靜靜地聽着。

　　靈魂對他説："在我所知道的一個城市裏，河邊上有一家客棧。我同水手們一塊兒坐在那兒，他們喝兩種顏色的葡萄酒，吃大麥麵包，還有和着醋放在桂葉裏的小鹹魚。我們正坐着取樂的時候，從外面進來一個老年人，他肩上搭了一幅皮氈，手中拿一張琴，琴上有兩個琥珀角。他把氈子鋪在地板上，用‘弦撥’彈着琴弦，一個戴面網的少女馬上跑進客棧，在我們面前跳起舞來。她戴的是紗面網，但是她卻光着雙腳。她的雙腳是光着的，它們在氈子上跳來跳去，好像一對小白鴿似的。我從沒有看見過像這樣美好的東西，並且她在那兒跳舞的城市離這個地方只有一天的路程。”

年輕的打魚人聽見了他靈魂的話，便想起來小人魚沒有腳，不能夠跳舞。於是一個大的慾望把他抓住了，他對自己說：“只有一天的路程，我能夠回到我愛人身邊的，”他笑了，便在淺水裏站起來，大步向岸上走去。

他到了岸上的乾地，又笑了，向着他的靈魂伸出了兩隻胳膊。他的靈魂快樂地大叫一聲，跑過來迎接他，進到他的身體裏面，年輕的打魚人便看見他面前沙灘上現出他身體的影子，那就是他靈魂的身體。

他的靈魂對他說：“我們不要耽擱了，快到那兒去吧，因為海神會妒忌，袖們又有不少的怪物可以聽袖們指揮的。”

他們便急急地走着，整個晚上他們在月亮下面趕路，第二天他們整天在太陽下面走，當天傍晚，他們到了一個城市。

年輕的打魚人對他的靈魂說：“你對我講的她就在這座城裏跳舞嗎？”

他的靈魂回答他說："不是這座城，是另外一座。不過我們還是進去看看吧。"

他們便走進城去，穿過一些街道，他們走過珠寶商街的時候，年輕的打魚人看見一個貨攤上擺着一隻漂亮的銀杯。他的靈魂對他說："拿起那個銀杯藏起來。"

他便拿起銀杯藏在他的袍子的褶縫裏，他們連忙走出城去。

他們離開城走了一里格路以後，年輕的打魚人皺起眉頭，把杯子扔掉了，對他的靈魂說："你為甚麼叫我拿這個杯子藏起來呢？這是一件壞事啊！"

可是他的靈魂回答他說："安靜點，安靜點。"

第二天傍晚他們到了一個城市，年輕的打魚人對他的靈魂說："你對我講的她就在這座城裏跳舞嗎？"

他的靈魂回答他說："不是這座城，是另外一座。不過我們還是進去看看吧。"

他們便走進城去，穿過一些街道，他們走過草鞋商街的時候，年輕的打魚人看見一個小孩站在水缸旁邊。他的靈魂對他說："打那個小孩。"他便動手打小孩把小孩打哭了，他們連忙走出城去。

他們離開城走了一里格路以後，年輕的打魚人生起氣來，對他的靈魂說："你為甚麼叫我打小孩呢？這是一件壞事啊！"

可是他的靈魂回答他說："安靜點，安靜點。"

第三天傍晚他們到了一個城市，年輕的打魚人對他的靈魂說："你對我講的她就在這座城裏跳舞嗎？"

他的靈魂答道："也許就在這座城裏，那麼我們進去吧。"

他們便走進城去，穿過一些街道，可是年輕的打魚人始終找不到那條河，也找不到河邊的客棧。城裏的人都張大眼睛好奇地望着他，他害怕起來，便對他的靈魂說：「我們走吧，那個用一雙小白腳跳舞的她並不在這兒。」

可是他的靈魂回答說：「不，我們住下來吧，因為夜太黑，路上又有強盜。」

他便在市場裏坐下來休息，過了一忽兒，來了一個戴頭巾的商人，身上披一件韃靼布的斗篷，打着一個牛角燈籠，吊在一根有節的蘆杆頭上。商人對他說：「你為甚麼還坐在市場上呢，你不看見貨攤都收了，東西也都打好包了！」

年輕的打魚人回答他說：「我在這座城裏找不到一家客棧，我也沒有一個親戚可以留我住宿。」

「我們不都是親戚嗎？」商人說。「不是都由一個上帝造出來的嗎？那麼你跟我來吧，我有一間客房。」

年輕的打魚人便站起來，跟着商人到他家去了。他穿過了一個石榴園進到屋裏，商人用一個銅盤盛了玫瑰香水來讓他洗手，又送來熟的甜瓜給他解渴，後來還給他端來一碗米飯和一塊烤小山羊肉。

他吃完以後，商人就引他進客房裏去，請他安睡休息。年輕的打魚人謝了主人，並且吻了商人手上戴的指環，隨後就倒在染了色的山羊毛毯上面。他拿一幅黑羔毛被子蓋好身子，便呼呼地睡着了。

到了天亮前三點鐘，還是黑夜的時候，他的靈魂喚醒了他，對他說：「起來，到商人的屋子裏去，就到他睡覺的屋子裏去，殺死他，拿走他的金子，因為我們需要它。"

年輕的打魚人便起來，爬到商人的房間裏去。商人的腳上面放着一把彎刀，商人身邊那個盤子裏有九包金子。他伸出手去拿刀，他的手剛剛挨到刀，商人便驚醒了，馬上跳起來，自己抓住刀，對年輕的打魚人喊着說："難道你以怨報德，我好心款待你，你反以流血來報答嗎？"

年輕的打魚人聽到他的靈魂對他說："揍他，"他把商人打得暈了過去，便拿起九包金子，連忙穿過石榴園逃走了。他朝着晨星的方向走去。

他們離開城走了一里格路以後，年輕的打魚人便打着他自己的胸膛，對他的靈魂說："為甚麼你教我殺那個商人，拿走他的金子呢？你實在很壞。"

可是他的靈魂回答他說："安靜點，安靜點。"

"不，"年輕的打魚人大聲說，"我不能夠安靜，因為你教我做過的那一切的事情我都恨。連你我也恨，我要你告訴我你為甚麼要教我那樣做法。"

他的靈魂回答他說："你從前把我送到世界上去的時候，你並沒有給我一顆心，所以我學會了做那一切的事，並且愛那一切的事。"

"你說甚麼？"年輕的打魚人喃喃地說。

"你知道的，"他的靈魂回答道，"你知道得很清楚。難道你忘記了你沒有給過我一顆心嗎？我不相信。所以你不要擔心你自己，也不要擔心我，你放心吧，世間並沒有你去不掉的痛苦，也沒有你享不到的快樂。"

年輕的打魚人聽到這些話以後，他渾身發顫，對他的靈魂說："不，是你壞，你使我忘記了我的愛人，你用種種的誘惑來引誘我，你使我的腳踏上罪惡的路。"

他的靈魂回答他："你沒有忘記吧：你把我送到世界上去的時候，你並沒有給我一顆心啊！來，我們到另一座城去，作樂去，我們還有九包金子呢！"

年輕的打魚人拿起九包金子，扔在地下，用腳踩着。

"不，"他叫道，"我用不着你，我再也不要跟你一塊兒去甚麼地方。我上次既然把你送走過，現在我還是要像那樣地送走你，因為你對我沒有好處。"他便轉過身把背朝着月亮，拿出帶綠蛇皮刀柄的小刀來，想把他身體的影子，也就是他靈魂的身體從他雙腳的四周切開。

可是他的靈魂並不動一下離開他一點兒，也不理會他的吩咐，卻對他說："那個女巫教給你的魔法再也不靈了。因為我不能離開你，你也不能把我趕走。一個人一輩子只可以把他靈魂送走一次，可是誰把他的靈魂送走以後又收了回來，就得永遠留住它，這是他的懲罰，也是他的報酬。"

年輕的打魚人臉色變白，捏緊拳頭，叫起來："她沒有把這一點告訴我，真是個騙人的女巫。"

"不，"他的靈魂答道，"可是她對於她所禮拜的'他'卻是很忠實的，她要永遠做'他'的僕人。"

年輕的打魚人知道他不能夠再去掉他的靈魂，並且那還是一個壞的靈魂，又得永遠跟他在一塊兒，他便倒在地上傷心地哭起來。

到了天亮以後，年輕的打魚人又站起來，對他的靈魂說："我要綁住我的手，免得我會照你的吩咐做事；我要閉緊我的嘴唇，免得我會說你要說的話；我要回到我所愛的她住的地方去。我甚至要回到海裏去，回到她平常在那兒唱歌的小海灣去，我要喚她，告訴她我做過的壞事和你對我做過的壞事。"

他的靈魂又誘惑他，說："誰是你的愛人，你得回到她那兒去？世界上有很多比她更漂亮的。薩馬利斯的舞女能學各種鳥獸的樣子跳舞。她們的腳用鳳仙花染上了紅色，她們的手裏捏着小小的銅鈴。她們一邊跳舞一邊笑，她們的笑聲跟水的笑聲一樣清朗。跟我來，我引你去看她們。你為着甚麼要擔心罪惡的事呢？難道美味可口的東西不是做來給人吃的嗎？難道味道甘美的飲料裏面就有毒藥嗎？你不要焦心了，跟我一塊兒到另一座城去。就在這裏附近有一座小城。城裏有一個百合樹的花園。在這個可愛的花園裏養着一些白孔雀和藍胸脯的孔雀。牠們向着太陽開屏的時候，那尾巴就像象牙的圓盤和鍍金的圓盤一樣。那個餵牠們的女人常常跳舞給牠們開心，她有時候用手跳，有時候用腳跳。她的眼睛染上了銻色，她的鼻孔形狀像燕子的翅膀。有一個鼻孔裏用一根小鈎子掛着一朵珍珠雕成的花。她一邊跳舞一邊笑，腳踝上一對銀鐲像銀鈴似地叮噹響着。所以你不要再焦心了，跟我一起到這座城裏去吧。"

可是年輕的打魚人並不答話，卻用沉默的封條封住他的嘴唇，用結實的繩子綁住他的雙手，動身回到他來的地方去，甚至走到他愛人平常在那兒唱歌的小海灣去。他的靈魂一路上不停地引誘他，可是他總不理睬，他也不肯去做它要他做的任何一件壞事；在他的心裏愛的力量太大了！

他到了海邊，把手上的繩子解開，將嘴上沉默的封條撕去，他喚起小人魚來。可是她並沒有應聲上來會他。雖然他喚了她一整天，求她出來，卻始終看不到她。

他的靈魂嘲笑他，對他說："你實在沒有從你愛人那兒得到多少快樂。你就像那個在天旱時候往漏船裏倒水的人。你把你所有的全給掉了，卻沒有得到一點兒報酬。你還不如跟我去，因為我知道歡樂谷在甚麼地方，那兒有的是些甚麼東西。"

可是年輕的打魚人並不理睬他的靈魂，他在一個岩石縫隙裏自己用樹條編造了一所房屋，在那裏住了一年。他每天早晨喚着人魚，每天正午又喚她，到了晚上他又叫她的名字。可是她始終沒有從海裏出來會過他，他在海裏任何地方都找不到她，雖然他在洞穴裏，在淺水中，在海潮的漩渦裏，在海底的井內到處找尋她，都不見她的蹤跡。

他的靈魂不斷地拿惡來引誘他，老是在他耳邊悄悄地講些可怕的事情。可是這對他並沒有效力，他的愛的力量太大了。

這一年過去了，靈魂暗暗地想道："我用了惡引誘過我的主人，可是他的愛比我強。現在我要用善去引誘他，他也許會跟着我走的。"

他就對年輕的打魚人說："我對你講過世界上的快樂，可是你不肯聽我。現在讓我告訴你世界上的痛苦，也許你要聽的就是這個。說句老實話，痛苦是這個世界的主人，沒有一個人能夠從它的網裏逃出來。有的人沒有衣服，有的人缺少麵包。有的寡婦穿紫袍，有的寡婦穿破衣。大痳瘋病人在沼地上走來走去，他們對彼此都很殘酷。討飯的在大路上來來往往，他們的乞食袋常常是空的。在各個城市大街小巷裏走着的是饑荒,坐在每道城門口的是瘟疫。來,讓我們去,設法改善這些事情,使它們不再發生。既然你愛人不肯應着你的喚聲出來,為甚麼你還老是留在這兒喚她呢?愛究竟是甚麼,你得為它付出這樣高的代價?"

可是年輕的打魚人並不答話,他的愛的力量太大了。他每天早晨喚着人魚,每天正午又喚她,到了晚上他又叫她的名字。可是她始終沒有從海裏出來會過他,他在海裏任何地方都找不到她,雖然他在海中的河裏,在浪下的谷裏,在被黑夜染成紫色的海裏,在被黎明塗上灰色的海裏到處找尋她,都不見她的蹤迹。

第二年又過去了,有天晚上年輕的打魚人孤單地坐在樹條房子裏的時候,他的靈魂對他說:"喂!我用惡引誘過你,我又用善引誘過你,可是你的愛比我更強。所以我不再引誘你了,不過我求你允許我進到你心中去,那麼我就可以像從前那樣跟你成為一體了。"

"你當然可以進來,"年輕的打魚人說,"因為你沒有一顆心在世界上飄流的那些日子裏,你一定吃了不少的苦了。"

"哎呀!"他的靈魂叫起來,"我找不到地方進去呢,你的心讓愛纏得那麼緊緊的。"

"可是我倒願意我能夠給你幫忙,"年輕的打魚人說。

他說話的時候,海裏起了很大的一聲哀叫,跟人魚族死的時候人們聽見的叫聲完全一樣。年輕的打魚人跳起來,走出他的樹條房子,跑到海灘去。黑色的浪濤急急地向岸上打來,載着一個比銀子還要白的東西。它跟浪頭一樣白,並且在海濤上面飄飄蕩蕩像一朵花似的。浪頭把它從浪濤中拿走,泡沫又把它從浪頭上拿開，後來是海岸接受了它，於是年輕的打魚人看見在他的腳下躺着小人魚的身體。她躺在他的腳下死了。

他哭得像一個痛苦萬分的人，撲倒在她身邊，他吻着她那冰冷的紅唇，撥弄着她頭髮上打濕了的琥珀。他撲倒在沙灘上，躺在她旁邊，他哭得像一個因快樂而打顫的人，他用他兩隻褐色的胳膊把她緊緊抱在懷裏。她那兩片嘴唇已經冷了，可是他仍然吻着它們。她頭髮上的蜜是鹹的，可是他仍然帶着痛苦的快樂去嚐它。他吻着緊閉的眼皮，她眼角上掛的浪沫還不及他的眼淚鹹。

他對着死屍懺悔起來。他把他的經歷的苦酒傾倒在她的耳朵裏。他把她兩隻小小的手挽在他的頸項上，他用他的手指頭去摸她那細細的咽喉管。他的快樂越來越苦了，他的痛苦裏又充滿了奇異的歡快。

黑色的海水愈來愈近，白色的泡沫像大痲瘋病人似地呻吟着。海水用它的泡沫的白爪來抓海岸。從海王的宮裏又響起了哀叫聲，遠遠地在海上半人半魚的海神們的號螺吹出嘶澀的聲音來。

"快逃開，"他的靈魂說，"海水越來越近了，要是你還在這兒耽擱的話，它會弄死你的。快逃開，我實在害怕，我知道因為你的愛太大了，你的心便攔住我不讓我進去。快逃到一個安全的地方去。你一定不會不給我一顆心就送我到另一個世界去吧？"

可是年輕的打魚人並沒有聽他靈魂的話，卻只顧喚着小人魚說："愛比'智慧'更好，比'財富'更寶貴，比人間女兒們的腳更漂亮。火不能燒毀它，水不能淹沒它。我在天明時候喚你，你不來會我。月亮聽見了你的名字，可是你也沒有理睬我。因為我不該離開了你，我跑開了害了我自己。可是你的愛永遠跟我在一塊兒，它永遠是有力的，沒有甚麼能夠勝過它，不管我面對着惡也好，面對着善也好。現在你死了，我一定要跟你一塊兒死。"

他的靈魂要求他走開，可是他不肯，他的愛太大了。海水逐漸逼近，它要用它的浪蓋住他，他知道他的死期就在目前的時候，他瘋狂地吻着人魚的冰冷的嘴唇，他的那顆心碎了。他的心因為充滿了愛而碎裂的時候，靈魂就找到一個入口進去了，它好像以前一樣地跟他成為一體了。海用浪蓋住了年輕的打魚人。

早晨神父出去給海祝福，因為海騷動得厲害。僧侶，樂手，拿蠟燭的，搖香爐的，還有一大堆人跟着他一塊兒去。

神父到了海邊，看見年輕的打魚人躺在浪頭上淹死了，懷裏還抱着小人魚的屍體。他便皺起眉頭往後退。他畫了一個十字架符號以後，就高聲叫着說："我不要祝福海，也不要祝福海裏的任何東西。人魚族是該詛咒的，凡是跟人魚族有來往有關係的人都是該詛咒的。至於他呢，他為了愛情的緣故離開了上帝，所以他現在同他那個被上帝的裁判殺死了的情婦一塊兒躺在這兒，搬開他的身體同他的情婦的身體，把它們埋在漂洗工地的角上，上面不要插甚麼標牌，也不要做甚麼記號，免得有一個人知道他們的安息地方。因為他們在生是該詛咒的，他們死後也是該詛咒的。"

人們照着他吩咐的做了，漂洗工地的角上，沒有長着一棵香草的地方，他們就在那兒挖了一個深的坑，把死屍放進裏面去。

第三年又過去了，在一個祭日，神父走到禮拜堂去，他要給人們看見主的傷痛，他要向他們講解上帝的憤怒。

他穿好法衣，走進禮拜堂，在祭壇前行禮的時候，他看見祭壇上放滿了他從未見過的奇怪的鮮花。這些花看起來很奇怪，而且有着異樣的美，它們的美使他心亂，它們的氣味在他的鼻孔裏聞着很香。他覺得很快樂，卻不知道他為甚麼快樂。

他打開了聖龕，在裏面的聖餅台前焚了香，把美麗的聖餅拿給人們看，然後又將它在帳幔後面藏起來。他開始對人們講話，他想對他們講解上帝的憤怒。可是那些白花的美使他心亂，它們的氣味在他的鼻孔裏聞着很香，另一種話到他的嘴唇來了，他講解的不是上帝的憤怒，卻是那個叫做"愛"的上帝。為甚麼他這樣説，他不知道。

神父説完了他的話，人們就哭了，他回到聖器所裏，眼中充滿了淚水。執事們進來，給他脱法衣，給他脱下了白麻布法衣，解下腰帶、飾帶和聖帶。他站在那裏就像在夢中似的。

他們給他脱下了法衣以後，他望着他們説："壇上放的是甚麼花，它們從哪兒來的？"

他們回答他："我們説不出它們是甚麼花，不過它們是從漂洗工地的角上採來的。"神父渾身發顫。他回到了自己的住處，開始禱告起來。

早晨，天剛剛發亮，他便同僧侶，樂手，拿蠟燭的，搖香爐的，還有一大群人走到海邊，祝福了海，以及海中的一切野東西。他也祝福了牧神和森林中跳舞的小東西，以及從樹葉縫中偷偷張望的亮眼睛的東西。在上帝的世界中所有的東西他都祝福了，人們充滿了快樂和驚奇。可是從此在漂洗工地的角上再也長不出任何一種鮮花來，那個地方仍然成了從前那樣的不毛地。人魚們也不再像平日那樣到這個海灣裏來，因為他們都到海中別的地方去了。

星孩

從前有一天晚上兩個窮樵夫正穿過一個大松林走回家去。這是冬天，又是一個非常寒冷的夜晚。地上雪鋪得很厚，樹枝上也是一樣地積了雪。他們走過的時候，兩旁的小樹枝接連地被霜折斷；他們走到瀑布跟前，她也靜靜地懸在空中，因為她已經被冰王吻過了。

這個夜晚真冷得厲害，連鳥獸也不知道該怎樣保護自己。

狼夾着尾巴從矮林中一顛一跛地走出來，嗥道："唔！真是很怪的天氣。為甚麼政府不想個辦法？"

"啾！啾！啾！"綠梅花雀叫道，"衰老的大地死了，人們用白壽衣把她收殮了。"

"大地要出嫁了，這是她的結婚禮服，"斑鳩在悄悄地說。他們的小紅腳凍傷得厲害，可是他們覺得對這個情景應當取一種帶浪漫性的看法。

"胡說！"狼咆哮道，"我告訴你們，這全是政府的錯，要是你們不相信我的話，我就要吃掉你們。"狼有着非常實際的頭腦，他永遠不愁沒有個好的理由。

“啊，至於我呢，”啄木鳥是一個天生的哲學家，他插嘴道，“我不喜歡這種原子論的解釋。一件事要是怎樣的，它便是怎樣的，現在天氣太冷了。”

天氣的確太冷。住在高高的杉樹上的小松鼠們接連擦着彼此的鼻子取暖，兔子們在他們洞裏縮着身子，不敢朝門外看一眼！惟一似乎喜歡這種天氣的就是大角鴞。他們的羽毛讓白霜凍得很硬，可是他們並不介意，他們骨碌碌地轉動他們又黃又大的眼睛，隔着樹互相呼喚着：“吐毀特！吐夥！吐毀特！吐夥！[22] 天氣多好啊！”

兩個樵夫只顧向前走着，一路上起勁地向他們的手指頭吹氣，用他們笨重的有鐵釘的靴子在雪塊上亂踏。有一回他們陷進一個雪坑裏去，爬起來的時候，他們一身白得就像正在磨麵的磨麵師；又有一回他們在堅硬光滑的冰（沼地上的水凍成了冰）上失了腳，他們的柴捆跌散了，他們不得不拾起來綁在一塊兒；還有一回他們覺得已經迷了路，害怕得不得了，因為他們知道雪對待那些睡在她懷裏的人素來是很殘忍的。不過他們信任那位守護着一切出門人的好聖馬丁，便順着原路退回去；他們小心地下着腳步，後來終於走到了樹林口，看見下面山谷裏遠遠地閃着他們村子的燈光。

他們看見自己出了險，高興得不得了，便大聲笑起來，在他們眼裏大地彷彿是一朵銀花，月亮就像一朵金花。

然而他們笑過以後，就憂愁起來了，他們想起了自己的貧窮，一個樵夫便對他的伙伴說：“我們為甚麼還要高興呢，既然生活偏向有錢人，不是向着像我們這樣的窮人？我們還不如凍死在林子裏，或者讓野獸抓住我們來弄死。」

「真的，」他的伙伴答道，「有的人享受得很多，有的人享受得很少。不平已經把世界分掉了，可是除了憂愁以外，沒有一件東西是分配得平均的。」

可是他們正在互相悲歎他們的貧苦的時候，一件奇怪的事情發生了。從天上掉下一顆很亮、很美的星來。它從別的星星旁邊經過，溜下了天邊，他們驚奇地望着它，他們覺得它好像落在小羊圈旁邊大約有一箭之遠的一叢柳樹後面。

「呀！哪個找到它就可以得到一罐金子！」他們叫道，便跑起來，因為他們太想金子了。

一個樵夫比他的伙伴跑得快，他追過了那個人，從柳樹叢中穿出去，到了柳樹外面，看呀！白雪上面的確有一個金的東西。他連忙跑過去，到它跟前，彎下身子，用兩隻手去摸它，這是一件精緻地繡着許多星星的金線斗篷，疊成了許多褶子。他大聲對他的伙伴說他已經找到天上掉下來的寶物了，等他的伙伴走近，他們就在雪中坐下來，打開斗篷的褶子，準備把金子拿來平分。可是啊喲！那裏面沒有金，也沒有銀，的確，連任何寶物都沒有，只有一個睡着的嬰孩。

他們中間的一個人便說：「我們的希望就只得着這個痛苦的收場，我們的運氣實在不好，一個小孩對男人有甚麼好處呢？我們還是把他丟在這兒，走我們的路吧。你我都是窮人，又還有我們自己的孩子，我們不應當把我們孩子的飲食分給別人。」

可是另一個人卻回答道：「不，把這個小孩丟在這兒，讓他凍死在雪裏，會是一件壞事情，雖然我跟你一樣窮，還要養活好幾口人，鍋子裏的東西又很少，可是我要把他帶回家去，我的妻子會照應他的。"

他很慈愛地抱起小孩來，用斗篷裹住小孩的身子，免得小孩受寒，隨後便走下山回到村子裏去，他的傻氣和他的軟心腸叫他的伙伴非常驚奇。

他們到了村子裏，他伙伴對他説："你得了小孩，那麼把斗篷給我吧，我們應當平分的。"

可是他回答："不，因為斗篷既不是我的，也不是你的，它是小孩一個人的。"他便跟他的朋友告了別，走到自己家裏去了。他敲着門。

他的妻子開了門，看見丈夫平安回來了，她摟住他的頸項接了吻，又把他背上的柴捆放下來，還刷去他靴子上的雪，然後要他進屋去。

可是他對她説："我在林子裏找到一個東西，我把它帶了回來要你照應。"他站在門外不進來。

"是甚麼呢？"她大聲問。"快拿給我看，我們家裏空空的，我們正需要很多的東西。"

他拉開斗篷，把睡着的小孩給她看了。

"啊喲，丈夫啊！"她喃喃地説，"難道我們自己的小孩不夠多，你還得帶一個換來的孩子到我們家裏來嗎？誰知道他會不會給我們招來厄運呢？我們又用甚麼來養他呢？"她對他生氣了。

"可是這是一個星孩啊，"他答道，他便把他怎樣奇怪地找到那個小孩的經過情形對她講了。

可是她還不肯息怒，她卻挖苦他，生氣地講話，並且嚷着：
"我們自己的小孩都吃不飽，難道還要養別人的小孩嗎？誰來照
應我們呢？誰又來給我們飲食吃呢？"

　　"不要這樣，上帝連麻雀也要照應的，上帝連牠們也養，"他
答道。

　　"麻雀在冬天不是也常常餓死嗎？"她問道。"現在不就是冬
天？"

　　她丈夫並不回答，卻站在門外不進來。

　　一股冷風從樹林裏吹進門內，她打了一個寒慄，顫抖起來。
她就對他說："你不把門關上嗎？一股冷風吹進屋裏來了，我冷
啊。"

　　"吹進硬心腸人家裏來的風不總是冷風嗎？"他反問道。妻子
並不回答，卻更靠近爐火了。

　　過了一忽兒，她掉過頭去看他，她眼裏充滿了淚水。他連忙
走進來，把孩子放在她的懷裏。她吻着孩子，把他放到一張小牀
上去，他們自己最小的孩子就睡在那兒。第二天樵夫拿開那件珍
奇的金斗篷，放進一個大櫃子去，他妻子也取下孩子頸項上戴的
琥珀項鏈放進櫃子裏。

　　星孩便跟樵夫的孩子們一塊兒養育起來，在同一張食桌上
吃飯，和他們在一處玩。他一年比一年地長得更好看，村子裏所
有的人都非常驚奇：怎麼大家都是黑色皮膚，黑頭髮，單單他一
個人又白又嬌嫩，像上等的象牙一樣，他的鬈髮又像黃水仙的花
環。他的嘴唇像紅色花瓣，他的眼睛像清水河畔的紫羅蘭，他的
身體像還沒有人來割過的田地上的水仙。

可是他的美貌給他帶來了禍害。因為他變得驕傲、殘酷而自私了。他看不起樵夫的兒女，也看不起村子裏別的小孩，說他們出身微賤，而他自己卻是很高貴的，從一顆星生出來的，他自命為他們的主子，稱他們做他的傭人。他毫不憐惜窮人，對瞎子或別的有殘疾的，有任何病苦的人，他沒有絲毫的同情心，他反而向他們丟石頭，把他們趕到大路上去，吩咐他們到別處去討飯。因此在他那個村子裏除了無賴漢外，就再沒有人第二次來求賙濟的。的確他迷戀美，瞧不起孱弱和醜陋的人，拿他們開玩笑；他愛他自己，在夏天風靜的時候，他會躺在牧師的果園內水井旁邊，望着水上映出的他自己的漂亮臉孔，並且因為他的美貌高興得笑起來。

樵夫夫婦兩人常常責備他，說：＂我們並沒有像你對待孤苦無助的人那樣地對待過你。為甚麼你對一切需要憐憫的人總是這麼殘酷呢？＂

老牧師常常找他去，想教會他愛一切生物，對他說：＂蒼蠅是你的弟兄。你不要害牠。那些在林子裏飛來飛去的野鳥有牠們的自由。不要圖你高興就把牠們捉來。蛇蜥和鼴鼠都是上帝造的，各有各的地位。你是誰，怎麼可以給上帝的世界帶來痛苦呢？就連耕田的馬、牛也知道讚美上帝的。＂

可是星孩並不注意他們的話，卻做出不高興和藐視的樣子，走開去找他那些同伴，又去領導他們。他的同伴都服從他，因為他長得很美，而且腳步輕快，會跳舞，會吹笛，會弄音樂。不管星孩引他們到甚麼地方，他們都跟他去；不管星孩吩咐他們做甚麼事，他們都做。他用一根尖的蘆葦刺進鼴鼠的矇矓眼睛裏的時候，他們都笑了；他拿石子去打大痲瘋病人的時候，他們也笑了。在無論甚麼事情上面他都支配他們，他們的心腸也變硬了，就跟他的完全一樣。

有一天一個窮苦的討飯女人走進村子裏來。她一身衣服破爛不堪，她的腳讓崎嶇不平的道路弄得血淋淋的，她的情形十分悲慘，她走乏了，坐在一棵栗子樹下休息。

可是星孩看見她，便對他的同伴們說："看啊！一個骯髒的討飯女人坐在那棵好看的綠葉子樹下面。來，我們把她趕走，她太醜、太難看了。"

他便走近她，朝着她丟石子，嘲笑她，她帶着驚恐的眼光看他，她目不轉睛地望着他。樵夫正在近旁一個草料場裏砍木頭，看見了星孩的行為，便跑過去責備他，對他說："你實在殘忍，沒有一點慈悲心，這個可憐的女人對你做了甚麼壞事情，你要這樣待她呢？"

星孩氣得一張臉通紅，頓着腳說："你是甚麼人，敢來管我的行動？我不是你的兒子，不要聽你的吩咐。"

"你說的是真話，"樵夫答道，"不過我在林子裏找到你的時候，我對你也動過憐憫心的。"

女人聽見這句話，大叫一聲，就暈倒了。樵夫把她抱進他家裏去，讓他的妻子看護她，等她清醒過來了，他們又拿食物和飲料款待她。

可是她不肯吃，也不肯喝，卻只顧問樵夫："你不是說這個孩子是在林子裏找到的嗎？是不是在十年前的今天？"

樵夫答道："是，我是在林子裏找到他的，就是在十年前的今天。"

"你找到他的時候，他帶有甚麼信物嗎？"她叫道。"頸項上不是有一串琥珀項鏈嗎？他身上不是包着一件繡着星星的金線斗篷嗎？"

"不錯，"樵夫答道，"恰恰跟你所説的一樣。"他從櫃子裏拿出斗篷和琥珀項鏈來，給她看。

她看見它們，高興得哭起來，她説："他正是我在林子裏丟失的小兒子。我求你快快叫他來。我為了找尋他，已經走遍了全世界。"

樵夫和他妻子便走出去，喚了星孩來，對他説："快進屋去，你會在那兒見到你的母親，她正在等你。"

星孩充滿了驚奇和狂喜跑進屋去。可是他看見她在那兒等他，便輕蔑地笑起來，説："喂，我母親在哪兒？這兒就只有這個下賤的討飯女人。"

女人回答他説："我就是你的母親。"

"你明明瘋了才説這種話，"星孩惱怒地嚷道。"我不是你的兒子，因為你是個討飯女人，又醜，又穿一身破衣服。你還是滾開吧，不要讓我再看見你討厭的髒臉。"

"不，你的確是我的小兒子，我在林子裏生的，"她大聲説，她便跪在地上，伸出兩隻胳膊向着他。"強盜們把你從我身邊偷走，丟在林子裏讓你死去，"她喃喃地説，"可是我一看見你，我就認得你，我也認得那些信物：金線斗篷和琥珀項鏈。我求你跟我來，我為了找尋你，已經走遍全世界了，我的兒，你跟我來，因為我需要你的愛啊。"

可是星孩連動也不動一下，她的話一點兒也打動不了他的心，在這屋子裏除了那個女人的痛苦的哭聲外再聽不見別的聲音。

最後他對她說話了，他的聲音是殘酷無情的："倘使你真的是我母親，那麼你還是走得遠遠的，不到這兒來讓我丟臉，倒好得多。因為我始終以為我是某一個星的孩子，沒有想到我是像你剛才告訴我的那樣，一個討飯女人的小孩。所以你還是走開吧，不要再讓我看見你。"

"啊喲！我的兒，"她叫道，"那麼我走以前你不肯親我嗎？我為了找尋你不知道吃了多少苦啊。"

"不，"星孩說，"你太難看了，我寧肯親毒蛇、親蟾蜍，也不要親你。"

那個女人站起來，傷心地哭着走進樹林裏去了。星孩看見她走了，他非常高興，就跑回他遊伴那兒去，還想同他們一塊兒玩。

可是大家看見他來了，都挖苦他，說："看啊，你跟蟾蜍一樣地難看，跟毒蛇一樣地可惡。你滾開，我們不許你跟我們一塊兒玩。"他們把他趕出了花園。

星孩皺着眉頭自言自語："他們對我講的究竟是甚麼意思？我要到水井旁邊去看看，水井會告訴我，我多漂亮。"

他便走到水井旁邊，往井裏看去，啊！他的臉就跟蟾蜍的臉一樣，他的身子就像毒蛇那樣地長了鱗。他撲倒在草上哭起來。他對自己說："這一定是我的罪過給我招來的。因為我不認我的母親，趕走了她，對她又傲慢又殘忍。所以我要去，要走遍全世界去找她，不把她找到，我就不休息。"

樵夫的小女兒走到他身邊來，她把她的手放在他的肩上，對他説：“你失掉了你的美貌，那有甚麼關係？請你留在我們這兒，我不會挖苦你。”

他對她説：“不，我待我母親太殘忍了，這個災難就是給我的懲罰。所以我應當走開，我應當走遍全世界，一直到我找着她，得到她饒恕的時候。”

他便跑進樹林裏去，一路上喚着他的母親，請她到他身邊來，可是他聽不見一聲回應。他喚了她一個整天，到太陽下山的時候，他便躺下來，睡在樹葉鋪成的牀上，鳥和獸看見他都逃開了，因為他們還不曾忘記他的殘忍，除了蟾蜍和毒蛇，他身邊沒有別的生物，蟾蜍守望着他，遲鈍的毒蛇在他面前爬過。

早晨他站起身來，從樹上摘下幾個苦果吃了，又傷心地哭着，穿過大樹林往前走去。不管他遇到甚麼東西，他都向他們探問，有沒有看見他的母親。

他對鼴鼠説：“你能夠在地底下走路。告訴我，我母親在哪兒嗎？”

鼴鼠答道：“我的眼睛已經給你弄瞎了。我怎麼會知道呢？”

他對梅花雀説：“你能夠飛過高樹頂上，能夠看見全世界。告訴我，你能夠看見我母親嗎？”

梅花雀答道：“我的翅膀已經給你在取樂的時候剪掉了。我怎麼會飛呢？”

他又問那隻住在杉樹上過着寂寞日子的小松鼠：“我母親在哪兒？”

松鼠回答：“你已經殺了我的母親。難道你還想殺死你的母親嗎？”

星孩哭了，他垂着頭，懇求上帝創造的生物們寬恕他，又繼續穿過林子走去，找尋那個討飯女人。到第三天他走完了樹林，又到平原上去。

他走過村子的時候，小孩們都嘲笑他，丟石子打他，鄉下人連穀倉也不讓他睡，他們看他那樣髒，怕他會使貯藏的麥子發霉，他們的長工也趕走他，沒有一個人憐憫他。他始終得不到一點關於那個生他的討飯女人的消息。雖然三年來他走遍了全世界找尋她，他常常覺得她就在他前面走着，他喚她，追她，一直到他的腳給又尖又硬的石頭弄出血來。可是他永遠追不上她，那些住在路旁的人都說沒有看見過她或跟她相像的女人，他們都拿他的悲痛來開玩笑。

三年來他走遍了全世界，在這個世界中他得不着愛，得不着親切，也得不着仁慈，然而這正是他從前得意的時候為他自己創造的世界啊。

有天晚上他走到一個城門口，這座城建築在河邊，四周圍着堅固的城牆，他雖然很疲倦，而且腳又痛，可是他還準備進城去。然而守城的兵士們橫着戟把城門攔住，粗暴地對他說：“你進城有甚麼事？”

他答道：“我找尋我的母親，我求你們准許我進去，因為她可能就在這個城裏。”

可是他們挖苦他，一個兵擺動他那部黑鬍鬚，放下他的盾牌，大聲說：“你母親一定不高興看見你，因為你比沼地上的蟾蜍和澤地上爬行的毒蛇還要難看。滾開。滾開。你母親不住在這座城裏。”

另一個手裏拿黃旗的兵問他道:"誰是你的母親,你為甚麼要找她?"

他答道:"我的母親就跟我一樣也是個討飯的,我以前待她很壞,我求你們准許我進去,讓我求到她的饒恕,說不定她會在這座城裏。"他們仍然不讓他進去,他們還拿長矛戳他。

星孩哭着轉身走了,可是有一個人走了過來,這個人穿一件嵌金花的鎧甲,他的盔上蹲着一頭有翅膀的雄獅,他向守兵詢問甚麼人要進城。守兵回答道:"那是一個討飯的,又是一個討飯女人的小孩,我們已經把他趕走了。"

"不必,"那個人笑着大聲說,"我們可以把這個醜東西當奴隸賣出去,會賣到一碗甜酒的價錢。"

旁邊正走過一個相貌兇惡的老人,他大聲說:"我願意出那個價錢買他,"便付了錢,拉着星孩的手帶他進城去了。

他們走了好幾條街,來到一戶人家,牆頭露出一棵石榴樹,就在樹蔭下牆上開了一道小門,老人用一隻雕花的碧玉戒指在門上挨了一下,門開了。他們走下五級銅階,進到一個長滿了黑色罌粟花的花園,園裏還放了不少綠色瓦罐。老人便從他的纏頭布上拿下一塊花綢巾縛在星孩的眼睛上,趕着星孩在前面走。等到他把綢巾給星孩取開的時候,星孩才看見自己在一個地牢裏,那裏燃着一盞牛角燈。

老人用一個木盤盛着發霉的麵包放到星孩面前說一句:"吃吧,"又用一個杯子盛着帶鹽味的水遞給他,說一句:"喝吧,"等他吃了喝了以後,老人便走出去,鎖上了門,又用一根鐵鏈把門拴牢。

第二天老人到地牢裏來。這個老人其實是利比亞魔術家中最能幹的，他的本領還是從一個住在尼羅河墳墓中的魔術家那兒學來的。他帶着兇惡的樣子看星孩，吩咐道：“在這兒邪教徒城的城門附近一個樹林裏，有三塊金錢。一塊是白金，另一塊是黃金，第三塊金錢卻是紅的。今天你把白金給我拿回來，要是你不拿回來的話，我就要打你一百下。你快點去，在太陽下去的時候，我在花園門口等你。當心你要把白金拿回來，否則會對你不利，因為你是我的奴隸，我花了一碗甜酒的價錢買了你的。”他又用那塊花綢巾綁住星孩的眼睛引着星孩走出房屋，穿過那個種罌粟花的園子，走上了那五級銅階。他又用那個戒指開了門，把星孩放到街上去了。

　　星孩走出了城門，走到魔術家所說的樹林前面。

　　從外面看來，林子是十分美觀的，好像裏面充滿了鳥語花香似的，星孩快樂地進去了。可是樹林的美對他並沒有好處，因為不管他走到哪裏，地上到處都有又尖又粗的石南和荊棘，攔住他的路，兇惡的蕁麻刺痛他，薊也拿它的刺來戳他，弄得他痛苦不堪。他從早到午，又從午到晚在林子裏到處找遍了，始終找不着魔術家所說的那塊白金。到了日落時候他傷心地哭着轉身回去，因為他知道有甚麼樣的命運在等待他。

　　可是他剛走出了林子，忽然聽見樹叢中一聲哀叫，好像是甚麼人在痛苦中發出來的叫聲。他忘記了自己的煩惱，又跑回到那個地方，他看見一隻小兔掉在獵人設下的陷阱裏給捉住了。

　　星孩可憐牠，把牠放了，對牠說：“我自己也不過是一個奴隸，可是我還可以給你自由吧。”

　　兔子回答他：“你的確給了我自由，我拿甚麼來報答你呢？”

星孩對牠說："我在尋找一塊白金，可是我到處都找它不到，要是我不把它給我主人帶回去，他就要打我。"

"你跟我來吧，"兔子說，"我帶你到它那兒，因為我知道它藏在甚麼地方，而且為甚麼要藏着。"

星孩便跟着兔子走了，看啊！在一棵老橡樹的裂縫中現出他正在尋找的那塊白金。他十分高興，抓起它來，對兔子說："我不過給你做了一點兒小事，你已經加上許多倍地償還我了，我對你不過施了一點兒恩惠，你已經加上一百倍地報答我了。"

"不是這樣，"兔子答道，"這不過是你怎樣待我，我也怎樣待你罷了。"它說完便連忙跑開了，星孩也就走回城去。城門口坐着一個大痲瘋病人。臉上罩着一塊綠痲布的頭巾，一對眼睛像燒紅的炭似地從痲布小孔裏射出光來。他看見星孩走近了，便敲着一個木碗，搖着他的鈴，喚着星孩道："給我一塊錢，不然我就要餓死了。他們把我從城裏趕了出來，沒有一個人可憐我。"

"唉！"星孩歎息說，"我袋子裏就只有一塊錢，要是我不把它帶給我的主人，他會打我，因為我是他的奴隸啊。"

可是大痲瘋病人不停地向星孩哀求，後來星孩動了憐憫心，便把白金給了他。

星孩回到魔術家那兒，魔術家給他開了門，帶他進去，問他："你拿到那塊白金嗎？"星孩答道："我沒有。"魔術家便撲到他身上去，打了他一頓，隨後放了一個空木盤在他面前，說一句："吃吧，"又給了他一個空杯子，說一句："喝吧，"最後又把他推到地牢裏去了。

第二天魔術家又來對他説：“要是你今天不把那塊黃金拿來，我一定要把你當作我的奴隸，給你三百下鞭子。”

　　星孩便動身到樹林去，他在林子裏尋找黃金找了一整天，卻始終找不着，到了日落時候他便坐下來，開始哭着，他哭得正傷心，他救過的那隻小兔子又跑來了。

　　兔子對他説：“你為甚麼哭？你在林子裏尋找甚麼東西？”

　　星孩答道：“我在尋找這兒藏的一塊黃金，要是我找不着它，我的主人就要打我，拿我當奴隸。”

　　“你跟我來，”兔子大聲説，它帶了他在林子裏跑着，一直跑到一個池子旁邊。那塊黃金就在池子底。

　　“我要怎樣謝你呢？”星孩説，“你看，這是你第二次救我了。”

　　“不啊，還是你先對我起憐憫心的，”兔子説完，連忙跑開了。

　　星孩拿了黃金，把它放進他的袋子，急急走回城裏去。可是那個大痲瘋病人看見他走來，便跑過去迎着他，跪在地上，嚷着：“給我一塊錢，不然我就要餓死了。”

　　星孩回答他：“我袋子裏就只有一塊黃金，要是我不把它帶給我的主人，他就要打我，把我當奴隸看待。”

　　可是大痲瘋病人再三要求，星孩又動了憐憫心，把黃金給了他。

　　星孩回到魔術家那兒，魔術家給他開了門，帶他進去，問他：“你拿到那塊黃金嗎？”星孩回答：“我沒有。”魔術家便撲到他身上去，打了他一頓，給他戴上鏈子，又把他丟進地牢裏去。

　　第二天魔術家又來對他説：“要是你今天把那塊紅金給我拿

了來，我就放你走，不過你要是不帶它回來，我一定要殺死你。"

星孩便動身到樹林去，他在林子裏尋找紅金找了一整天，卻始終找不着。到了傍晚，他坐下，哭起來，他哭得傷心的時候，小兔子又跑來了。

兔子對他說："你尋找的那塊紅金就在你背後那個洞裏面。所以你不要再哭，你要高興啊。"

"我怎樣報答你呢？"星孩叫道，"你看，這是你第三次救我了。"

"不啊，還是你先對我起憐憫心的，"兔子說完，連忙跑開了。

星孩進了洞，在洞中最遠的角落裏找到了紅金。他把它放在他的袋子裏，急急走回城去。那個大痲瘋病人看見他走來，便站到路中間喚他，對他說："給我那塊紅的錢，不然我就得死了。"星孩又動了憐憫心，給了他那塊紅金，一面說："你的需要比我的更大。"然而他的心卻是很沉重的，因為他知道有甚麼樣的惡運在等待他。

可是看啊，他走過城門的時候，守兵都躬身，對他行禮，說着："我們的皇上多漂亮！"一群市民跟在他後面，歡呼："的確世界上再沒有更漂亮的人了！"星孩聽見卻哭起來，一面對自己說："他們瞧不起我，拿我的不幸開心。"人越聚越多，他在擁擠中迷了路，後來發覺自己在一個大廣場上，前面就是一座王宮。

宮門大開，僧侶和大臣們一齊跑來迎接他，對他躬身行禮，說道："您是我們在恭候的皇上，您是我們國王的兒子。"

星孩回答他們說："我不是國王的兒子，我是一個窮討飯女人的兒子。你們怎麼說我漂亮呢？我知道我很難看。"

這時候那個甲上嵌着金花、盔上蹲着一頭雙翼雄獅的人拿起一面盾牌，大聲説：“皇上怎麼説他不漂亮啊？”

星孩看那面盾牌，他的臉又是從前那樣的了，他的美貌恢復了，並且他還看見他的眼睛裏有一種從前不曾有過的東西。

僧侶和大臣們跪在地上對他説：“從前有人預言過那個應該來統治我們的人要在今天來。所以請我們皇上接受這頂王冠和這根節杖，在公正與仁慈這兩點上做統治我們的國王吧。”

可是他對他們説：“我是不配的，因為我不認我的生母，除非我找着她，得到她的饒恕，我不能夠休息。你們還是讓我走吧，因為我還得走遍全世界去找她，雖然你們把王冠和節杖拿給我，我也不該在這兒耽擱。”他這樣説了，便把臉掉向通往城門的街道，看啊！在兵士們四周擁擠着的一大群人中間，他看見了那個生他的討飯女人，在她旁邊站着的便是那個坐在路旁的大痲瘋病人。

他忍不住發出一聲歡呼，連忙跑過去，跪下來，親他母親腳上的傷口，拿他的眼淚去洗它們。他把頭俯到塵埃，抽泣着，像一個心碎了的人一樣，他對她説：“母親，我在我得意的時候不認你。現在在我卑屈的時候你收了我吧。母親，我恨過你。現在請你愛我吧。母親，我拒絕過你。現在請你收留你這個孩子吧。”可是討飯女人連一個字也不回答。

他又伸出手去拖住大痲瘋病人的一雙沒有血色的腳，對那個人説：“我對你動過三次憐憫心。請你叫我母親對我講一次話吧。”可是大痲瘋病人也不回答他一個字。

他又哭起來，説：“母親，我的痛苦大得我實在不能忍受了。饒恕我吧，讓我回到林子裏去。”討飯女人把她的手放在他的頭上，對他說："起來，"大痲瘋病人也把手放在他的頭上，說："起來。"

他站了起來，望着他們，啊！他們原來是國王和王后。

王后對他說："這是你的父親，你曾經救過的。"

國王說："這是你的母親，你用眼淚洗過她的腳。"

他們抱住他的頸項，吻他，帶他進宮裏去，給他穿上華貴的衣服，把王冠戴在他的頭上，把節杖放到他的手裏，他治理着這個建築在河邊的大城，做它的主人。他對所有的人都表示公正和仁慈，趕走了那個壞魔術家，又送了許多值錢的禮物給樵夫夫婦兩人，對他們的兒女也賜了大的恩典。他不許任何人虐待鳥獸，卻拿愛、親切和仁慈教人，他讓窮人吃得飽，對赤身露體的人他給他們衣服穿。在他的國裏充滿著和平與繁榮的景象。

然而他治理的時間並不長久，他受的苦太大了，他受的磨煉也太苦了，所以他只活了三年。他死後繼承他的卻是一個很壞的國王。

註

1	花園	12	水池
2	翅膀	13	一點
3	這裏	14	詞
4	那裏	15	一會
5	留	16	慢慢地
6	擬聲詞	17	樹林
7	一起	18	築巢
8	為甚麼	19	圈
9	鳥	20	隻
10	花	21	做
11	哪裏	22	擬聲詞